LaVyrle Spencer
Romance Writers of America
Golden Medallion Award Winner

Hummingbird

"Fine . . . witty . . . an authentic recreation of a small-town life of an earlier time makes this memorable reading."
— *Rocky Mountain News*

Twice Loved

"A beautiful love story . . . emotional . . . refreshing."
— *Rocky Mountain News*

Separate Beds

"A superb story capturing many human complexities and emotions, that transcend both age barriers and genres. 'Must' read for anyone who has lived and loved."
— *Los Angeles Daily News*

Years

"A splendid job . . . more than a story of two people enamored with each other."
— *Publishers Weekly*

The Gamble

"Novel of the Month . . . a grand new bestseller!"
— *Good Housekeeping*

continued...

LaVyrle Spencer

TWICE LOVED

JOVE BOOKS, NEW YORK

TWICE LOVED

A Jove Book / published by arrangement with
the author

PRINTING HISTORY
Jove edition / June 1984

ISBN: 0-515-09065-4

Jove Books are published by The Berkley Publishing Group,
200 Madison Avenue, New York, New York 10016.
The name "JOVE" and the "J" logo
are trademarks belonging to Jove Publications, Inc.

PRINTED IN THE UNITED STATES OF AMERICA

30 29 28 27 26 25 24 23 22 21 20

*To the three
people I love most—
my wonderful husband Dan
and our darling daughters
Amy and Beth*

Chapter 1

1837

IT HAD BEEN five years, one month, and two days since Rye Dalton had seen his wife. In all that time only the salty kiss of the sea had touched his lips, only its cold, wet arms had caressed him.

But soon, Laura, soon, he thought.

He stood on the deck of the whaleship *Omega*, a two-masted schooner riding low in the brine just beyond the shoals of Nantucket Bay, her hold crammed with brimming oil casks, "bung up and bilge free," so that none of the precious cargo would be lost. The hand on the larboard rail was burnished to the shade of teak, as was the face that contrasted starkly with thick brows and unruly hair bleached almost colorless by years of sun and salt. That hair, badly in need of cutting, added a ruggedness to the bold Anglican features. A thick tangle of side-whiskers swooped almost to his jaw, emphasizing its squareness, then jutting toward the hollow of his cheek. A handsome man with a mariner's wide stance, he stood rock-ribbed and anxious, studying the distant shore.

Just short of Nantucket Shoals, the *Omega*'s sails were reefed, her anchors dropped, and the lighters used for unloading were lowered from their davits. Her crew boarded the boats, babbling eagerly, their ribald banter laced with excitement. *They were home.*

The lighter slipped through the calm waters of Nantucket

Bay, but across the sun-splashed surface it was difficult to make out the crowd awaiting their arrival at Straight Wharf. The May sun transformed the top of the water into a million gilded mirrors, each shaped like a tiny, flashing fish, blinding the blue eyes of the man who squinted quayward. He need not see her—she'd be there, he knew, just as most of the town would be. The watchtower out on Brant Point had spotted the *Omega* long since, and word would have spread; she was coming in, plowing deep: the voyage had been successful.

The bright reflection paled and the crowd came into view. Weeping women waved handkerchiefs. Old retired sea-dogs scraped crusty wool caps from graying pates and hailed the returning whalers with flapping arms, while lads with salt in their dreams gaped in awe, impatiently awaiting their day for becoming heroes.

The lighter thumped against the pilings, and Dalton's eyes scanned the crowd. Within minutes the wharf was a melee of happy reunion: sweethearts hugging, fathers holding children they'd never seen, wives dabbing happy tears from their eyes, while horse-drawn buggies and carriages waited to bear the arriving seamen away to their homes. Other lighters were already arriving from the *Omega*, and stevedores began unloading heavy wooden casks of whale oil and blubber, rolling them down a wooden gangplank with a rumble like low, constant thunder. Horse-drawn drays waited to haul the cargo off to warehouses along the waterfront.

At last Rye's boots touched solid planking that neither rolled nor pitched. He shouldered his heavy sea chest, caught his pea jacket under one arm, and moved through the crowd, searching anxiously. All about were skirts flared over baleen hoops and waists pinched tight by whalebone corsets. His gaze swept them cursorily, searching for only one.

But Laura Dalton was not there.

Frowning, Rye swayed up the length of Straight Wharf, picking his way between clusters of townspeople, his stride wide and balanced even under the weight of the sea chest. In his wake, matrons gaped at each other in stunned surprise. A pair of young girls tittered behind their palms, and old Cap'n Silas, knees crossed, back hunched against the weather-bleached wall of a bait shack, nodded silently to Rye, squinted at the tall young cooper as he moved up the street, puffed on his pipe, and grunted, "Uh-oh!"

Leaving the excitement of the wharf behind, Rye passed warehouses redolent with tar, hemp, and fish. From the noisome tryworks where blubber was melted down into whale oil came its omnipresent reek, mingling with billows of gray smoke from the cauldrons.

But the rangy seaman scarcely noticed the stench, certainly not the occasional eye peering inquisitively at him from chandlery, ropewalk, and joiner's shop as he strode along the cobbled streets toward the heart of the village. At the head of the wharf he entered the lower square of Main Street itself. Before him, rising from the great harbor and ascending in gently rising slopes toward the Wesco Hills, spread the town where he'd been born. Ah, Nantucket, my Nantucket!

A lonely outcropping in the North Atlantic, the island lay thirty miles asea, off the clay cliffs of Martha's Vineyard, to the west and the windswept moors of Cape Cod, due north. The Little Gray Lady of the Sea, Nantucket had come to be called, and she certainly looked it today, sleeping beneath an arch of blue sky, her silvery cottages gleaming like rough-hewn jewels in the high May sun. The cobbled streets contrasted sharply with the startling green of new spring grass along the walkways, giving way to paler paths of sand and shells farther inland. Salt breezes swept across the open heath, carrying with them the fragrance of blossoming beach plums and bayberries, while in dooryards apple trees bloomed in scented explosions of white.

Rye paused long enough to pick one, hold it to his nose, and savor the delicate fragrance, made the more precious for being a product of land instead of sea. He drank deep, as if he might make up for the five-year dearth of such pleasure. Then, thinking again of Laura, he frowned in the direction of home and strode on purposefully.

Within minutes he came to a quaint lane of startlingly white scallop shells. They clicked beneath the crush of his boots, and he hoisted the sea chest higher, reveling in the remembered sound, the scent of the apple blossoms, and the familiarity of the cottages he passed. A wild thrum of expectation pounded through his vitals at the thought that he was, at last, *walking* home.

He reached a *Y* in the path, the left branch leading away to Quarter Mile Hill, the right narrowing toward a gentle rise upon which rested a little story-and-a-half saltbox, typical of most on the island, its sides and roof sheathed in silvered shingles, unpainted, polished by wind and salt and time until each board gleamed like a lustrous gray pearl. Its leaded windows were long gone, melted down for bullets, decades before as a sacrifice to the Revolution, but on either side of the door small panes gleamed in wooden frames and white shutters spread like open arms to allow the spring day inside.

Geraniums—Laura's favorite—had already been set out beside the wooden step. A new line of evergreen shrubs bordered the west end of the house, where a lean-to—called a linter on Nantucket—snuggled against the fireplace wall. Surprised, Rye scanned its angled roof. The linter had been added on since last he was home.

As he crunched his way the last twenty feet up the shelled path, the noon clarion rang out from the tower of the Congregational church below. Fifty-two times a day it struck, and had for as long as Rye remembered. It now called Nantucket's citizens to take their midday meal, but the reverberations seemed to explode within Rye Dalton's heart as a personal welcome home.

Just short of the house, he stepped off the path to approach silently. The front door was open, and the smell of dinner drifted out as if in welcome. A thrill of expectation again lifted his heart, and suddenly he was grateful she'd chosen to await him in the privacy of their home instead of on the public wharf.

He set his sea chest beside the path, ran four shaky fingers through the bleached hair that lay about his face like tangled kelp, heaved a nervous sigh that momentarily lifted his chest, and stepped to the open doorway.

It faced south, leading directly to the yard from the keeping room into whose shadows Rye peered blindly, his eyes still dazzled by the brilliance outside. He made not a sound, though it seemed his heart clattered aloud and must forewarn her of his presence.

She leaned before a giant stone fireplace, dressed in a blue flowered floor-length dress and a white homespun apron, which she held like a potholder while stirring the contents of an iron cauldron hanging on the crane.

He stared at the back of her head with its heavy knot of nutmeg-colored hair, at her slender back, at the faint outline of hip beneath blue cotton. She was humming quietly to the accompaniment of the spoon clanking against the pot.

His palms went damp and he felt almost dizzy at finding everything so dearly close to the way he'd left it. In silence he watched her, basking in the simple familiarity of homing to such a woman, such a house.

She clapped the cover back on the pot and reached up to set the spoon on the mantel while he imagined the lift of her breasts, the coffee brown of her eyes, and the curve of her lips.

At last he knocked softly on the open door.

Laura Dalton looked over her shoulder, startled. A tall man was silhouetted in the door space, haloed by the blaze of noon light behind him. She made out broad shoulders, a full shock of hair, something bulky draped between wrist and hip, feet spraddled wide as if against a hearty wind.

"Yes?" She turned, wiping her palms on the apron, then lifting one to shade her eyes. She squinted, and moved forward with uncertain steps until the hem of her dress was lit by the sunlight slanting across the wooden floor. There she stopped, making out familiar blue eyes, copper skin, bleached brows and hair . . . and the first lips she had ever kissed.

She gasped, and her hands flew to her mouth. Her eyes widened in disbelief while she stiffened as if struck by lightning.

"R . . . Rye?" Her heart went wild. Her face blanched, and the room seemed to spin around crazily while she stared at him, shocked. At last her hands fluttered downward and she stammered again in a choked voice, "R . . . Rye?"

He managed a shaky smile while she struggled to comprehend the incredible: Rye Dalton, hale and vital, was standing before her!

"Laura," he got out, half choking on the word before continuing with gruff emotion. "After five years, is that all y've got t' say?"

"R . . . Rye . . . my God, you're alive!"

He dropped his pea jacket to the floor and took one long step, head bending, arms reaching, while she flew forward to be gathered high and hard against him.

Oh no, oh no, oh no! her thoughts protested, while those long-remembered arms hauled her close against a rough striped shirt that smelled of the sea. She pinched her eyes shut, then opened them wide as if to steady the senses that careened off kilter. But it was Rye! It was Rye! His embrace threatened to crack her ribs and his body with its wide-spread legs was pressed against the length of hers, his cheek of bronze very warm and rough, and very much alive! Her arms did what they'd done a thousand times before, what they'd ached to do a thousand times since. They circled his tough, wide shoulders and clutched him while her temple lay pillowed against his swooping sideburn and tears scalded her eyes. Then Rye lifted his head. Hard calluses framed Laura's face as he bracketed her jaws with broad hands and kissed her with an impatience that had been growing for five years. Wide, warm, familiar lips slanted over hers before reason interfered. His tongue came hungering, searching and finding the depths of her mouth as the years slid away into oblivion. They crushed each other with the sweet torment of reunion driving their hearts into a ramming dance as the embrace and kiss pushed all sense of time aside.

At last they separated, though Rye still held her face as if it were a precious treasure, gazing down into her eyes as he whispered in a racked voice, "Ah, Laura-love." Tiredly, he leaned his forehead against hers while his eyes sagged shut, and he basked in the scent and nearness of her, running his palms over her back as if to memorize its every muscle.

After a long moment she lifted his face, traversing it with fingertips and eyes, familiarizing herself with five added years of creases that webbed its bronzed skin. The days of gazing into high sun seemed to have bleached not only his hair and brows, but the very blue of his eyes.

With those eyes he drank her in, standing a small space

away. He lifted one long palm, as tough as the leagues of rigging it had hauled, and lay it on her cheek, pink still from the heat of the fireplace. His other palm fell from her shoulder to the gentle hillock of her breast, caressing it as though to affirm that she was real, that he was here at last.

She reacted as she always had, pressing more firmly against his palm, letting her eyelids slide closed for a moment, cupping the back of his hand with her own as her heartbeat and breathing hastened. Then, realizing what she was doing, she captured his hand in both of hers, turned her lips into it, and pressed it instead to her face, while dread and relief raised a tempest of emotions within her.

"Oh, Rye, Rye," she despaired, "we thought you were dead."

He placed his free hand on the knot of hair at the nape of her neck, wondering how far down her back it would fall when he freed it. His rough palm caught in the fine strands he remembered so well, had dreamed of so many lonely times. Once more he circled her with both arms, holding her lightly against him while asking, "Didn't y' get any of my letters?"

"Your letters?" she parroted, gathering enough common sense to push at his inner elbows and back out of his embrace, though it was the last thing she wanted to do.

"I left the first one in the turtle shell on Charles Island."

There was, atop a certain rock in the Galapagos Islands, a large white turtle shell known to every deep-water whaling man in the world. No New England vessel passed it by without putting in to check for letters from home or, if heading eastward around Cape Horn, to pick up any seamen's letters it held and deliver them to loved ones in towns such as Nantucket or New Bedford. It often took months for these letters to reach the right hands, but most eventually did.

"Y' didn't get it?" Rye studied the brown eyes with long charcoal lashes that had seen him through a hundred storms at sea and brought him safely into harbor at last.

But Laura only shook her head.

"I left that first one in the winter of 'thirty-three," he recalled, frowning in consternation. "And I sent another with a first mate from Sag Harbor when we crossed paths with the *Stafford* in the Philippines. And another from Portugal . . .

why, I know I sent you at least three. Didn't y' get any of them?''

Again Laura only shook her head. The sea was wet and ink was vulnerable. Voyages were long, destinies uncertain. There were myriad reasons why Rye's letters had failed to reach their destination. They could only stare at each other and wonder.

"B . . . but word came back that the *Massachusetts* went down with . . . with all hands." Unsmiling, she touched his face, as if to reaffirm he was no ghost. It was then she saw the small craters in his skin—several on his forehead, one that slightly altered the familiar line of his upper lip, and another that fell into the smile line to the right side of his mouth, giving him an appearance of rakishness, as if he wore a teasing grin when he did not.

Dear God, she thought. Dear God, how can this be?

"We lost three hands just this side of the Horn. They jumped ship, too scared t' face roundin' 'er after all. So we put into the coast of Chile t' sign on some shoalers and walked into an epidemic of smallpox. Eleven days later, I knew I had it, too.''

"But you took the cowpox inoculation before you left." She touched the scar on his upper lip.

"Y' know it's not foolproof." Indeed, it wasn't. The current method of inoculation was to let the pus of the cowpox scabs dry on the ends of threads, then apply the virus to a scratch in the skin. Though it didn't always prevent the disease, it nevertheless greatly reduced its severity.

"Anyway, I was one of the unlucky ones who caught it. At least, I thought I was unlucky when they put me off ship. But later, when I heard that the *Massachusetts* had piled up on Galapagos and gone down with all hands . . .'' A haunted look came into his eyes and he sighed deeply at his near brush with death and memories of his lost shipmates. Then he seemed to draw himself back to the present with a squaring of his shoulders. "When the fever and rash were gone, I had t' wait for another ship in need of a cooper. I made my way t' Charles Island, knowin' they all put in there, and I got lucky. Along came the *Omega*, and I signed articles on her, then headed into the Pacific, all the time believin' my letter would reach y' and y'd know I was still alive.''

Oh, Rye, my love, how can I tell you?

She studied his beloved face—long, lean, handsome, and hardly marred by the scars. She counted each one—seven, she could find—and resisted the urge to kiss each of them, realizing that the physical scars of this voyage were nothing compared to the emotional scars yet to come.

His thick hair was the color of corn shocks darkening in the weather, and her eyes followed the L-shaped side-whiskers as they jutted toward his cheeks, then she lifted her gaze to his beautifully shaped eyebrows, far less unruly than his hair, which always seemed styled by the whims of the wind, even after he'd just combed it. She smoothed it now—ah, just this once—unable to resist the familiar gesture she'd performed so often in the past. And while she touched his hair she became lost in his eyes, those eyes that had haunted her so when she'd thought him dead. All she'd had to do was step to the doorsill and scan the skies on a clear day to know again the color of those pale, searching eyes of Rye Dalton.

She looked away from them now, haunted anew by all he'd suffered, by all he must yet suffer, through no fault of his own.

They had fought before he left, bitter arguments, with him promising to go whaling just this once, to return to her with his cooper's "lay"—his share of the profits—and put them on easy street. She had begged and pleaded with him not to go, to stay and work the cooperage here on Nantucket with his father. Riches mattered little to her. But he'd argued, just one voyage—just one. Didn't she realize how much a cooper's lay could be if they filled all their barrels? She had expected him to be gone perhaps two years and at first had schooled herself to accept an absence of this duration. But the Nantucket whalers could no longer fill their barrels close to home. The entire world sought whale oil, baleen, as whalebone was called, and ambergris, a waxy substance used in making perfume; those who went in search of these products of the deep found them harder and harder to find.

"But five years!" she half-moaned.

Moving again to cradle her face in his hands, he said now, "I'm not sorry I went, Laura. The *Omega* chocked off! Filled 'er hold! Do y' know how rich—"

But just then a small voice interrupted. "Mama?"

Laura leaped backward and pressed a hand to her hammering heart.

Rye spun around.

In the doorway stood a lad whose pale blond head reached no higher than Rye's hip. He peered up uncertainly at the tall stranger while one finger shyly tugged at the corner of a winsome mouth. A burst of emotion flooded Rye's chest. A son, by Jesus! I have a son! His eyes sought Laura's, but she avoided his questioning glance.

"Where've you been, Josh?"

Josh, Rye thought joyously. Shortened from my father's Josiah?

"Waiting for Papa."

Panic tore through Laura. Her mouth went dry, her palms damp. She should have told Rye immediately! But how do you tell a man a thing like that?

His face, alit with joy only seconds ago, suddenly lost its smile as he turned a quizzical expression to his wife. She felt the blood leap to her cheeks and opened her mouth to tell him the truth, but before she got the chance, steps crunched on the shell path outside and a square-built man stepped to the doorway. His attire was very formal: square-tailed black frock coat, bowed white cravat, and twilled pantaloons stretched faultlessly taut between hidden suspenders and the straps riding under his shoes. He removed a shiny beaver top hat and hung it on a coat tree beside the door in a smooth, accustomed movement. Only then did he look up to find Laura and Rye standing like statues before him. His hand fell still halfway down the row of buttons on his double-breasted topcoat.

Laura swallowed. The face of the man in the doorway suddenly blanched. Rye's glance darted from the dapper man to Laura, to the beaver hat on its peg, and back to the man again. The sound of stew bubbling in the pot seemed as loud as the roar of a nor'easter, so silent had the room become.

Rye was gripped by a sick feeling of dread, a dread much stronger than any he'd experienced while rounding Cape Horn in the jaws of two oceans that ripped at one another and threatened to dismember the ship.

Daniel Morgan was the first to recover. He forced a welcoming smile and came forward with hand extended. "Rye! My God, man, have you been regurgitated from the bowels of the sea?"

"Dan, it's good t' see you," Rye returned automatically, though the words were suddenly half lie, if his suspicions proved true. "The fact is, I wasn't aboard the *Massachusetts* when she went down. I'd been left ashore with a case of smallpox."

The men, dear friends all their lives, clasped hands and pounded each other's shoulders, but the hearty sincerity of the handclasp did little to lighten the strained atmosphere. Neither was certain of what the situation was.

"Saved . . . by smallpox?" Dan said.

The irony of it made them laugh as they broke apart. But the laugh drifted into uncomfortable silence and each glanced at Laura, whose eyes skittered from one to the other, then fell to Josh, who studied the three of them in puzzlement.

"Go out back and wash your hands and face for dinner," Laura ordered gently.

"But, Mama—"

"Don't argue, now. Go." She gave the child a nudge, and he disappeared out the rear door while the pale blue eyes of the seaman followed.

The tension was as thick as the shroud of fog that covered Nantucket one day out of four. Casting about, Rye took in the trestle table for the first time—it was set for three. A humidor stood on a finely made table of cherrywood beside an uphol-stered wing chair with a matching cricket stool. The bed that had been in the room when he left was no longer there. In its place was an alcove bed, a single bunk situated above a built-in storage chest, the entire setup fronted by folding doors, open now, revealing some carved wooden soldiers standing at attention upon the counterpane—obviously the child's bed. Rye's gaze moved to the new doorway that had been cut into the wall on the left side of the fireplace. It led to the linter room beyond, where a corner of the familiar double bed was visible.

Rye Dalton swallowed hard. "Y've come t' have lunch with Laura?" he questioned his friend.

"Yes, I . . ." It was now Dan Morgan's turn to swallow,

and it appeared he didn't know where to put his hands.

Both men silently appealed to the woman, whose fingers were clenched tightly before her. The room had the kind of pall usually presaged by the news that someone had died, brought about now, ironically, by the news that Rye Dalton lived.

Laura's voice was strained, her cheeks blazing, as she worked her palms together nervously. "Rye, we . . . we thought you were dead."

"We?"

"Dan and I."

"Dan and you," Rye repeated expressionlessly.

Laura's eyes sought Dan's for help, but he was as speechless as she.

"And?" Rye snapped, looking from one to the other, his dread growing with each passing second.

"Oh, Rye." Laura reached a beseeching hand toward him, and her face seemed to melt into lines of pity. "They said *all hands*. How could we know? The log was never found."

They stood, appropriately enough, in a perfect triangle. Finally, Dan suggested quietly, "I think we should all sit down."

But being a man of the sea, Rye Dalton was used to facing calamities on his feet. He faced them both, challenging. "Is it . . . is it what it looks like here?" His eyes made a quick arc around the room, encompassing all the signs of Dan's residence in that single sweep, and came to rest on his wife. Her lips were open, trembling. Her hands were folded so tightly the knuckles were white. Her brown eyes were luminous with unshed tears and bore an expression of deep remorse.

Softly, she admitted, "Yes, Rye, it is. Dan and I are married."

Rye Dalton groaned and sank into a chair, burying his face in his hands. "Oh my God."

It was all Laura could do to keep from going to him, kneeling before him, comforting him, for she felt the keen agony as sharply as he. She wanted to cry out, "I'm sorry, Rye, I'm sorry!" But Dan stood there, too. Dan, Rye's best friend. Dan, whom Laura also loved, who had seen her through the worst times of her life; who had comforted her when the news of Rye's death came; who had been so much stronger than she in the face of their mutual loss; who had cheered her during her utterly despondent pregnancy and given her the will to go on; who had been her right hand whenever she needed the strength of a man for the thousand things she, as a pregnant woman, was unable to do; Dan, who had grown to love Rye Dalton's child as if he were his own, who had taken Josh as his son when he took Laura as his wife.

Josh came charging in now, face shiny, a rooster tail of hair standing straight up from the crown of his head. He ran directly to Dan, hugging the man's legs, gazing up his body with a cherubic smile that tore at Rye Dalton's heart.

"Mama made one of your favorites—guess what."

Rye watched Dan Morgan ruffle the boy's hair, then smooth down the rooster tail, which immediately popped up again.

"We'll play our guessing game at supper, son," he said without thinking, then immediately colored, and glanced up to meet the pained expression on Rye's face.

The pale blue eyes dropped to the boy—how old? Rye wondered frantically, Four? Five? But he couldn't tell.

His slumped shoulders straightened by degrees, and he raised his gaze to Laura, silently asking the question. But the boy was there, and Rye understood that she could not answer before him. He looked down at the lad again, wondering, Is he mine or Dan's?

The tension built and Laura felt like the rope in a tug-of-war. She felt light-headed and nauseated and removed from herself, as if this farce must certainly be happening to someone else. Some sense of propriety surfaced and made her lips move to say, "You're welcome to stay for dinner, Rye." Even to her own ears it sounded strange, inviting a man to a table that was his own.

Rye Dalton heard her stilted invitation and held back a bark of tormented laughter that almost escaped his lips. For five years he'd sailed the seas, eating unsavory ship's biscuits, unpalatable lobscouse stew, and salt fish, all the while savoring the anticipation of his first meal at home. And now he was here; in his nostrils was the aroma of the meal he'd dreamed of. Yet he could not possibly sit and share it with Laura and her . . . her *other* husband.

Rye reeled to his feet, suddenly in a hurry to get away and sort out his thoughts. The boy still looked on, making questions impossible. "Thank you, Laura, but I haven't seen my parents yet. I think I'll go down and say hello t' them." His parents would know the truth.

Laura's heart seemed to drop to the pit of her stomach. She and Dan exchanged a secret glance while she telegraphed a silent plea for him to understand. "I'll walk a little way down the path with you, Rye," she offered.

"No . . . no, that's not necessary. I remember the way well enough."

Quickly, Dan interjected, "You go with him, Laura. I'll spoon up for Josh and me."

The tension grew while Rye pondered whether to gesture Laura ahead of him or insist again that she need not go.

Josh lifted his face to Dan, asking, "Is that man going to go for a walk with Mama?"

"Yes, but she'll be right back," Dan answered.

"Who is he?" Josh inquired innocently.

"His name is Rye, and he's an old friend of mine . . . and your mother's."

Josh perused the tall, strapping stranger whose clothes were whitened by salt rime, whose hair was streaked by sun, whose boots were soaked with whale oil, and whose speech was clipped and different from theirs.

"Rye?" repeated the child. "That's a funny name."

With an effort, Rye smiled at the precocious child, taking in every freckle, every gesture, every expression, wondering yet if Josh was his.

"Yes, it is, isn't it? It's because m' mother's name was Ryerson when she was a girl."

"I gots a friend, his name is Jimmy Ryerson."

He's your cousin if you're my son, thought the man, whose blue eyes moved to Laura, only to have the answer forestalled once more while she knelt down on one knee to speak to the boy.

"You and . . . and Papa get started. I'll only be a minute."

Hearing her own hesitation over the word *Papa*, Laura felt guilty, confused, and embarrassed. Dear Lord, what have I done? From the corner of her eye she saw Rye lean to scoop his pea jacket off the floor, then stand waiting.

As Laura preceded Rye out the door, Dan watched their backs, a tight-lipped expression on his face. He remembered the three of them as children, running the dunes together, barefoot and carefree. Down through his memory drifted his own voice, cracking into a high falsetto.

"Hey, Laura, wanna go with me and see if the wild strawberries are ripe?"

And Laura, calling after Rye's retreating back. "Hey, Rye, you wanna come with us?"

Rye, looking over his shoulder, still walking away. "Naw, think I'll go up to Altar Rock and watch for whalers."

Then Laura again, choosing as she always chose. "I'm gonna go with Rye. Strawberries prob'ly ain't ripe yet anyway."

And Dan, following the two of them, hands in his pockets, wishing that just once Laura would follow him the way she followed Rye.

Outside, Rye again hefted his sea chest onto his shoulder and moved down the scallop-shell path beside Laura while both of them carefully kept their eyes straight ahead. But she was conscious of his salt-caked cuffs, and he of her sprigged skirts. It seemed an eternity before they were beyond earshot of the house, and he asked without preface, "Is Josh my son?"

"Yes." She knew a wheeling jubilation at being able to tell him at last, even as uncertainties came to crowd out the momentary joy.

Rye's feet stopped moving. The sea chest slid off his back and landed on the shells with a crunch. They had reached the *Y* in the path. To their left was a grove of apple trees rioting with blossom. Patches of violet-colored crocus nodded in the sun. Below, the bay twinkled, bright and blue as the eyes that sought and held Laura's. "He's really mine?" Rye asked incredulously.

"Yes, he's really yours," she whispered, a tremulous smile lending her face a brief serenity while she watched the stunned reactions parade across Rye's face. Suddenly he plopped backward and sat on the sea chest, drawing deep breaths, as if recovering from having the wind knocked out of him.

"Mine," he repeated to the shells, then to her brown smiling eyes, "Mine," as if it were too incredible to grasp yet.

He reached for her hand, and she could no more deny her own hand its rightful place in his at this moment than she could turn the irreversible tides of fate that had brought them to this impasse. His broad, brown hand enfolded her much narrower, much lighter one, and he drew her closer, to stand within the vee of his thighs, then rested his palms on her hips while gazing up at her with a wealth of emotions in his eyes. With a slight pressure at her waist, he brought her still closer until her knees touched the juncture of his legs, then he softly groaned and pressed his face against her midsection.

"Oh, Laura . . ."

A pair of screeching gulls arced overhead, but she did not see them, for her eyelids were closed against the sight of the coarse, pale hair resting just below her breasts, the full crown of his skull, which she wanted so badly to pull securely against her.

"Rye, please . . ."

He lifted his pained eyes to search hers. "How long have y' been married to him?"

"It'll be four years in July."

"Four years." A succession of uninvited pictures flashed through Rye's head, of Laura and Dan and the intimacies they had inevitably shared. "Four years," he repeated, disheartened, staring at the hem of her skirt. "How could something like this happen? How!" Angrily, he leaped to his feet, turning his back on her, feeling helpless and thwarted. "And Josh . . . he doesn't know?"

"No."

"Y' never told him anything about me?" He turned to face her again.

"We . . . we didn't consciously keep it from him, Rye. It's just that . . . well, Dan's been here since Josh was born, since *before* Josh was born. He grew up loving Dan as a . . . a father."

"I want him t' know, Laura. And I want y' back, and the three of us livin' in that house the way it ought t' be!"

"I know, but give me time, Rye, please." Her face was etched with creases and her voice cracked. "This is . . . well, it's all so sudden, for all of us."

"Time? How much time?" He glowered.

Her eyes met his directly as she wondered exactly what it was he was asking. But seeing the intensity there, the determination, she dropped her gaze to his chest, and she didn't know how to answer.

"I've been waitin' five years for this day, and y' ask me t' give you time. How long do I have t' keep waiting?" He moved toward her.

"I don't . . . we shouldn't . . ." Her glance flickered past his lips. "I . . . please, Rye . . ." she stammered.

"Please, Rye?" With his eyes riveted on her mouth, he reached slowly for her elbow. "Please what?"

"We . . . we could be seen here." But her cheeks were flushed, her eyes bright. Her breath came fast between open lips.

"So what? You're my wife."

"I didn't walk down here with you for this."

"I did." His voice was throaty, and he tugged inexorably at her elbow, his gaze shifting to the top of the hill to make sure they could not be seen from the house. "It's been five years, Laura. My God, do y' know how I've thought of y'? How I've missed y'? And all I've had is a single kiss when I want so much more." His eyes were an azure caress, his voice a husky temptation. "I want to take y' right here under these apple trees, and the world be damned, and Dan Morgan be damned along with it. Come here."

His fingers tightened. Her heart leaped crazily as he pulled her closer, closer, erasing the space between them while his blue eyes roved the features of her face and his broad hand found the curve of her waist. He pulled her flush against him, and though her elbows folded between them, she knew the instant their hips met, that Rye had blossomed as fully as the apple trees. His kiss was wide, wet, and demanding, a thorough invasion of her mouth, telling her without doubt that it would take only her acquiescence for him to invade the rest of her as well.

He groaned into her open mouth, his tongue dancing lustily over hers, his fingers feeling the sun's heat captured in her bountiful spice-brown hair, careful not to mess it, though he wanted nothing so much as to untether it and send it flying free in a circlet upon the grass as he possessed her the way he'd dreamed of doing for so long.

His hand drifted down her neck, found her shoulder blades, her back, her ribs—but there it encountered the firm lashing made of the very substance that had sent him onto the high seas to lose her: whalebone!

"Damn all whalers!" he cursed thickly, tearing his mouth away from hers, examining the stays of her corset with his fingertips. They started just below her shoulder blades and extended to the lumbar regions of her spine, and he traced them through the blue cotton of her dress while his breath beat heavily against her ear.

She couldn't help smiling. "Thank God for whalers right this minute," she declared shakily, backing away.

"Laura?"

It was the first she had admitted to wanting him. But when he would have tipped her chin up for another kiss, she would not allow it. "Stop it, Rye! Anyone on the island could happen along here."

"And see a man kissin' his wife. Come back here, I'm not through with y' yet." But again she eluded him.

"Rye, no. You must understand, this has got to stop until we can get this awful situation untangled."

"The situation is clear. You were married t' me first."

"But not longest." Difficult as it was to say, she had to make it clear she would not willfully hurt Dan.

The tumescence wilted from Rye's body with a suddenness that surprised him. "Does that mean y' intend t' stay with him?"

"For the time being. Until we get a chance to talk, to—"

"Y're my wife!" His fists bunched. "I will not have y' living with another man!"

"I have as much to say about it as you do, Rye, and I'm not

. . . not walking out on Dan in an emotional fit. There's Josh to consider, and . . . and . . .'' Frustrated, she clenched her hands together and began pacing in agitation, finally whirling on him and facing him head on. "We've believed for more than four years that you were dead. You can't expect either of us to adjust to the fact that you're not, in one hour."

Rye's jaw looked as hard as teak as he scowled out across Nantucket Bay. "If y're goin' t' stay with him," he said icily, "just give me the word, because—by God!—I won't stay around t' watch it. I'll be gone on the next whaleship that leaves port."

"I didn't say that. I've asked you to give me some time. Will you do that?"

He turned his eyes to her once again, but it took extreme effort to be so close to Laura and not embrace her . . . kiss her . . . more. He gave a brusque New England nod, then gazed out at the bay again.

The lonely ringing of a bell buoy drifted up to them from the hidden sandbars of the shoals. The ever-present rush of the ocean to shore created a background music neither of them heard, after living their entire lives to its beat. The cry of gulls and the sound of hammers from the shipyards below became part of the orchestration of the island, taken in unconsciously, as was the scent of its heaths and marshes, the damp salt air.

"Rye?"

Belligerently, he refused to face her.

She lay a hand on his arm and felt the muscles tense beneath her touch. "The reason I walked out here with you is that I wanted to talk to you before you walk down the hill."

He still would not look at her.

"I'm afraid I have some . . . some bad news."

He snapped a glance at her, then turned away again. "Bad news?" he repeated sardonically, then laughed once, mirthlessly. "What could be worse than the news I've already got?"

Rye, Rye, her heart cried, you don't deserve to return to all this heartache. "You said you were going down to see your parents, and I . . . I thought you should know before you got there . . ."

He began to turn his head, and there was a wary stiffness

about his shoulders, as if he'd already guessed.

Laura's hand tightened on his arm. "Your mother . . . she's not at home, Rye."

"Not at home?"

But even though she sensed that he knew, the words seemed to stick in Laura's throat. "She's down there on Quaker Road."

"Qu . . . Quaker Road?" He looked in its direction, then back to her.

"Yes." Laura's eyes filled, and her heart ached at having to deliver yet another emotional blow to him. "She died over two years ago. Your father buried her in the Quaker cemetery."

She felt a tremor pass through his body. He whirled about, ramming his hands hard into his pockets, squaring his shoulders while fighting for control. Through tear-filled eyes she watched the pale, pale hair at the back of Rye's neck fall over his collar as he raised his face to the blue sky and a single sob was wrenched from his throat.

"Is anything the way it was before I l . . . left here?"

She was torn by sympathy. It welled high in her throat, and she had a sudden overwhelming need to gentle and comfort. She moved close behind him and lay a hand on the valley between his shoulder blades. Her touch brought forth another sob, then another.

"Damn whaling!" he shouted at the sky.

She felt his broad back tremble and suffered at the tormented sounds of his despair. Yes, *damn* whaling, she thought. It was an inhuman taskmaster who little valued life, love, or happiness. These a whaler was asked to forfeit in the pursuit of oil, bone, and ambergris. Windjammers plied the seven seas for years at a time, their barrels slowly filling, while ashore mothers died, children were born, and impatient sweethearts wedded others.

But homes glowed at night. And ladies perfumed themselves with scents congealed by ambergris. And they pretended that whalebone corsets could effectively guard their virtue because a stiff-spined queen across the Atlantic led the vanguard of prudishness that was spreading across the waves like a pestilence.

The inhumanity of it swept over Laura, and unable to hold herself apart from Rye any longer, she circled his ribs and held him fast, her forehead pressed against the small of his back. "Rye darling, I'm so sorry."

When his weeping had passed, he asked only one question. "When will I see y' again?"

But she had no answer to ease his misery.

The May wind, heedless of human misery, too, scented with salt and blossom, ruffled his hair, then skittered on to dry the caulking of yet another whaleship being readied for voyages, and to carry away the smoke from the tryworks that brought prosperity, and sometimes pain, to the people of Nantucket Island.

Chapter 2

WHALING WAS THE loom that wove together the warp of sea and the woof of land to create the tapestry called Nantucket. Not an islander was unaffected by it; indeed, most earned their living from it, whether directly or indirectly, and had since the late 1600s, when the first sperm whale was taken by a Nantucket sloop master.

The island itself seemed predestined by nature to become the home of whaling, a new economic force in Colonial America, for its location was close to the original migratory routes of the whales, and its pork-chop shape created a large natural anchorage area ideal for use as a waterfront and needing no modification. As a result, the town was laid out contouring the edge of the Great Harbor and virtually rising from the rim of the sea.

The pursuit of the sperm whale had become not only an industry on Nantucket, but a tradition passed down from generation to generation. The sons of captains became captains themselves; the sailmaker passed down his trade to his son; ships' riggers taught their sons the art of splicing the lines that carried the sails aloft; shipwrights apprenticed their sons in the trade of ship repair; ships' carvers taught their sons to shape the figureheads, believed to be good-luck charms, that would see the ships safely back to shore; the retired shipsmith often saw his son take his place with anvil and hammer aboard an outgoing whaler.

And so it was with Josiah Dalton. A fifth-generation cooper, he had passed down his knowledge of barrel making to his son and had watched Rye sail away as he himself had done when he was younger.

Barrels were constructed on shore, then dismantled and packed aboard ships to be reassembled as needed when whales were captured. Coopers, therefore, had the advantage of plying their trade either on land or aboard a whaleship, choosing the risk of a voyage for the chance of high stakes, for a cooper's portion of the profits—his lay—was fourth only to those of the captain and the first and second mates.

Josiah Dalton had, in his time, earned himself three substantial lays, but had, too, suffered the miseries of three voyages, so now he shaped his barrels with both feet on solid ground.

His back was hunched from years of straddling the shaving horse and pulling a heavy steel drawknife toward his knees. His hands were rivered with bulging blue veins and were widespread from clutching the double-handled tool. His torso seemed wrought of iron and was so muscular that it outproportioned his hips, giving him the burly look of an ape when he stood.

But his face was gentle, seamed with lines reminiscent of the grains in the wood he worked. The left cheek was permanently rounded in a smile from accommodating the brierwood pipe that was never absent from between his teeth. His left eye wore a perennial squint and seemed tinted by the very hue of the blue-gray smoke that always drifted past it, as if through the years it had absorbed the fragrant wisps somehow. The frizzled hair about his head was gray and curly, as curly as the miles of wood shavings that had fallen from his knives.

Rye paused in the open double doors of the cooperage, peering in, taking a minute to absorb the sights, sounds, and scents on which he'd been weaned. Shelves of barrels lined the walls—plump-waisted barrels, flat-sided hogsheads, and an occasional oval, which could not roll with the pitch of a ship. Partially constructed barrels sat like the petals of daisies in their hoops, while the staves of the next wet barrel soaked in a vat of water. Drawknives were hung neatly along one wall while the grindstone sat below them in the same place as always. The croze—planes for cutting grooves at each end of the barrel stave—adzes with their curved blades, and jointing planes were up high off the damp floor, just as Josiah had always taught they must be.

Josiah. There he was—with a billow of fresh wood curls covering his boot, which pressed against the foot pedal of the shaving horse, clamping a stave in place as he shaped it.

He's grown much older, Rye thought, momentarily saddened.

Josiah looked up as a shadow fell across the door of his cooperage. Slowly, he raised his veined hand to remove the pipe from his mouth. Even more slowly, he swung his leg over the seat of the shaving horse and got to his feet. Telltale tears illuminated his eyes at the sight of his son, tall and strapping in the doorway.

The thousand greetings they'd promised themselves, if only they could ever see each other alive again, eluded them both now, until Josiah broke the silence with the most mundane remark.

"Y're home." His voice was perilously shaky.

"Aye." Rye's was perilously deep.

"I heard y'd docked aboard the *Omega*."

Rye only nodded. They stood in silence, the old man drinking in the younger, the younger absorbing the familiar scene before him, which he'd sometimes doubted he'd ever see again. The emotions peculiar to such homings held them each, for the moment, bound to the earthen floor, until at last Rye moved, striding toward his father with arms outflung. Their embrace was firm, muscular, crushing, for Rye's arms, too, had known their share of pulling drawknives. Clapping each other's backs, they separated, smiling—blue eyes gazing into bluer—quite unable to speak just yet.

An old yellow dog with graying muzzle filled the breach by shambling to her feet and lurching forward, her tail wagging in joyful welcome.

"Ship!" Rye exclaimed, going down on one knee to scratch

the dog's face affectionately. "What're y' doing here?"

Ah, what a sight, his father thought, to see the lad's head bent over that dog again. "Beast seemed t' think y'd come here if y' ever made it back. Left the house on the hill and wasn't anybody gettin' 'er t' stay up there without y'. Been waitin' here these five years."

Rye lowered his face, one hand on either side of the dog's head, and the old Labrador squirmed as best she could, swiping her pink tongue at the man's chin as Rye laughed and backed away, then changed his mind and leaned forward for a pair of wet slashes from the tongue.

He'd had the dog since he was a boy, when the yellow Labrador was found swimming ashore from a shipwreck off the shoals. Put up for grabs, the pup had immediately been appropriated by young Rye Dalton and named Shipwreck.

Finding old Ship waiting, whining a loyal welcome, Rye thought: Here at last is something the same as it used to be.

The old man clamped his teeth around his pipestem, watching Rye and the dog, joyful at the boy's return, but sorrowed that Martha wasn't here to share the moment.

"So the old harpy didn't get y' after all," Josiah noted caustically, chuckling deep in his throat to cover emotions too deep to be conveyed any other way.

"Nay." Rye raised his eyes, still scratching the dog's ears. "She tried her best, but I was put off ship just before the wreck, with a case of smallpox."

The pipestem was pointed at Rye's face. "So I see. How bad was it?"

"Just bad enough to save my life."

"Ayup," Josiah grunted, scrutinizing with his squint-eye.

Rye stood up, rested his hands on his hips, and scanned the cooperage. "Been some changes around here," he noted solemnly.

"Aye, and aplenty."

Their eyes met, each of them saddened by the tricks five years had played on them.

"Seems we've each lost a woman," the younger man said gravely. The dog nudged his knee, but he hardly noticed as he gazed into his father's eyes, noting the new lines etched about them, the threatening tears glistening there.

"So y've already heard." Josiah studied his pipe, rubbing its warm bowl with his thumb as if it were a woman's jaw.

"Aye," came the quiet reply.

The dog reared up and leaned against Rye's hip, pushing him slightly off balance. Again he seemed not to notice. His hand unconsciously sought the golden head, moving on it absently as he watched his father rub the bowl of the brier-wood pipe. "It won't seem the same, goin' upstairs without her there."

"Well, she had a good life, though she died sad to think y'd been drowned at sea. Seemed she never quite got over the news. Reckon she knew you was safe long before I did, though," Josiah said with a sad smile for his son.

"How'd she die?"

"The damps got her . . . the cold and damps. She got lung fever and was gone in three short days, burnin' up and shiverin' both at once. Wasn't a thing that could be done. It was March, and you know how gray the Gray Lady can be in March," he said. But he spoke without rancor, for anyone born to the island knew its foggy temperament and accepted it as part of life . . . and of death as well.

"Aye, she can be a wicked bitch then," Rye agreed.

The old man sighed and clapped Rye on the shoulder. "Ah well, I've got used t' life without y'r mother, as used t' it as I'll ever get. But you—" Josiah left the thought dangling as he studied his son quizzically.

Rye's glance went to the window.

"Y've been up the hill, then?" Josiah asked.

"Aye." A muscle tightened and hardened the outline of Rye's generous mouth, then he met his father's inquisitive eyes and the mouth softened somewhat.

"I've lost only one woman, lad, but y've lost two."

Again the mouth tensed, but this time with determination. "For the time bein'. But I mean t' reduce that number by half."

"But she married the man."

"Thinking me dead!"

"Aye, as we all did, lad."

"But I'm not, and I'll fight for her until I am."

"And what's she got t' say about it, then?"

Rye thought of Laura's kiss, followed by her careful withdrawal. "She's still in shock, I think, seein' me walk into the house that way. I think for a minute she believed I was a ghost." Rye turned his stubborn jaw toward his father again. "But I showed her I wasn't, by God!"

Josiah chuckled silently, nodding his head as his son colored slightly beneath his tan. "Aye, lad, I'll bet my buttons' y' did. But I see y've hauled y'r chest down here and set it on me floor as if y've come expectin' to share me bunk."

"It's Ship I've come t' bunk with, not you, you old salt, so y' can wipe the smirk off y'r briny face and have done with teasin'!"

Josiah broke into an appreciative roar of laughter, the pipe in jeopardy, scarcely anchored between his yellowing teeth. At last he removed it. "Haven't changed a bit, Rye, and it's my guess y'r woman's wonderin' what t' do with that spare husband of hers, eh? Well, stow y'r gear and welcome to y'. Ship and I are happy enough for y'r company. 'Tis been a quiet house f'r two years now. Even y'r sharp tongue will be welcome." Again he pointed at Rye's nose with his pipestem, and added, "Up to a point." Their eyes met and they shared the moment of levity—an aging parent and the child who'd grown taller and stronger than himself.

At the saltbox on the hill, Laura was still trembling from the shock of seeing Rye again, of kissing him. As soon as he disappeared down the path, none of it seemed real. But facing Dan made reality sweep back, along with the need to accept the bizarre truth and deal with it.

At the door, Laura closed her eyes for a moment, pressed a hand to her fluttering stomach, then stepped inside.

Dan sat at the table, but his elbows rested on either side of an untouched plate and his mouth was hidden behind interlaced fingers. His eyes followed her across the room, hazel eyes she'd known for as long as she'd had memory. Hazel eyes she now found difficult to meet.

She stopped beside the trestle table, wondering what to say,

and if the man who sat studying her so silently was still her
husband. His eyes moved to her hands, and she realized her
fingers were nervously toying with the waistband of her apron,
so she dropped them quickly and took her place on the bench
across from Dan. Her nerves felt as if they were made of spun
glass. The room was painfully silent, all but for the constant
sounds of the island: hammers, gulls, bell buoys, and the
faraway breath of a steam whistle from the Albany packet as it
pulled into Steamboat Wharf below.

Suddenly Laura wilted, resting her elbows on either side of
her own plate and burying her face in her palms. Several long,
silent minutes passed before she raised her eyes to confront
Dan again. He was absently toying with a spoon, pressing it
firmly against the tabletop and cranking it around as if to
screw it into the wood.

When he realized she was watching, he stopped, and his
well-groomed hand fell still. He sighed, cleared his throat, and
said, "Well . . ."

Say something, she berated herself. But she didn't know
where to begin.

Dan cleared his throat again and sat up straighter.

"Where is Josh?" she asked quietly.

"He finished and went out to play."

"You haven't eaten anything," she noted, eyeing his plate.

"I . . . I wasn't very hungry." His eyes refused to meet hers.

"Dan . . ." She reached to cover his hand with her own, but
his did not move.

"He looks healthy as a horse, and very much alive."

She couched her hands in her lap, studying the plate that
Dan had filled for her sometime while she was outside. "Yes,
he does . . . he . . . he is."

"Was he here long?"

"Here?" She looked up quickly.

"Here. In the house."

"You know when the *Omega* came in."

"No, not exactly. Nobody said a word to me about Rye's
being on board. Funny, isn't it?"

Again she covered his hand with hers. "Oh, Dan, nothing is
changed . . . nothing."

He jerked his hand free and spun to his feet, turning his back on her. "Then why do I feel as if the world just dropped out from under my feet?"

"Dan, please."

He turned and took a step nearer. "Dan, please? Please what? Sit here . . . at *his* table, in *his* house, with *his*—"

"Dan, stop it!"

He whirled away again, the words *his wife* echoing through the room as distinctly as if he'd uttered them. Almost everything here was Rye Dalton's, or had been at one time—people and possessions both. Dan Morgan found himself floundering for a way to accept the fact that his friend was very much alive and had walked in here expecting to reclaim it all.

From behind, Laura watched as Dan grasped the back of his neck with one hand and dropped his chin onto his chest.

"Dan, come and sit back down and eat your dinner."

His hand fell to his side and he turned to face her. "Laura, I've got to get back to the countinghouse. Will you . . . are you going to be all right?"

"Of course." She rose and accompanied him to the door, where she held his jacket while he slipped it on. She watched as he retrieved his beaver top hat from the tree, but instead of donning it, he brushed his fingertips distractedly along its brim, his back to Laura. Studying his despondent pose, her throat constricted and her fingers twisted into a tight knot.

Dan took a step toward the open door, halted, drew a deep breath, then spun and clasped her against his chest so hard, the breath swooshed from her lungs. "I'll see you at supper," he whispered in a tortured voice, and she nodded against his shoulder before he tore himself away and quickly stepped out the door.

As Dan Morgan moved down the scallop-shell path in the footsteps of Rye Dalton, it seemed to him that was where he'd been walking all his life.

When Dan was gone, Laura found tears in her eyes. She went back inside to find she must confront countless objects that bore witness to the curious melding of their three lives. At the trestle table she touched Dan's fork, which still rested in the unfinished food on his plate, realizing that years ago Rye, too, had eaten with this very fork; he very likely owned it. Distracted, she put away the remainder of the interrupted meal, but still the memories persisted. She closed the doors of the alcove bed, cutting off the sight of the place where Rye Dalton's son slept at night beside a row of wooden soldiers that had belonged to Dan Morgan as a boy. The humidor beside the wing chair had been a gift to Dan from Rye. The chair itself was one Dan had chosen after marrying Laura, though the cricket stool before it was a piece given to Rye and Laura by some guest at their wedding.

Almost against her wishes, Laura found herself at the door of the linter room, her eyes moving to the bed—how painful it was to look at it now—where she and Rye had conceived Josh and upon which Josh had been born and where Dan had come to sit beside the new mother and peer into the flannel blankets at the squirming pink bundle and predict, "He'll look just like Rye." Laura's eyelids trembled shut as she remembered Dan's words and how they'd been spoken because he'd sensed it was what Laura had needed to hear at that moment. This bed, above all, seemed a testimony to their convoluted history. It had been used by all three of them; the pineapple carving on its headposts had held the jackets of both men and the rails in between had been clasped by Laura's hands in the throes of both ecstasy and pain.

Her throat constricted and she turned away.

Which of them is still my husband? Above all, this question needed answering.

Thirty minutes later, Laura had her answer. She stepped out of the office of Ezra Merrill, the island's attorney, suddenly unable to face the house again, with all its reminders. And though she was twenty-four and a mother herself, Laura was smitten by the overwhelming urge to run to her own mother's arms.

Having left Josh at the Ryersons' house, Laura made her way to the silver-brown saltbox on Brimstone Street where she'd grown up. Returning to it, the memories grew stronger, of Rye and herself and Dan trooping in and out at will, in those days before commitments had been made. Nostalgia created a deep need to talk about those days and these, with someone who knew their beginnings.

But Laura had scarcely put foot inside her mother's keeping room before realizing Dahlia Traherne wasn't gong to be much help.

Dahlia could scarcely handle the everyday decisions of her own life, much less offer advice to others on how to handle theirs. An inveterate whiner, she had learned to get her way through chronic complaining about the most trivial problems; when trivialities failed to surface, she invented imaginary problems.

Her husband, Elias, had been island-born, a sailmaker who had sewn canvas all his life but had never sailed beneath it, for at the merest mention of his signing articles, Dahlia had come up with some new malady to make him promise never to leave her. He had died when Laura was twelve, and there were those who said Dahlia had driven him to an early grave with her habitual complaining and hypochondria, but that he'd probably gone to it gladly, to get away from her. Some said Dahlia should have stepped down a little harder on her daughter after Elias Traherne's death, for the girl ran free as a will-o'-the-wisp after her father was gone, tramping the island without curfew or call, following the boys, and learning the most unladylike habits while Dahlia sat home and made not the slightest effort to control her. And there were still others who condescendingly explained away Dahlia's weak nature by pointing out, "Well, after all, she's an off-islander."

No, Dahlia had not been born on the island, though she'd lived here for thirty-two years. But if she lived on Nantucket another hundred, she would still bear the stigma from which no mainland-born person could ever be free, for once an off-islander, always an off-islander. Perhaps it was because she sensed this wry disdain that Dahlia lost confidence and became so weak and puling.

Greeting her daughter now, she wheezed like the airy whine of a calliope. "Why, Laury, I didn't expect to see you today."

"Mother, could I talk to you?"

The expression on Laura's face made her mother suddenly suspect there was a problem, and the older woman hesitated, as if reluctant to invite her daughter in. But Laura swept inside, dropping to a bench at the table, heaving an enormous sigh, and saying in a shaking voice, "Rye is alive."

Dahlia felt a pain stab her between the eyes. "Oh no."

"Oh yes, and he's back on Nantucket."

"Oh dear. Oh my . . . why it's . . . what . . ." Dahlia's hands fluttered to her forehead, then massaged her temples, but before she could dredge up an ailment, Laura rushed on. The whole story tumbled out, and long before it ended, Dahlia's expression of dismay had intensified to one of alarm.

"You . . . you aren't going to . . . to see him, are you, Laury?"

Disheartened, Laura studied the woman across the table. "Oh, Mother, I already have. And even if I hadn't, how could I avoid it on an island the size of Nantucket?"

"B . . . but what will Dan think?"

Laura resisted the urge to cry out, What about me? What about what I think? You haven't even asked me. Instead, she replied tonelessly, "Dan's seen him, too. Rye came to the house."

"To the house. . . . oh my . . ." Dahlia's fingertips fluttered from her temples to her quivering lips. "Whatever will I say to people?"

Insecurity had always been Dahlia's fundamental problem. Laura realized her folly in expecting her mother to analyze a situation in which security was clearly personified by Daniel Morgan, who had been the stalwart in Laura's life for so long, while Rye had gone away and left her "high and dry," as Dahlia had often said. But Laura couldn't help herself from admitting, "I've already talked to Ezra Merrill and found out Dan is still my legal husband." She raised troubled eyes that needed comfort. "But I . . . I still have feelings for Rye."

Immediately, Dahlia presented her palms. "Shh! Don't say such a thing. It will only cause trouble. You shouldn't even have *seen* him!"

Laura became exasperated. "Mother, it's Rye's house. Josh is his son. I couldn't possibly keep him away."

"But he could . . . could take everything from you!"

"Mother, how could you think such a thing of Rye!" How

typical of Dahlia to be concerned about such a thing at a time like this. Laura sprang to her feet and began pacing.

"Laury, you mustn't get yourself worked up. Are you feeling all right? I'll have to speak to Dan about getting you some drops to calm this—"

"There's nothing wrong with me!"

But to a woman who could conjure up a convenient ache at the mention of anything disagreeable, it seemed imperative to discover an ailment. She came forward, attempting to press a palm to Laura's forehead, but Laura adroitly sidestepped.

"Oh, Mother, please."

The fussy hand dropped. The pinched face with its ever-present expression of suffering seemed to take on several new wrinkles. Frustrated by her mother's inability either to cope or sympathize, Laura felt perilously close to tears.

Oh, Mother, can't you see what I need? I need reassurance, your cheek against my hair. I need to go back with you into the past so that I can sort out the present.

But Dahlia had never been a calming influence; whatever had possessed Laura to believe she would be now? Dahlia's flustered twittering only made things worse, and Laura was not surprised when her mother drifted to a chair, rested the back of her hand against her forehead, and said, "Oh, Laury, I fear I have a frightful headache. Could you mix up a tisane for me? There . . ." She fluttered a hand weakly. "On the shelf you'll find some valerian root and anise. Mix it up . . . with some water . . . please." By now she was breathless.

Thus, Laura found herself administering to her mother instead of being comforted, and by the time she left the house on Brimstone Street, she herself had a headache. She returned home to pass a tense afternoon reflecting upon the past and worrying about the future.

When Dan returned at the end of the day, his eyes scanned the keeping room as if he half expected to find Rye there. He hung up his jacket and caught Laura's glance from across the room, but neither of them seemed able to speak.

Dan's stare followed Laura as she put supper on the table, but throughout the meal the strained atmosphere remained while they avoided the subject of Rye Dalton.

But in the evening, Josh, with the intuitive accuracy of a child, shot a question that hit two marks at once. Dan was sitting at a small oak desk with a pen in his hand when Josh leaned across his lap and asked, "Why did Mama get scared today when that man was here?"

The entry on the ledger sheet went awry. Then Dan's hand stopped moving over the page, Laura's over her crocheting. Their eyes met, then Laura dropped her gaze.

"Why don't you ask Mama?" Dan suggested, watching the red creep up Laura's cheeks while he wondered again what had gone on between the two of them when Rye first got here.

Josh galloped over and flung himself across his mother's lap. "Are you scared of that man, Mama?"

"No, darling, not at all." She ruffled Josh's hair.

"You looked like you was. Your eyes was big and you jumped away from him like you make me jump away when I get too close to the fire."

"I was surprised, not scared, and I did not jump away from him. We were talking, that's all." But guilt flared Laura's cheeks to an even brighter hue, and she could tell Dan was studying her carefully. She lit into her crocheting as if the doily had to be finished by bedtime. "I think it's time you marched your soldiers to the shelf and got your nightshirt on for bed."

"You and Papa wanna talk grown-up talk, huh?"

Laura couldn't hide her smile. Josh was a bright and witty child, though there were times when she'd cheerfully have gagged him for his innocent comments. But there was a new discomfort between Laura and Dan that would have been there with or without Josh's remark, and as the evening rolled on toward bedtime, it became more and more palpable. By the time they retired to their room, Laura felt as if she were walking on fishhooks. And to make matters worse, there was the problem of disrobing.

Clothing of the day was styled for ladies with maids; both dresses and whalebone corsets were laced up the back, so it was impossible to don or doff them without aid. Laura had protested when Dan insisted on her purchasing such dresses instead of making her own, but he had a fierce pride in his ability to provide for her, thus she'd obliged and bought the inconvenient garments, though twice daily she needed his assistance to get the infernal things on and off.

But tonight she felt a disquieting reluctance to ask the favor, though it had come to be part of their bedtime ritual, as automatic as the pinching of the last candlewick.

But tonight was different.

Dan set the candle on the commode table, untied his cravat and hung it on the bedpost, followed by his shirt. Laura, trussed up like a stuffed turkey ready for the spit, silently rebelled at women's plight. Why did women dress in such absurdly restrictive clothes? Men had no such inconveniences with which to contend.

How she wished she might unobtrusively slip out of her things and into her nightie and quickly duck beneath the covers. Instead, she was forced to ask, "Dan, would you loosen my laces please?"

To her horror, his face went red. She whirled to present her back. After nearly four years of unlacing her, Dan was blushing!

He released the brass hooks down the back of her dress and tugged at the laces, which were strung through metal grommets along the back of her corset. She felt him fumble, then he muttered under his breath. When at last she was free, she stepped from the garment, laid her corset over the cedar trunk, and unbuttoned her petticoat. That left only her pantaloons, which buttoned at the waist, and the chemise—it tied up the front with a satin ribbon.

The wrinkles of her chemise had been pressed into her skin all day, leaving a crisscross of red marks that itched terribly. Often Dan teased her when she slid into bed and immediately began scratching.

But tonight all was quiet after they'd dressed in nightgown and nightshirt—standing back to back—and lay beneath the coverlets, with only the after scent of candle smoke remaining. From outside came the incessant wash of sea upon land, and from nearer, the cluck of a whippoorwill that always precedes its song. Again it clucked, and Laura lay in the dark, equally as tense as Dan, telling herself there were many nights when they went to sleep without touching. Why was she so aware of it tonight?

She heard him swallow. Her ribs itched, but she forced her hands to be still. The silence stretched long, until at last, when the whippoorwill had called for the hundredth time, Laura reached for Dan's hand. He grasped it like a lifeline and squeezed so hard, her knuckles cracked softly, while from his side of the bed came a throaty sound, half relief, half despair. She heard the shush of the feather pillow as he turned to face her and ground his thumb into the back of her hand with possessive desperation.

When he finally spoke, his voice was guttural with emotion. "Laura, I'm scared."

A thorn seemed to pierce her heart. "Don't be," she reassured, though she was, too.

There were things he could not say, would not say, understood things that neither had ever admitted but that were suddenly implicit between them.

During their childhood and adolescence it had always been the three of them, forever comrades. But it had never been any secret that Laura had eyes only for Rye. When news of his death reached Nantucket, Dan had suffered with her, the two of them walking the windswept beaches, knowing that particular torment reserved for those who mourn without the benefit of a corpse. Helplessly, they'd wandered, needing the proof of death's finality. But that final proof was denied them by the greedy ocean, which cared little for man's need to lay a spirit to rest.

During those restless, roaming days, Dan's despair was shorter-lived than Laura's, for with Rye gone, he was free to court her as he'd always dreamed of doing. But he lived those days under a mantle of guilt, grateful that Rye's death had cleared the way for him, yet sickened by that very gratitude.

He had won Laura mainly by becoming indispensable to her.

She had awakened one morning to the sound of the ax in her back yard and had found Dan there, chopping her winter wood. When the crisp weather warned of imminent winter, he had come again, unasked, with a load of kelp with which to ballast the foundations of the house against the intrusive drafts of the harsh climate. When she grew cumbersome with pregnancy, Dan came daily to carry water, to fill the woodbox, to bring her fresh oranges, to insist that she put her feet up and rest when backaches riddled. And to watch her eyes fill with sorrow as she brooded before the fire and wondered if the baby would look like Rye. When she went into labor, it was Dan who fetched the midwife and Laura's mother, then paced the backyard feverishly, as Rye would have done had he been there. It was Dan who came to her bedside to peep at the infant and smooth Laura's brow with a promise that he would always be there when she and Josh needed him.

Thus, she grew to depend on Dan for all the husbandly support he was more than willing to give, long before he ever asked her to be his wife. They drifted into marriage as naturally as the bleached planks of ancient vessels drift to Nantucket's shores at high tide. And if intense passion was not a part of Laura's second courtship, security and companionship were.

As in most marriages, there was one who loved more, and in this one it was Dan. Yet he was secure at last, for the rival who'd once claimed Laura was no longer there. She was Dan's at last, and she loved him. He had never dissected that love, never admitted that much of it was prompted by gratitude, not only for his physical and financial support, but because he truly loved Josh as if the boy were his own and was as good a father as any natural father could be.

But when Dan had stepped into the house this noon and found Rye Dalton standing there, he'd felt the very foundation of his marriage threatened.

Lying beside Laura now, his throat ached with questions he did not want to ask for fear her answers would be those he dreaded hearing. Yet there was one he could not withhold, though his heart swelled with foreboding at the thought of putting it to her. His thumb ground against her hand. He swallowed and sent the question through the dark in a strange, tight voice.

"What were you and Rye doing when I walked in today?"

"Doing?" But the word sounded pinched and unnatural.

"Yes . . . doing. Why did Josh say you jumped when he walked in?"

"I . . . I don't know. I was nervous, naturally—who wouldn't be when a . . . a dead man has just walked in your door?"

"Quit hedging, Laura. You know what I'm asking."

"Well, don't, because it doesn't matter."

"Meaning he kissed you, right?" When she made no reply, he went on. "It was written all over your faces when I interrupted."

"Oh, Dan, I'm sorry, I really am. But he took me completely by surprise, and it didn't mean anything except hello." But she knew in her heart it did.

"And what about when you walked down the path with him—did he kiss you then, too?"

"Dan, please tr—"

"Twice! He kissed you twice!" He gave her hand a hurtful yank. "And what was the second time, another hello?"

She had never known jealousy from Dan before, for there'd never been cause. The vehemence of it quite frightened her as she frantically searched for a reply.

"Dan, for heaven's sake, you're hurting my hand." Though he eased his grip, he didn't release it. "Rye had no idea, when he walked in here, that we were married."

"Does he mean to take up his old place as your . . . husband?"

"You're my husband now," she said softly, hoping to placate him.

"One of them," he said bitterly. "The one you haven't kissed yet today."

"Because you haven't asked," she said even more softly.

He came up on one elbow, leaning over her. "Well, I'm not asking," he whispered fiercely. "I'm *taking* what's mine by rights."

His lips came down violently, moving over hers as if to punish her for circumstances that were not of her doing. He kissed her with a fierce determination to force Rye Dalton from her thoughts, from her life, from her past, knowing all the while that it was impossible to do.

His tongue plundered deep, wounding her with a lack of sensitivity she'd never before known from him. Hurt, she pulled sharply aside, making him suddenly realize how rough he'd been.

At once penitent, he scooped her tightly into his arms and crushed her beneath him, speaking raggedly into her ear. "Oh, Laura, Laura, I'm sorry. I didn't mean to hurt you, but I'm so afraid of losing you after all the years it took to finally have you. When I walked in here and saw him, I felt like I was back ten years ago, watching you trail after him like a love-sick puppy. Tell me you didn't kiss him back . . . tell me you won't let him touch you again."

He had never before admitted that he'd been jealous of Rye all those years ago. Pity moved her hands to the back of his neck to smooth his hair. She cradled him, closing her eyes, kissing his temple, suddenly understanding how tenuous his security was, now that Rye was back. Yet she was afraid to make promises she wasn't at all sure she could keep.

But this much she could say, and say with all truthfulness: "I love you, Dan. You never have to doubt that."

She felt a shudder run through him, then his hands started moving over her body. But at his touch came the wish that he would not make love to her tonight. Immediately, she was deluged with guilt for the thought. Never before had she even considered denying him. Dutifully, she caressed his neck, his back, telling herself this was the same Dan she'd made love with for three years and more; that Rye Dalton could not come walking up the lane and give her the right to turn this man away.

Yet she wanted to—God help her, she wanted to.

He ran his hand down her hip, pulled her nightgown up, and she understood his need to reestablish himself. She opened her body to him and moved when she knew it was expected, and held him fast when he groaned and climaxed, and hid the fact that she felt faithless to another for what last night would have been the most natural and welcome act in the world.

In the loft above the cooperage, Rye Dalton lay on his back, disquieted by the emptiness of the womanless house. At each familiar piece of furniture he had pictured his mother, sitting, working, resting, her presence felt as much now as it had been when she was there in the flesh.

His first meal at home was an improvement over ship's fare, but fell far short of the tasty stews his mother or Laura would have prepared. His boyhood bunk, though larger than that on the *Omega*, was a sorry substitute for the large rosewood featherbed he'd thought to be sharing with Laura tonight. When he lay down, his body expected to ride the sway and swell it had known for five years; the steadiness of the bed beneath him kept Rye awake. Outside, instead of the whistle of wind in the rigging, he heard hooves on new cobbles, occasional voices, the crack of a whip, the closing of a street lantern's door.

Not disturbing sounds—just different.

He rose from his bunk and padded to the window facing south. Were it day-bright, he could have seen the tip of his house, for trees here on the island were stunted things, pruned by the wind so that few grew taller than the edifices built by man.

But it was dark, the hill obliterated by a near-moonless night.

Rye imagined Laura in the bed he'd once shared with her, but lying in it now with Dan Morgan. He felt as if a harpoon had been thrust into his heart.

In his bed nearby, Josiah moved restlessly, then his voice came through the dark. "Thinking of 'er will do y' little good tonight, lad."

"Aye, and don't I know it. She's up there in bed with Dan this very minute, while I stand here making wishes."

"Tomorrow is time enough to tell her how y' feel."

"I needn't tell her—she knows."

"So she put y' off, did she?"

Rye leaned his elbow against the windowframe, frustrated anew. "Aye, that she did. But the lad was there, thinking Dan is his father, lovin' him as if he is, the way she tells it. That'll be somethin' t' reckon with."

"So she told y' about the boy?"

"Aye."

The incessant sound of the ocean seemed to murmur through the rough walls of the building while Rye remained as before, studying the dark square outside the window. When he spoke again it was quietly, but with inchoate pride nearly making his voice crack. "He's a bonny lad."

"Aye, with the look of his grandmother about his mouth."

Rye faced the spot where his father's bed was, though he could not clearly make him out. "Y've lost your grandchild just as I've lost my wife. Did she never bring him around for the two of y' t' get acquainted?"

"Aw, she has little business in the cooperage, and I doubt the lad lacks for grandparents' love, with Dan's folks playin' the part. I've heard they love him like their own."

The entanglements of the situation were ever increasing. Remembering days when he felt as free to run uninvited into the Morgans' house as he did into his own, Rye asked, "They're still well, then?"

"Aye, sound as dollars, both of 'em."

Silence followed again for a moment before Rye asked, "And Dan . . . what does he do t' keep her in such fancy furniture up there?"

"Works at the countinghouse for old man Starbuck."

"Starbuck!" Rye exclaimed. "You mean Joseph Starbuck?"

"One and the same."

The fact stung Rye, for Starbuck owned the fleet of whaleships that included the *Omega*. How ironic to think he himself had gone in search of riches only to lose Laura to one who stayed behind to count them.

"You see those three new houses up along Main Street?" Josiah continued. "Starbuck's buildin' them for his sons. Hired an architect clear from Europe to design 'em. The Three Bricks, he's callin' 'em. Starbuck's had good times. The *Hero* and the *President* came home chocked off, too, and he expects the same of the *Three Brothers*."

But Rye was barely listening. He was ruing the day he'd set out after riches—and riches he'd have, for his lay at one-sixtieth a share, would be close to a thousand dollars, no small amount of money by any man's standards. But the money could not buy Laura back. It was obvious she had a good life with Dan; he provided well for both her and the boy. Rye swallowed, peering through the dark to where the tip of his house must be, remembering his and Laura's bed in the new private linter room.

Damn! He takes her in my very own bed while I sleep in my boyhood bunk and eat bachelor's rations.

But not for long, Rye Dalton vowed. Not for long!

Chapter 3

THE FOLLOWING DAY, fog had again settled over Nantucket. Its dank tendrils sniffed at Rye Dalton's boot tops like a keen-nosed hound, then silently retreated to let him pass untouched. As he strode toward Joseph Starbuck's counting-house, the thick mist shifted and curled about his head while beneath his boots it turned the dull gray cobbles jet black and left them sheeny with moisture. On the iron bowl of the horse-watering fountain beads gathered, then ran in rivulets before dropping with irregular *blips*, each magnified into a queer resounding musical note by the enshrouding fog. Almost as an afterbeat came the click of Ship's toenails as she followed her master.

But in spite of the damp, gray day, Rye Dalton reveled in the unaccustomed luxury of being dry and clean after five years of being splattered by ceaseless waves and wearing oily, salt-caked "slops."

He was dressed in a bulky sweater Laura had knit for him years ago, its thick turtleneck hugging high against his jaw, nearly touching the side-whiskers that swept down to meet it. Those whiskers closely matched the color and texture of the tweedy wool, while down his sleeves twisted a cable knit that seemed to delineate the powerful curvature of the corded muscles it followed. His black wool bell-bottom trousers were

43

waistless, rigged out with twin lacings just inside each hip, creating a stomach flap inside which his hands were pressed for warmth as he crossed the cobbles with long, masculine strides that parted the fog and sent it roiling behind him.

The salmon-colored bricks of the countinghouse appeared specterlike, a hazy backdrop for the dazzling white paint of its door, window casings, and signpost that stood out even under the leaden skies. When Rye's hand touched the latch, Ship dropped to her haunches, taking up her post with tongue lolling and eyes riveted on the door.

Inside, the fires had been lit to ward off the spring chill, and the place swarmed with activity, as it always did after a whaleship came in. Rye exchanged greetings with countless acquaintances while he was directed to the office of Joseph Starbuck, a jovial mutton-chopped man who hurried forward with hand extended the moment Rye appeared at his doorway.

Starbuck's grip was as firm as that of the cooper. "Dalton!" he exclaimed. "You've done me proud this voyage. Chocked off and bringing a dollar fifteen a gallon! I couldn't be happier!"

"Aye, greasy luck for sure," Rye replied, in the idiom of the day.

Starbuck quirked an eyebrow. "And are they makin' a landlubber of y' or will y' sail on the next voyage with the *Omega?*"

Rye raised his palms. "Nay, no more whaling for this fool. One voyage was enough for me. I'll be content t' make barrels with the old man for the rest of m' life, but right here on shore."

"Can't say I blame y', Dalton, though your lay is a healthy one. Are y' sure I can't tempt y' to try 'er one more time—say for a one-fifteenth share?" Starbuck kept a shrewd eye on Rye's face while he moved again to the enormous roll-top desk that dominated the room.

"Nay, not even for a one-fifteenth. This voyage has cost me enough."

A frown settled over Starbuck's features, and he hooked his thumbs in his waistcoat pockets as he studied the younger man. "Aye, and I'm sorry for that, Dalton. Hell of a mix-up

for a man to come home to—hell of a mix-up." He scowled at
the floor thoughtfully before looking up. "And be assured
both Mrs. Starbuck and I extend our deepest sympathies at the
loss of your mother, too."

"Thank y', sir."

"And how is your father?"

"Spry as ever, and cutting barrel staves over there faster
than that punk apprentice of his can keep up with."

Starbuck laughed robustly. "Since I cannot convince you to
cooper my ship on the ocean, perhaps I can convince you and
your father to put up my order for barrels this time around."

"Aye, we'd be happy t' do that."

"Good! I'll be sending my agent over to agree on a price
with you before the day is out."

"Good enough."

"I expect you've come to collect your lay."

"Aye, that I have."

"You'll have to see your . . . ah, friend . . . Morgan." Starbuck looked slightly uncomfortable. "He's my chief accountant now, you know. His office is on the second floor."

"Aye, so I've heard."

Starbuck studied Dalton's face at the mention of Dan
Morgan, but his expression remained unchanged, only a polite
nod of the head acknowledging Starbuck's statement. Starbuck extracted a ten-cent cigar from a humidor, offered one to
Rye, who refused, snipped the end, and soon blew fragrant
smoke into the room.

"You know, Dalton, there are aspects of this business
which I cannot say I relish. A man leaves his home with the
best of intentions, tryin' to be a proper provider for his wife
and family, but his rewards are often grim in the final outcome. Now it's not his fault, though neither is it mine. Yet I
feel responsible, damnit!" Starbuck thumped a fist on the
elbow-worn arm of his captain's chair. "Though it's small
consolation, Mrs. Starbuck and I wish to show our apprecia-
tion by inviting the officers under my employ to a dinner party
at our house Saturday night, to celebrate the return of the
Omega. You'll come, won't you?"

"Aye, and happily." Rye grinned. "Especially if Mrs. Starbuck plans t' serve anything my old man hasn't cooked.''

Though Dalton smiled and bantered, Starbuck realized what a hell of a shock the man had suffered, landing to the news that his wife had been usurped by his best friend. It was damn sure Dalton missed more than just his wife's cooking. There was little Starbuck could do about the situation, but being a fair man, the thought rankled, and he promised himself to see that Dalton received a generous contract on barrels.

Upstairs, Rye approached the broad pigeonholed desk before which Dan Morgan sat on a high stool. A candle in the hurricane lamp with a bowl-shaped reflector shed light onto the open books spread out on the desk, for though Nantucket lived by whale oil, ironically, it rarely lit itself by it. As the saying went, "Why burn it up when you can sell it and get rich?"

Morgan glanced up as Rye's footsteps echoed on the oiled pine floor. His quill pen paused, and the corners of his mouth drooped. But he eased from the stool to greet Rye on his feet.

Rye stopped beside the desk, his feet planted wide in a new way to which Dan was not yet accustomed, his thumbs caught up on his stomach flap. It seemed suddenly intimidating, this seaman's stance, so solid, so self-confident. And he was reminded that Rye was half a head taller.

Rye, too, assessed Dan. After five years he was still trim and fit. He was dressed in a stylish coat of twilled mulberry worsted, his neckpiece impeccably tied, and a striped waistcoat hugged his lean ribs. He was dressed like a man who enjoyed financial security and wanted to display it in even so reserved a fashion.

Momentarily, Rye wondered if Laura was equally as proud of Dan's natty mode of dress.

He extended his hand, thrusting jealousy aside, and for a moment he thought Dan would refuse to greet him civilly. But at last Dan's hand clasped Rye's briefly. Their touch could not help but bring back memories of their years of friendship. There was, within each, an ache to restore that friendship to its original vigor as well as the realization that it would never again be recaptured.

"Hello, Dan," the taller man greeted.

"Rye."

They dropped hands. Clerks and subordinates moved around them, carrying on business within full view and earshot. Curious eyes turned their way, making their exchange cautious.

"Starbuck sent me up t' collect my lay."

"Of course. I'll make out the bank draft for you. It'll only take a minute." Rye even talked in a new clipped seaman's vernacular, Dan noted.

Dan again sat down on his stool, pulled out a long ledger, and began making an entry. Standing above him, watching his hands, Rye remembered the hundreds of times they'd threaded bait for each other, gone gigging for turtles in Hummock Pond, or digging clams at low tide, sharing their catch over an open fire on the beach, often with Laura sitting between them. Rye stared at Dan's well-shaped hands as he penned the figures in the ledger, then wrote in an elegant, swirling English roundhand—square, competent hands with a faint spray of light hair on their backs—and he realized those hands had known as much of Laura as his own. The conflict between old loyalty and new rivalry created a maelstrom of emotion within Rye.

My friend, my friend, he thought, must you now be my enemy?

"Y've provided well for Laura, I can tell," he said, speaking quietly so nobody else could hear. "I thank y' for that much."

"There's no need to thank me," Dan replied without looking up. "She's my wife." Here he did look up, a challenge in his eyes. "What would you expect?"

They confronted each other silently for a moment, knowing well that each would suffer in the days ahead.

"I expect a hell of a good fight for her, from the looks of it."

"I expect no such thing." Dan stood up and extended the check, scissored between two fingers. "The law is on my side. You were reported lost at sea. In such cases there is what is legally referred to as an assumption of death, so in the eyes of the law, Laura is *my* wife, not yours.''

''Y' haven't wasted any time checkin' on legalities, have y'?''

''Not a day.''

So a fight it will be, Rye thought, disappointed at this new disclosure. Yet if Dan had gone to all that trouble, it meant Laura had cast some doubt into his mind about her intentions.

''And so the battle lines're drawn, old friend?'' Rye asked sadly.

''Put it as you will. I will not give up either Laura or my son.'' His meaning was clear. His posture was stiff.

So, that was how it was to be. But Rye could not resist placing one well-aimed barb as he pocketed the check and gave a brief salute.

''Give them both my love, will y', Dan?'' Then he turned on his heel and left.

But once outside, his jaunty attitude vanished. In its place came a worried frown as he paused to glower in the direction of Crooked Record Lane. Ship lifted her head off her paws and lumbered to her feet, raising patient eyes. Rye seemed unaware of the dog's rapt attention, but presently he slipped his palms inside his stomach flap and spoke softly. ''Well, Ship, it seems she's truly his wife after all. And what are we t' do about that, mate?''

The dog's mouth opened while she looked up Rye's length, waiting for some signal. At last the man turned away from the spot he'd been studying and strode off in the opposite direction, the click of canine toenails accompanying him across the square.

But the pair had not gone ten yards before approaching footsteps echoed eerily and came to a halt before them. Rye looked up and stopped in his tracks. The familiar creased eyes of Dan's father were relaxed on this sunless day, so the lines radiating from their corners were strikingly white in the mahogany face. He'd grown thinner, and there was less hair on his head than ever. For a moment neither spoke, then the pleasure at the sight of the long-loved man forced Rye to move forward again.

''Zach, hello.'' He extended a hand, and Zach came forward to take it. He had hard, horny hands, those of a fisherman who'd hauled both sail and nets all his life. They were burned by sun, cured by salt to the color and texture of brine-soaked ham.

"Hello, Rye." The handshake was brief and bone-crushing. "I heard the news." Zachary Morgan lifted his eyes momentarily to the countinghouse behind Rye's shoulder where his son was working, then met Rye's again self-consciously. "It's good to hear you're alive after all."

"Aye, well, it's good to be back on dry land, I can say that for sure."

But the unsaid hovered between the two men. They shared a history that commanded them to care, but there were new obstacles between them.

Zach bent to scratch Ship's head. "Ah, and the old girl's glad to have you back, aren't you, Ship? Haven't seen you for a long time." The dog was a convenient diversion, but only temporary. When Zach straightened, they were ill at ease again. "Sorry about your mother, Rye."

"Aye, well . . . things change, don't they?"

Their eyes met, spoke silently. And now my boy is your grandson, Rye thought, and his mother your daughter-in-law. I won't be runnin' in and out o' your house like I used to. "But the old man tells me your missus is healthy and spry."

"Ayup, same as always."

An enormous void fell, a void five years wide. It used to be so easy to talk to each other.

"You're not out fishin' today."

"Fog's too thick."

"Aye."

"Well . . ."

"Give my best to Hilda," Rye said.

"I'll do that. And say hello to Josiah."

They'd said nothing. They'd said everything. They'd said, Understand, this is hard for me—I love them both, too. They turned their backs on each other and their footsteps parted in the fog, then Rye turned to watch Zach disappear into the countinghouse, presumably to talk with his son about this queer quirk of fate.

The fog seemed the perfect accompaniment to Rye's morose mood. He and Ship plodded through its shreds, both with heads hung low. Along the silent streets the silvery saltboxes blended into the enveloping whiteness, their painted shutters the only glimmer of color in the otherwise bleak day. Occasionally those shutters were blue, the color reserved for captains of whaleships only. The close-pressed yards were surrounded by picket fences that soon gave way to those into which the ribs of whales were woven. Out near the tryworks the odor of putrefaction hung in the air, the gray smoke of decomposing blubber inescapable, locked as it was about the island by the veil of fog.

Whaling! It was everywhere, and suddenly the despondent Rye Dalton wanted to escape it.

Seeking the solace of isolation, he made for Brant Point Marshes. The low-lying land spread out like a sea of green, providing a nesting area for thousands of species of birds. Their voices lilted through the haze that pressed close above the cattails and sedge. There was a constant flutter of activity about the thickets of highbush cranberry as the birds fed, and the scene was lent a surreal quality by the swirling mists that were constantly on the move. How many times had three children come here in search of nests and eggs? Rye pictured the three of them as they'd been then, but immediately Laura's face alone emblazoned itself upon his memory, not as she'd been yesterday, surprised and stunned, but as in the days of their awakening sexuality, when she'd first looked at him through a woman's eyes—wondering and tremulous. Next he pictured her turning from the hearth with the spoon handle wrapped in her apron; then his son running in, heedless . . .

And a great loneliness overwhelmed him.

He moved on through the marshes, making useless wishes, wondering what she was doing at this very moment.

He stopped on a high bank where last year's sea oats now drooped, laden with heavy water droplets. The fog swirled about his knees and obscured the distant view of the shore. But from out of the lost beyond came the incessant throb of incoming waves while in the foreground the Brant Point Shipyard was vignetted by a frame of fog. There, below, the

Omega was already undergoing a complete overhaul. Like a beached whale, she'd been hoisted onto the skeletal "ways" and careened—turned on her side for cleaning. Workers scurried over her like ants, scraping every inch of her hull, recaulking seams, holystoning, or scrubbing, and revarnishing decks. Already six new cedar whaleboats were being constructed for her davits, while in town, at the ropewalk, new hemp was being woven for standing rigging and manila for running rigging from which the ship's rigger waited to splice the intricate network of shrouds, sheets, and stays for the upcoming voyage. And in a sailmaker's loft above a chandlery on Water Street, needles and fids were flying as new sails were being stitched.

But on an embankment above Brant Point Shipyard, a lonely man stood beside his dog, forlornly contemplating the implacable cycle that never ceased in this whaling empire. *Whaling!* He clenched his fists.

Damn you, you merciless bitch! I have lost my wife to you!

He studied the *Omega* below, painfully considering whether it would be preferable to sign on another voyage rather than stay here to see Laura remain married to Dan.

But then, with a determined grimace, he turned back the way he had come, stalking the ocean path while seagulls squawked and hammers echoed through the shrouds of mists behind him.

Dan is at his desk in the countinghouse, and she is home alone.

The long stride grew longer, and the dog at his heels broke into a trot.

Laura Morgan had been expecting the knock, but when it came she started and pressed a hand to her heart.

Go away, Rye! I'm afraid of what you do to me!

The knock sounded again, and Laura caught her trembling lower lip between her teeth. Resolutely, she moved toward the door, but when it was opened, only stared transfixed at Rye, who stood outside with his weight slung on one hip, his hands tucked inside the stomach flap of his britches. A myriad of impressions danced across her mind, all too quick to grasp—he stands differently; he's wearing the sweater I made; his hair needs trimming; *he's* spent a sleepless night, too.

"Hello, Laura."

He didn't smile, but stood at ease, waiting patiently on the stoop. And it happened, as it had happened since she was fourteen—that total surge of gladness at the sight of him. But now caution tempered it.

"Hello, Rye." Resolutely, she held the edge of the door.

"I had t' come."

Somewhere in the recesses of her mind she noted the abbreviated speech he'd picked up on the high seas, realizing it added to his magnetism: a thing she needed to explore, for it made him somewhat a stranger. Her fingers clenched upon the door, but her eyes remained steadily on his.

"I was afraid you might."

At the word *afraid* his eyebrows puckered, and his lips seemed to thin. She noted again the pockmark on the top one and steeled herself against the urge to touch it with her fingertip.

He studied her as if she were a rare diamond and he a gem-cutter.

She stared at him as if expecting him to rattle some ghostly chain. The Nantucket mists formed an appropriate background, as if they had levitated Rye Dalton and borne him to her, then hung back to watch what she'd do.

"Can I come in?"

How preposterous the question. This was his house! Outside it was damp and cold, and behind her a fire burned. Yet while he tucked his hands against his stomach for warmth, she hesitated like a gatekeeper.

She glanced nervously down the scallop shell-path, then dropped her hand from the door. "For just a minute."

As he stepped forward, the dog instinctively moved with him.

"Stay."

At the word, Laura noticed Ship for the first time. Immediately, she smiled and bent to greet the Lab.

"Ship . . . oh, Ship . . . hello, girl!" With a whine and a wag, Ship returned the greeting. Laura hunkered in the doorway, holding the dog's chin with one hand and scratching the top of her head with the other. Her pale gray skirt billowed wide, hiding Rye's boots as he stood studying the top of her head. But it was on the dog that she lavished her affectionate greeting.

"So you've come to see me at last, silly girl . . . and it's about time, too. You could have dropped by now and then . . ." There followed a chuckle as Laura was bestowed a brief whip of a pink tongue on her cheek. She jerked back, but laughingly invited, "No need for you to stay outside, girl. Your rug's still there."

Looking down at the two of them, it was all Rye could do to keep from pulling the woman up into his arms and demanding the welcome he, too, deserved.

She rose and led the way inside. When the door was closed, she faced it while Rye paused with his back to it, and they both watched Ship give a brief sniff to the air, then circle twice before dropping to the braided rug beside Rye's ankles, with a grunt of satisfied familiarity.

The blue eyes of Rye Dalton lifted to meet the brown ones of Laura. The sense of homecoming was overwhelming. Ship lowered her chin to her paws with a sigh while Rye once more slipped his fingers inside his stomach flap, as if they were safest there. His voice, when he spoke, was pulled from deep in his throat.

"The dog's had a more affectionate welcome than her master."

Laura's eyes dropped, but unfortunately they fell to the sight of his palms tucked just inside his hip laces. She felt an unwanted heat pressing upward to steal across her cheeks. "She . . . she remembers her old spot," Laura managed in almost a whisper.

"Aye."

The unfamiliar term scarcely reached the far walls while she again fought the urge to explore the differences in him. She saw one dark hand slip into the open and reach for her elbow. "Rye, you can't—"

"Laura, I've been thinking of y'."

His fingers curled around her arm, but she pulled it safely

out of reach and moved back a step while her eyes flew to his.
"Don't!"

His hand hung in midair for a tense moment, then fell to his
side. He sighed thickly, dropping his chin to stare at the floor.
"I was afraid y'd say that."

She glanced nervously toward the alcove bed and whispered, "Josh is napping."

Rye's head came up with a jerk, and he, too, looked across
the room. She watched an expression of longing cross his face.
Again his blue eyes sought hers. "Can I see him?"

Indecision flickered in her eyes while she threaded her fingers tightly together. But finally she answered, "Of course."

He moved then, crossing the room with light steps that
seemed to take eons of time before he stopped in front of the
alcove bed and peered into its shadows. Laura remained where
she was, following him with her gaze, watching Rye pause,
hook a thumb into the top of his trousers again, and lean
sideways from one hip. For a long moment he stood silent, unmoving. Then he reached into the recesses of the alcove to take
the binding of Josh's small quilt between index and middle
fingers. The fire burned cozily. The only sound was that of
falling ash. A father studied his slumbering son.

Rye . . . oh, Rye . . .

The cry was locked inside Laura's throat, and her eyes were
drawn into an expression of pain while she watched him slowly
straighten and even more slowly look back over his shoulder at
her. His blue gaze moved down to her stomach, and she realized both of her palms were pressed hard against it, as if she
were only now in the throes of labor. Flustered, she dropped
them to her sides.

"When was he born?" Rye asked softly.

"In December."

"December what?"

"Eighth."

Rye's eyes caressed the sleeping child again, then he turned
away and moved with silent deliberation to the door of the
new linter room. There he stopped again, looking in, his eyes
moving across its interior to linger on the bed.

A queer mixture of feelings seemed to turn Laura's stomach

over: familiarity, caution, yearning. She studied Rye's broad shoulders, covered by the sweater she had knit years ago, as they filled the bedroom doorway. He looked at once relaxed and tense as he stood contemplating her and Dan's bedroom, and Laura wondered if Rye had deliberately chosen to wear that particular sweater today. It strikingly emphasized his ruggedness, and the sight of him in it gripped her with a sudden flush of sensuality as she watched him slowly turn her way and take a slow walk around the edge of the keeping room, eyeing objects, running a finger along the edge of the mantel, taking in the new as well as the familiar. When he reached Laura again, he stood before her with that wide-legged stance of a seaman.

"Changes," he uttered in a broken voice.

"In five years they were inevitable."

"But all these?" Now his voice had taken on a harder note. Again he reached for her; again she avoided his touch.

"Rye, I went to see Ezra Merrill." Laura was grateful that her announcement distracted Rye, and he refrained from reaching again.

"You too? That makes two of y'."

"Two?" She looked up, puzzled.

"It seems Dan visited Merrill yesterday."

Yesterday, thought Laura. Yesterday?

At her look of consternation, Rye went on. "He gave me the news this mornin' when I saw him at the countinghouse."

"Then you know already?"

"Aye, I know. But I know that the law can't dictate how I feel."

Rather than face his determined eyes, she turned away. But from behind he saw her lift a hand to touch her temple.

"This is such a muddled mess, Rye."

"It appears the law can't dictate y'r feelings, either."

She spun to face him again. "Feelings are not what I'm speaking of, but legalities. I am his wife, don't you understand? You . . . you shouldn't even be here at this very minute!"

Her head was tipped slightly to one side, and her upper body strained toward him in earnestness. He spoke with deadly calm. "Y' sound rather desperate, Laura."

Immediately, she straightened. "Rye, I have to ask you to leave and not to be seen here again until we can get this thing straightened out. Dan was . . . he was very upset last night, and if he should find you here again, I . . . I . . ." She stammered to a halt, her eyes on the strong curve of his jawbone, where the new side-whiskers nearly met the thick turtleneck of his sweater, giving him a brawny and wholly unsettling appeal. "Please, Rye," she ended lamely.

For a moment she thought he would raise his fist and shout at the heavens, releasing his tightly controlled rage. Instead, he relaxed—albeit with an effort—and agreed. "Aye, I'll go . . . but the lad is asleep."

His eyes flashed to the alcove bed, then back to her, and before she could prevent it, he'd taken a single long step forward and grasped the back of her head, commandeering it with one mighty hand while his mouth swooped over hers. She pressed her palms against the wool sweater, only to find his heart thundering within it. She strained to pull away, but his grasp was so relentless it pushed the whalebone hairpins into her scalp. His tongue had already wet her lips before she managed to jerk free. When she did, her lips escaped his with a frantic, sucking sound.

"Rye, this—"

"Shh . . ." From violent to gentle, his quick change confused her as his admonition cut off her words. "In a minute . . . I'll leave in a minute." Recklessly, he'd clasped the back of her neck and forced her forward, the action in direct contrast to his repeated, soft, "Shh . . ."

She allowed herself to stay as she was, though rigidly, with his chin pressed against her forehead while his eyes sank shut. Beneath her fingers his heart still pounded, and she closed her fists about the rough, textured wool of his sweater, grasping and twisting it as if it could keep her from sinking. But both she and Rye were trembling now.

"I love y', Laura." The words rumbled from his throat while her knees went wobbly. "Josh . . . ." She heard Rye swallow. "Josh looks like my mother," he uttered thickly. Then, as suddenly as he'd demanded the kiss, he was gone,

spinning away to jerk the door open with only one more word.
   "Come!"
   But Ship was already on her feet.
   And Laura Morgan was left behind to wish desperately that
she could follow that order as freely as Ship could.

Chapter 4

THE FOLLOWING SATURDAY NIGHT, Joseph Starbuck's home was brightly lit with whale oil, appropriate for an occasion honoring the successful voyage of a whaleship.

When Laura Morgan stepped through the front door, it was into a fairyland of artificial brightness such as few Nantucket homes boasted at night. Chandeliers gleamed, reflecting off polished oak floors and the highly waxed bannister of the staircase. On a refectory table in the main hall, smaller lanterns glimmered into the depth of a crystal punch bowl of persimmon beer beside another of syllabub, a rich mixture of sweet cream and wine. Around the edges of the room, small Betty lamps highlighted the array of colorful silk gowns whose skirts were held aloft by whalebone hoops, making the women appear to glide as if on wheels.

Dan had been taciturn and brooding all evening, ever since helping Laura lace her stays and hook her gown. He had looked up to find the whalebone corsets thrusting her breasts up higher than usual, helped along by the stiff boning that shaped the bodice of the dress itself. A sour look had overtaken his face and was still there.

The dress front was modest, topped by a stiff yoke of narrow pleating which swept from the crest of one shoulder to the other with scarcely a dip at the center. When she'd bought the dress, Laura had laughingly said there was no escaping whaling on Nantucket, for she even *looked* like a whaleboat! Indeed, the shadows of the pleating resembled the overlapped planking on a dory. But there was no mistaking Laura for anything except what she was—a shapely young beauty whose contours were ripe within her bodice.

Her muslin gown was interwoven with cream silk stripes between sprays of pink roses on a delicate background of tiny green leaves. Artificial roses of pink rode on the crests of her shoulders, from which the sleeves of the gown were also tightly pleated to the elbow before an enormous puff of muslin billowed out beneath a band of pink ribbon.

The dress set off her fine-boned fragility: the delicate jaw, chin, and nose, and an adorable mouth shaped like the leaf of a sweetheart ivy. Her dainty features made Laura's dark-lashed brown eyes appear even larger than they were, as did the style of her hair, most of which was pulled high onto the crown of her head in an intricate knot entwined with thin pink ribbons, while above her left ear nested another rose, from which fell a gathering of sausage-shaped curls. Around her face, tiny angel-wisps had been cut shorter than the rest and curled like an auburn halo about her delicate features.

Her femininity was further enhanced by the styles of the day, with their elongated waists and enormous skirts, which served to make the fat look fatter, the thin look emaciated, but the lucky ones, like Laura Morgan, look like a Dresden doll.

At the moment, however, Laura felt far from lucky. Her waist was pinched into a miserable little hourglass and felt as if it would surely snap in half a minute! A wide whalebone stay ran up the front of the dress and already it was digging into her stomach whenever she bent, and into the valley between her breasts each time she inhaled. Her discomfort had made her decidedly testy, to say nothing of light-headed.

Laura never went out for a social evening without silently cursing the rigging into which she was forced. But tonight's occasion demanded that she smile cordially and uncomplainingly, for it was a business dinner, Dan had said, meaning that Starbuck's more important employees had been invited, along with such honored guests as Captain Blackwell, of the *Omega,* and Christopher Capen and James Childs, the mason and carpenter whom Starbuck had contracted to build the Three Bricks for his sons.

The conversation seemed centered around the success of the *Omega* and the progress on the houses, which were well under way. Laura listened with half an ear to Annabel Pruitt, the wife of Starbuck's purchasing agent, who had a habit of releasing news even before the town newspaper did. Though it was of little interest to Laura that the bricks for the houses had come all the way from Gloucester, her attention was captured when the subject abruptly changed.

"They say Mr. Starbuck has offered Rye Dalton a substantial lay to sail on the *Omega* next time she goes out." Mrs. Pruitt closely watched the faces of Dan and Laura Morgan as she divulged this tidbit.

Laura felt Dan's fingers tighten on her elbow and suddenly scanned the hall in search of a fainting bench, that abominable invention created by men who'd never had to bear being trussed up like a Thanksgiving turkey! But in the next moment Dan's fingers dug in even harder, and Laura realized it was not the mere mention of Rye's name that had made her husband go stiff. He tugged on her elbow so sharply that the syllabub went sloshing in her glass.

"Why, Dan, whatever—" she began, jerking back to avoid soiling her dress, and sending the whalebone digging sharply into her stomach.

But in that instant, following the course of Dan's glare, the discomfort she endured to look so beautiful became suddenly justified. There, at the door, Rye Dalton was being greeted by the Starbucks. Laura's heart leaped. She could not help staring, for Rye was dressed like a fashion plate—no sweater or pea jacket in sight.

He wore stirruped pants of forest green with a matching tailcoat boasting a stiff, high collar, with the newest feature—notches—on its lapel. Long, tight sleeves dropped well below his wrist, half covering his bronze hands. His sea-tanned face was the color of a ripe chestnut above a pristine white stock wound tightly about his neck and tied in a small bow, half hidden behind his double-breasted jacket.

As a mallard finds its mate in a flock, so Rye found Laura in the throng of people that filled the room. His eyes met hers and sent a shaft of heat down her body. Forgotten were the pains in her stomach; instead, she was filled with pride at how she looked in the dress. As those blue eyes lingered on hers, then traveled down her body and back up, she realized her mouth was open, and snapped it shut.

They had not seen each other for four days, and she certainly hadn't expected him to be here tonight. Nor had she expected his eyes to seek her out so brazenly, nor the slight bow he gave her even before the footman reached for his beaver top hat.

Immediately, Laura hid her flaming cheeks behind her glass of syllabub, but not before Dan noted the exchange of glances between the two. With an acid look, he gripped Laura's elbow and turned her away from the door, circling her waist and leaving his hand there possessively, something rarely done here in public, in this city where Puritan founders had left their indelible mark.

Knowing Dalton watched their backs, Dan leaned intimately close to his wife's ear. "I didn't have any idea he'd be here tonight, did you?"

"Me? How could I have known?"

"I thought he might have told you." He watched her face carefully to see if he was right.

"I . . . I haven't seen him since Monday," she lied. She'd kissed him on Tuesday.

"If I'd known he'd be here, we wouldn't have come."

"Don't be silly, Dan. Living in the same town, we're bound to run into him now and then. You can't isolate me, so you'll just have to learn to trust me instead."

"Oh I trust you, Laura. It's him I don't trust."

Almost thirty minutes passed before the guests were called to dinner. By the time they entered the dining room, Laura had a backache from standing so rigidly and the beginnings of a headache from the tension. Try though she might to forget that Rye was in the room, she couldn't. It seemed each time she turned to visit with another guest, he managed to be in her line of vision, studying her from beneath those perfectly shaped eyebrows of his, smiling boldly when no one was looking. His hair was neatly trimmed now, but the new sideburns remained, bracketing his jaws in brawny appeal. Though she tried to keep from looking at him, she had little success, and once—she couldn't be sure—she thought he mimed a kiss to her, but he was lifting his glass at that moment, and the kiss, if it was one, became a sip.

He was in one of his devilish, teasing moods tonight. Laura remembered them well.

At dinner, as if her hostess had intentionally planned to compound Laura's misery, she and Dan were placed directly across the table from Rye and a talkative young blonde named DeLaine Hussey, whose forefathers, along with those of Joseph Starbuck, had settled the island.

Miss Hussey immediately engaged Rye in conversation about the voyage, sympathizing effusively over his bout with smallpox, studying the few marks left on his face, and claiming they'd done nothing whatever to mar his appearance. She followed this statement with a fluttery smile that made Laura wish the woman would get the pox herself! But Rye—damn him!—was lapping it up, grinning down at the woman, the grin enhanced by the pockmark that fell in the crease of his cheek and dimpled him beguilingly.

In no time at all Miss Hussey pursued a subject that raised Laura's temperature to that of the clam chowder she'd just been served. "The *Omega* was gone five years . . . that's a long time."

"Aye, it is."

Laura felt Rye's eyes upon her as she lifted a spoonful of steaming soup, but she carefully refrained from returning his glance.

"You don't know, then, about the group of women here on Nantucket who've organized and call themselves the Female Freemasons?" chirped the blonde across the way.

And Laura blew too hard on her soup, making some of it fly onto the table linen. DeLaine Hussey, she thought, had been aptly named! She'd been trying to get her claws into Rye for as long as Laura could remember, and she certainly wasn't wasting any time, now that word was out Rye had been refused admittance to the saltbox on the hill.

"No, ma'am," Rye was answering. "I've never heard of 'em."

"Ah, but you will now that the *Omega's* come in with full barrels."

"Full barrels? What do full barrels have t' do with a women's group?"

"The Female Freemasons, Mr. Dalton, are sworn to refuse to be courted by or to marry any man who has not killed his first whale."

Laura burned her tongue on the chowder and nearly overturned her water glass in her haste to cool her mouth.

Mr. Dalton, indeed! Laura thought. Why, the two of them had gone to school together. Just what did DeLaine Hussey think she was up to?

The servers came then to remove the chowder bowls and Laura realized she should not have eaten the entire helping, but she'd become preoccupied with the conversation and hadn't realized she was putting herself in jeopardy. Her restrictive whalebones were already causing extreme misery, but the servers were now bringing in a steaming veal roast ringed with glazed carrots and herbed potatoes.

Laura had no choice but to accept the main course when it came her turn. But the veal stuck in her throat, along with the flirtatious conversation continuing on the other side of the table.

The smitten Miss Hussey continued to delineate the doctrines of the chivalric order of island ladies devoted to loving only proven whalers, until Rye was forced to ask politely, "And are you a member of th' group . . . Miss Hussey?"

At that precise moment, Laura nearly choked on a piece of veal, for something soft and warm was working her skirts up and caressed her calf beneath the table.

Rye's foot!

"Indeed I am, Mr. Dalton," DeLaine Hussey simpered.

The gall of the man to do a thing like that while innocently smiling down at DeLaine Hussey! Why, he knew full well it was his and Laura's old playful signal that they wanted to make love when they got home!

While Rye's foot made shivers ripple through Laura's flesh, the doe-eyed Miss Hussey continued batting her sooty lashes and gazing devastatingly into Rye's eyes while pointedly asking, "Have *you* killed your first whale yet, Mr. Dalton?"

Rye laughed uninhibitedly, leaning back until his jaw lifted before he grinned engagingly at his table companion again. "Nay, Miss Hussey, I haven't, and y' well know it. I'm a cooper, not a boatsteerer," he reminded, using the official name of the harpooners.

At that moment Rye's toes inched up and curled over the edge of the chair between Laura's knees, all the while he smiled into DeLaine Hussey's eyes. This time Laura visibly jumped and a chunk of veal lodged in her throat, sending up a spasm of coughing.

Dan solicitously patted her back and signaled for the server to refill her water glass. "Are you all right?" he asked.

"F . . . fine." She gulped, struggling for composure while that warm foot brushed the insides of her knees, preventing her from clamping them shut.

The coughing, unfortunately, brought her hostess's attention to Laura's plate, and Mrs. Starbuck noted how little her guest had eaten and inquired if the food was all right. Thus, Laura felt compelled to lift yet another bite of veal and attempt to swallow it.

Just then Rye smiled nonchalantly at Laura and said, "Please pass the salt." He could see she was in misery: he remembered well enough her abhorrence of whalebone corsets.

To Laura's surprise, she then felt a *tap! tap! tap!* against the inside of one knee. And while across the table Rye and De-Laine Hussey engaged in a seemingly innocent conversation about coopering, Rye cut two pieces of his own veal, ate one, and covertly dropped the other on the floor, where the Starbucks' fluffy matched Persian cats immediately cleaned up the evidence.

Laura raised her napkin to her lips and smiled behind it. But she was grateful to Rye, for at the next possible opportunity she practiced the same sleight-of-hand he'd just demonstrated, which ultimately saved her from embarrassing either herself or her hostess—or both.

The meal ended with a rich rum-flavored torte, which neither of the cats liked—a barely perceptible shrug of Rye's shoulders made Laura again take smiling refuge behind her napkin—so she was forced to eat half her serving, which left her stomach in a perilous state.

By the time Rye chose to remove his foot, Laura was not only queasy but flustered. Their host and hostess were rising from their chairs when Laura could tell by the look on Rye's face that he was searching for his lost shoe. She let him suffer, slipping it further underneath her chair while up and down the table guests were getting to their feet and repairing to the main hall. Dan moved behind her chair, and for a moment she considered leaving the shoe where it was, but if it were spied there, it would convict her as well as Rye, so his scowl was rewarded a second later by the safe return of the shoe.

A string quartet played now in the main hall, and some couples danced while others visited. A small group of men stepped outside to smoke cigars, among them Joseph Starbuck and Dan, who reluctantly left Laura's side at his employer's request. But first he observed that Rye was still in the clutches of DeLaine Hussey, so he assumed Rye would have no chance to bother Laura.

Laura, meanwhile, did not need Rye Dalton to be bothered. She realized if she didn't soon ease her whalebone corsets she was going to either vomit or faint.

As soon as it was gracefully possible, she escaped through the back door, inhaling great gulps of night air. But the air alone did little to relieve her, for it was laden with fog tonight, and she nearly choked on the tang of tar, spread as it was beneath the fruit trees of Starbuck's orchard, to control canker worms. Picking up her skirts, she ran at a most unladylike clip between the apple trees, where the cloying scent of blossoms only worsened her nausea. She groped futilely for the row of brass hooks and eyes at the back of her dress, but knew full well there was no reaching them. Her mouth watered warningly. Tears stung her eyes. She clutched her waist and bent over, gagging.

At that moment cool fingers touched the back of Laura's neck and quickly began releasing the hooks while she broke out into a quivering sweat.

"What the hell're y' doin' in these things if y' can't tolerate them?" Rye Dalton demanded.

For the moment she was unable to answer, battling the

forces of nature. But finally she managed to choke out a single word.

"Hurry!"

"Damn idiotic contraptions!" he muttered. "Y' should have more sense, woman!"

"Th . . . the laces . . . please," she gasped when the dress was open.

He yanked at the bow resting in the hollow of her spine, then jerked it free at last and began working his fingers up the lacings until Laura breathed her first easy breath in three hours.

"May you b . . . burn in hell, Rye D . . . Dalton, for ever bringing whalebones to shore and m . . . making women all over the world miserable!" she berated between huge gasps.

"If I burn in hell, might's well do it for a lot better reason than that," he said, moving close behind her, slipping his hand inside her loosened corset.

"Stop it!" She lurched away and spun on him while all her frustrations boiled to the surface. This incredible trap he'd caused by insisting on going whaling, the torture of these damned insufferable whalebones, the cozy little piece of flirtation she'd just been forced to witness—it all sparked an explosion of temper that suddenly raged out of control. "Stop it!" she hissed. "You have no right to sail in here after . . . after *five years* and act as if you'd never left!"

Immediately, his temper flared, too. "I left for *you*, so I could bring you—"

"I begged you not to go! I didn't want your . . . your stinking whale oil! I wanted my husband!"

"Well, here I am!" he shot back sarcastically.

"Oh . . ." She clenched her fists, almost growling in frustration. "You think it's so simple, don't you, Rye? Playing footsie under the table, as if the most important thing I have to decide is whether or not to take my shoe off. Well, you can see what a state it's put me in."

"And what about the state I'm in!"

She turned her back disdainfully. "I'm fine now. Thank you for your help . . . *Mister* Dalton," she retorted, imitating DeLaine Hussey, "but you'd better go back before you're missed."

"I did that so y'd see what I'm forced t' go through every time I see you and Dan together. It bothered y', didn't it—seeing your *husband* with another woman?"

Again she whirled to confront him. "All right . . . yes! It bothered me! But I realize now I have no right to be bothered by it. As I said before, you'd better go back before you're missed."

"I don't give a damn if I'm missed. Besides, all I'm doin' is standin' in an orchard visiting with my wife. What's wrong with that?"

"Rye, Dan won't like—"

At that moment Dan's voice came from just beyond the nearest row of apple trees.

"Laura? Are you out there?"

She turned toward the voice to reply, but Rye's hand found her elbow and he moved close, placing a finger over her mouth, breathing softly beside her ear, "Shh."

"I've got to answer him," she whispered while her heart drummed. "He knows we're out here."

He grabbed her head with both hands and brought her ear to his lips. "You do, and I'll tell him your corsets are loose because we were just enjoyin' a little roll beneath the apple trees."

She jerked away angrily, frantically scrabbling to retie her rigging. But it was futile, and Rye only stood by grinning.

"Laura, is that you?" came Dan's voice. "Where are you?"

"Help me!" she begged, turning her back on Rye as Dan's footsteps came closer. He was walking between the trees now; they could hear the branches snapping.

"Not on your life," Rye whispered.

In a panic she grabbed his wrist, picked up her skirts, and ran, pulling him along after her. Down the rows they went, ducking between trees, skimming silently through the fog-shrouded night, which buffered the sound of their passing. Foolish, childish thing to do! Yet Laura was unable to think beyond the fact that she could not let Dan discover her half undressed out here in the misty night with Rye.

The orchard was wide and long, stretching away in a maze of white-misted apple trees which gave way to quince, then to plum. The fog blanketed everything, obscuring the two who moved through it like specters. Laura's wide skirt might well have been only another explosion of apple blossoms, for the trees cowered close to the ground, protecting themselves from the incessant ocean winds, until they took on the same bouffant shape as a hooped skirt.

At last Laura stopped, alert, listening, one hand pressed against her heaving breasts to hold the dress up. Rye, too, listened, but they heard not the faintest strains of the music drifting from the house. They were surrounded by billows of white, lost in the swirling fog, alone in a private scented bower of quince, where they'd be neither seen or heard.

She still clutched his wrist. Beneath her thumb she could feel his pulse racing. She flung the hand away and cursed, "Damn you, Rye!"

But his good humor was back. "Is that any way t' talk to the man who's just loosened your stays?"

"I told you I had to have time to think and work things out."

"I've given y' five days . . . just what have y' worked out?"

"Five days—exactly! How can I get a mess like this worked out in five days?"

"So y' want to string me along and lead me out t' the apple orchard where we used t' do it right under Dan's nose even when we were kids?" He moved closer, his breath coming heavy, too, after their run.

"That's not why I came out here," she protested, and it was true.

"Why, then?" He put both wide hands on her waist to pull her closer. Immediately, she grabbed his wrists, but he would not be waylaid. He caressed her hipbones while his voice blended with the soft fog to muddle her. "Remember that time, Laura? Remember how it was . . . with the sun on our skin and both of us so scared Dan would find us right there in the daylight, and—"

She clapped a hand over his mouth. "You're not being fair," she pleaded, but the memory had been revived, as he'd intended, and already served Rye's purpose, for her breath was not easing. Instead, it came heavier and faster than when they'd first stopped running.

So he kissed the fingers with which she'd stifled his words. Immediately, she retracted them, freeing his lips to vow, "I'll tell y' right now, woman, I've no intention of playin' fair. I'll play as dirty as I have to t' win y' back. And I'll start right here by soilin' your dress in this apple orchard if y' won't take the damn thing off."

His hands pulled her against his hips again, then slid up her ribs and onto her back, finding the openings in her laces, pressing against her shoulder blades until her breasts touched his jacket.

She turned her mouth aside. "If I kiss you once, will you be satisfied and let me go back?"

"What do y' think?" he whispered gruffly, nuzzling the side of her neck, biting it lightly, sending goosebumps shivering across her belly.

"I think my husband will kill me if I don't get back to the house soon." But she inched her lips closer to his even as she said it.

"And I think *this* husband will kill y' if y' do," he said, almost at her mouth. He smelled of cedar and wine and the past. She recognized his aroma, and it prompted her response. The silence hemmed them in, so immense and total that within it their heartbeats seemed to resound like cannon shot. The first day when he'd kissed her, she'd been in shock. The second time he'd taken her by surprise. But now—if he kissed her now, if she let him, this one would be deliberate.

"Once," she whispered. "Just once, then I have to go back. Promise you'll lace me up," she pleaded.

"Nay," he returned gruffly, breathing on her lips. "No promises."

Sensibly, she pulled back, but it took little effort for Rye to change her mind. He simply touched the corner of her mouth with his lips.

And the old thrill was back, as fresh and vital as always. He had that way about him, Rye did, that she'd tried to forget since being married to Dan. Call it technique, call it practice, call it familiarity—but they'd learned to kiss together, and Rye knew what Laura liked. He let their breaths mingle, then wet the corner of her mouth, dipping to taste before savoring fully. She liked to be aroused one tiny step at a time, and she waited now, her neck taut, her breathing labored, while he held her with one hand around the side of her neck, his thumb massaging the hollow beneath her jaw. The thumb circled lazily. Then came his tongue, wetting the perimeter of her lips with patient, faint strokes, as Rye sensed the fire building within her.

The memories came flooding back to Laura . . . being fifteen in a dory with lips tightly shut and eyes safely closed, being sixteen in a boathouse loft and knowing well the use of tongues; moving toward full maturity and learning together how a man touches a woman, how a woman touches a man to create impatience, then ecstasy.

As if he read her mind, Rye now murmured, "Remember that summer, Laura, up in the loft above old man Hardesty's boathouse?"

And he took her back to those beginnings, pressing his mouth fully over hers, his tongue inviting hers to dance. His silky inner lips were just warm enough, just wet enough, just hesitant enough, just demanding enough, to wipe away today and take her back through the years to those first times.

She shivered. He felt the tremor beneath his palm on her neck and drew her against him, then slipped that warm, seeking palm within the dress that hung loosely from her shoulders. But when he would have pulled it down, she quickly flung her arms about his neck so that he couldn't. The dress was doing its intended job, for through spikes of whalebone and clumps of gathers there was little chance of his touching her intimately. The hoop was pressed tightly against his thighs and flared out behind her as if blowing in a hurricane.

But the hurricane blew not on her skirts but within her head and heart, for the kiss now had substance. It was a hot, whole giving of mouths, with neither holding back anything. Her tongue joined his and she knew the immediate shock of difference, as anyone knows who has kissed only one person for a long time, as she had Dan. It should have sobered her, reminded her she was not free to do these things with this man, but instead she welcomed it and realized that ever since she'd married Dan, she'd been comparing his kiss to this and finding it lacking.

That traitorous admission brought her somewhat to her

senses, and she hoped fervently that Rye would be content with this kiss for now, because her resistance was fast slipping as he held her firmly and ran his hands along the exposed skin of her back, which was the only bareness he could reach.

He tore his lips away and spoke with savage emotion. "Laura—my God, woman, does it give y' joy to torture me?" He raised one hand and slid it along her arm, capturing one of her hands from the back of his neck, carrying it down, and placing it on his swollen body. "I've been five years at sea and this is what it's done t' me. How long would y' make me wait?"

Shock waves sizzled through her body. She tried to pull free, but he held her palm where it had too long been absent, the heat of his tumescence insistent through the cloth of his trousers. Clutching the back of her neck, he drew her wildly against him once more, kissing her, his hot, demanding tongue stroking rhythmically in and out of her mouth, reminding Laura that it was he who had taught her these things in a boathouse loft years ago. Her hand stopped resisting and conformed to the shape of him, and he thrust against her caress, still pressing the back of her wrist and knuckles and fingers.

Against her will, she again compared him to the man who waited at the house for her now. Her palm moved up, then down, measuring, remembering, while Rye begged her with the motion of his body to seek the touch of his satin skin if she would not allow him to seek hers.

The fog curled its tendrils about their heads, and the seductive scent of blossoms filled the night. Their breathing scraped harshly with desire, like ocean waves rushing upon sand, then retreating.

"Please," Rye growled into her mouth. "Please, Laura-love. It's been so long."

"I can't, Rye," she said miserably, suddenly withdrawing her hand and covering her face with both palms, a sob breaking from her. "I can't . . . Dan trusts me."

"Dan!" he growled. "Dan! What about me?" Rye's voice trembled with rage. He grasped her arm and jerked her almost onto tiptoe. "I trusted you! I trusted y' t' wait for me while I sailed on that . . . that *miserable* whaleship and floundered in the stink of rancid oil and rottin' fish and ate flour with the

weevils sifted out of it and smelled men's unwashed bodies day
after day, and one of them my own!'' His fingers closed
tighter, and Laura winced. ''Have y' any idea of how I longed
for the smell of y'? I nearly lost my mind at the thought of it.''
But now he thrust her away almost distastefully. ''Lyin' there
adrift in the doldrums, at the mercy of a windless sky, while
days and days passed and I thought of the wasted time when I
could've been with you. But I wanted t' bring y' a better life.
That's why I did it!'' he raged.

''And what do you think I was going through?'' she cried,
her shoulders jutting forward belligerently, tears now coursing
down her cheeks. ''What do you think I suffered when I
watched you stuffing clothes in your sea chest, when I saw
those sails disappear and wondered if I'd ever see you alive
again? What do you think it was like when I discovered I was
carrying your baby and I got the news that that baby would
never know his father?'' Her voice shook. ''I wanted to kill
you, Rye Dalton, do you know that? I wanted to *kill* you
because you'd *died on me!*'' She laughed a little dementedly.

''But y' certainly wasted no time findin' someone t' take my
place afterward, did y'!''

She clenched her fists and shouted. ''I was pregnant!''

''With my child, and y' turned to him!'' They stood almost
nose to nose.

''Who else could I turn to? But you wouldn't understand!
When's the last time your stomach swelled up like a baloon-
fish so you couldn't even walk without hurting or . . . or
shovel a walk or carry wood or lift a water pail! Who do you
think did all those things while you were gone, Rye?''

''My best friend,'' Rye answered bitterly.

''He was my best friend, too. And if he hadn't been, I don't
know what I'd have done. He was there without being asked,
whenever I needed him, and whether you want to believe it or
not, it was as much because he loved you as because he loved
me.''

''Spare me the dramatics, Laura. He was there because he
couldn't wait t' get his hands on y', and you know it,'' Rye
said coldly.

''That's a despicable thing to say, and *you* know it!''

"Are you denyin' that y' knew how he felt about y' all the years we were growing up?"

"I'm denying nothing. I'm trying to make you see what two people suffered at the news of your death . . . suffered together! After we heard that the *Massachusetts* had gone down, we got through those first days by walking the dunes where the three of us used to play, telling ourselves one minute that it couldn't be true, that you were still alive out there someplace, and the next minute telling each other to accept it —you'd never be back. But I was the weaker one by far. I . . . I told myself I was acting exactly like my mother, and I hated it, but the despair was worse than anything I'd ever known. I found I didn't care if I lived or died, and at times I felt the same about the child I carried. After the funeral was the worst . . ." Her voice cracked with remembrance, and she shuddered. "Oh God, that funeral . . . without a corpse . . . and me already awkward with your child."

"Laura . . ." He moved near, but she turned her back and went on.

"I couldn't have made it through that . . . that horror, if it weren't for Dan. My mother was perfectly useless, as you can well imagine. And she was no better when Josh was born. It was Dan who was my strength then, Dan who sat beside me through the first of my labor, then paced outside where you should have been pacing, then came to praise the baby and tell me he looked like you, because he knew those were the words I needed to give me the will to get strong again. It was your best friend who promised he'd always be there for Josh and me, no matter what. And I owe him for that." She paused a moment. "You owe him."

He studied her back, then stepped close and roughly began lacing up her stays.

"But *what* do I owe him?" His hands stopped tugging. "You?"

Laura shivered, unable to answer. What did they owe Dan? Certainly something better than stealing off into the night and indulging in sex play. Again Rye continued lacing.

"You've got to understand, Rye. He's been Josh's father since the day Josh was born. He's been my husband three times as long as you've been. I can't just . . . just fling him aside carelessly, without a thought for his feelings."

At her back came one irritated tug, harder than the rest, then the tension disappeared around Laura's ribs as Rye fumbled. "I'm not much good at this . . . I haven't had much practice."

There was an icy insinuation in his tone. He was still angry with her, and with this seemingly unsolvable confusion into which their lives had been thrust. When he'd finally managed to close both corset and dress, his hands continued resting on her hips. "So y' intend t' stay with him?"

Laura closed her eyes tiredly, inhaled deeply, no closer to solutions than Rye. "For the time being."

His warm hands slipped away. "And y' won't see me?"

"Not this way . . . not . . ." But she stammered to a halt, uncertain of her ability to resist him.

His anger was back, roiling just beneath the surface as he gritted his teeth. "We'll see about that . . . *Mrs. Morgan!*"

Then he spun and walked into the silent fog.

Chapter 5

THE DAYS THAT followed found Laura and Dan uncomfortable and distant. Since the night of the Starbucks' dinner, Dan had grown more and more stoical toward her, often wearing a wounded look that pricked Laura's conscience each time she glanced up and encountered it. She had not lied when he asked if she'd been with Rye that night, but Dan had seen her red-rimmed eyes and guessed the worst hadn't happened—not if there'd been tears. Yet those tears themselves told Dan that Laura still had feelings for Rye. And the tension grew.

On a warm golden evening in late May, when the sun hovered over the rim of the ocean like a ripe melon, Laura watched from the window above her zinc sink while Dan and Josh played together in the yard. Dan had made a pair of stilts and was patiently trying to teach Josh to walk with them. He held them upright, and Josh clambered up onto the footblocks once more while Dan supported him, keeping the sticks steady. But the minute Dan let go, Josh's legs spread apart like two halves of a wishbone. A single halting step, then the stilts went crashing to the ground in one direction and the boy in another, rolling over and over and over, playfully exaggerating, and Dan right with him, the two of them laughing joyously. They tumbled to a halt and Dan lay flat on his back, arms outflung while Josh straddled his chest as if he had Dan pinned. Then over they went in the other direction, and this time Dan pinned Josh, whose childish giggling drifted through the spring evening . . . the music of love.

The sun was behind the pair, turning their bodies to silhouette as Laura observed with a lump in her throat. Dan pulled Josh to his feet and brushed his clothes off, turning him around to tease with a playful spank on the boy's backside. Josh whirled around to get his giggling revenge, but in the next instant Dan's brushing slowed . . . then stopped . . . then his arms went around Josh and their two outlines melted into one.

Laura's heart expanded. Quick tears stung her eyes, seeing the desperation in that sudden embrace, the way Dan laid his cheek atop Josh's golden head, the way he hugged a little too tenaciously, and Josh squirming free, galloping toward the stilts once more while Dan knelt on the ground for a long moment, his eyes following the romping child.

He turned and looked down toward the house then, and Laura jumped back from the window, her throat constricting. Her eyes slid closed. Her fingers made a steeple before her mouth. How could I ever separate those two?

Later that night Laura and Dan made love, but she felt in his embrace that same desperation she'd seen in his clutching grasp of Josh earlier. He held her too hard. He kissed her too avidly. He apologized too profusely if he thought he'd done the smallest thing to displease her.

She wondered, after Dan at last fell into a restless sleep—would it ever be the same between them again? As long as Rye lived within touching distance, how could it be? Whether she saw Rye or not, kissed him or not, made love with him or not, he was there again, accessible, and this fact alone thwarted her and Dan's relationship.

Conscience-torn, Laura lay in the dark, the back of one wrist draped across her forehead, mouth dry, palms damp, willing her thoughts to take the straight and narrow.

But her reflections had a will of their own and would plague her with comparisons she had no right to be making. For what did it matter, the proportions of a man's body, the turn of his shoulder, the texture of his palm, the shape of his lips? None of this mattered. What mattered were his inner qualities, a man's values, the way he cared for a woman, worked for her, respected her, loved her.

But Laura wasn't fooling herself one bit. The physical comparisons were the ones that now brought her the most discontent. The undeniable truth was that Rye was the better lover and had the more desirable body. Deep in her heart she had recognized this during her years of marriage to Dan, but she had effectively suppressed the thought whenever they made love. But now Rye was back, and his superiority as a lover plagued her, causing great guilt each time she let the fact intrude between herself and the man to whom she was still wed.

Dan had always approached her almost as a supplicant approaches an altar, whereas she and Rye had always met on equal terms. She was no goddess, but a woman. She didn't want adulation, but reciprocation. Yes, there was a vast difference between making love with Dan and making love with Rye. With Dan it was sobering, with Rye intoxicating; with Dan it was mechanical, with Rye shattering; with Dan a ceremony; with Rye a celebration.

How could this be, and why should it matter? Yet it was . . . it did. Laura felt her body—only now, after Dan had left it—growing aroused at the memory of herself and Rye in the orchard with fog tendrils binding them closer and the scent of spring ripening in the damp night about them.

Oh, Rye, Rye, she despaired, you know me so well. We taught each other too well, you and I, to be able to live in the same town together and not be tempted.

Her hand rested on her stomach. She raised it to her breasts, finding them hard, tight peaks at the very thought of him. She pictured his lips, remembered that first time he'd kissed her . . . out in the bayberry patch up on Saul's Hill . . . and the first time he'd touched her here . . . and here. First times, first times . . . when they'd been trembling and afraid but burgeoning with sexuality as they treaded that fine line between adolescence and adulthood. It had begun with that innocent touch on his bare back . . .

They'd been swimming along the sandy beach at the head of the harbor near Wauwinet, ending, as always, by trudging along the place called the Haulover—a narrow stretch of sand separating the calm waters of the harbor from the pounding Atlantic, where fishermen often hauled over their dories from one side to the other.

She followed Rye through the reedy yellow-green beach grass that swept the strand and barred the intrusion of the mighty ocean from the quiet bay. To their left swept Great Point, crooking its narrow finger as if beckoning the ocean waves against it. But Rye gave it only a cursory glance before squatting in his customary way on the sand, hunching forward with his arms wrapped around his knees, searching the Atlantic for sails.

Grains of sand clung to his back, so Laura reached out and did as she'd done a hundred times before, whisking them off.

Only, this time he flinched and whirled around and shouted, "Don't!" Then he stared at her as if she'd committed some horrendous crime, while Laura gawked at him in owl-eyed amazement.

"All I did was brush the sand off."

He glowered at her silently for several seconds, then abruptly jumped to his feet and ran as hard as he could across the beach toward the Coskata cedars while she watched him disappear and hugged her stomach, where a queer light feeling had settled.

It had never been the same after that. They were no longer three—Rye and Laura and Dan—but two plus one.

As children they'd played whaler the way mainland children play house. Laura was always the wife, Rye the husband, and Dan the child. Rye would plop a dry peck on her sunburned lips and stride off across the strand to his "whaleship"—a beached skeleton of a rowboat that would never again split the brine—while she'd take Dan's hand and the two of them would wave goodbye, pretending that five minutes were five years, before Rye came striding back, some driftwood over his shoulder, the sailor home from the sea.

But those kisses didn't count.

The first time Rye really kissed Laura was long after those gamish pecks. Kissless years had gone by between then and the afternoon she'd brushed the sand from his back, but since that day, neither had thought of anything else.

Dan was with them, as usual, the next time they met to go clamming over at the creeks in the salt marsh at the harbor. They divided their catch, but Laura and Rye made excuses to linger together after Dan trudged off up the road past Consue Spring. Rye said he was going to help Laura carry her clams home, but when Dan was gone, he just stood there with his rake in his hand, nudging a buried shell up from the sand with his toe.

After a long silence, Laura asked, "Wanna walk home along the road or on the commons?"

He looked up. The wind blew skeins of nutmeg-colored hair across her mouth, and he seemed to stare at it a long time before swallowing hard and answering in a falsetto, "The commons."

They headed west, across the sweep of land between Orange and Copper streets, toward the undulating terrain beside First Mile Stone, through the low hills toward the shearing pens at Miacomet. Fall had swept the island with her paintbrush, and they walked through gay patches of sweet fern, huckleberry, and trailing arbutus that covered the moorlands like a blazing carpet. Rutted footpaths led them through fragrant thickets of bayberry whose scent was heady when crushed beneath their soles. As if by mutual consent, they veered off the trail into a thick patch of the berries, to lend excuse for that which really needed no excuse.

Neither of them had a container for carrying berries, anyway.

Once off the path, Laura wondered how to get Rye to make the first move, for though they were in the concealing underbrush, he seemed to have lost his nerve. So she spilled her basket of clams, and when he knelt down to help her scoop them up, she managed to nudge his arm, and the touch of her autumn-warmed skin on his was all it took.

Their eyes met, wide and wondering and uncertain, fingers still trailing in the clams before finally touching, and clinging. They held their breaths while each leaned forward haltingly. Their noses bumped, then their heads tipped just enough, and it happened! Childish, dry, tongueless first kiss. But expertise lacking, emotion was not.

And that kiss led the way to others, kisses for the sake of

which they filled that colorful autumn with countless walks through the bayberries, each kissing session growing more bold, until the touch of tongue upon tongue no longer sufficed.

But winter came, stripping the heath of color and cover. They lost their camouflage and found fewer times together. Miserably, they waited out the icy months until, in March, the mackerel started running and they at last found a place, an excuse.

That first time Rye touched Laura's breast she had not been wearing whalebones, for she yet had some growing to do. And neither had his hand grown to its full man's-width, nor had the blond hair sprouted on the back of it.

They'd been sitting in the dory facing each other, with their knees almost touching, pretending they were enjoying fishing when actually it was only keeping them from doing what they'd both thought about all winter.

Laura pulled her line in and dried her hands on her skirt, looking up to find Rye staring at her, his Adam's apple bobbing convulsively, as if he had a popcorn husk stuck on his tongue.

"I don't feel much like fishing," she admitted.

"Neither do I."

He licked his lips and swallowed once more, and without a word, he edged over and made room for him on her seat.

The boat rocked while he moved toward her and sat down without taking his eyes from her face. Her hands were freezing, clenched tightly between her knees.

When at last he kissed her, his nose and cheeks were cold, but his lips were as warm as that autumn day they'd first bumped noses on the blazing heath amid its scented colors. While his lips lingered on hers, Laura clamped her knees tighter upon the backs of her hands, wondering if Rye felt as grown-up as she did since the passing of winter. A moment later the touch of his tongue confirmed it, for it sought hers with a new insistence that made her turn on the seat and put both arms around him while she told him with her kiss how long the wait had been for her, too.

She felt Rye shiver, though he wore a bulky wool jacket to ward off the stiff March breeze. The dory rocked, swaying their bodies while their lips remained locked, bumping them first against each other, then tugging them apart.

At first she wasn't sure what Rye was doing, for her jacket was as bulky and cumbersome as his. But a moment later she realized his fingers were loosening the buttons. She jerked back, staring into his eyes.

"M . . . my hand is cold," he choked, voicing the first excuse he could think of.

"Oh." She gulped and let the rocking of the boat sway her against him, waiting, waiting for that first adult touch with the breathless eagerness of untutored youth. Then his hand slipped inside, where it was warm and secret and forbidden, and she knew they were doing wrong.

"Rye, we shouldn't," she protested.

"No, we shouldn't," he agreed hoarsely. But that didn't stop his hand from knowing its first of her, from learning the shape of her budding breasts through her dress, from discovering the way a woman's nipples grow rigid as they plead for more. As with all first times, it was more exploration than caress, a search for the differences that were making her woman, him man.

Laura's breath came jerky and fast. Her heart thumped madly beneath Rye's hand.

"Put your hand inside my jacket, Laura," he ordered, and she did his bidding for the first of many times to follow. She slipped her hand between jacket and sweater, and felt his ribs rising like sea swells, he was breathing so hard.

"Ouch! Not so hard!" she exclaimed when his exploration of her nipple grew a little too insistent.

From that moment on they remained open and vocal about their sexuality.

When the weave of her linen chemise abraded her tender breast, she reached and pushed his exploring hand to her other breast, saying against his lips, "That one's sore."

Laura and Rye used the excuse of going mackerel fishing again two days later, but not until just before they made for shore did their lines get wet. They sat in the vast privacy of the open water, surrounded by Nantucket Bay, while the boat bobbed up and down and the sun came skipping up at them from the rippling sea. Only the inquisitive gulls observed the first time Laura followed Rye's instructions and slid her hands beneath his sweater to feel his warm, bare skin underneath.

There followed an excruciating week during which Josiah commanded all of Rye's time, for Rye was already a four-year apprentice and was nearly as adept at coopering as his father.

By the time Sunday came and Rye was free to be with Laura again, they both felt tense and desperate. Rye had planned all week where they would go to be alone. Old man Hardesty had a boathouse on the waterfront near Easy Street where he kept old lobster traps and seines. He'd given Rye free use of any of the abandoned equipment anytime Rye wanted it.

"Ma wants me to get her a couple lobsters for tomorrow," Rye said when he came to fetch Laura. "Wanna come along with me over to old man Hardesty's and pick up a trap?"

"I suppose."

They didn't look at each other along the way. Rye stalked with his hands in his pockets, whistling, while Laura watched her toes and tried to match her stride to his—impossible to do anymore since his legs had grown so long.

They climbed the steps of the silvery old boathouse, and at the top Rye stood back, holding the door open for her. She stopped with her hand on the rail, staring up at him: Rye had never bothered with courtesies in all his sixteen years! He looked up and nervously scanned the waterfront, then he shifted his feet, and she hurried up the steps.

Inside it was dry and dusty, cobwebs lacing the corners and junk everywhere. Coils of old rope lay on the floor, along with buckets of rusty clews, battered oars, and lanterns with missing side glass; trennels and tar pots, piggins and barrel rings. While Laura stood taking it all in, a calico cat jumped out of nowhere, startling her into a shriek.

Rye laughed and picked his way across the littered floor to pluck the cat from an old nail keg and bring her back to Laura. Standing close together, they scratched the cat, who purred contentedly between them as if happy that company had come to call. Both Laura and Rye studied the creature as she stretched her neck and squinted her eyes closed in ecstasy while their fingers moved on her fur but itched to move over each other.

Laced over the cat's back, their fingers touched, warm fur

and warm flesh blending as they raised their eyes. For a long moment they stood still, the only movement the hammering of their hearts and the drifting of dust motes in the dry old loft. Rye leaned forward and Laura raised her lips, the kiss a gentle thing at first, until they lunged together and the cat squawked, making them leap apart and laugh self-consciously.

The cat took up her post on a barrel. She began to give herself a bath while Rye scanned the floor. He found an old mainsail rolled up and abandoned years earlier to mice and dust, and he tugged Laura's hand, leading her to it.

They knelt down, one on either side of the brittle, gray canvas, and together began smoothing it out. Sunlight slanted in through a single window, falling across their sail bed in an oblique slash of gold, while from below the lap and swash of waves continued lazily nudging the pilings of the building.

Rye looked down at the waiting canvas, then up at Laura. They were both on their knees, facing each other, afraid now, and hesitant. From outside came the cry of gulls, wheeling lazily above the wharf. On his knees, Rye moved to the center of the canvas, and after a moment Laura followed suit. She watched the sunlight play across his beautiful arched eyebrows and light the tips of his eyelashes to gold as they slid closed and he leaned forward to kiss her. He found her fingers and clasped them tightly, as if for courage. When the kiss ended, he sat back on his haunches, searching her eyes while he squeezed her fingers till she thought the bones would crack.

He swallowed, lowered his gaze to the center of her chest, rose again to kneeling height, and slowly began unbuttoning her jacket. She shuddered as he pushed it from her shoulders, and Rye looked up, startled.

"Are you cold, Laura?"

She hunched her shoulders and gripped the skirts in her lap. "No."

"Laura, I . . ." But he gulped to a stop, and she could see it was her turn to make a move.

"Kiss me, Rye," she said in a voice she'd never heard before, "the way I like it best." For by this time they had practiced it many ways.

He picked up her hands from her lap, gripping them tightly, and they met halfway, his tongue touching the seam of her lips even before they opened beneath his, her girl's ignorance clashing with her woman's intuition.

His hand found her breast across the vast distance that seemed to separate their bodies except for knees and lips. And for the first time ever, her hand nudged his toward the buttons at her throat, verifying that it was time. He hesitated, then shakily, inexpertly, opened the polished whalebone buttons all the way to her waist.

As if suddenly realizing what he'd done, he sat back on his haunches, staring into her eyes now with a frightened look in his own.

"It's okay, Rye. I want you to."

"Laura, it's different than just . . . just kissing, you know."

"How do I know?" she asked, experiencing her first heady recognition of the power of her feminine mystique, wielding it as surely as if she were an experienced woman of the world.

"You sure?" He gulped, still scared of all the unknowns.

"Rye, I didn't come up here to get any lobster trap. Did you?"

His lips were open, blue eyes wide and not a little frightened as he touched one shoulder inside her open dress, then the other, then carefully pushed the garment back to stare at her chemise.

The dark circles of her nipples showed against the linen cloth, and she followed the movement of his eyes from one to the other, then dropped her gaze to watch his hand reach for the streamer of the satin bow between her breasts. A moment later the cool air touched her bare skin as Rye pushed the chemise to her waist.

She held her breath, waiting for him to touch her, and when he didn't, her eyelids fluttered up to find his face red to the roots of his hair, while he stared as if struck dumb.

"Golly . . ." he muttered thickly, and she knew he was afraid to touch, now that he'd come this far. "Laura, you're so . . . so pretty."

Her face was red, too, but it ceased to matter when, a moment later, his scratchy wool sweater was pressed against her bare skin, then within seconds, it drifted back to make way for Rye's shaking hand.

His palm was damp with nervousness, but warm and

already callused hard from working the drawknives. She wondered how it could possibly be wrong to let Rye touch her this way, because for the first time ever, she'd found justification for the growing pains she'd endured during the last year while her breasts had begun developing. At first he only brushed her breasts with callow timidity, but soon he explored the nipple with his fingertips, finding the hard little pebble of growth that would be there yet for some months.

It hurt, and though she only shrugged her shoulder away in response, he reacted as if she'd cried out in pain. He jerked his hand back, a stricken look on his face.

"Did . . . did I hurt you, Laura?"

"N . . . no, not really . . . just . . . I don't know."

He moved more cautiously after that, experimenting with great care until their kisses became wilder and it seemed their bodies could not press together hard enough, kneeling as they were.

He urged her backward, a little at a time, until she listed beneath the pressure of his chest and tumbled with him to the floor. Her arms twined up around his shoulders as he pressed his length against hers, and they kissed with the all-consuming fire that only first times ignite.

When at last he pulled away, she knew where his lips were headed, but lay very still, very cautious, her shoulder blades pressed solidly against the floor. His breath dampened her neck, stopping there a long, tremulous time before proceeding down, down, by inches, until his lips were at her breast. Once there, they only brushed the nipple, not so much as the dew of his breath dampening it, for his mouth was closed.

Her stomach and chest hurt, tight bands of expectancy and fear binding it strangely. But the urge to know, to understand this thing called growing up, made her touch his hair experimentally. And with that touch, his lips opened and she felt the sleek texture of his tongue stroking the bright rosebud not yet fully blossomed. A sound came from her throat and her shoulders lifted off the canvas as she was overcome with some new compulsion to reach toward him with her breast.

Liquid fire coursed through her veins. Her head fell back as he tasted her other nipple, and she felt her body go all limp and tense at once. His weight felt welcome as Rye lay across her body, and she learned with each new motion of his tongue why he had leaped up angrily and run away when she had brushed that sand from his shoulder the summer before.

Her eyes flew open as Rye suddenly sprang to his knees beside her, reaching for the bottom of his sweater, yanking it viciously over his head, then falling still a moment, again looking down at her for permission.

She had never seen hair on his chest before, but it was there now—a soft shadow of blond, sparkling in the light from the window, across the high square twin muscles of his chest. She reveled in discovery, moving her gaze downward eventually to the spot where his navel made a round, secret shadow, just above his waistline. He knelt before her with his knees apart, each of them satisfying curiosity for a moment before going any farther.

"Rye, you're all muscly," she said, amazed.

"And you're not," he said, unsmiling.

She could see—actually see!—the way his pulse pounded in the hollow of his throat, and wondered if hers did the same, for it seemed to be thrumming everywhere, in her temples, in her stomach, and in the secret part of her that now seemed the center of all feeling.

He fell toward her, one hand on each side of her head, and kneeling over her that way, kissed her before easing his bare, golden chest onto hers, their hearts thundering uncontrollably while hard muscle flattened soft.

There was wonder and astonishment then, feeling the difference between their textures, experimentally grinding those textures against one another in a touch that somehow proved silken.

Again he caressed her breasts. Again he kissed them, his tongue already dancing more masterfully on the puckered tips. She threaded her fingers through his hair, and she writhed in unknowing invitation, begging him to lay his full length over hers, for without it she felt incomplete and searching.

He bent a knee, lifted it, and pressed it on her leg while she sucked in a breath and held it. The knee passed heavily up her thigh, across the juncture of her legs, to her stomach, making her skirts whisper alluringly against her legs. The weight of that knee seemed to anchor her to earth, from which her body wanted to soar. Then, before long, a greater weight pressed her to the sail bed, for Rye shifted his hips to cover hers, lying flat on her now with not so much as a muscle moving while she marveled at how good it felt to know the curves and warmth of another this closely.

Then, somehow, her legs had parted and made a space where his knee fit securely, and he moved it against her in an altogether satisfying way that made her press and lift rhythmically against it.

When Rye's knee moved back and his weight slipped to one side, she felt his hand skimming along her skirt, raising layers of petticoats as he searched along the length of her leg. Her heart clamored crazily, and his breath beat like wild waves against her ear. His fingers touched the legband of her pantaloons, then moved higher . . . higher . . . until his palm covered the gentle swell between her legs, and she realized, horrified, that the linen fabric there was damp. She felt his hesitant surprise when he encountered the dampness, but when he pressed her hard, it felt wonderful and right and relieved some inner yearning even while Laura waited for the hand of Providence to reach out and smite her dead.

Instead, the hand of Rye Dalton explored her through the last barrier of linen, but when it ventured to the buttoned waist of her pantaloons, caution intruded. She caught his wrist and whispered shakily, "No more, Rye. I . . . I think we'd better get dressed. I have to go."

For a moment his eyes blazed down at her with an untamed intensity she'd never seen there before. She hadn't known he was holding his breath until it came out in a mighty gust that seemed to leave him weak. Immediately, he rolled to his knees, turning his back on her while yanking his sweater over his head. She pulled up her chemise, smoothed her skirts, and slipped her arms into her sleeves. He smoothed his hair, and his blue eyes met hers as he looked over his shoulder to find her buttoning her dress. His glance skittered away in self-consciousness. She studied his back a long time.

"Rye?"

"What?"

When she said nothing for a long moment, he looked over his shoulder again.

"Are we gonna go to hell now?"

They stared at each other, wide-eyed, for some seconds.

"I suppose so."

"Both of us, or just me?"

"Both of us, I think."

She experienced a sick feeling of dread in the pit of her stomach, for she didn't want Rye suffering in hell because of her.

"M . . . maybe if we don't ever do it again and if we pray real hard, we won't."

"Maybe." But his morose tone held little hope. He got to his feet. "I think we'd better go, Laura, and we'd better not come up here together anymore. I'll get those traps, and . . . and . . ." He half turned to find her sitting on her haunches, a look of dread on her face.

His words faded away. Below them, the old pilings of the boathouse creaked as the tide came in, while above them gulls reeled and screeched. Then suddenly they pitched together, holding each other tightly, their hearts hammering with this new awareness they didn't yet know how to handle.

"Oh, Rye, I don't want you to go to hell."

"Shh . . . maybe . . . maybe you don't for just one time."

Chapter 6

THE NEXT DAY in church, Rye avoided her eye all through services. Guilt was evident on his face, and it filled Laura with an awesome fear of retribution even while her mind was dominated by memories of what they'd done together. Furthermore, whenever she relived those moments, that liquid sensation began to build in her body and she was certain it alone was sinful. He avoided her in the churchyard, leaving her feeling bereft and abandoned while he walked off toward home without so much as a hello.

He kept away for nine days, but on the tenth, she went to Market Square to buy fresh haddock for her mother and was wending her way through the carts and drays when she saw Rye approaching. As he glanced up and saw her, his step faltered, but he continued in her direction until they met and he was forced to stop.

"Hi, Rye." She gave him her brightest smile.

"Hi."

Her heart fell to her feet, for he neither said her name nor met her eyes. "I haven't seen you for over a week," she said.

"I've been busy helping the old man." He studied something across the square.

"Oh." He seemed impatient, and she searched for something to keep him a minute longer. "Did you catch any lobsters in those traps?"

His gaze met hers fleetingly, then skittered away. "A few."

"You take the traps back yet?"

"No, I set 'em every morning and haul 'em at the end of the day."

"You gonna haul 'em today?"

His mouth pursed slightly, and he seemed reluctant to answer, but finally grunted, "Yeah."

"What time?"

"Four o'clock or so."

"You . . . you want some help?"

He looked at her from the corner of his eye, then turned his gaze toward Nantucket Bay. But instead of his usual bright invitation, he only shrugged. "I gotta go, Laura."

Her heart felt broken as she watched him walk off.

But she was waiting at the dory at four o'clock. When Rye spotted her, he came up short, but she stubbornly stood her ground. Neither said a word while she stooped to release the bow line and he the stern line. Neither did they talk while they headed out to collect the traps and haul them in. He had two good-sized lobsters, which he put in a burlap sack before heading again for shore.

When the dory bumped against the pilings, Rye hefted one of the traps up onto the wharf.

Laura looked up, surprised. "What you gonna do with that?"

He reached for the second trap and thumped it down beside the first, avoiding her eyes. "I've had 'em long enough. Time I return 'em to old man Hardesty's boathouse."

Her heart careened with a mixture of joy and foreboding.

Together they secured the dory, then each picked up a trap and they walked wordlessly side by side past old Cap'n Silas, who nodded and puffed his pipe without saying a word. When they'd passed him, they peered at each other guiltily but continued in the direction of the boathouse.

Inside, the boathouse was just as they'd left it, except today, with a shroud of fog at the windows, it seemed more secret and forbidden. Just inside the door Laura came to an abrupt halt, her fingers clinging to a bar of her lobster trap as it rested against her knees. She jumped and spun around when Rye dropped his trap with a clatter. He took hers and set it down, too, but when he straightened, neither of them seemed to know where to look. He slipped his hands inside the back waistline of his pants while she folded hers tightly together before her skirts.

"I gotta go," he announced abruptly. "My ma said to bring the lobsters home for supper." But the burlap bag lay forgotten near the door.

"I gotta go, too. My ma likes me to come and help her with supper."

He turned toward the door but had taken only three steps before she dared to speak the word that stopped him.

"Rye?"

He spun around and gave her a searching look that revealed what had possessed his thoughts for ten days now. "What?"

"Are . . . are you mad at me?"

His Adam's apple bobbed. "No."

"Well then, what's wrong?"

"I . . . I don't know."

Laura felt her chin tremble, and suddenly Rye's image seemed to grow wavery while she tried her hardest to keep the tears from showing. But Rye saw the glisten, and suddenly his lanky legs were covering the space between them, and a minute later she was crushed against his chest. The strength of his not-yet-adult arms was as powerful as that of any full-grown man as he pulled her hard against him, and she clung to his neck. Their kiss, too, held an adult intensity, and a wondrous letting go happened inside Laura when his tongue came into her mouth and circled hers, then licked the insides of her cheeks and made her own tongue arch so sharply that it ached sweetly.

Their lips broke apart and he hugged her close, rocking back and forth and dropping his face into the lee of her neck. Standing on tiptoe, she clung to him; he'd grown so tall in the past winter, they no longer matched in height.

"Rye, I was so scared when you wouldn't look at me in the square today." Her words were muffled against his thick brown sweater as he continued rocking her in a motion meant to pacify but that only inflamed. Laura pulled back to look at him. "Why did you act that way?"

"I don't know." His blue eyes appeared haunted.

"Don't ever do that again, Rye."

He only swallowed, then spoke her name in a strange, adult way. "Laura . . ."

Then she was pulled roughly against him again while they kissed and kissed, frightened of the needs of their bodies, yet hearkening to them nonetheless, for soon they were moving, hardly aware of their action, toward the canvas where they'd lain once before. By some unspoken agreement they went down on their knees, still kissing, then fell to their hips, then elbows, seeking that closeness they'd experienced and could not forget.

And this time when his hand slid beneath her skirts, Laura's limbs opened readily, anticipating the thrill of his intimate touch. As before, her body craved his exploration and blossomed at his caress. When his hand moved to the button of her pantaloons, she knew she should stop him, but was incapable. His palm slipped inside, exploring the warm surface of her stomach, then gingerly encountering the nest of new-sprung hair, hesitating at the threshold of femininity until she moved restlessly and made a soft sound in her throat.

Her heart felt as if it would explode with anxiety as she waited on the brink of the forbidden. But when at last his fingers slipped those final inches to discover the wherefore of her silken femininity, she jumped.

Immediately, he recoiled and withdrew. "Did I hurt you?" His blue eyes were wide with fright while carnality and morality waged war within her.

"N . . . no. Do it again."

"But what if . . ."

"I don't know . . . do it again."

When his inexperienced fingers plumbed her for a second time she did not jump, but closed her eyes and knew a great wonder. Naïvely he went on, far from mastering the touch yet, but needing not to master, only to explore.

"Rye," she whispered after some moments, "we're sure going to hell now."

"No we're not. I asked somebody about it, and it takes a lot more than this before you go to hell."

She pulled back sharply and shoved his hand away. "You . . . you asked somebody?" she repeated, horrified. "Who?"

"Charles."

She sighed with relief when he named an older, married cousin of his whom she scarcely knew.

"What did you ask him?"

"I asked him if he thought a man would go to hell for touching a woman."

"And what did he say?"

"He laughed."

"He laughed?" she parroted, amazed.

"Then he said if that was any man's idea of hell, he could do without heaven. And he told me . . ." Rye stopped in mid-sentence, and his hand moved toward that secret place again.

But she stopped it, demanding, "What did he tell you?" She saw Rye color and look away. Somewhere in the loft the cat made a soft sound.

At last Rye looked at her again and drew a deep breath. "How to do things."

She stared at him speechlessly and suddenly knew an overwhelming fright at these mysteries to which Rye was now privy.

She sat up abruptly. "It's getting close to supper time. Mother will be expecting me." Then she was on her feet and heading for the door before he could detain her. He sat up, too, raising one knee and draping an elbow across it. "Meet me here tomorrow after supper," he said quietly, studying her back as she hesitated with her hand on the doorknob.

"I can't."

"Why not?"

"We're going to Aunt Nora's."

"The next night, then."

"We're going to get in trouble, Rye!"

"No we're not."

"How do you know?"

" 'Cause I found out from Charles."

But nothing made sense to Laura, for *trouble* was only a vague notion in her mind. When she'd said the word she'd only meant that by hanging around up here, they risked getting caught. But she sensed he meant something else.

"You afraid, Laura?" Rye asked.

"No . . . yes . . . I don't think I can come." Then she went out quickly and slammed the door.

But nature's curiosity ran rife through Laura's changing body. That night as she lay in bed, she recalled Rye's touch —his touch, oh his touch, what it had done to her!—and brushed her palms over her breasts, trying to recapture the exquisite sensation of Rye's rough fingers. But her own were somehow incompetent and left her wanting. She ran her fingers down to test the entrance to her virginity and found it sleek at the very thought of Rye. What would he teach her if she met him tomorrow night? So many mysteries, yet one thing was sure. Touching herself left her filled only with the longing to be touched instead by Rye. He'd be waiting at the boathouse, she knew, and the thought of advancing the next step with him filled her with queer feelings she both welcomed and resisted.

The following day crept by like a decade, but when at last the appointed time came, Laura was there before Rye, sitting on a rolled up tarp with the cat on her lap. When footsteps sounded on the outside stair, her heart hammered in trepidation. Suppose it was somebody else—old man Hardesty maybe, or . . . or . . .

But it was Rye, wearing a clean muslin shirt and black straight-legged pants with brass buttons, his hair freshly combed, his boots gleaming from an unaccustomed polishing.

This time their eyes met steadily, holding deep while he stood at the door, some ten feet distant from her perch. The evening shadows were long; only the lip of the window ledge was limned in gold. Already the loft felt secure and familiar.

"Hi," he greeted quietly.

A smile broke upon her face. "Hi."

Her heart thrilled at the sight of him. Her body welled with anticipation. But she scratched the cat's jaw with feigned poise while he crossed and sat down on the hard canvas roll beside her. His fingers, too, reached to stroke the cat and, as with that first time, touched Laura's accidentally, then not so accidentally until finally they stopped making excuses and clasped hands tightly, both of them staring at his thumb as it rubbed the base of hers.

With one accord their gazes were lifted and their eyes met, and Laura felt a great impatience to learn more of what

Charles had told Rye. Her brown eyes were wide, her lips open with womanly waiting, while Rye squeezed her hand so hard she felt the soft skin bruise. He tipped his head aside and she lifted her face, eyelids closing as their lips met in a tender first hello, the fragile touch of a moth's wing against an evening leaf.

Rye pulled back his head and their eyes met again, filled with longing and uncertainty and the absolute awareness of sin.

"Laura," he croaked.

"Rye, I'm still scared."

She flung her arms around his neck and felt his smooth jaw against her temple while they clung, perched like two gulls on a yardarm. He slid to the floor and tugged her along, both of them resting on their sides, facing each other while their eager lips and arms held fast. They kissed with fiery impatience, bringing their breasts and hips together as hard as nature allowed, until Rye's hand slowly moved from her shoulder blade to her breast, caressing it through thin spring cotton, making it bud like the lilacs outside their lofty nest. She rolled forward against his palm, then back, like a body being sucked and pushed by breakers on a shore, until finally his hand went down to her waist, where it lingered, garnering courage before finally drifting down her petticoats to lift them during long minutes of expectation.

Every inch of the way she knew she should stop him, remind him again of hell. But instead, she breathed harder and made the way clear and unencumbered. He touched her bare leg and she did nothing. He touched the hem of her pantaloons and still she did nothing. He unbuttoned the waist and she stretched acquiescently.

Then his hand slid down and her legs parted to accept his touch again. Her whole body felt liquid and hot, her pulse driven. Soft sounds came from Rye's throat, half groan, half accolade, until at last he spoke gruffly in her ear.

"You're supposed to touch me, too, Laura."

Instinctively, she knew he meant in the same place he was touching her, but her fingers seemed spliced into the threads of his shirt. His lips rested on hers, then his tongue rode across her bottom lip and nuzzled toward her ear.

"Laura, don't be scared."

But she was. She had come here knowing a little bit about what he might do to her, but nothing about a woman's part in all this. He kissed her ear, and she squeezed her eyes shut and bit her lower lip. He had asked Charles, hadn't he? Charles must know. She understood that boys were shaped differently than girls, but had never before questioned why. What would happen if she let her hand slide down? Would he grow wet, too? Then what? *How* should she touch him?

Her palm, resting on his ribs, grew damp. She held her breath and eased her hand to his hip, then stopped, afraid. He kissed her encouragingly, murmuring her name and nudging her hand until it began moving by degrees—until it halted with the backs of her knuckles touching the buttons of his fly. His hips began a series of slow undulations and she brushed lightly back and forth, feeling little except the woolen texture of his pants and the coolness of brass buttons.

Without warning his hand captured hers, turned it over, and pressed it hard against the brass buttons. Wild questions burst into her mind. Why wasn't he shaped as she'd thought men were shaped? What was this ridge which, even through wool and brass, she could tell was bigger than what her peeps at naked infants had led her to expect?

He held her hand firmly, playing it up and down before finally cupping it firmly against him, way down low, where his trousers felt warm and damp. Suddenly he rolled away and fell back against the tarp, eyes closed, legs outstretched. But he still held her wrist, guiding her hand up and down, up and down the mysterious ridge. Her fingertips grew brave and began exploring, counting buttons—one, two, three, four, five—the ridge stopped at the fifth button.

Rye rolled his head to face her, and opened his eyes. He licked his dry lips and she stared at his familiar blue eyes, which held an expression she'd never before encountered in them. She was sitting up now, higher than he, breathing hard through trembling lips, her own eyes wide and unsmiling, filled with discovery. His hand fell away and his hips began rising and falling rhythmically, and only when he felt her palm stay to complement the rhythm of his thrusts did his eyes close again.

She stared down at her hand, feeling the brass buttons grow warm as they scraped along her palm, watching Rye's stomach and ribs heaving torturously, as if he'd just completed a league's swim.

"Laura?"

The throaty word brought her eyes back to his with a snap.

"Kiss me while you do that."

She bent over him, and when their tongues met, hot and wet, his thrusting grew more pronounced. And then she felt his fingers circle her wrist again and haul her hand to the top button at his waist. Instinctively, she knew what he wanted of her and began to pull away. But he clapped a hand around the back of her neck and forced her to stay as she was.

She managed to free her mouth, shaking her head once and twisting free of his hand. "Rye, don't!"

"I did it to you. Don't you think I was scared, too?" His eyes seemed suddenly to blaze with anger while her clenched fist was held captive at his waist.

"I can't."

"Why not?"

"I . . . I just can't, that's all."

He braced himself up against the tarp, rolling slightly toward her, the anger now replaced by a new tone of encouragement. "Aw, Laura, come on, don't be scared. I promise nothing bad will happen." He bestowed fluttering touches of his lips upon her face until her fingers relaxed. He was rubbing the back of her hand softly, where it rested against the hard muscles of his stomach, just above his waistband. "Laura, don't you want to know what I feel like?"

Oh . . . she did, she did. But it was easier letting somebody touch you than being the one who touched. A moment later, though, he was releasing the brass buttons himself while her trembling palm still lay on his stomach and he half leaned over her, kissing her tenderly as if to reassure her it was all right. He raised his hip and pulled the tail of his shirt up, and its barrier was suddenly gone from between her palm and his skin. Then he found her wrist again and drew her hand down to something that was so hot, she flinched away. But relentlessly, Rye took her hand to his flesh again and covered her shaking fingers with his own, making a sheath of her hand into which his long, silken surprise slipped. My God, had there ever been skin so smooth or so hot? It was smoother than the tender flesh of his inner lip, which her tongue had grazed many times. It was hotter than the inside of his mouth, which she knew as well as her own. He held her fingers closed tightly and forced them to stroke up and down while her heart threatened to explode inside her body. I'm going to hell! I'm going to hell! But no threat of hell could tear her hand from his body now. She experimented, moving the silken skin with tender exploration, learning each ridge and hollow of the masculine shaft until he fell back in abandon, his hand now fallen away from hers. She looked down and saw what she held then for the first time. In the deepening shadows it appeared to be the color of the deepest of the cosmos in her mother's garden. Abashed at having viewed it, she felt the same color suffuse her face and tore her eyes away. But now Rye made a guttural sound at the crest of each stroke and a moment later his body began a frightful trembling, his hips seeming to shake in a way that scared Laura much more than anything that had happened so far. But when she would have pulled away, he held her, and a moment later something warm and wet cascaded over the back of her hand and between her fingers.

"Rye, oh Rye, stop!" Her voice was choked with fright. "Something's wrong. I think you're bleeding." She was afraid to look down and find out. It must be blood. What else could it be, warm and wet? She started to cry.

"Laura, shh . . ." They were lying on the floor, her head resting in the crook of his elbow, and he turned to pull her cheek beneath his lips. "Are you crying?"

"I'm scared. I think I hurt you."

"It's not blood, Laura . . . look."

But she was afraid to look down, sure now that when she did, she'd find her hand scarlet with Rye's blood. His blue eyes seemed so sure, looking deeply into hers, but her voice trembled and tears rolled down her temple.

"I . . . I told you I didn't want to . . . and now . . . now something awful has happened, I just know it."

Unbelievably, Rye smiled. Laura was incensed to think he could be smiling at a time like this.

"I said look, Laura. If you don't believe me, look."

She did at last. White. It was white and slick and had dampened a circle on the tarp between them.

Her eyes flew to his. "Wh . . . what is it?"

"It's what makes babies."

"Babies! Rye Dalton, how dare you put it on me if you knew that all the time!" Instinctively, she sat up, searching frantically for something with which to clean her hand so that one didn't start in her. At last she used her petticoat.

"Button your britches up, Rye Dalton, and don't you ever do that to me again. If I got a baby, my mother would kill me!" Disdainfully, she turned her back on him while fastening her buttons. When her clothing was all adjusted, she knelt with her hands clenched tightly between her knees, horrified to think of what he'd done to her.

On his knees, Rye moved close behind her. "Laura, haven't you ever heard how a woman gets pregnant?"

Her chin was trembling and the tears rolled freely. "No, never before tonight." Distressed by his thoughtlessness in jeopardizing her, she swung around angrily. "Why didn't you tell me before we . . . I . . . we did it?"

"Laura, I promise you you're not going to get pregnant. You can't."

"But . . . but . . ."

"That stuff's got to get inside you before you can get pregnant, but I wasn't inside you, was I?"

"Inside me?" Her puzzled eyes probed his.

"Haven't you ever seen animals do it, Laura?"

"Animals?"

"A dog or . . . or even chickens?" But her confused expression needed no further interpreting. It clearly spoke of ignorance.

"Do what?" No animal could do what they'd just done!

They knelt facing each other with their knees almost touching. Dusk had settled, so only the pale outlines of their faces were visible in the dusty old loft. His face wore an expression of deep tenderness.

He reached for her hand and placed it on his brass buttons. "This part of me goes into this part of you." He pressed his palm into her lap. "Then there are babies."

Her lips fell open. Her blue eyes were wide with disbelief.

Could Rye be right? Her face burned, and she yanked her hand away from his.

"What happened in your hand has to happen inside your body, Laura. That's how a man gives a woman a baby." He touched her jaw, but she was too ashamed to look up at him. But he went on earnestly. "I promise I'll never do that to you, though, until after we're married."

Now her eyes flew to his. Her heart beat crazily and a flood of relief surged through her. "M . . . married?"

"Don't you think we should get married, Laura, after . . . well . . . after this?"

"M . . . married?" Her astonishment began to grow. "You want to marry me, Rye, really?"

His astonishment, too, blossomed into manly realization, then a grin. "Why, I can't imagine marrying anybody besides you, Laura."

"Oh, Rye!" Suddenly she was up against him, her arms about his neck, her eyes squeezed tightly shut at the thought of it. Until just this minute she hadn't thought of how awful it might have been *not* to marry Rye after what they'd done together. "I can't imagine marrying anybody besides you, either."

He held her, and they rocked back and forth while her face remained securely against his neck.

"Do you think that makes it all right . . . I mean . . . you know?" came her muffled question.

"Touching and stuff, you mean?"

"Mmm-hmm."

"I don't think husband and wives go to hell for touching."

She released a sigh of relief, then backed away and looked eagerly into his face. "Rye, let's tell Dan."

"Tell Dan?"

"That we're going to get married."

Rye looked skeptical. "Not yet. We'll have to wait until my apprenticeship is served, Laura. Then, when I'm a master cooper, we can afford to live in a house of our own. I don't think we should tell Dan till then."

Slightly disappointed, she sank back on her heels. "Well . . . all right, if you think it's best."

*   *   *

But it was hard for Laura to keep from telling Dan the very next time they met, for she wanted to share her new joy—after all, the three of them had always shared everything.

It was a week later. An immense storm had blown up, and afterward, Laura and Dan went out together to scour the shingle for driftwood, a precious commodity here on Nantucket, where there was little wood to spare, since most was hauled over from the mainland. The coast along the south side of the island caught the worst of the Atlantic's wrath and also turned up the greatest rewards after storms. Laura and Dan were working their way eastward when they came upon Rye, standing some twenty yards away, across the wet, hard-packed shingle that was strewn with shells, kelp, and tidepools where small fish had been trapped. The storm itself had passed, but the skies were still low, with scudding gray clouds hemming in the island, making it a world apart.

Rye wore a heavy pea jacket, its collar turned up around the flaxen hair that whipped about his face in the wind. Laura, in a yellow slicker and red bandana, raised her arm to wave as soon as she saw him.

The three of them moved down the beach together after that, their burlap sacks scraping triple tracks as they dragged along. It was the first time Laura had seen Rye since the evening in the boathouse, and she immediately got that curious wanton feeling in the pit of her stomach and wondered how they could get rid of Dan. The natural way was to ask if his mother had anything good to eat, and when the answer was "gingerbread," they made Dan's house their first stop back in town.

By the time Laura and Rye left Dan's house, she felt ready to burst with impatience, yet he seemed calm and unaffected by the last two hours—the last seven days! But when they were moving down the street toward Josiah's, Rye did something he'd never done before: he took her sack from her and hoisted it over his shoulder with his own, refusing to heed her insistence that she could handle it herself. The waterlogged wood was as heavy as dead weight, and secretly Laura was pleased by Rye's chivalry. He even managed to open the door of the cooperage for her despite his burden.

Dropping the sacks just inside the door, he looked up when his mother called from overhead.

"Rye, is that you?"

He placed a finger over his lips in warning, and Laura bit off the greeting she'd been preparing to call up.

"It's me," he called. "I got some driftwood. Gonna make a fire and lay it around the fireplace to dry out."

It was Sunday, and the lower level of the cooperage was abandoned. The damp, windy clouds made the room shadowed and secret. As Laura and Rye stood silently staring at each other, they could hear the sounds of his parents moving back and forth above their heads. Then he dragged their two sacks over to the fireplace and began laying a fire. When it was crackling, he methodically began pulling wet driftwood from the sacks and arranging it in a circle on the dirt floor. When the bags were empty, he took them to the far wall and draped them over a tool bench. Returning to Laura, he silently reached for her slicker, and without a word she let him slip it from her shoulders. He pulled up one of the long shaving horses and positioned it near the hearth, where warmth already spread. The bench was four feet long, widened at one end to form a seat, the opposite end rising like a hunter's bow, forming the wooden clamp for holding the stave in place with a foot pedal. He swung a leg over and sat down at the wide end, then reached up a hand to Laura in invitation. Her gaze, of its own accord, dropped to his lap when he'd spread his knees wide to straddle the bench. Color flared in her face, and she diverted her gaze to his waiting hand, then placed her own in it, and let him pull her down to sit before him, her body at a right angle to his, with both knees touching only one of his thighs. He touched her face with his fingertips, seeming to search it avidly before kissing first one eyelid, then the other.

"I've missed you," he whispered so softly it might have been only the hiss of the fire.

"I've missed you, too." She snuggled against his pea jacket.

"You didn't tell Dan, did you?"

She shook her head, no.

"When I saw you together, I felt . . ." His whisper floundered, but his eyes were stormy, looking down into hers.

"What . . . tell me what you felt." Her hand lay on his chest. She felt his heart driving hard against it.

"Jealous," he admitted, "for the first time ever."

"Silly Rye," she whispered, and kissed his chin. "You never have to be jealous of Dan."

They kissed then, but in the middle of it the bracings overhead creaked, startling them apart. Their eyes turned toward the dark beamed ceiling, and they held their breaths. But no further sound came, and their eyes moved once again to each other. The fire was warm now, and Laura wondered why Rye hadn't removed his jacket. But with the next kiss she understood as he led her hand to the warmth between his open legs, hidden in the shadows behind his heavy garment, should anyone intrude.

"Laura . . ." he begged in a shaky whisper, "can I touch you again?"

"Not here, Rye. They'll catch us," she whispered.

"No they won't. They don't know you're here with me." He pulled her into his arms and slid her up firmly against his open legs, and she was immediately tempted.

"But what if they come?"

"Shh, just turn around here and lean back against me. We'll hear them coming, and if they do, go over and sit on the other shaving horse as if we were just warming up by the fire." He turned her until her back rested against his chest. "Swing your leg over," he ordered behind her ear.

Her leg went over the shaving horse and his hand up under her skirts, scarcely hesitating at the button before finding her feminine warmth with one hand and her breast with the other. She squirmed back against him, listening to his harsh breathing beside her ear, grasping his knees as the delight of sexuality kindled again at his touch. But when he touched a strangely sensitive spot, she jerked upright and sucked in a breath, trying to escape.

"Laura, don't pull away."

"I can't help it."

"Shh. Charles told me how to do something to you, but you have to sit still while I try it."

"Wh . . . what?"

"Shh . . ." he soothed, and again she settled back against

him, but stiffly. He murmured softly in her ear, "Be still, Laura-love. Charles says you'll like it."

"No . . . no, stop, Rye, it . . . it . . ."

But her objections died aborning, and she leaned her head back against his shoulder as his touch seemed to rob her of the will to move or speak. Her breasts rose and fell deeply as his caress worked some sort of magic. And in a few short minutes she felt her body quicken with the same sort of rhythmic quaking Rye's had. Something tightened the tips of her toes, worked its way up the backs of her legs like creeping fire, and a minute later her body was convulsed by a series of inner explosions that stunned her, shook her, and brought a groan to her lips. Then Rye was clamping his free hand over her mouth to stifle the sound while, in the throes of ecstasy, she gripped his knees with her finger.

She tried to speak his name behind his palm, but he held her prisoner in a world so exquisite, her body was shattered with delight. The undulations grew, peaked, and were suddenly stilled.

She became foggily aware of a dim pain and realized Rye's teeth had clamped on her shoulder. She fell back into a panting near swoon, her limbs overcome by a tiredness such as she'd never imagined.

"Rye . . ." But his hand was still over her mouth. She reached to free her lips and whispered, "Rye . . . oh, Rye, what did you do?"

His voice shook. "Charles says . . ." He swallowed. "Charles says that's what you do if you don't want to have babies. Did you like it?"

"At first no, but then . . ." She pressed a kiss on his callused fingers. "Oh, then," she crooned, quite unable to express her new, soaring discovery.

"What was it like?"

"Like . . . like I was in both heaven and hell at once." But at the mention of hell, Laura sobered and straightened. Her voice became edged with guilt. "It's a sin, though, Rye. It's . . . it's what they call fornication, isn't it? I never knew what it meant before when—"

"Laura—" He swung her around by the shoulders, taking her jaw in both hands, rubbing her cheeks with his thumbs.

"Laura, we have to wait three years before we can get married."

Her brown eyes met his blue ones with a new understanding. "Yes, I know."

She knew also that morality weighed little against this new-found heaven-hell, for they had found a way . . . together. And they would be man and wife, just as they had pretended to be as children, when Rye had stalked off to sea with a kiss good-bye. Only there would be no good-byes after they were married, just hellos each morning, noon, and night.

And so they told themselves as they bounded through that wild, wicked, wonderful spring, pleasuring each other countless times without fulfilling the act of love. In the old boathouse, out in the dory, on the borders of Gibbs Pond within sweet groves of Virginia creeper, and in the stands of beech trees that grew in the protected shallows of the hilly heathlands, which became their playground.

They fled to privacy each chance they got, scattering herds of grazing sheep as they raced, laughing, across hilly pastures —carefree nymphs learning more and more about love as each day passed, running through the salt air of summer, bound for more of each other, yet never quite getting enough.

Chapter 7

THE SAME MEMORIES had been plaguing Rye Dalton in the cooperage on Water Street; Laura was rarely absent from his thoughts. After the meeting with her in the orchard, he threw himself into his work with reckless zeal, pressing his body to limits he had no right to expect of it as two weeks passed, and then three, and he heard nothing from her.

But she was there before him even while he shaved away with a drawknife or hunched his shoulders over the howel or cranked the windlass about the resisting staves of a barrel to draw them in tight. She was there before him, her face beckoning, body bending. He saw her features in the grain of wood, imagined the outline of her breasts as he ran his fingers delicately along the bowed edge of a stave. When he wound the ropes of the windlass around the flaring barrel staves to cinch them together for banding with a hoop, he imagined her waist being tightly cinched by lacings, knowing it was Dan who did that daily.

And it was all he could do to keep from flinging the windlass aside and marching up the hill to claim her. But she had asked him for time, and though he wondered how much she would need, he'd do her bidding in the hope that she'd eventually come to a decision in his favor.

There was, for Rye, a modicum of contentment in being back at the cooperage again, toiling beside his father, bending to labor in the sweet-scented confines of the place where he'd grown up.

On foggy days there was always a fragrant blaze in the fireplace, with never an end of wood scraps to supply it. Josiah, when he finished a cedar pail, would set the tailings aside and dole them into the fire prudently, just often enough to provide a steady fragrance that wafted through the air like incense, to mingle with his pipe smoke.

On sunny days the wide double doors were thrown open to the street and the scent of lilacs drifted in to accent the aromas of wood, both wet and dry. There was a steady passing of townspeople, many of whom stepped inside for a brief greeting and to welcome Rye back. Everyone knew of the curious situation to which he had returned, yet not a soul mentioned it; they only watched and waited to see what would come of it.

The old man asked no questions either, but Josiah was shrewd enough to note the growing restlessness that made Rye jumpy and distracted. Tolerance was not Rye's long suit, and his father wondered how long it would take before things came to a head.

It was early June, a sparkling day of flawless blue sky and warm sun, when the old man took a midmorning break, shuffling to the open doorway to puff at his pipe and flex his back. "Takin' that boy long enough to get back with them hoops," Josiah commented in his rich New England drawl. He spoke of his brother's boy, Chad Dalton, his newest apprentice, who was off to the smithy to fetch a pair of hoops. But now that Rye was back, the lad slacked off at times, taking advantage of his Uncle Josiah's good mood.

Rye didn't even look up, which scarcely surprised Josiah. His son was standing at the fixed blade of a five-foot-long jointer plane, drawing the edge of a stave across it. It took keen judgment, a steady hand, and your eyes on your work to shape every edge identical. No, it didn't bother Josiah that Rye didn't look up; what bothered him was that he didn't even seem to hear.

"Said it's takin' that boy long enough to get back with them hoops!" Josiah repeated louder.

At last Rye's hands stilled and he glanced up, frowning. "I heard you, old man, or is it y'r ears goin' bad?"

"Not a thing wrong with m' ears. Just don't like talkin' to m'self."

"Boy's probably rollin' those hoops the opposite direction from Gordon's smithy—you know a boy and a hoop." Again Rye set to planing.

"Had in mind t' send him after some fresh oranges from the square—just come in from Sicily. Time he gets here, oranges'll be rottin' in the noon sun." Even from here Josiah could hear the calls of the vendors on Main Street Square, where the daily market was in full swing.

"Go get 'em yourself. Do y' good t' take a walk and get out of here for a few minutes."

Josiah, his back still to the cooperage, puffed his pipe and watched ladies pass with baskets over their arms. "Knees're a little stiff today—can't imagine why m' rheumatism's actin' up on a clear day like this." He scanned the flawless blue skies. "Must be foul weather blowin' in."

Behind him, Rye measured the shaped length of wood with a stave gauge. Ignoring the old man's hint, he studied it critically, found it to his liking, and took up a finished stave to compare the two. Finding them perfectly matched, he tossed them onto a completed stack and chose another rough-hewn piece to begin edging.

In the doorway, Josiah slipped his fingers between waistband and shirt back, rocked back on his heels, and complained to the azure sky, "Ayup! Sure could go for a fresh orange about now." A loud clatter sounded behind him as Rye flung the board down. Josiah smiled to himself.

"All right, if y' want me t' run to the damn market for your oranges, why don't y' just say so?"

Now Josiah turned his squint-eye back to his son. "Gittin' a little twitchy lately, ain't cha?"

Rye ignored him as he clumped across the cooperage and brushed around the older man with irritation in every step.

"Looks t' me like it's you needs gettin' outa here for a while, not me."

"I'm going! I'm going!" Rye barked.

When he stomped off up the street, Josiah smiled again, puffed his pipe, and muttered, "Ayup, y' sure are, boy—to-hell-in-a-rowboat crazy, and drivin' me right with y'."

Rye Dalton made an impressive sight storming along the cobbled street in close-fitting tan breeches and a drop-shouldered shirt of white cotton with wide sleeves gathered full at the wrist. The open collar left a deep vee of exposed skin behind the buttonless garment, and coarse gold hairs sparkled there against his dark flesh. Around his neck a red bandana was tied sailor fashion, the habit adopted from his shipmates and continued now, for the bandana was convenient for swabbing his temples when he sweated in the cooperage.

It was a warm morning, filled with the sounds of exuberant gulls and the grinding of wheels along the streets as Rye jumped around the tail of a passing wagon and leaped to the new, cobbled sidewalk. The wind ruffled his sunstreaked hair, whipped his full sleeves as he strode, long-legged and angry, toward Market Square.

Farmers were selling fresh flowers and butter from big-wheeled wooden carts. Fishermen peddled fresh cod, herring, and oysters while butchers kept fresh meat covered with heavy wet cloths in the backs of drays. At one end of the square, an auctioneer called out his gibberish as furniture and household items went up for sale.

Rye scanned the vendors until he spotted the bright splashes of citrus fruits—limes, lemons, and oranges piled in pyramids on the wagons, creating a tempting array of colors. The scent was heavenly, the fruit always coveted, for it was available only seasonally.

Rye took a long-legged step off the curb and took up a shiny-skinned orange, his mouth watering as he grudgingly admitted the old man was right—the fruit was tempting, and it was good to get out into the fresh air and activity of the market. There was a steady mingling of voices, the sharp staccato of the auctioneer, the indolent calls of wagon owners, and the musical hum of shoppers exchanging pleasantries, while over it all the gulls interjected their demands for scraps of fish, crumbs of bread, or anything else they might scavenge.

Rye squeezed the orange, selected another, and put it to his nose to sniff its pungent fruitiness, telling himself he'd be mellower to the old man; it wasn't Josiah's fault that Rye was in this damnable predicament. The old man had been more than patient with him during the past couple of weeks when Rye's temper flared or he became brooding and silent. He smiled now, in resolution, making his selections from the pyramid of fruit. He had chosen three flawless oranges when a voice at his elbow purred, "Why, Mr. Dalton, you out doing the daily marketing?"

"Miss Hussey . . . good morning," he greeted, turning at the sound of her voice. She peered up at him from beneath the crescent of a lavender bonnet brim, a becoming smile on her face.

"Aye, the old man had a cravin' and thinks I'm still an apprentice in kneepants." He laughed indulgently.

She laughed, too, and turned to the selection of oranges for herself. "My mother sent me out for the same reason."

"I have t' admit they're temptin'. I can't wait t' peel one m'self." He grinned mischievously and angled her a glance. " 'Course, don't tell the old man that or he'll have me runnin' down here every mornin' like a housemaid."

"If you had a wife, Mr. Dalton, you wouldn't have to worry about running to the market for oranges."

"I have a wife, Miss Hussey, but it doesn't seem t' do me much good."

It was out before he could stop it, but immediately he was sorry, for he'd brought a most unbecoming blush to DeLaine Hussey's cheeks, and he could see she was at a loss for something to say. She quickly became intense about her selection of oranges and refused to meet his eyes. He touched her hand briefly. "I apologize, Miss Hussey. Five years at sea, and I forget m' manners. I've made y' uncomfortable. That was a most indulgent thing for me t' say."

"It's true nevertheless. The whole town's wondering what she means to do about it, though, living up there in your house with your best friend . . ." But she stammered to a halt, her eyes widening in surprise as she stared at the woman and boy who'd quietly appeared on the other side of the wagon.

Rye noticed Laura a second too late, but immediately withdrew his hand from DeLaine Hussey's. Next to her overblown dressiness, Laura was a vision of feminine simplicity, standing in the sun with the brim of a becoming yellow bonnet angling over her face, a large satin bow caught just below one ear. Her dress was narrow-waisted, but she wore no billowing hoops to-day, and he couldn't help but wonder if she was pinched up in stays—she was thin enough that he could not tell by looking.

She held the hand of the boy tightly, and while Rye stared at Laura, he forgot everything but the welcome sight of her. Suddenly seeming to remember the presence of the other woman, he stepped back as if to acknowledge her, but before he could, Laura smiled and said, "Hello, Miss Hussey. It's nice to see you again."

In a pig's eyes, Laura thought all the while she beamed at the woman. She was very conscious that Rye's hand had been on DeLaine's.

"Hello," DeLaine replied shortly, a sour expression on her face.

"Hello, Rye," Laura said then, turning her bonnet brim up to him, hoping DeLaine Hussey could not tell the way her heart suddenly flew to her throat at the sight of him, tall and handsome and looking good enough to eat right along with those three oranges he held in his wide-spread palm. The sun tinted his blue eyes bluer and glanced off the narrow slit of exposed chest, turning it to rich gold behind the white shirt.

"Hello, Laura," he managed, oranges and DeLaine Hussey completely forgotten as he took in the face that had haunted him night and day.

Laura's expression instantly gave away her feelings, for her pink lips suddenly lost their smile and fell open slightly. Her eyes, refusing to obey her edict of caution, stared widely into his before fluttering to his bronze chest, then back up. And she'd squeezed Josh's hand so hard, he now squirmed and howled, then yanked free.

Reminded of the boy's presence, Rye smiled down at him. "Hello, Josh."

"You're the man with the funny name."

"Aye, and do y' remember it?"

"It's Rye."

"Aye, it is. So next time I'll expect a proper hello when I meet y'."

But again he turned his eyes to Laura, and she could not resist asking sweetly, "Are the two of you shopping for oranges?"

Rye colored deeply, the flush barely discernible on his face, which was already tanned to the shade of an old copper penny, darker than Laura ever remembered seeing it before the voyage of the *Omega*.

"Ah, no . . . well, I mean, yes, I was out buyin' oranges for Josiah."

"And I was out buying oranges for my mother," Miss Hussey put in, a pinched expression about her mouth.

"And we was out buyin' oranges for Papa," Josh piped innocently.

At the word, Rye's mouth sobered, and he studied Laura's face.

DeLaine Hussey noted the exchange of glances, but remained stubbornly at Rye's side.

"Well, how about if we all have one now—my treat," Rye offered, unable to think of any other way to ease the tension.

"Mmm . . . I *like* oranges!" Josh exclaimed, bright-eyed and eager.

"Then which one will it be?"

It was plain to Laura that Rye was suddenly as eager as Josh. He looked at the chubby hands that touched every orange as if it mattered a great deal which was chosen. And this first innocent encounter beneath the bright June sun in the bustling market square suddenly seemed representative of all the experiences of fatherhood Rye had missed. Laura hadn't the heart to deny him such a small joy. His eyes shone with delight when Josh finally picked an orange and plopped it into Rye's big hand with a "There!" as if he'd solved a great and important riddle.

Rye laughed, jubilant and handsome and capturing Laura's heart as she watched his dark, lean fingers tear into the orange skin for his son.

DeLaine Hussey, feeling a complete outsider in this little scene *en famille,* decided it was time to withdraw and aimed a flashing good-bye to Rye, and to Laura a nod so brisk it was undeniably rude.

No sooner was she out of earshot than Rye caught Laura's eye. "I've been wondering when I'd see you again," he said, extremely aware of the understatement, and quelling the urge to touch her.

"I come to the market every morning," she said.

"Every mornin'?" he repeated, cursing himself for wasting all these opportunities.

"Hey, hurry up, Rye!" Josh demanded, seeing that the peeling process had suddenly slowed while Rye and Laura indulged themselves with the sight of each other's faces.

"Aye-aye!" Rye snapped nautically, tearing his attention away from Laura long enough to finish the job. He handed half an orange to Josh, then began sectioning the rest, his eyes again on her.

She watched each dexterous movement of his fingers, the square nails separating the delicate filaments so expertly that not a drop of juice escaped. Hands, hands, she thought, there is no forgetting hands.

Just then one of his came toward her, offering a bright crescent of fruit. Her eyes flew to his. It was nothing, she thought, just a piece of an orange, so why was there a little drum tattooing the message through her veins that she was answering some unspoken innuendo as she reached breathlessly for Rye's offering?

Without taking his eyes from hers, he lifted a section of orange to his lips. They opened in slow motion to receive the ripe, plump fruit, and as he bit down, a succulent spurt of orange juice flew into the warm, summer air.

As if mesmerized, she answered by lifting her own delicacy, tasting old memories as she bit into its sweetness, her every sense heightened by awareness of the man before her.

In his turn he ate a second piece, and this time a sweet rivulet of juice drizzled down his chin, and her eyes followed it, unable to do otherwise.

Suddenly he laughed and broke the spell, Laura following suit, while he untied the red bandana from about his throat and wiped his chin, then offered it to her.

It smelled of salt and cedar and of him as she brushed her lips with it. He peeled another orange for Josh, whose eyes were too busy to note the looks being exchanged between his mother and the tall cooper.

"So y' come to the market every mornin'?" Rye asked.

"Well, almost. We come to get milk, Josh and I."

"And I carry it, too," Josh declared proudly, backhanding

his orangy lips, making them both laugh down at him.

Something powerfully sweet swelled Rye's heart. He'd missed being this child's father, didn't even know if it was a great accomplishment for a four-year-old to safely carry a pitcher of milk. But it was heady learning, sharing such first revelations with the boy.

"You do!" Rye exclaimed, bending down to test Josh's biceps. "I can see why. Y've a fine set o' muscles in that arm. Y' must've been haulin' traps or pullin' rigging."

Josh laughed gaily. "I ain't old enough for that yet, but when I get big like my papa, I'm gonna be a whaler."

Rye's eyes flashed briefly to Laura's, then back to their son. "Whalers get mighty lonesome out there on the big ships, Josh, and sometimes they miss out on lots of fun, bein' gone so much of the time. Maybe you'd be better off bein' a clerk like . . . like y'r papa."

"Naw, I don't like it in the countinghouse. It's dark in there, and you can't hear the waves as good." Then, with typical childish caprice, Josh scarcely paused as he changed subject. "I wanna hear the auctioneer, Mama. Can I go over and listen to him?" He squinted up at her.

Aware of Rye suddenly turning pleading eyes to her, aware of her own heart thumping away in double time, Laura knew it was safer to keep Josh beside her, yet answered as her heart dictated. For what could happen out here in the middle of Market Square? "All right, but stay right there until I come for you, and don't go anywhere else."

"Aye-aye!" he answered, imitating Rye, then scampering away toward the lower end of the square.

Rye's gaze followed the boy. Softly, he said, "Ah, but he's bonny."

"Yes . . . yes, he is."

They were alone now, but hesitated to look at each other or say another word. Laura sought equilibrium in the oranges, turning to test them, selecting some to place in her drawstring bag. But while her hand moved from fruit to fruit, Rye's hovered beside it, doing likewise. He squeezed one, took it away, then squeezed another, but at last his hand fell still. A long motionless moment passed before Laura looked up to find his eyes upon her, full of her, taking their fill now as they hadn't been able to while Delaine and Josh had been with them.

His gaze moved up to the tiny springing curls beneath her bonnet brim, then to her lips, softly parted, and to her brown eyes, which seemed caught in his. "Jesus, but I've missed you," he breathed.

Her lips fell open further, and she stammered, "D . . . don't say that, Rye."

"It's the truth."

"But better left unsaid."

"And now I can be miserable thinking about the boy as well?"

But she was as miserable as he at the thought. She'd read his longing plainly enough in each glance he'd given Josh, each exchange of words they'd shared, and the small insignificant gift of peeled orange: a father's first offering to his son.

"Rye, I'm sorry."

"He's dreamin' of makin' the same mistakes I've made."

"He has a good fath . . . a good man to steer him."

"Aye, he does, and it cuts me t' the quick t' know it."

"Rye, please don't. You're only making it harder."

Momentarily, he glanced at the brick building across the square where even now Dan Morgan worked at his desk. "Have y' talked to him yet? Have y' told him . . . asked him . . ."

She shook her head, chin lowering, oranges suddenly becoming blurred by tears. "I can't. It would kill him to lose Josh now."

"And what about me? Josh is my son—have y' had a thought for what I'm feelin'?"

"I've had a thousand thoughts for what you're feeling, Rye." She raised tormented eyes and he saw tears sparkling on her lashes. "But if you could see the two of them together—"

"I have! I do! I see them in my nightmares, just the way they were the day I came home. But it doesn't alter the fact that I want t' be his father now, though it's four years late I'll be startin'."

"I've got to go, Rye. We've been together too long as it is. Dan is sure to find out about it."

"Wait!" He reached out quickly to stay her with a wide

hand on her yellow sleeve. Shivers radiated through her from his touch. Reading her reaction in those brown, startled eyes, he immediately withdrew his hand. "Wait," he entreated more softly. "Will y' meet me here in the market tomorrow mornin'? I've somethin' to give y' . . . somethin' I made for y'."

"I can't accept gifts from you. Dan will ask questions."

"He'll know nothin' about this one. Please."

She looked up to find his face filled with pain and longing, just above hers, and wondered if it was not just a matter of time before she gave in to him—all the way in. She backed up a step, guilty for the thought, once again withdrawing to a safe distance, yet unable to deny his request. "We'd best not meet at the oranges again."

He glanced around, searching the crowded square. "Have y' planted y'r garden yet?"

"Most of it . . . not all."

"Do y' need seeds?"

"Parsnips."

"I'll meet y' by the flower carts. They sell seeds there, too."

"All right."

Their eyes clung for a last look.

"Y' won't disappoint me, now, will y', Laura-love?"

She swallowed, wanting nothing so much as to fling her arms about his neck and kiss him right here, and the whole square be damned.

"No, I won't disappoint you, Rye, but I must go now." She turned away, her heart knowing a delight it had not felt in years, that rapturous torture of first love happening all over again. The giddiness of secret meetings, of sharing small intimacies under the noses of others. How often they'd dared such things in years past. To do so again was dangerous, yet the idea seduced Laura in a way that made her feel more vibrant, more alive, than she'd been since Rye Dalton had sailed away.

When she'd taken a mere three steps, his voice came softly from behind her. "Bring the boy. I've known too little of him, too."

Without turning around, she nodded, then headed for the lower square.

*   *   *

Josiah noted the difference in Rye but offered no comment as his son sauntered into the cooperage, flipping three oranges up for grabs in quick succession, almost faster than Josiah could nab them. "There, y' old sea dog. Y' needn't worry about the scurvy catchin' up with y' now. Is the boy back yet?"

"Ayup, and gone again. I fear he's takin' advantage of me, but I've got a soft old heart, as y' well know, lettin' all m' help run out in the sun and leavin' me here to molder in the shadows of the place and carry on business without a bit o' help." Josiah chuckled softly.

"I've an errand for Chad t' run when he comes back, so keep him under y'r thumb next time he chooses t' darken the doorway for a minute."

When Chad returned, Josiah pretended to pay no attention as Rye fished a penny from his pocket and ordered, "I want y' to run t' the apothecary on Federal Street and fetch me as many sarsaparilla sticks as this will buy. And have one y'rself, but don't break the rest while y're dallyin' on the way back t' work."

He had promised Laura that Dan wouldn't find out about what he had for her, but he'd said not a thing about any treat he might bring to Josh, knowing full well word of sarsaparilla sticks would reach Dan's ears. If he couldn't get Laura to make the first move toward separation from Dan, maybe he could get Dan to.

That night Rye opened his sea chest, still thinking of the sight of Laura and the boy standing in the sun against a backdrop of bright fruit and a pony cart filled with daisies, lilies, and tulips. It had been so unexpected, looking up to find her there after so many lonely days of searching faces on the streets each time he walked them.

How many times during the past five years had he thought of that face just as it had looked today, with its wide, bright eyes, delicate lips alluringly open, and that look about her that said she still felt the same?

Laura's face had been with him through the empty first days of the voyage while the weight of guilt for leaving her still lay heavy on his soul. It had accompanied him during endless hours of listening to the rush of the curling waters climbing the flared planking of the *Massachusetts*'s bow, washing the wooden knees of the figurehead, the only lady to make the voyage. It had been his reason to exult during the brief hours when a whale was hauled against the side of the ship and he sat on the quarterdeck sharpening spades while the second mate cut away blubber. The scent of her had been his sustenance while he erected barrels, with the sickening stench of half-decomposed blubber filling his nostrils as the trypot sizzled and spat on the deck, melting down fat in various stages of putrefaction. Laura had been the prayer on his lips during the terror-filled days rounding the Horn, when he was certain he would make her not a rich wife but a poor widow.

And during those fevered days of smallpox, when his senses dimmed, Laura had come to him in his delirium, giving him reason to fight for life.

Now, picking from his sea chest a small, flat piece of carved whalebone, he remembered how images of Laura's face and body had guided his hands as he'd filled the worst hours of all, those nerve-racking days considered the most excruciating by any man, be he deck hand or captain, who'd ever sailed a windjammer—the doldrums.

The doldrums, when the fickle wind denied them her breath, leaving the ship to drift motionlessly upon a merciless, windless sea. The doldrums, when the urge for home became agonizing. The doldrums, when wasted days only lengthened the voyage, profiting nothing, bringing a feeling of utter helplessness until tempers flared and vicious fights broke out on board.

He had shared the doldrums with shipmates who fought the lassitude with the only pastime available—scrimshaw. At first when Rye took up a knife to carve the whalebone, he was inept and impatient. The initial pieces he turned out were rough and hardly worth keeping, so he tossed them overboard. But he persisted, with the help of the others, and soon he produced a smooth splicing fid—a pin for separating the strands of a rope—then a walking stick. Next he tried a jewelry casket, and when it was finely polished, its etchings deep and true, the men started teasing him about making a busk, for they knew he'd left a wife ashore.

The busk was a foot-long strip of bone, fingernail-thick, that could be slipped into a casing along the front of a woman's bodice, like a batten on a sail. Its purpose was to uplift, it was extremely personal, and was meant to serve as a reminder to the woman who wore it that she must remain true to her seafaring man until he returned.

Yet for all their teasing, no skrimshander carved any piece as caringly as he did a busk, for in the end it became a vent for his loneliness and his hope for the journey's end.

When Rye finished the busk for Laura, it was smoother than anything he'd done before, and he polished the striated grooves with silicon carbide until it was as satiny as Laura's very breast. He'd carved on it an entwined design of Nantucket wild roses, among which he and Laura had played as children, adding gulls and a delicate scallop-edged heart. Then he deliberated long over the carved message, rephrasing the brief poem for weeks before deciding on the exact words.

Lifting the busk from his sea chest now, he read:

> Until upon your rosy breast
> My loving lips are fondly press't
> Wear thee this token made of bone
> And know I long for thee alone.

Never while he'd been carving the busk had Rye dreamed it would take on the poignant relevance it did now. He wondered if she'd bury it deep in some bureau drawer or wear it pressed secretly against her skin.

He thought of her sunlit face this morning beneath the brim of a yellow bonnet and recalled gay shafts of sunlight piercing a succulent section of orange, lighting it to near transparency as her straight white teeth broke it. He remembered her brown eyes and how they'd measured his awareness, and orange juice glistening on her lips. He thought of the way she'd clutched Josh's hand at first, then allowed Rye his first father's privileges.

And his heart swelled with hope.

Chapter 8

SLEEP WAS IMPOSSIBLE for Rye that night. Eagerness kept him tossing fitfully until finally, at four A.M., he pulled a thick turtleneck sweater over his head and found his boots in the dark, along with the cold nose of Ship, who woke at the sound of his rustling and came to investigate.

They crept out together to sit on the bottom step while Rye pulled on his boots and whispered, "What do y' say we climb up the rock like we used to, old girl?"

Ship's tail answered, and her tongue lolled pink from the side of her mouth.

Rye scratched the dog's jaws, then got to his feet, whispering, "Let's go, girl."

They walked side by side through the somnolent town, the dog's warm bulk pressed against Rye's leg. The cobblestones were shiny and damp, but they soon left them behind for a sandy street that led eventually to the foot trails of Shawkemo Hills, which were still shrouded in fog as Rye and Ship made their way toward Altar Rock, the highest spot on the island.

They climbed up and sat side by side as they'd done a hundred times before, the rangy man folding his limbs, crossing his calves, and wrapping his knees with both arms, while beside him the dog sat on its haunches. Like a pair of monoliths, they awaited the spectacle they'd many times shared, and as it began the man rested a hand on the dog's back.

Summer was near her solstice, the dawn silent-still. In those last purple minutes before the sun intruded, the harbor lay like a mirror beneath tier upon tier of lavender mist. Between these foggy strata, the undulations of the island appeared like purple mountains whose feet were made of nothing more than the ocean's breath.

Then up stole the sun to peer over the sea's rim and cast her red-hazed eye over Nantucket, transforming those fog arms into lazy, pink limbs, now stretching, now flexing, now moving restlessly, yawning awake in ever widening chasms until the red-gold of morning spilled through.

The harbor's forest of masts was a study in stillness, each craft with its twin lying beside it on the glassy surface of the water.

And for that moment, at least, it seemed that all creatures of earth, sky, and sea waited, as did Rye and his dog—silent, respectful—paying homage to the spectacle of light and color that announced the day.

Then one by one the coots swam out, wrinkling the reflections of masts, spars, and stays in their search for silver minnows. The spotted sandpiper made her first run along the deserted shore, stopping to teeter in her drunken way, as if intoxicated, too, by the show just staged by morning.

Next came the gulls, lazy scavengers awaiting the first moving boat to follow, and with the gulls, their sisters—the terns —awaiting the first moving boat to lead.

Below Rye, the bell in the Congregational church tower tolled its peaceful wake-up peal over the harbor town, and a first catboat eased from its slip, then another and another, heading for the place called the "cord of the bay," just inside the bar, where bluefish schooled now that June was here.

Rye lingered as long as he dared, till his spine grew numb and the dog's stomach growled, along with his own.

The scent of wood smoke drifted up from the fires of blacksmith, candle maker, tryworker, and baker. Soon the repetitive clang of the smith's hammer sounded from below, and the scent of ship's biscuits baking in beehive ovens told Rye he must go.

Reluctantly, he got to his feet and, followed by the yellow Labrador, made his way back down through the heathland to

the quayside, where weathered wooden doors were now turned
back as shops came to life. He passed the ropewalk, and from
within came the rumble of steel wheels riding steel rails as the
forming machine rolled backward, twisting yarns of manila
into strands of rope. From inside the shop of a ship's carver
came the soft rap of hammer on chisel, and farther up the
street Rye nodded good morning to the clerk who was tacking
up a sign in a window: "Spermaceti Candles—Exceeding all
Others in Beauty and Sweetness of Scent when Extin-
guished—Duration Double that of Tallow Candles."

Ah, Nantucket—even though at times he felt trapped by it,
he loved it just the same. He had forgotten the beauty of these
intermingling sounds and smells and sights that seemed to
symbolize the close correlation of all the island's livelihoods.

Rye stopped to buy a roll for his breakfast, ordering Ship to
wait outside the shop until he emerged, eating a crispy bun. He
offered one to the dog, and took another home for Josiah,
who'd just arisen, his cold pipe already between his teeth,
awaiting its first tamping of the day.

They set to work together, hooping a thirty-gallon wet
barrel whose staves had been soaking overnight. They worked
amiably now, for Rye's testy temper of the previous day
seemed to have evaporated, replaced by a barely concealed
eagerness that Josiah could not quite understand until later
that morning, when Rye jogged up the steps to their lodgings
above and then returned a few minutes later, whistling, in
clean shirt and ducks, his hair neatly brushed.

Offhandedly, he announced, "Those oranges took the edge
off y'r tongue. I'll run out and get y' y'r day's supply."

"Ayup, y' do that." The old one grinned around his pipestem.

This morning his grin was returned as Rye left the cooperage, again whistling, his step sprightly.

For both Laura and Rye it was a heady feeling, walking
toward the square to meet. Innocent yet illicit, callow yet
knowing; for though they'd been man and wife before and
had shared the deepest intimacies of marriage, here they were
plunged back to the beginning like sea-green children. As they
approached the square from opposite sides, they were reckless

spirits, straining toward that first glimpse of one another, hearts hammering, palms damp.

Laura picked out Rye with the canny instinct of a bufflehead diving for plankton. As his blond head moved toward her amid vendors, wares, and shoppers, she suppressed the urge to smile and wave, and the even greater one to hurry toward him.

It was hard to control the smile that wanted to burst over her face at the sight of him advancing, full sleeves luffing in the breeze, head bare to the June sun, his hair already coming in darker at the roots, and his eyebrows losing their bleached look even after so few weeks away from sea. And on his dark-skinned face she read the anticipation he, too, strained to conceal.

At his approach her heart went weightless, lifting with a fluttering expectancy every bit as poignant as during those long-ago days in the loft when they were learning together the thrill of first love.

"Hello," he said, as if it were not the most glorious day ever created.

"Hello," she answered, fingers trailing in a bin of parsnip seeds, as if parsnip seeds mattered in the least.

"It's nice to see you again." I love you! You're beautiful.

"And you." I cannot forget. I feel the same.

"Hi, Rye." It was Josh, looking up. The man went down on one knee, producing the sarsaparilla sticks.

"Hello, Joshua. Did y' come to hear the auctioneer again?"

Josh beamed, his eyes whipping from the candy to Rye's face, then back again as he answered, "Aye."

Rye laughed with fatherly ebullience. " 'Aye,' is it? Yesterday it was 'yes.' "

"I like aye better."

Pleased, Rye gave the lad the treat and ordered, "Well, be off with y', then. I'll keep an eye on y'r mother."

Immediately, Josh darted away. Laura studied Rye as he knelt with an elbow braced on a knee, his full white sleeve drooping on a tight blue trouser leg.

Just then he looked up at her and slowly straightened to his full height to stand beside her and savor the look of her, her brown eyes agleam before her gaze dropped again to the parsnip seeds.

"I've brought it," he said softly, eyeing the square to make sure they were not being listened to or watched.

"Oh?" She tipped her head aside and peered up at him, then back at the seeds. When she refrained from asking what the gift was, he teased her by delaying the giving.

"Y' have a lovely bonnet today."

"Thank you."

"And a lovely set o' curls peepin' around it."

"Thank you."

"And the prettiest mouth I've seen t'day." It tipped up at the corners while her cheeks nurtured roses.

"Thank you."

"And I wouldn't mind kissin' it again as soon as possible."

"Rye Dalton, stop that!" She, too, looked around warily.

He laughed and captured her hand in the bin of parsnip seeds.

"What is it you've brought for me?" she couldn't resist asking at last.

He slipped the busk from inside his full sleeve and partially concealed the exchange under the seeds. Her color grew rosier as she hid it in her sleeve, unable to read what he'd written on it until she was alone.

"Oh, Rye, a busk!" Her eyelids flew up and she touched a fingertip to her throat.

"Will y' wear it?"

"I . . . it's very—"

"Personal," he finished.

"Yes." She demurely studied the seeds.

"And intimate."

"Yes."

She let her hand drift along to the bin of pumpkin seeds while he continued, "Like my feelings for you when I made it . . . like my feelings for you right now." He studied her forehead in the shadow of her bonnet, wishing she would meet his eyes again.

"Shh, Rye, someone will hear you."

"Aye, they well might, so tell me you'll wear it or I'll shout t' the square at large that Mrs. Daniel Morgan's got somethin' up her sleeve and it's a scrimshawed busk carved by Rye Dalton.''

His willful teasing made Laura delight in being with him. Now she smiled prettily, raising her eyes, which had a teasing glint of their own. "And just what did you write on it?"

"What was on m' mind from the minute I sailed away from y'."

"Will it make me blush?"

"I hope so."

It did, when she got home later. She read the verse with a curious mingling of guilt and arousal; nevertheless, she secretly sewed the busk into its casing, where it rested intimately between her breasts through the days that followed. To have such words pressed against her skin did, indeed, keep her aware of Rye's wish to possess her again, and forbidden though it was to dwell on the thought, she did. She was woman, and carnal, and having the busk touch her was like having Rye touch her, tempt her, every minute of the day.

"I'm wearing it," she volunteered breathlessly the next time they met.

His eyes lit up with a knowing glint, and he lazily examined her bodice while the new dimple creased his right cheek. "Show me where."

She interlaced her fingers, folded her arms between her breasts, and rested her chin on her knuckles while all about them fishmongers sold 'blues.' "Here."

"How soon can I take it off y'?" he asked, raising her color to a very telling hue.

"Rye Dalton, you've not changed one bit."

"Thank God, no!" He laughed, then sobered only a little. "When?"

"You're harassing me."

"It's me bein' harassed. I want to take y' up into the bayberries and crush a few while I do what I wrote on that busk . . . and more." Her flustration was his only reward as she blushed prettily and turned away to buy butter.

There followed a heady string of sun-swelled days during which Rye and Laura met that way, hearts, thoughts, and eyes communicating even before they reached each other across the square. They gave themselves these meetings as consolation, neither asking where the encounters were leading. They never touched—they couldn't. And they never met privately—they dared not. But their eyes spoke messages that voices could not, except on those rare days when they were gifted with a few sterling minutes alone. Then, the brief intimacies they spoke threatened to undo them.

Summer came on full, enticing them to roam the island's beloved floral landscape as they had years ago. In the village of Siasconset tame ivy thickened and greened upon the small silvery cottages of 'Sconset's narrow lanes while poison ivy climbed merrily up the trunks of scrub pines in the wilds. Bayberry and heather carpeted the heath while in the swamps and lowlands the wax myrtle glistened. The delicate lavender blossoms of the trailing arbutus, nicknamed the mayflower by the Pilgrims who'd first found it, gave way to the fragrant blooms of pasture roses. Marsh marigolds burst forth like droplets of sun fallen to earth while the higher slopes broke out in Solomon's seal and false spikenard.

Laura and Rye, meanwhile, hovered on the brink of accepting the invitation of the hills that seduced them with the promise of privacy. But before privacy became theirs, Dan Morgan paid a call at the cooperage.

Rye, his back to the door, was arranging the staves of a slack barrel into a temporary hoop when he heard Josiah say, "Well, been some time since I seen you, young feller."

"Hello, Josiah. You've been well, I hope." But Dan's eyes were on Rye, who continued working without turning around.

"Got no complaints. Business is good, fog's been scarce."

Dan directed his glance back to Josiah. "Working on the order for the *Omega*'s next voyage?"

"Aye, we are," the old man confirmed, then, following Dan's glance back to Rye, he decided it would be provident to quietly disappear for a while.

Silence fell as Rye set the final two staves in a wooden band that held them at the bottom while they flared out on top like the petals of a daisy.

"Could I talk to you a minute, Rye?" Dan asked with strained courtesy.

The cooper glanced up briefly, then back down at his work. He took up a windlass to loop its rope about the petallike staves. "Aye, go ahead." He began cranking the windlass handle and felt Dan move close behind him while the ropes began squeakily closing up the daisy petals.

"Word has it you've been seeing Laura in the square each day."

"We've run into each other a time or two."

"A time or two? That's not the way I've heard it."

"Might have been a few times, come t' think of it." With each turn of the crank the staves cinched closer, the rope drawn as taut as the facial muscles of the visitor.

"I want it stopped!" Dan ordered.

"We've talked in the square before a hundred watchful eyes and with the boy right there beside us."

"People still talk—it's a small town."

The staves were now joined, ballooning out at the middle. Rye reached for a permanent metal hoop, placed it around them, and tapped it down with mallet and drift. "Aye, it is, and they all know she's my wife."

"Not anymore she's not. I want you to stay away from her."

At last Rye's hands fell still, and his eyes met Dan's. "And what's she had t' say about that?"

Dan paled and his jaws tensed. "What's between us is none of your business."

"What's between y' is my son, and plenty of my business." This was one fact Dan Morgan could not deny and the one that sent fear piercing through him. His voice trembled slightly. "You'd use him to try to get her away from me?"

Rye spun away angrily and flung the tools onto a high tool bench with a clatter. "Damnit, what do y' take me for, Dan? He has no idea I'm his father. I've no wish to turn the boy against y', nor t' make him pick between us. She's only brought him t' the square so I could see a little of him, talk to him, get acquainted."

"He tells me you bring him candy sticks, and the other day he showed me a whale's tooth he said you carved for him."

"Aye, I gave it to him, I'll not deny it, but if y' were in my place, could y' keep yourself from doin' the same?"

Their eyes met, Rye's expression defensive, Dan's angry. Nevertheless a shaft of grudging guilt shot through Dan, followed by a lonely premonition of what it would be like if he himself were asked to withdraw as the boy's father. But he went on sternly.

"Since the day Josh was born, I've watched him grow up. I was there beside Laura that day while you were off to sea, where she'd begged you not to go. I was there for his christening, and when he got sick for the first time and she needed moral support and somebody to talk her fears away. And after we were married, I took my turn walking the floors with him at night when he got whooping cough and teeth and earaches and the . . . the hundred things that make babies cry! I was there for his first birthday, and every birthday after that, while you were off . . . *whaling!*" Now Dan turned away. "And I never once loved him less because he was yours. Maybe I loved him more because of it, wanting to make up to him for the fact that he'd . . . lost you."

Rye glared at Dan's shoulders. "So what do y' want now? My thanks, is it? Well, y've got 'em, but not the right to keep me from seeing him."

Again Dan swung around angrily. "And her along with him?"

Their eyes clashed while they faced off, one on each side of a half-made barrel, then suddenly Rye swung to work again, flipping the barrel over to begin hooping its other end. "I said I expected you t' fight for her, so did y' expect any less of me? Be happy I haven't come up there t' claim that bed y' take her to—it belongs to me, too, y' know."

The cruel barb stung, and immediately Dan retaliated. "And I think it's all you want her for, judging from things I remember."

"Damnit, man, you go too far!" Rye Dalton roared, his fists bunching as he took one menacing step forward, the mallet still in his right hand.

"Do I? Do you think I was so ignorant I didn't know what the two of you did together all those times you ran off alone when we were sixteen? Do you think I didn't suffer, wanting her then while I watched her scamper after you as if I weren't even alive? But if you think I'll let her do it again, you're sorely mistaken, Dalton. She's mine now, and I paid dearly, waiting to have her to myself."

Anger and embarrassment bubbled up in Rye, for like most who've stolen kisses, he never suspected others had guessed. "I love her," he said unequivocably.

"You left her."

"I'm back. Suppose we let her make the choice?"

"I'm her legal choice, and I intend to see to it these meetings stop."

Almost nonchalantly now, Rye picked up a hand adz and began evening off the irregular ends of the staves. "Y've a right t' try," he granted. "Good luck."

Having gained no more than he'd expected, Dan gave up, frustrated by the fact that Rye denied nothing and was waging a fair fight, frustrated even further by the fear that his rival might win. He turned on his heel and strode angrily out the door, swinging past Josiah, who sat indolently on an upturned keg out front.

When Josiah went back inside, he found Rye wielding the adz with a vengeance, all semblance of nonchalance now gone. The old man puffed on his pipe, watching wordlessly while the scowl on Rye's face warned that his temper was strained.

But it was nothing compared to the rage spawned later that day, when one Ezra J. Merrill appeared at the double doors and stepped diffidently inside. "Good day, Josiah." He sounded nervous.

"Ezra." The grizzled cooper nodded. His eyes narrowed as he watched Ezra looking about for Rye, who was working in the rear of the shop. "Somethin' I can do for y'?"

"Actually, I'm here to see Rye."

"Well, there he is."

Ezra cleared his throat and moved toward Rye, who stopped tapping a barrel bottom into place and looked back over his shoulder. "Hello, Ezra." Rye turned, the hammer still in his hand. "Need something made?"

Again Ezra cleared his throat. "N . . . no, actually. I'm here in an official capacity. I've been hired by Dan . . . er, Daniel Morgan, that is, to act on his behalf."

The hand holding the hammer tightened perceptibly upon its handle. Ezra's eyes shifted downward nervously, then back up.

"What the hell's he up t' now?"

"Are you the owner of a saltbox house at the end of the lane commonly called Crooked Record?"

Rye glanced at his father, then back at the lawyer. His eyebrows were drawn down into a scowl. "Well, for God's sake, Ezra, you know as well as I do that I own that house. Everybody on the island knows I own it."

Ezra Merrill's face was as red as an autumn apple. "I've been authorized by Daniel Morgan to make you an offer of seven hundred dollars for the purchase of the house, exclusive of any furnishings within it that have been there five years or more, which you are free to take."

The cooperage seemed to crackle in the silence before a storm.

"You what!" Rye growled, took a step toward Ezra, grinding the head of the hammer against his palm.

"I've been authorized to make you an offer—"

"The house is not for sale!" Rye barked.

"Mr. Morgan has instructed me to—"

"You go back and tell Dan Morgan my house is not for sale any more than my wife is!" Rye raged, now advancing on the retreating Ezra, whose mouth was pursed tightly while his eyes blinked rapidly in fright.

"You . . . I . . . shall I tell . . . er, Mr. Morgan, then, that you are rejecting his offer?"

The roof fairly shook as Rye Dalton backed the trembling attorney to the door, emphasizing his words with nudges of the steel hammer against Merrill's chest. "You tell Dan Morgan the goddamn house is not for sale and never will be so long as I draw breath. *Is that clear?*"

Rye watched the lawyer scurry up the street, clutching his hat to his balding head. Rye grasped the hammer so tightly, the hickory handle seemed to depress. Josiah merely puffed his pipe. Ship retreated to the shadows under the tool bench, whined once, laid her head on her paws, and kept a wary eye on her master.

Never in her life had Laura seen Dan as angry as he was that night after his confrontation with Rye. He waited until Josh was in bed before saying without preamble, "It's all over town that you've been meeting Rye in the square, as bold as brass."

"Meeting? I'd hardly call the exchange of hellos meetings."

"I saw him today, and he didn't deny it."

"You saw him—where?"

"At the cooperage. I had to swallow my pride and troop down there and demand that he stop courting my wife under the curious eyes of the entire town, and making a fool of me in the process!"

She colored and turned away. "Dan, you're exaggerating," she lied, the hidden busk seeming to scorch her skin as she spoke the words.

"Am I?" he snapped.

"Yes, of course. Josh and I have talked to him when we've gone to do the marketing, but nothing else . . . I assure you." She looked up entreatingly, and her voice softened as she appealed, "Josh is his son, Dan, his son. How can I keep—"

"Stop lying!" Dan shouted. "And stop using the boy to hide behind. I won't allow it, do you hear? He's not to be made a pawn while the two of you create a scandal right out in public!"

"Scandal? Who calls it a scandal—we've done nothing wrong!"

He wanted badly to believe her, but doubts ate at him, strengthened by things he suspected from their past.

"You've been . . . been doing *wrong* with him since—" His eyes narrowed on her accusingly. "Since when, Laura?" His voice turned silky. "When did it start with you and Rye? When you were fifteen? Sixteen? Or even before that?"

The blood drained from her face and she could think of no answer, could only stand before him appearing guilty as accused. She was stunned to think he'd known all these years yet had never said anything before.

"Don't," she begged in a tiny voice.

"Don't?" he repeated, a hard edge to the word. "Don't remind you of the times you left your . . . your *shadow* behind, thinking he didn't see the berry stains on your back when you came trooping down from the hills with your mouths still puckered, and you with your cheeks rubbed raw from his whiskers before he'd even learned how to shave."

She turned away, chin dropping to her chest. "I'm sorry you knew. We never meant to hurt you, but it has nothing to do with now."

"Doesn't it?" Dan grabbed her arm, forcing her to turn and face him. "Then why do you turn away, blushing? What happened between you two out in the orchard the night of Joseph Starbuck's party? Why were you missing for so long without a trace? Why didn't you answer when I called to you? And how do you think I felt when I went back inside looking for you and found you still gone?"

"Nothing happened . . . nothing! Why won't you believe me?"

"Believe you! When I walk through the streets and people snicker behind my back?"

"I'm sorry, Dan, we . . . I . . ." She choked to a stop.

He glowered at her stricken face, watching her swallow repeatedly in an effort to keep from crying. "Yes, dear wife, we . . . you . . . what?"

"I didn't think of how it would look to others when they saw us together. I . . . I won't see him again, I promise."

Immediately, Dan was sorry he'd jerked her around so roughly. Never in his life had he touched her without tenderness or caused fear to spring into her eyes. Forcing the picture of Rye Dalton from his mind, he clutched Laura tightly against his chest, sensing that he was losing her even as she vowed to be faithful. He buried his face in her neck while fear and passion coursed through him. Yet Josh was hers and Rye's, and Dan was muddled with guilt for denying Rye the right to his son.

"Oh God, why did he have to come back?" Dan said thickly, holding Laura so tightly it seemed he would force the very flesh from her bones.

"Dan, what are you saying?" she cried, struggling out of his arms. "He's . . . he was a friend you loved. How can you say such a thing? Are you saying you wish he'd died?"

"I didn't mean I wanted him dead, Laura . . . not dead." With a horrified expression, Dan sat down heavily and dropped his face into his hands. "Oh God," he groaned miserably, shaking his head.

Studying him, Laura, too, suffered. She understood the

conflict of emotions that was changing Dan in ways that made him dislike himself. These same conflicts warred inside Laura at times, for she loved two men, each in a different way, yet enough to want to hurt neither.

"Dan," she said sadly, moving to rest her hands on his stooping shoulders, "I'm very mixed up, too." Her eyes sparkled with unshed tears as he lifted his tortured face to hers. He willed her not to put voice to her feelings, but she went on, a note of growing weariness in each word as she crossed to the far side of the room and turned to face him.

"It would be a lie for me to say I feel nothing for him. What is between Rye and me is of a whole childhood's making. I can't cause it to disappear or pretend it never existed. All I can do is sort it out and try to make the right decision for . . . for four people."

Her words could have come from his lips and been equally true—what was between Dan and Rye was also of a whole childhood's making—but the realization only added to his wretchedness. Hearing it at last put into words made him realize that his place as Laura's husband was tenuous at best, for seven hundred dollars and a deed to this house were not necessarily the deed to her heart.

Dan contemplated her across the shadowed room. Her hands were gripped together tightly, her face a mask of torn emotions. Suddenly, he could not face the truth and made for the door, jerking his jacket from the hook and shrugging it on.

"I'm going out for a while."

The door slammed abruptly, leaving an absence so profound it seemed about to swallow Laura. It took several minutes before she believed he was actually gone, for he never went out in the evenings, except perhaps to take Josh for a walk or visit his parents. But tonight was different. Tonight Dan was escaping.

He was gone for two hours. Laura was waiting up for his return. When he came in, he stopped abruptly. "You're still up!" he exclaimed, surprised, a glint of hope lifting his brows.

"I needed your help with my laces," she explained.

The hope faded. He turned, hung his jacket on the coat tree, but his hand seemed to rest on the prong and hover there for several seconds, as if he were steadying himself.

Finally he turned, still near the door. "I'm . . . I'm sorry I kept you up."

"Oh, Dan, where did you go?" Her expression was grieved.

He stared at her absently for several seconds before his voice came, quiet and hurt. "Do you care?"

Pain darkened her eyes. "Of course, I care. You've never gone out like this before. Not . . . not angry."

He tugged the hem of his waistcoat down and came halfway across the room. "But I am angry," he said, with no apparent trace of that emotion. "Should I stay here and be? Would you prefer that?"

"Oh, Dan, let's just . . ." But she didn't know how to finish. Let's just what? Let's just go to bed and forget it? Let's just pretend everything is the same? That Rye Dalton doesn't exist?

As they studied each other, they both knew the reason her words had trailed away: there *was* no pretending. Rye was there between them every hour of the night and day.

Dan sighed tiredly. "Come," he said. "It's late. I'll help you get undressed so we can both get some sleep." His shoulders drooped as he crossed to Laura and turned her by an elbow toward the linter room.

Beside the bed, she presented her back to Dan, but when he stepped up behind her, she caught the smell of brandy on his breath. But Dan was no drinking man! Guilt swept her as his fingers moved down the row of hooks at her back. When she was free of the dress, she stepped from it and waited. There followed a long, tense moment when nothing happened, and she knew his eyes were on her exposed back. Finally, he untied the stays and worked them loose, but when she bent forward to step out of the circlet of stiff whalebone, her backside bumped him and she realized he hadn't moved. She straightened and suddenly his arms circled her ribs, jerked her backward, and held her possessively. His mouth came down hard against the side of her neck while his tongue flavored her skin with brandy.

"Oh, Laura, don't leave me," he pleaded, cupping her breasts tightly, holding her firmly against his body.

Through the single layer of her pantaloons, she could feel his sexual arousal. The smell of his breath made her want to pull away, but she didn't. She covered the backs of his hands with her own and let her head tip back against his shoulder.

"Dan, I'm not leaving you. I'm here."

He ran his hand down the front of her, cradling the mound of womanhood in a tight, upward clutch that almost lifted her from the floor. "Laura, I love you . . . I've always loved you . . . you'll never know how much . . . I need you·. . . don't leave me . . ." The litany went on and on, desperate, pleading words meant to inflame her, but filling her with pity instead. He unbuttoned her waistband and slid his hand over her bare stomach while she willed her body to respond. But there was only dryness, and she flinched when he touched her intimately. This recklessness was unlike Dan, and she realized the extent of his desperation. She told herself she must reassure him, but when he turned her in his arms and kissed her, the taste of brandy revolted her.

"Touch me," he begged, and she did, only to be reminded of Rye's so different body. The thought brought an immediate backlash of guilt, so she put more into her kisses and caresses than she felt. But the thought of Rye released the first faint sensation between her legs, so she went on thinking of him, to make this easier, even as Dan shed his clothes and blew out the light, then took her down. As his body moved over hers, she thought of orange sections—sweet, bright, and juicy—slipping between Rye's lips, leaving succulent droplets on his smiling mouth. She pictured Rye's tongue taking the droplets away, though it was Dan's tongue moving in her mouth. But at last her body was receptive, and his hips moved against hers for a brief time before he plunged hard and shuddered. It was over for him while it had scarcely started for her.

With Dan's body heavy on hers, Laura pictured the loft over old man Hardesty's boathouse, remembering all those times with Rye. And she wanted to weep. Oh, Rye, Rye, if only it were you beside me . . .

But as Dan settled into sleep, Laura was steeped with shame at her own duplicity, using thoughts of one man to arouse herself for another.

Chapter 9

THE FOLLOWING DAY, Josiah said nothing when Rye went upstairs at the usual time, then came back down with fresh comb marks in his hair and his shirt tucked tightly into his waistband.

"I won't be gone long," the younger man said, setting off through the wide double doors with a confident step.

But he was gone longer than usual, having waited and watched and searched the square only to give up after thirty minutes. His booted feet clumped out a warning even before he strode angrily through the door of the cooperage, his lips narrowed tightly, a look of suppressed rage about him.

Josiah squinted behind his pipe smoke; his gaze followed Rye.

"So, she didn't show up t'day," he noted tersely.

Rye's fist came down like a battering ram on top of the tool bench. "Goddamnit, she's mine!"

"Not so's Dan's admittin'."

"She wants t' be."

"Aye, and what does it count for when the law's on Dan's side?"

"The law can free her, just as it tied her to him."

Josiah's scowl nearly hid his blue-gray eyes beneath grizzled eyebrows. "Divorce?"

Rye pierced his father with a look of determination. "Aye, it's what I'm thinkin'."

"On *Nantucket?*"

The two words needed no further embellishment. The rigid Puritanical beliefs of Nantucket's forefathers still clung; in his whole life Rye had never heard of any couple from the island divorcing.

With a sigh, he sank onto an upturned barrel, bending forward to twine his fingers into the hair at the back of his head while staring at the floor.

Josiah braced one handle of his drawknife on the floor, withdrew his pipe, and abruptly changed the subject. "Been thinkin'. Y're not much good t' me lately, swingin' tools as if y'd like t' kill somebody, breakin' perfectly good staves and forgettin' y' left the wet ones out of the water."

Rye looked up: his father never complained—Josiah was the most patient man Rye knew. Now his dry New England drawl continued.

"Be needin' t' set up our agreements with the mainlanders for our winter supply of staves."

With no source of wood on Nantucket, Josiah got his rough-rived staves from the mainland farmers, whose wood supply was limitless and whose hands would otherwise have been idle during the long winter. Each spring a full year's supply of dimensional boards was delivered in exchange for finished barrels and pails, the arrangement benefiting both farmer and cooper.

"Best be gettin' over there and talk t' them Connecticut farmers." Here Josiah pointed his pipestem at Rye. "Thought y' might be talked inta goin' and gettin' the job done."

At Josiah's words, Rye's anger began losing sway.

Josiah bent his curly gray head over his work again, and the drawknife created more spiral shavings and the smoke wreathed and dissipated overhead. As if to himself, Josiah muttered, "If it was me sittin' on that barrel, I'd be thinkin' about chattin' with them mainland lawyers about what my rights was. Wouldn't take the word of Ezra Merrill that things was all cut 'n' dried."

Still leaning his elbows on his knees, Rye studied the old

man's back. It flexed rhythmically as his burly forearms pulled, then retreated for a new bite at the cedar billet. Watching, mulling, Rye felt a softening about his heart. Silently, he unfolded, got to his feet, and crossed to stand behind his father, on whose tough, flexing shoulder Rye clasped a hand. Beneath his touch the muscles bunched and hardened as Josiah completed the stroke. Then, wordlessly, he let the knife rest and lifted his wise gaze to his son, who looked down at Josiah with eyes erased of anger. Josiah's lips pursed closed. They opened and a puff of smoke came out. Rye squeezed the shoulder and said quietly, "Aye, I'll go, old man. It's just what I need . . . thank you." Josiah nodded agreement, and Rye squeezed his shoulder once more before his hand fell away.

Laura heard that Rye had left the island, and it made it easier for her to keep her promise to Dan. But she felt as if her husband could see into the hidden recesses of her mind. More and more often she'd glance up to find him watching her with a look of consternation on his face, as if he had detected secret thoughts at work in his wife. It became an irritation to her to realize he had a right to mistrust her, for though in body she remained true to him, in her mind she again wandered the hills with Rye.

She owed Dan so much. He *had* been a good husband, and if possible, an even better father. He'd taught Josh how to fly a kite, how to walk on stilts, how to tell a gull from a tern, and how to handle the difficult quill pen. Why, already Josh was learning the alphabet, his shaky letters a constant inspiration for praise from Dan. The two spent long sessions bent over the trestle table with their heads side by side. And when the ink spilled, there was patience instead of anger; when the letters were inept, there was encouragement instead of criticism.

But most evenings when the lessons were over, Dan remained in the house only a short time before donning his coat and hat and heading toward the solace that alcohol seemed to provide. Then Laura would wander about the house restlessly, touching the countless luxuries Dan had bought for her—the zinc sink, the brass roasting kitchen before the fireplace, and at its top the clockjack for turning meat. Sometimes her fingers skimmed along the mantel as she paced the quiet room and stared at the pieces of whitewear that Dan had insisted upon her having so that she need not be constantly melting down and recasting the pewter, which was forever breaking or bending or springing holes.

Then he started bringing her presents, coming first with fragrant soap and discouraging her from the drudgery of making her own. When she protested, he made light of his gift, insisting it was inexpensive, since every candler on the island made it with the same materials and processes used in candle making. When a ship from France put in, he came home and presented her with a colorfully painted and varnished sugar box and tea caddy made of the new French toleware.

But she knew why he'd been bringing her gifts more and more often, and these constant offerings created an ever-growing sense of guilt within Laura. For even while she accepted them, she was wondering how to break away from the good life he'd provided her and her son, without bringing lasting hurt to all of them.

Rye returned from his trip to the mainland to find a check had been delivered—from Dan. House rent. Rye stubbornly refused to cash it, bellowing to Josiah that it'd be like accepting rent for Dan's use of Laura!

She, meanwhile, needed someone to talk to, someone who could help sort out the mixed emotions of a woman who pondered her duty to one man and resisted the temptation to seek out another man, whose busk was still pressed to her heart by day and whose image filled her dreams by night.

Laura discarded the possibility of going to have a talk with her mother. Her married friends, too, were out, for they were Dan's friends as well. That left Laura's sister, Jane, who lived on Madaket Harbor, a half-hour's walk to the west.

Jane's husband was a commercial fisherman who followed the seasonal schooling of fish on and about Nantucket—in March, the herring that crowded the island's channels, in April, the cod and haddock off the east end of the island. But now Laura knew John Durning's ketch would be out taking cod off Sankaty Head, so she and Jane could talk privately.

Laura took a warm hooded cloak and crossed the hills west of town paralleling the high cliffs along the island's inner curve, happy to be once again on the salty heath, though the day was overcast and threatened rain. With Josh skipping ahead, she followed Cliff Road as it bent between the strung-out sections of Long Pond. As she approached the hills on the northwestern edge of the island and looked out beyond Madaket Harbor, Tuckernuck Island was scarcely visible through the dimming drizzle that was falling. She shivered and hurried on.

Jane's house was a weathered gray saltbox to which two linters had been added as her family grew, for Jane had six children, all under nine, and on any given day at least three extras seemed to be underfoot, until it seemed children squirted from between the wallboards! Jane managed the noise and fighting with surprising calmness, taking in stride the spats she was asked to arbitrate, the constant demands for food, and the cleaning up that inevitably followed the children's treats of milk and jam tarts.

The moment Laura walked into Jane's house, she knew it was a mistake to have chosen a rainy day for a confidential talk with her sister. The weather had chased all six of her nieces and nephews inside, and it seemed as if each had brought along a battalion of friends. Josh was in his glory, for he was immediately included in their game of hide-the-thimble, which sent the tribe scrambling to every corner of the keeping room, sometimes even across Laura's and Jane's laps, as the children probed the two women's pockets, their ears, their high-topped shoes, and even their chignons in search of the hidden thimble.

Jane laughed and abetted their scramblings by suggesting likely hiding places, while Laura grew more and more impatient. But just when it seemed that no chance would come to broach the subject, Jane herself introduced it.

"The whole island's talking about you and Rye . . . and Dan, of course."

"They are?" Laura looked up in surprise.

"They say you've been meeting Rye secretly."

"Oh, it's not true, Jane!"

"But you have seen him, haven't you?"

"Yes, of course I've *seen* him."

Jane studied her sister for a moment, then confided, "So have we. He looks wonderful, doesn't he?"

Laura felt herself color, and she knew Jane watched her closely as she went on.

"He stopped by here, brought some little things he'd carved for the children, though he didn't know we'd had the last three. Surprised him plenty to see us with enough to man a whaleboat." Jane chuckled, then her expression sobered as she leveled her hazel eyes on Laura. "He's been seen out walking the moors a lot, and they say he haunts the shore with that dog at his heels, looking like a lost dog himself."

The picture of a forlorn Rye walking the islands with Ship at his heels at last made Laura's face crumple. "Oh, Jane, what am I to do?" She covered her eyes, which were suddenly streaming tears.

A child came squealing past, but Jane ignored him for once and laid a sympathetic hand on her sister's hair. "What do you want to do?"

"I want to keep everyone from getting hurt," Laura sobbed miserably.

"I don't think that's possible, little one."

At the endearment, Laura grasped her sister's hand and held it against her cheek for a moment before lowering it to the tabletop, where she held it between them. "I have made them both miserable then, if what you say is true. Rye, wandering the hills with the dog, waiting for me to tell him yes, and Dan leaving the house every night to drink away his fear that I'll tell him no. And between them, Josh, who doesn't have any idea Rye is his father. I wish I knew what to do."

"You have to do what your heart tells you to do."

"Oh but, Jane, y . . . you haven't seen the look on Dan's face when he comes home at the end of the day bringing me another gift, hoping . . . oh, it's just awful." Again Laura dissolved into a pool of tears. "He's been so good to me . . . and to Josh."

"But which of them do you love, Laura?"

The red-rimmed eyes lifted. The trembling lips parted. Then she swallowed and looked down again. "I'm afraid to answer that."

Jane refilled Laura's teacup. "Because you love them both?"

"Yes."

Jane moved her hand across the tabletop and gently rubbed the back of Laura's. "I can't tell you what to do. All I can say is this: I was married already when . . . well, when you and Rye turned from children into adolescents. I saw you both growing up before my eyes. I watched what happened between the two of you, and the way Dan followed you with the same look he's probably got in his eyes now when he brings you gifts in an effort to win your love. Laura dear . . ." With a single finger Jane lifted Laura's trembling chin and looked into her troubled brown eyes. "I know how it was with Rye and you long before you married. I knew because John and I were so happily in love at the time that it was easy for me to recognize it in someone else. The two of you couldn't keep your eyes off each other—nor, I suspect, your hands either, when you were by yourselves. Would I be out of line to ask if your misery now's got something to do with that?"

"Jane, we haven't done anything since he's been back. He . . . we . . ." But Laura stumbled into silence.

"Ah, I see how it is. You want to."

"Dear God, Jane, I've fought it."

"Yes." Jane's pause was eloquent. "So Rye walks the hills with his dog, and you come to my kitchen to cry."

"But I was married to Rye for less than one year and to Dan for four. I *owe* Dan something!"

"And yourself—what do you owe yourself? The truth, at least? That if the false rumor of Rye Dalton's death had never reached Nantucket, you would no more have married Dan Morgan than you would've at the age of nineteen, when you chose Rye over him."

"But what about Josh?"

"What about him?"

"He loves Dan so much."

"He's young, resilient. He'd bounce back if he learned the truth."

"Oh, Jane, if only I could be as . . . as sure as you."

"You're sure. You're just scared, that's all."

"I'm legally married to Dan. It would require a divorce."

"An ugly word. Enough to scare anyone raised in these Puritan parts, and enough to make the most benevolent of do-gooders scorn you on the street. Is that what you're thinking?"

Laura shook her head tiredly and leaned her forehead on the heel of a hand. "I don't know what to think anymore. I had no idea everybody on the island has been watching Rye and me so closely."

Jane pondered for a long, silent moment, then squared herself in her chair, drummed on the tabletop with a palm in much the manner of a judge lowering a gavel, and mused, "They say Rye has become a familiar sight wandering the moors. If you were to run into him out there, who's to say it was no accident? And who'd be there to watch?"

"Why, Jane—"

But before Laura could say more the door opened and John Durning swept in, robust and big-voiced, booming a hello to his children and plopping a forthright kiss on his wife even before he slipped out of his yellow oilskins. With a smile and cheery hello for Laura, he stood behind Jane's chair and put his wide hands on the sides of her neck, kneading it with his thumbs while teasing, "And what's waiting at home to warm a man's body in weather like this?"

Jane craned around to grin up at him. "There's tea, among other things."

The affection between the two of them was so obvious, and the way they enjoyed each other and teased made Laura remember how it used to be with Rye when he'd come sweeping into the house. It had been like this—the smile, the bold caress, the words with second meanings. The simple events of every day had been enhanced to something sublime simply because they were shared.

If you were to run into him out there someplace, who's to say it was no accident?

And though it was undeniably tempting, Laura astutely avoided the moors after that day.

The sight of the listless, wandering Rye Dalton and his dog had indeed become familiar to the islanders. The pair could be seen at day's beginning and day's end, trekking along the myriad paths of the inner island or along any of its white, sandy shores, the man in the lead, the dog tramping faithfully at his heels.

In the dew-spattered dawns, their silhouettes were often etched against the colorful eastern sky as they sat atop Folger Hill or Altar Rock, the highest points of the island, with the panoramic view of the white-rimmed spit of land and the restless Atlantic beyond. Or if the dawn was murky, it was not uncommon for the old fishermen who lived in the tiny weatherbeaten cottages along 'Sconset's shores to see the pair emerge from the shrouds of mist at the ocean's edge, ambling listlessly, heads down, the man's hands buried deep in his trouser front, the dog giving the impression that were it possible, she'd have imitated her master's posture.

At other times the inseparable pair ran along the hard-packed shingle, Rye's heels digging deep into the flat-washed sand, his footprints disappearing as waves lapped behind him while Ship, with her tongue trailing from the side of her mouth, galloped just within the surf, keeping up with the man who seemed to run with a vengeance, his breath beating ragged while he pushed his body to its physical limits. Exhausted, they'd fall, panting, onto the sand flats, Rye lying supine, studying the deep sky, the dog searching the undulating horizons as if for sails.

Evenings, they could sometimes be seen standing on the high bluffs overlooking deserted Codfish Park, where in spring and fall, when the cod ran, fishermen hauled up their dories and lay their catch out to dry on the wooden "flakes" below.

Mornings, just after high tide had strewn the Atlantic's offerings on the island's southern shores, Rye and Ship often encountered kelp seekers, rummaging through the tide wrack for oarweed and tangle, though Rye would scarcely be aware that others occupied the same stretch of beach he haunted.

Other times, he and Ship picked their way around the boulders on Saul's Hill, scattering flocks of blackbirds which in days of old had been such a nuisance that each male islander was issued a quota he must kill before he was allowed to marry. "Ah, Ship," the man sighed, reaching blindly for the dog's head. "If only I could simply kill five hundred blackbirds and be free t' marry her.''

A day came when not a breath of wind stirred, while the two stared at a nearly calm sea. Ship's ears suddenly perked up, and the hair along her spine bristled. She turned, alert, on guard, checking behind her for the source of the sudden, violent hissing sound that came out of nowhere. But there was naught to be seen, only an eerie sibilance as of something letting off a giant eruption of steam. The rare, unexplained sound emitted by the ocean was called a rut by the old-timers. Yet none knew its origin, only that it was sure to be followed by shrewish winds that would work their way east and bring rain.

And true to its prediction, before the day was out, the sky had lowered to a menacing greenish-gray. It found Rye and Ship watching the wild, broken waters of Miacomet Rip, where hidden currents tugged and sucked at the island's feet while the winds tore at the man's hair and whipped it about his head like spindrift.

There followed three days of punishing rain that lashed the island from the south and kept Rye and Ship indoors. On the fourth morning, though, the rain had disappeared, leaving in its wake a fogbank so dense it obscured even the scalloped curves of Coatue Peninsula's shores.

The three days' forced confinement had left Rye jumpy and irritable. Therefore, when in late morning of the fourth day the sun broke through and blue sky spread slowly from west to east, Josiah suggested Rye go up to Mill Hill and negotiate the exchange of barrels for flour that was periodically made between the cooper and the miller, Asa Pond.

Shortly after noon, Rye set out on the errand with Ship in tow, grateful to be free of the cooperage once again. The island looked crisp and fresh-washed after the rain. The cobblestones along Main Street shone brightly in the high sun, and along the narrower lanes gay splashes of red and coral geraniums spilled from windowboxes. Rye thought of the geraniums beside Laura's door and wondered if they bloomed, too, but with an effort he put her from his mind.

With Ship at his heels he walked past Sunset Hill, where the home of Jethro Coffin, one of the island's first settlers, had been standing for almost 150 years now. He passed along Nantucket Cliffs, beyond which the pale green waters marked the bar and the darker blue told of deeper waters in the sound beyond. Above, a pair of white mackerel gulls pursued a single black one, the ragged shred of their voices tossed aloft in the August afternoon.

He moved on toward the four "post" windmills of Dutch design that rode the breasts of four hills to the south and west of town. Asa Pond's mill had been built in 1746 of timbers taken from shipwrecks, but as it came into view over the hill, it appeared ageless, its four lattice-veined arms backed by new linen sails, now facing southwest, from which a gentle breeze blew. Like its sister mills, it was at once graceful and ungainly; graceful for its gently turning arms whose sails, like those of a windjammer, could be reefed in high winds; ungainly for its long tail pole extending from the rear, like the rump of an awkward beast squatting on the ground. This thick wooden spar projected from the structure and rested on a wheel by which the entire building could be turned to face windward. The wheel had worn a deep circular rut into the earth, and Rye now leaped over it, crossed the circle of grass, and climbed the ladder to the grinding floor high overhead.

Inside, the mill was adrift in bran- and corn-dust, ever present in the air as grain was poured down the hopper to the grinding wheel and meal was sifted by apprentices into varying grades of fineness. The elevated floorboards vibrated constantly from the thumping of wooden gears as giant pins meshed with oak pinions on the windlass drive. To Rye's nose the grain scent was pleasant, but he peered across the dust motes to find Asa with a handkerchief tied over his nose and mouth while he worked. The miller raised a hand in greeting and pointed to the doorway; the noise of the grating millstones and the thud of gears precluded speech. Following Rye back outside, Asa pulled the hanky from his face while they stood at the base of the building, conducting their business in the pleasant summer sun while the vanes creaked a quiet accompaniment.

Josh, too, had been restless and bored during the three days of inclement weather. As soon as the sky began clearing, he begged Laura to take him out bayberrying, one of his favorite things to do. When she patiently explained that the bayberries weren't quite ripe yet, Josh pleaded for another walk to Aunt Jane's. When that suggestion failed, he thought of his other favorite diversion, a trip to the mill, where he was sometimes allowed to ride aboard the spar while the oxen turned the building into the wind. But to this Laura answered almost gruffly, "No, I don't have time. The garden needs weeding, and right after the rain is the best time."

"But, Mama, Mr. Pond might—"

"Joshua!" She rarely called him Joshua.

Josh's mouth turned down and he hung around the garden while she worked, obviously bored, asking questions about June bugs and cabbage moths and baby cucumbers. He squatted between the rows, pointing an inquisitive finger at each weed that Laura touched, asking, "What's that one?" and "How can you tell it ain't a bedjtable?"

"I can just tell, that's all. I've been doing it a long time."

He watched her pull up a few more. "I could do that."

She scarcely looked up. "Why don't you just go play, Josh?"

"Papa would let me."

"Well, I'm not Papa, and I have a lot to do!" Laura went on weeding while Josh hung there beside her, his cheek now resting on a knee as he hummed tunelessly, poking in the dirt with one finger.

Laura moved farther down the row, and Josh continued to study her. A few moments later he came to squat beside her and proudly presented an uprooted plant. "Here, Mama, I can help . . . see?"

"Ohhh, Josh," she moaned, "you've pulled up a baby turnip."

"Oh." He stared at it disconsolately, then flashed a bright smile. "I'll put it back in!"

Impatiently, she retorted, "No, it won't work, Josh! Once it's pulled out, it'll wilt and die."

"It will?" Josh asked, mystified, and disappointed because he'd only intended to help.

"Yes, it will," she answered disgustedly before returning to her weeding.

Josh stood beside her a moment longer, studying the turnip

green, which was already growing limp. "What's die?" he asked innocently.

Unbidden came the thought: die is what we thought your father did and why I married somebody else. Upset with herself, impatient with him, she snapped, "Josh, just throw it away and go find something else to do! I'll never get done here if you keep pestering me with your everlasting questions!"

Josh's little mouth trembled and he pulled at his cheek with a dirty finger. Immediately, Laura hated herself for being so short with him when he'd only meant to help. This had happened more and more lately, and each time it did, she vowed not to let it happen again. She wanted to be like Jane, whose patience with her mob of children was close to saintly. But Jane was incredibly happy, and happiness made a difference! When you were happy you could handle things more easily. But Laura's growing tension sought a vent at some very unexpected times, and unfortunately her son often got the brunt of it. To make matters worse now, Laura realized Josh was right —Dan would have patiently shown him how to tell the weeds from the vegetables, regardless of how much efficiency he forfeited.

Josh was trying valiantly not to cry, but tears winked on his golden lashes as he studied the sad little turnip plant, wondering why his mama was so upset.

Laura sighed and sank back on her heels. "Josh darling, come here."

He dug his chin deeper into his chest as a tear went rolling, followed by another.

"Josh, Mama is sorry. You were just trying to help, weren't you, darling?"

He nodded his head forlornly, still looking at the earth.

"Come here before Mama cries, too, Josh." He lifted his teary eyes to her, dropped the turnip, and rushed into Laura's arms, hugging her fiercely, his sunny head buried in her neck. She knelt in the garden row holding Rye's son tightly against her apron front, just short of crying herself.

I am changing, she thought, in spite of my fight to preserve equanimity in my marriage. I'm becoming short-tempered with Josh and unhappy with Dan, and I'm not treating either one of them fairly. Oh, Josh, Josh, I'm sorry. If only you were old enough to understand how much I love your father but that I honestly love Dan, too. She closed her eyes, her cheek against her son's hair, his cheek pressed against her breast, where the busk was hidden even now. She rocked him gently, swallowing tears as she pushed him back to look down into his lovable face.

"You know, I really don't feel like weeding the garden at all. Suppose we take that walk up to the mill. I do need to order some flour from Asa."

"Really, Mama?" Josh brightened, tears forgotten just that quickly.

"Really." She tweaked his nose. "But you'll have to wash your hands and face first and comb your hair."

But he was already four rows away, jumping turnips, beans, peas, and carrots on his way to soap and water. "I bet I can beat you!" he hollered as he ran.

"I bet you can't!" And Laura, too, was up, skirts lifted, racing him through the backyard.

Chapter 10

IT WAS A glorious day, the sky as blue as a jay's wing, a light breeze chasing through the grass. An afternoon hush lay on both land and sea, for few boats moved in the harbor below as Laura and Josh left the scallop-shell path and threaded their way toward the open moor and the gently rising hills beyond. Meadowlarks came to watch the mother and child passing, accompanying them with the sweetest music in all of summer. Field flowers seemed to be drying their cheeks as their faces arched toward the warm sun. Katydids droned lazily while an occasional gull wheeled overhead.

Josh stopped to examine an ant hill and Laura joined him, taking time to bask in the joy of watching him instead of the ants. His mouth formed an excited *O* and he exclaimed, "Look at that one! Look at the big rock he's carrying!" Laura laughed, and looked, and shrank for the moment into the miniature world of insects, where a grain of sand became a boulder.

In time they moved on up the sandy path. All around, the treeless hills were trimmed with creamy heads of Queen Anne's lace nodding in the breeze.

"Just a minute!" Laura called, and left the path to pick several stems of lace, adding a few brown-eyed Susans when they passed a patch, and later tucking wild yarrow into the bouquet.

"I see it! I see it!" Josh cried as the latticed vanes appeared at the crest of the hill. "Do you think Mr. Pond will let me ride the spar?"

"We'll have to see if the oxen are hooked to it today."

Laura was hatless and half-blinded as she turned her face toward the two-o'clock sun that formed an aureole behind the windmill. The vanes rotated slowly. And then a dark core seemed to separate itself from the sun and become distinct from it, and she shaded her eyes with a forearm to watch it take the shape of a man coming downhill in their direction.

He stopped when he saw them. Though she could not make out his face, she saw long, slender legs in calf-high boots and white sleeves billowing in the breeze. A moment later another dark shape moved around his ankles and stopped beside him. A dog . . . a big yellow Lab.

"Rye," she whispered, not realizing she had, the name coming to her lips as if in answer to a long-repeated prayer.

For a moment both man and woman paused, he with the grass feathering about his knees on the hill above her, she with skirts clutched in one hand and the shadow of a nosegay of wildflowers painting fernlike images across her features. The child scampered up the hill and the dog scampered down, but neither Rye nor Laura noticed. The breeze caught her pink calico skirt and held it abaft while two hearts soared and plunged.

Then Rye leaned forward and came down the hill at a dog-trot, half jumping, elbows lifting slightly as he took the decline with an eagerness that sent her hurrying upward, skirt caught up in both hands now. They met with Josh and Ship between them, exuberant child and overjoyed dog completely taken with each other, just as man and woman were. Josh fell to his knees while Ship wagged not only her tail but her whole body.

"Gosh, is he yours, Rye?" Josh asked, oblivious of all but the dog and the pink tongue he tried gaily to avoid.

"*She*," Rye corrected, his eyes riveted on Laura.

"She," Josh repeated. "Is she yours?"

"Aye, she's mine." the blue eyes took in nothing but the face of the woman before him.

"Boy, I'll bet you really love her, don't you?"

"Aye, son, I love her," came the husky reply.

"You had her a long time?"

"Since I was a boy."

"How old is she?"

"Old enough t' know by now who she belongs to."

"Gee, I wish she was mine."

But to that came only the soft reply, "Aye."

There followed a long, trembling pause, filled only with the sigh of the wind in a woman's skirts and the shush-shush of whispering grass. Laura felt as if the field of wildflowers had just blossomed within her breast. Her lips were parted, and her heartbeat leaped wildly within her bodice of pink calico. The hills of Nantucket embraced them, and for that moment all else was wiped away.

And suddenly she had to touch him . . . just touch him.

She extended her hand to be shaken.

"Hello, Mr. Dalton. I didn't think I'd . . . we'd run into you out here."

His palm enfolded hers, held it like a treasure while he gazed into her eyes above the golden head of their son, frolicking at their feet.

"Hello, Laura. I'm glad y' did."

His palm was callused, hard, and familiar. "We're on our way up to the mill to order flour and bran."

He slipped his index and middle fingers between her cuff and the delicate skin of her inner wrist, then covered the back of the hand with his other. Her pulse raced wildly beneath his fingertips.

"And I was at the mill takin' an order for barrels."

"Well," she said, laughing nervously, "it seems everyone is out enjoying the sunny weather."

"Aye, everyone." Just then Josh scrambled to his feet, and only then did it strike them how long, how caressingly, they'd been holding hands. Immediately, Rye released hers. But Josh and Ship only leaped and cavorted in circles about them, leaving them to gaze at each other.

"Do you . . . do you come up this way often?" she questioned.

"Aye, Ship and I, we do a lot o' walkin'."

"So I've heard."

"And you?"

"Me?"

"Do y' come up this way often?"

"No, sometimes on the way to Jane's house is all."

"And when you order flour." He smiled into her eyes, and she smiled back. "And pick wildflowers."

She nodded and dropped her gaze to the cluster in her nervous hands.

"I stopped by Jane's myself one day," Rye said.

"Yes, she told me. It was nice of you to bring gifts for the children. Thank you."

There they stood, feeling as if they were smothering, talking of inconsequential things when there were a thousand things they wanted to tell each other, ask each other. Most overwhelming of all was the compulsion to touch. Laura let her gaze meander over his hair, his features. She wanted to reach up a fingertip and trace the new jutting line of the side-whiskers that followed his hard jaw. She wanted to thread her fingers through his thick rye-colored hair and say what was on her mind: *It's gotten darker since you've been back, but I like it better this way, the way I remember it.* She wanted to kiss each of the seven new pockmarks on his face and say, *Tell me about the voyage. Tell me everything.*

Josh interrupted their visual reverie to ask, "What's her name?"

Rye pulled his eyes away from Laura and went down on one knee—safer that way; in another moment he would have reached for Laura again, but this time it would have been for more than a handshake.

"Ship."

"That's a funny name for a dog, ain't it? You both got funny names."

Rye's rich laughter spilled across the flower-strewn field. "Aye, we both got funny names. Hers is really Shipwreck, 'cause that's where she came from. Found her swimmin' ashore when a bark piled up on the shoals."

The dog was taking swipes at Josh's face with her tongue, and he got her around the neck, giggling in delight. Then over they went, Josh on the bottom, eyes closed tightly while he giggled and the dog nuzzled and licked. Laura and Rye, too, joined in laughing as Josh curled up like an armadillo and the big Lab worried him.

Rye bent forward, resting an elbow on his knee, and smiled up at Laura. "If y' don't mind, Josh could stay here and play with Ship while you go on up and talk to Asa. We'll be waitin' when y' come back down."

She could no more have refused him than alter the changing of tides. Rye himself would have been invitation enough, kneeling in the strong sunlight, handsome and honed, with his shoulders slanted forward, sleeves flowing loosely as he held the back of one wrist with the opposite hand. His smiling eyes were raised to Laura, awaiting her answer.

Josh came out of his crouch to appeal, "Yeah, please, Mama! Just while you go up to the mill."

Laura teased, "What about riding the spar?"

"The oxes ain't hitched up anyway, so I wanna stay down here and play with Ship." The two rolled over in the long grass.

"All right. I'll be right back."

Her eyes met and held Rye's before he silently nodded. Then, seemingly of its own accord, her hand did a most surprising thing. It reached out to rest on the back of his neck—half on his hair, half inside his collar—while she passed behind him.

Rye's head snapped around and his elbow slipped from his knee, blue eyes smoldering in surprise. But she had turned and was already making her way up the hill. He watched her retreating form, the way her pink skirt bunched at the hip as she took long, high steps in her climb. When she disappeared over the crest of the hill, he returned his attention to Josh and Ship. They cavorted together until Ship tired and flopped down to pant.

Soon Josh flopped down, too, beside Rye and struck up a conversation. "How come you know my Aunt Jane?"

"I've lived on the island all my life. I knew Jane when I was a boy not much older than you."

"And Mama, too?"

"Aye, and your mama, too. We went t' school together."

"I get t' go to school, but not till next year."

"You do?"

"Uh-huh. Papa already bought me my hornbook, and he says he's gonna give his share of the firewood so I won't have to sit far away from the fire."

Rye laughed, but he knew it was true that those students whose parents donated firewood got the choicest seats, close to the fireplace. "Do y' think y'll like school?"

"It'll be easy. Papa's already taught me most of my letters."

Rye plucked a blade of grass and put it in the corner of his mouth. "Sounds like you get along real well with your papa."

"Oh, Papa's better'n just about anybody I know . . . 'cept Mama, o' course."

"O' course." Rye's gaze wandered up the hill momentarily, then back to his son. "Well, y're a lucky boy."

"That's what Jimmy says. Jimmy—" But Josh stopped, screwed up his face quizzically. "You know Jimmy?"

Rye shook his head, enchanted by the elfin child. He thought it best not to admit Jimmy Ryerson was a second cousin.

"Oh. Well, Jimmy, he's my best friend. I'll show him to you someday," Josh said matter-of-factly, "if you'll bring Ship along so Jimmy can see 'er, too."

"It's a deal." Rye stretched out on the grass while Josh continued.

"Well anyways, Jimmy, he says I'm lucky cause Papa made me stilts and he says I'm the onlyest one he knows that's got 'em. I let him use 'em sometimes, but Jimmy, he can't stand up too good on 'em—not like me, 'cause Papa, he taught me to get the sticks behind my—" Josh stretched an elbow over his head, rubbed his armpit, and strove to remember. "What do you call these things again?"

Rye controlled the urge to laugh, answering most seriously, "Armpits."

"Yeah . . . armpits. Papa, he says to put the sticks behind 'em and stick your butt out, but Jimmy, he falls over, cuz he holds the sticks in front of him, like this, all the time." Josh leaped to his feet to demonstrate. Then he dropped to his knees like quicksilver.

Delight filled Rye Dalton. The child was as lovable as his mother, quick-witted and spontaneous.

"Your papa sounds like a smart man."

"Oh, he's smarter 'n anybody else! He works at the counting-house."

"Aye, I've seen him there." Rye plucked a new blade of grass. "Your papa and I went t' school together, too."

"You did?"

Josh's eyes were so like Laura's as they expressed surprise. "Aye."

Josh's expression became thoughtful before he asked, "Then how come you say aye and Papa says yes?"

" 'Cause I've been on a whaleship and heard the sailors sayin' it so much I don't remember startin' t' say it m'self."

"You talk funny, though." Josh giggled.

"Y' mean short-like? That's b'cause on a ship y' don't always have time t' give speeches. Y' got t' get things said fast or y're in trouble."

"Oh." And a moment later, "You like it on that whaleship? Was it fun?"

Rye's glance again swept the crest of the hill, then turned back to his son, finding an expression on the child's face that he sometimes encountered in his own mirror when he was thoughtful. " 'Twas lonely."

"Din't you take Ship along?"

Rye shook his head.

"Where'd she go?"

Rye reached for the Lab's big head and rested his hand on it. The dog opened lazy eyes and closed them again. It was difficult for the father to keep from giving the answer that was on his mind: *Ship lived with your mother at first, and maybe even with you when you were a baby. Maybe that's why you two like each other so much now. She remembers you.*

Instead, he said, "She went t' live with my father at the cooperage."

"Then I guess you *was* lonely," Josh sympathized.

"Well, I'm back," Rye said brightly, flashing the boy a smile.

Josh smiled, too, and piped, "You're nice. I like you."

Heady emotions sprang up within Rye at the boy's words, so impetuous, so honest. He wished he could be equally free, that he could hug this child and have him know the truth. Josh was a lovable sprite, untarnished, unspoiled. Laura and . . . and Dan had done a good job with him.

Laura stopped at the top of the hill as Josh and Rye came into view below. They were distant enough that Josh's childish laughter carried only faintly on the breeze, then Rye's could be heard more distinctly for a moment. They were stretched out on the grass alongside the dog. Rye lay on his side, ankles crossed, his jaw propped on a palm, chewing a blade of grass. Beside him, his son was sprawled with his head pillowed on the sleeping Lab, who'd collapsed beside her master with chin on paws, taking a breather. It was a scene of great repletion such as Laura had dreamed of countless times. The son she loved, beside his father, whom she also loved, and it took only herself to complete the family circle.

Again Jane's question came back to Laura. *Who's to know it wouldn't be an accident if you ran into him on the moors?*

She studied the man stretched out below her in a field of Queen Anne's lace. Who's to know? Who's to know? With the wind on her face, sun on her hair, and a heart dancing triple-time, she headed down the hill.

Laura knew the exact moment Rye saw her coming, though he lay as before, relaxed, only his blue eyes moving as they followed her progress. When she came within earshot, he shifted the blade of grass to the corner of his mouth to say, "Here comes your mother." Then, slowly, he uncrossed his ankles and sat up, rolling onto one buttock, lifting a knee, and draping a forearm over it.

"Do we hafta go yet? Do was hafta?" Josh pleaded, charging up the path to meet Laura, throwing himself into an enormous hug that pulled her skirts against her thighs.

She smiled down at him, ruffled his hair, but her eyes passed to Rye as she answered softly, "No, not yet."

The boy let go, and Laura moved to stand near Rye's outstretched foot. The hem of her skirt brushed his pant leg as his gaze drifted down the line of her shoulder, breast, and midriff, then rose once more to her brown eyes.

"Would y' like t' go for a walk around Hummock Pond?" he asked.

Instead of answering directly, Laura asked Josh, "Would

you like to go for a walk around Hummock Pond?''

He spun toward Rye. "Is Ship coming, too?"

"Aye." The grass bobbed in the corner of Rye's mouth.

"Then, aye . . . me too!" the boy answered his mother.

She watched Josh and Ship scamper off ahead while Rye remained where he was, his eyes following the boy until Josh was safely out of hearing. Then he looked up at Laura and his gaze drew hers as the shore draws the surf. For a moment neither spoke, then Rye spit out the blade of grass. "I asked if *you'd* like to go for a walk around Hummock Pond," he said.

"More than anything else in the world," she answered simply.

He raised his palm. Her glance shifted from it to the child trudging up the hill, then back to the calluses. And without further hesitation she laid her hand in Rye's, and his strong fingers closed about hers as she tugged him to his feet.

Hummock Pond was one of a chain stretching north to south across the western center of the island. It was shaped like a lazy *J* whose lower curve extended to Nantucket's southern shore, where the pond's fresh water almost touched the briny Atlantic. As children, Rye and Laura had fished it for white and yellow perch, and he'd taught her how to bait her hook with angleworms. Years ago they'd picnicked in Ram Pasture and walked as they walked now, from North Head toward the ocean, which could be heard in the distance but not seen.

"I've dreamed about doing this with you and Josh," Rye said, just behind her shoulder.

"So have I. Only in my dreams you taught Josh to fish like you taught me."

"Y' mean he doesn't know how yet?"

"Not yet."

"Then y' haven't raised him proper." But his voice held a smile.

"He does all right with kites and stilts."

"Aye, he told me all about his stilts." His tone grew serious. "You and Dan've done a good job of it. He's a delightful child, Josh is."

They moved through a patch of white violets, the sun on their cheeks, conscious solely of how close they were, of how much closer they wanted to be. So much to say, so much to feel, so little time.

"I want Josh to know you, Rye, and to know you're his father."

"I, too. But I begin t' see the problem we'll have tellin' him. He loves the one he's got as much as I love my own."

The earth had grown tussocks here. Rye reached for her elbow to steady her. Red-winged blackbirds bobbed on thready reeds of cattail and sedge along the pond's marshy shore, scolding, holding tight while Rye, too, held tight to Laura's elbow as she leaped along to more even ground.

"But I do want us t' be a family," he wished aloud.

"So do I."

They held the thought and moved on slowly through the gift of afternoon, their time together at once luxuriant yet metered by the walk's length. They circled the pond's irregular shoreline, coming upon places where thick broom crowberry—mattress grass—invited them with its resilient cushion. But they could only walk, contenting themselves for the moment with an occasional touch of fingers or a meeting of eyes while the boy and the dog explored ahead.

The thrum of the ocean grew louder, its breakers now white feathers in the distance. Soon its boom surrounded them and they stood on the outwash before an ebbing tide that had scattered jellyfish, which the boy and dog found.

"Don't touch!" Rye called. "They sting!"

The dog knew and kept her distance. The boy waved back before moving on to the next find. Rye hid half his hands within his waistband while taking up that wide-legged stance he'd acquired on a listing deck. His expression was loving as he followed Josh. "There's so much I've missed. Just callin' out a small warnin' t' him that way becomes a joy t' me."

Their eyes met, a mingling of the sweet and the bitter in the exchange.

"When I heard you'd gone to the mainland, I thought you meant not to come back."

"I went t' contract for rough staves." He turned his eyes back to the ocean. "But while I was there, I spoke to a lawyer about this . . . this situation we're caught in. I'd hoped he'd tell me different, but it seems y' truly are Dan's wife."

Laura watched the rim of the world undulate far out on the horizon. "I've thought of divorcing him," she said softly, surprising even herself, for she hadn't meant to admit it.

She sensed Rye turn to her in surprise. "It's not often done."

"No, but it's not often a dead sailor returns from the bowels of the sea. They'd have to understand." She turned to search his face pleadingly. "How could I have known?" she asked with a plaintive note in each word.

"Y' couldn't."

They were on open sand with nothing but surf, a boy, and a dog visible for the white stretch of a mile. But resolutely, Rye refrained from taking her in his arms.

"Rye, does it bother you, what we'll be doing to Dan?"

"I try not t' think about him."

"He's taken to drinking almost every night."

"Aye, I've heard." His head moved sharply toward Miacomet Rip, and his face looked drawn.

"I feel as if I've forced him to start that," she said.

He turned back to her with a new intensity. "It's not our fault anymore than it's his. It's . . . providence."

"Providence," she repeated sadly.

He felt her slipping away and scowled down at her. "Laura, I can't . . . ." he began, then his hand came up and worked across his unsmiling lips before he asked abruptly, "Will I have t' wait until then—until a divorce is granted?"

"No."

His eyes snapped to hers, but she was looking out at the horizon. "How long, then?"

"Until tomorrow," she answered quietly, still searching the sea.

His fingers closed on her elbow, and he gently turned her toward him. "I want to kiss you."

"I want to be kissed," she confessed. Not even when contemplating her first time with him had she known sexual impatience such as this. "But not here . . . not now."

His breath hissed out and he released her elbow. They turned and watched a sandpiper trotting the waves, eating sea fleas, and he understood her great trepidation at the decision she was making.

"I tried very hard to do the right thing. I kept away from you," she was saying. "But today, when I saw you coming down that hill . . ." She looked down at her feet. "I . . . I don't know anymore what's right and what's wrong."

"I know. It's the same with me. I keep walkin' in all my spare time, but I can't walk y' out of my system. Y're there in all the old spots we used t' haunt."

"I've thought of a way," she told the sandpiper.

"A way?" He looked at her askance.

"Josh has been begging to spend a day at Jane's."

"Will she suspect?"

"Yes, I think so. No, I know so."

"But—"

"She already knows how I feel. I've never been able to hide much from her. She's told me she knew about you and me and what we did together even before we were married. She'll help us now."

"What about . . . him?"

"I'll tell him tonight."

"Aye, and he'll come into the cooperage tomorrow morning and I'll have t' kill him t' keep from gettin' killed myself."

A smile touched her lips. "No, I won't tell him *that*. I mean I'll tell him I want to divorce."

Rye turned serious again. "Do y' want me there when y' tell him?"

She looked up into his face, his hair lifting like seaoats in the breeze. "I want you . . . everywhere I am. But, no. I'll have to do that part on my own."

He checked the beach in both directions. It was empty but for them. Josh was teasing the edges of waves as they crept up and back. Impulsively, Rye dipped his head and gave Laura a quick kiss.

"I'm sorry, I couldn't help it. I thought I'd been through hell on that whaleship, but I've never been through such hell in my life as the last ten weeks. Woman, when I get y' back, I'm never letting y' out o' my sight again."

"Rye, let's look for a place."

They smiled into each other's eyes, scarcely able to resist this craving.

"It should be easy. We know 'em all, don't we?"

A shiver of anticipation skimmed her arms. "Aye," she replied, low and sensuously. "Aye, we know them all, Rye Dalton."

He gave a sharp whistle between his teeth. The boy and dog perked up. "Come on! Let's head on!" he called.

They found a spot in the lee of Hummock Pond, where its south end looped around, almost closing in on itself. Here, within a sheltered woodlet of pine and oak, they found a secret clearing where bramble and briar seemed to have walled out the rest of the world. Upon these natural trellises wild grapes clung, creating an arbor of fluttering green tiers. Hip-high grass carpeted the glade while tiny wildflowers peeked through shyly. In spots the grass was flattened where deer had made their beds. Squirrels chased and chattered in the oaks. The wind was absent while the sun beat down on them, and on Ship and Josh, playing across the meadow.

"Here?" Rye asked, looking down at Laura.

"Here," she confirmed.

And their hearts raced, and they prayed for sun.

Chapter 11

THEIR PRAYERS WERE ANSWERED, for the following day was as faultless and clear as a perfect diamond. Laura delivered Josh to Jane's house and arrived at the clearing first. Parting the grapevines, she ducked inside to stand motionless for a moment, listening. The afternoon was so still, she thought she could hear hammering from the shipyards four miles away. But maybe it was only the hammering of her own heart as she surveyed the woodsy oval before her—protected, private, perfect.

It smelled of grass and pine and time alone as Laura lifted her skirts to her ankles, then her face to the sun, eyelids closing, feeling only warmth and a sense of rightness upon her skin. She opened her eyes and turned in a slow circle, but all around were only shades of green enclosing her in a summer world of her own. She whirled faster, faster, arms flung wide in gay abandon, skirts twisting about her legs like a pinwheel.

He's coming! He's coming!

The thought of him tightened her chest and sent currents of anticipation to her limbs.

A movement flashed at the corner of her eye and she stopped twirling, the fingers of one hand moving to the underside of one breast as if to keep her heart confined within her body.

At the edge of the clearing Rye poised, the dog, as usual,

coming to a halt beside the knees of her master. Blue eyes took in a vision in airy white dimity turning round and round while the shadow of a wide-brimmed straw hat flitted across her uplifted face. A mint-green ribbon fluttered from its crown, trailing over her shoulder and drifting to rest on the bare skin above the square-cut neckline of her bodice.

Their eyes met. Their senses thrummed while Laura remained totally unabashed at being caught in such a display of abandon, for she loved Rye too well to hide her impulses from him today.

He was dressed in tight tan breeches and a white muslin shirt that stood out strikingly against the green grape leaves behind him. One thumb was hooked in his waistband, the other in a drawstring bag slung over his shoulder.

He surveyed the waiting woman, neither smiling nor moving, but his heart drummed wildly. Laura, you came! You came!

Around her slim waist was tied a green satin ribbon to match that about her hat brim. Wide, white skirts, like a puffy cloud, were lifted by the grass while the bodice hugged Laura's ribs tightly and pressed firmly upward on breasts, which —even from a distance, Rye could clearly see—rose and fell more sharply at first sight of him.

He let the bag slip slowly to the ground, eyes riveted on Laura while he gave a soft command. "Stay."

Across the silence she heard him utter the word, and while the dog dropped to the ground to wait, Laura stood stalk still and breathless, as if the command were spoken for her.

He took a first slow step, then another, coming on deliberately, eyes never wavering from her. The grass whispered as his high boots brushed through it. Her heart clamored beneath the slim fingers still pressed to her breast. When he stood close, they drank in each other's faces for a long, silent moment before he lazily lifted a hand to the side of her ear, caught the green streamer in the crook of a finger, and trailed it slowly downward until he grazed the bare skin above her straining bodice.

"Satin," he said quietly, rubbing the back of the index finger up and down between her chest and the ribbon.

Beneath his knuckle her flesh rose and fell faster. She watched his eyes travel the path of the green streamer to the fullest part of her breast, then slowly back up to her lips. From low in her throat came a single, strained word. "Aye."

It brought an easy smile to his lips. "It's in my way." Still, he toyed with the skein of ribbon, brushing up and down, up and down, while the flutter of satin against her collarbone made goosebumps erupt along her arms. He stood so close, his shiny boots were buried within the mountainous billows of her skirts.

His eyes, as blue as the skies behind him, lingered on her every feature while hers traversed his face with its skin lit to nut-brown by the afternoon sunshine, his hair with its new sideburns making him seem partly stranger. Curiously, Laura's fingers still cupped her own breast. She could feel her hastened heartbeat there and wondered if he, too, detected it as he leaned slowly, knuckle slipping away to be replaced by his warm, open lips. Lightly, he touched the satiny skin of her collarbone, pushing the ribbon aside.

An ecstasy of emotions flooded Laura as her eyelids drifted shut and she touched his face for the first time. "Oh, Rye," she breathed, cupping his jaw, resting her lips against his hair. The scent of him was as she remembered, a mixture of cedar and his father's pipe tobacco and the flavor she thought of as sea breeze, knowing no other name for it.

He raised his head, seemingly unhurried, though within, he, too, knew great impatience. But it was too good to hurry, too fine, with Laura, to plunge through the luxury they'd been afforded in this golden afternoon.

"Turn around," he ordered gently, still having touched no more than that tantalizing bit of skin at her collarbone.

"But . . ." His lips were too inviting, his touch too enticing.

"Turn around," he said more softly, putting his wide brown hands on her tiny waist. She covered them with her own, turned away from him very slowly, scarcely able to breathe. His hands slipped from under hers and she felt the tug of the brass pin leaving her hat while he asked, "What am I wearing?"

"A white muslin shirt, the tan summer breeches you wore

the day we ate oranges in the market, new black boots I've never seen before, and a whale's tooth on a silver chain in the open collar of your shirt.''

"Ahh . . . very good. You get a reward." The hat was pulled from her head and rustled onto the grass at her side. His hands, spread wide, came back to span her ribs, as if she were a ballerina he was guiding in a spin. Then his lips touched the side of her neck above the scooped back neckline. She tilted her head to one side, luxuriating in the touch of his mouth on her skin.

"You're very stingy with your rewards, Mr. Dalton," she murmured, feeling as if her body would rebel if it couldn't soon know more of him than he chose to dole out in tantalizing deliberation.

"I seem to remember y' liked it lingery . . . or have y' changed? Do y' want it all at once?"

She laughed throatily, for her head was thrown back, the sun warm on her jaw as he bit the side of her neck and wet it with his tongue.

"Mmm, y' taste good."

"Like what?"

"Lilacs."

"Aye, lilac water." She moved sensuously. "You, too, get a reward." She knew he was smiling, though his face was buried in her neck and hers turned toward the Nantucket sky. She covered his hands with her own. For a moment neither of them moved but for his driving breaths against her shoulder and hers that raised their joined hands on her ribs. The backs of his hands were wider than hers, the fingers longer, the skin harder. She guided them slowly, slowly upward while the smile dissolved from her lips, which parted as she held his palms cupped tightly against both of her breasts. For a moment his breath stilled beside her ear and she pictured him with eyes closed as hers were, sunspots dancing in crazy, exhilarating patterns against her lids.

"Laura-love," he said gruffly as his hands started moving, caressing, relearning, while hers lingered on them, absorbing the very feel of his touch. "Am I dreaming or are y' really here at last?"

"I'm here, Rye, I'm here."

As they shared this first caress, the faraway notes of the bell in the church tower drifted across the meadow, chiming out the musical prelude to the hour, then the hour itself . . . one! . . . two! They had grown up to the chiming of that bell, had often gauged their waning time to it, and knew its message well.

"Two o'clock. How much time do we have?"

"Until four."

One hand left her breast and tipped her chin up. Twisting half-around, she met his lips at last over her shoulder. And as they kissed, each wished the bell had not rung. He dropped his hands to her waist and spun her around almost viciously. She looped one of her arms around his neck, the other around his ribs, while he held her so demandingly, the whalebones bit into her skin. His mouth blended with hers as their tongues possessed one another, thrusting and tasting, hungry for full intimacy. He grasped the sides of her head and slanted his mouth across hers in one direction, then another, low sounds coming from his throat, as if he were in pain. All pretense of nonchalance had disappeared with the ringing of the church bell, but it had left its reverberations within their bodies, which moved rhythmically against each other when he pulled the length of her against him.

He dropped to the earth, taking her with him, and fell across her lap in a billow of white dimity. Reaching an arm up, he hooked the back of her neck and bent her to him while she pressed kisses on his closed eyelids, his temple, the hollow beneath his nose, the corner of his mouth, and his throat. "Oh, Rye, I would know the smell of you if I were blindfolded. I could pick you out from all the men of this world with my nose alone." Without opening his eyes, he chuckled, letting her go on nuzzling and kissing her way around his face and hair.

"Mmm . . ." She made a humming sound of delight with her nose buried in the soft waves above his ear.

"What do I smell like?" he asked.

"Like cedar and smoke and salt."

He laughed again, then returned his mouth to hers for a long, ardent intermingling of tongues. She ran her hands along the firm muscles of his chest while he pressed his palm

along the side of her breast, exploring with a long thumb until
the nipple ached sweetly for release from its tight restraints.

She slipped her hand within his shirt. The chain was warm,
the hairs silken, his nipple tiny-hard as her fingertips fluttered
across it. His chest muscles tensed beneath her hand, then with
a groan he turned his face toward her breasts, opening his
mouth greedily against the dress front, forcing his warm
breath through it before catching the fabric between his teeth
and tugging it as he made inarticulate sounds deep in his
throat.

"Are y' wearin' it?" He backed away, freeing his lips from
the white dimity.

Their eyes met as with a single fingertip she traced the outline of a swooping sideburn, from the pulsebeat that rapped at
his temple to the curve beneath his firm cheekbone. "Yes, I'm
wearing it."

"I thought so. I could feel it."

"I've worn it every day since you gave it to me."

"Let me see." But he remained across her lap for a minute,
studying her delicately pink cheeks and the brown eyes, heavy-
lidded with anticipation. He braced up, resting a palm beside
her hip, his eyes now on a level with hers. "Turn around," he
ordered gently.

He moved back off her skirts to kneel behind her as the
fabric rustled and puffed high, totally covering his thighs.
Her hair was gathered in a cascade of ringlets, which she
moved aside, presenting the nape of her neck. He touched it
with his fingertips, sending shivers preceding his touch along
the line of hooks down her vertebrae. She pictured his hands,
tough and capable, hands that knew well how to control both
oak and a woman's flesh. The contrasting pictures unleashed a
rush of sensuality within Laura while he parted the dress down
to her waist, then beyond.

The dress fell forward and she pushed it past her wrists,
then, still sitting, reached for the button at the waistband of
her petticoat. Watching, he pressed a hand to her shoulder
blade, just above the corset, and stroked the soft hollow up
the center of her back with his thumb. Dress and petticoats lay
now like a newly blossomed lily, with Laura its pistil. Like a
bee gathering nectar, he dipped his head to kiss her soft shoul-

der before straightening once more to free the laces along her back. Inch by inch they separated, revealing a wrinkled chemise. With a touch he urged her to stand, and she rose on shaky knees, resting a hand on his shoulder to steady herself as she stepped out of the cylinder of whalebone and buckram.

Rye raised his eyes, but she stood partially turned away from him, clad now in pantaloons and chemise. Strong, tan hands squeezed her hipbones, turning her slowly to face him while he gazed up, then reached for the ribbon between her breasts. But his hands stopped, then captured the backs of hers as he spoke into her eyes.

"You take it off. I want to watch y'. Out at sea, the picture of you undressing was the thing I remembered best." He turned one soft palm upward, then the other, leaving a lingering kiss in each before placing them at her laces. Then he sat back on his haunches, watching, remembering first times with her.

Slowly, Laura loosened the ribbons, and along with them a series of ricocheting feelings that made her feel wanton and shy, sinful and glorified, while his gaze remained steadily on her. She grasped the hem of the waist-length garment and worked it over her head, then dropped her arms to her sides, leaving the chemise dangling, forgotten, from her fingertips.

His eyes scanned her bare breasts, their dusky nipples exposed to the sun, then the criss-cross tracery of red lines on her skin. She watched, standing perfectly still, as his Adam's apple glided up and down before he rose to his knees, placing warm palms gently over her ribs to pull her near and kiss the imprint made by the busk along the center of her stomach and chest. Other impressions had been left by the whalebone stays on either side, and he treated them likewise, tracing each with the tip of his tongue, starting at the warm hollow beneath her breast, gliding down to her waist. His palms caressed her warm back, gathering her close against him as his lips at last covered a dark, sweet nipple.

Laura closed her eyes, adrift upon a liquid rush of desire, one hand seeking his hair, the other his shoulder, taking a fistful of shirt and twisting it tightly as he moved to her other breast, where he tugged and sucked, sending spasms of desire knifing through her limbs.

Rye clamped a strong arm about her hips, pulling her against his chest as he took his fill of this woman he'd wanted for five yearning years. Long, delighted minutes later, he leaned away to look up at Laura. She dropped her gaze to see him framed by her naked breasts, and smiled at the sight of his dark fingers stroking her white, soft flesh, shaping and re-shaping it, a wonderous expression on his face. Unashamed, she watched and thrilled, letting the tide of emotions build.

"I thought I remembered perfectly, but y' were never this good in my memories. Aw, love, your skin is so soft." His tongue circled the outer circumference of one orb, then its crest, wetting a wide circle of skin. Then he sat back and watched as, the air touching it, evaporating, cooling, the nipple drew up tightly into a ripe, ready berry of arousal, which he again teased with tongue and teeth.

She reached over his shoulder to tug his shirttail free of his pants, needing to touch more than just his clothing. He sat back and obediently raised his arms while the shirt skimmed past ribs and wrists. Holding the garment, she plunged her face into the soft cloth to breathe deeply of his scent, which lingered there.

An impatient hand stole the shirt and flung it aside.

"Sit down," he ordered, the words rough-textured.

Immediately, Laura complied, dropping back onto ruffled pantaloons, bracing her palms on the grass behind. She watched in fascination while he lifted one foot and started re-moving her shoe. Over his shoulder it went before he peeled away her stocking and reached for her other foot.

He managed the second shoe without taking his eyes from her face, while she watched every movement of the arousing process, each shifting muscle of his hands undressing her. The second shoe and stocking joined their mates, then he held her foot in both hands, running a thumb over the sensitive instep. While he fondled the foot, his eyes traveled her disheveled hair, bare breasts, and pantaloons.

"Y're beautiful."

"I have wrinkles on my belly."

"Even y'r wrinkles are beautiful. I love every one of 'em."

Sitting back on his haunches with knees widespread, he

lifted her foot and kissed its arch, then the small hollow beneath her anklebone, while he watched her beguiling mouth drift open and her tongue catch between her teeth. He pressed the sole of her foot against the high, hard center of his chest, moving it in small circles while her eyes followed . . . silky-soft hair, hard muscle, the chain, and whale's tooth trailing on her bare toes.

Senses that had lain dormant for five years sprang to life in Laura while Rye gradually lowered her foot down the center of his chest to his hard belly, then to his waistline, settling it finally against the hot, hard hills of his tumescence. A shuddering breath fell from him and his eyes closed. She pressed her heel against him and he rocked forward on his knees while her fingers clutched handfuls of grass behind her. When he opened his eyes again, they were fraught with passion.

"I want y' more right now than I did in Hardesty's loft when we were sixteen." The heat of his body burned through his breeches while he soothed a hand over her ankle.

Elbows locked, she let her head drop backward, and her eyes drifted shut as she said chokily, "I thought I'd never feel your hands on me again. I've wanted this since . . . since the day you sailed away from me. What's happening inside me now has never happened since that day . . . only with you."

"Tell me what's happening." He moved sharply up beside her, bracing one hand on the grass, the other at last cupping the ripe readiness between her legs as he leaned over her, kissing her exposed throat.

But her only answer was an impassioned sound more expressive than any words she might have chosen as, with head slung back, palms braced firmly on the earth, she thrust her hips upward in invitation. He explored her through cotton pantaloons as he'd first done years ago, dipping his head to kiss the tip of her chin while she moved rhythmically against his hand.

"Let me see the rest of you," he begged against her throat.

She drew her heavy head up. "In a minute." She pressed a palm against his breast until he went backward onto the grass, catching himself on his elbows, Laura's and his positions now reversed. "Your boots."

Unceremoniously, she took up his left foot, working assiduously at tugging the boot off. But her efforts proved futile. He couldn't help smiling as her face contorted with a grimace.

"Why do you wear . . . your . . . boots . . . so . . . tight?" She grunted. "They never . . . used to be."

"They're new." He enjoyed every minute of her struggle, then she changed positions and his smile grew broader at the sight of her pink soles facing him, one on each side of his long leg.

"Laura, y' should see y'rself, sittin' there in nothin' but those ruffly pantaloons, pullin' at my boot like some hoyden."

"It . . . won't . . . come . . ." But just then the boot slipped off, nearly tumbling her backward. She laughed into his eyes and threw the boot over her shoulder, then ran her hands up inside the leg of his breeches to peel away his woolen sock.

"Did I make this?" she asked, holding the stocking aloft.

"No, another woman did."

"Another woman?" Her eyebrows puckered.

His blue eyes twinkled mischievously. "Aye, m' mother. An old pair I found in a chest at home."

"Oh." Laura's smile was reborn as the sock sailed away, and she made quick work of the second boot and sock, which soon joined the others.

In a swift movement, Rye came up off the ground, tackling Laura with an arm around her waist, rolling her over and over on the grass until her hair was tumbled and her breasts heaved. Sprawled across the length of her body, he looked down into brown, eager eyes and a mouth across which a strand of hair had fallen during their tussle. His mouth slammed down across hers, heedless of the lock of hair, opening fully in a wild, voluptuous exchange of tongues while his left hand clamped the back of her head and his right kneaded a breast almost hurtfully. His knee came up hard between her legs and their bodies writhed together in reckless thrusts while they rolled to their sides, kissing with an unleashed ardor in which gentleness, for the moment, had no part.

Her fingers twisted in his hair and her eyelids shut out the blue sky background as he tore his mouth from hers and opened it on the breast, which he cupped high and hard, sending a sweet pain through her as she rejoiced, "Oh, Rye, Rye, is it really you at last?"

"Aye, it's me, with five years t' make up for." But his breath wheezed like a high wind and his chest heaved torturously as his blue eyes burned into her brown ones. Then suddenly she was released, and he sat up abruptly, straddling her hips as his hands roughly began jerking open the buttons of his breeches while his eyes blazed with the unmistakable fire of intent. Her own blazed an answer as she freed the single button at her side. Their eyes did not waver while he sat her straight and tall, like a rider in a saddle, then a moment later dismounted, swinging a knee back and pulling her to her feet all in one fluid motion.

Trousers and pantaloons drifted to the ground and a moment later they faced each other with but the distance of a glance between them, nature's children, dressed in no more than a whale's tooth and a criss-crossing of red lines, which even now were fading from her skin. Their eyes feasted for a brief time as they stood naked beneath a blue bowl of sunshine, surrounded by salt-scented grass and a wreath of grapevines.

When Laura and Rye's arms went about each other, the force nearly knocked the breath from their bodies. She felt her toes leaving the ground while he held her aloft, kissing her mouth, turning in a circle of ecstasy. Then she was struggling, squirming.

"Rye, put me down so I can touch you."

"You touch me, and I'm gone," he declared roughly. "Christ, it's been five years."

"Aye, love, I know. For me, too." His eyes pierced hers with a question, and she immediately realized she should not have admitted it. "Rye—" Her voice trembled. "—put me down . . . love me . . . love me . . ."

The trees tipped sideways as his hard brown arm slipped behind her knees to lift her, and a moment later Laura's shoulders were pressed to the grass. She looked at his face, framed by blue sky, then at his nodding tumescence, for which she immediately reached, then guided home. . . . He was solid

velvet, she liquid, and his first thrust brought to Laura a
bursting sensation of desire which this act had not brought
since she'd last celebrated it with Rye. And then the beat
began, rhythmic and fluent. And they ceased to be him and
her and became simply them—one.

They arched together beneath the summer sun, which rained
on his back as he moved, sending hovering shadow across her
face and shoulders. The whale's tooth dangled across her
breastbone to the hollow of her throat, then took up a pen-
dulous tapping on her chin.

She lifted herself in reception to each thrust, watching Rye's
pleasured face while he bared his teeth and sucked in great
shuddering gulps of air. He hung his head to watch their
bodies mingling, and her eyes followed. When his beat accelerated, the grass bit into her shoulders and her head was
pressed back harder onto the earth. She closed her eyes and
rode the swells with him, while his body beckoned her response. It built and it burned until the inward embraces began,
forcing a throaty cry from her lips. He grunted as his climax
neared, coming against her so hard she skittered beneath him
along the earth, then unknowingly closed her fingers around
the grass for a handhold.

She welcomed every inch of the force as her body quivered
to its completion. His cry carried over the meadow as he
spilled into her, and the final shudder sent sparkling beads of
perspiration glinting on his shoulder.

He fell across her breasts, exhausted, and lay there panting
until he felt silent laughter lifting her chest. He raised his
weary head to meet her eyes. "Look what we've done." She
rolled her head to peer past his shoulder and along her hip.

He craned around to find in her hand a fistful of turf,
pulled up by its roots. He smiled and checked her other hand.
It, too, was clasping a clump of grass. Suddenly, she lifted
both hands high off the ground and let the clods tumble from
her fingers in a kind of jubilation, then flung her arms tightly
about his shoulders. He rolled them to their sides, one hand
reaching to brush off her palm.

"Was I too rough with y'?"

She smiled tenderly into his eyes. "No, oh no, love. I
needed it just as it was."

"Laura . . ." He cradled her gently, closing his eyelids against her hair. "I love y', woman, I love y'."

"I love you, Rye Dalton, just as I've loved you since I first knew what the word meant."

They lay together with their heartbeats joined, letting the sun dry their skin. After several minutes, he rolled back his shoulder and flung an arm out, palm up. She did likewise, and they closed their eyes as they basked and rested. She lay on his left and with her right hand reached lazily to idle through the hair on his chest. Blindly, he reached for it and brought the fingertips to his lips before replacing it on his chest.

"Laura?"

"Hm?"

"What did y' mean before when y' said it'd been five years for y'?"

For a moment she didn't answer, but finally replied, "Nothing. I shouldn't have said it."

He studied the sky, where a single white cloud drifted. "Dan doesn't take you all the way, does he?"

Immediately, she rolled near and covered his lips with her fingertips. "I don't want to talk about him."

He braced his jaw on a palm and lay on his side facing her. "That's what y' meant, isn't it?" He trailed the tip of a finger down between her breasts to her belly, and on to the nest of hair that held the warmth of the sun in its tangles, the warmth of him in its shelter. He watched goose pimples ride her skin, though her eyes were closed. He pressed the brown triangle. "This is mine. It's always been mine, and the thought of him havin' it has kept me miserable every night that I've slept alone since I've been home. At least he didn't have it all." He kissed her chin lightly. "I'm glad."

Her eyes opened to his. "Rye, I had no right to say it. I sh—"

His lips cut off her words. Then he lifted his head and stroked her jaw with a knuckle. "Laura, I taught you, you taught me. Learnin' together gave us rights."

But she didn't want to mar the day with any talk that might rob them of the smallest slip of joy. Brightly, she smiled, then studied his face, from hairline to chin. "Do you know what I've been wanting to do ever since you've been back?"

"I thought y' just did it." The dent appeared in his cheek.

"No, not that."

"What, then?"

"To explore each of these tiny pockmarks with the tip of my tongue, and to touch these—" she pressed both palms against his side-whiskers. "—like this."

With a smile, he fell onto his back, flipping her over on top of him. "Explore all y' like."

She wet each tiny mark, ending with the seventh, on his upper lip. Raising her head, she smoothed her palms over the side-whiskers, studying him, delight in her face. "I like these, do you know that? They're . . . very masculine. When I first saw you, they made you seem . . . well, almost like a stranger, somebody enticing but forbidden."

He lazily caressed her hipbones, then moved his hands down over her bare buttocks. "And do I still seem like a stranger?" he asked, grinning up at her.

"You're different in some ways." She flipped his lower lip down with an index finger, and let it slip closed again.

"How?"

"The way you stand, like the ship is going to yaw at any minute. And the way you talk. You used to talk just like I do, but now you say aye and nay and cut off the ends of words." She pouted and pondered. "Say, 'Laura darling.' "

"Laura darlin'," he repeated obediently.

"See? Laura, darli*nnn* . . ." She giggled, and he, too, laughed.

"Well, y' are my Laura darlin'," he said.

But she laughed again. "I fear it's there to stay, but it's charming, so I don't mind."

He gave her an affectionate slap on the rump. "Are y' hungry?"

"There y' go again, m' briny lad," she answered in her best imitation of a New England tar. "Aye, I'm rav'nous!"

He laughed, white teeth flashing in the sun, slapped her again, and demanded, "Then get up off me. I've brought food."

The next minute she was dumped away, and sat Indian-fashion while he strode off to where Ship lay guarding the drawstring bag. She watched the strong muscles of Rye's buttocks and thighs flexing as he crossed the clearing to retrieve his cache. The dog immediately sat up, alert. Rye went down on one knee, giving Ship a scratch and a muffled assurance of her master's affection. Then the two of them came back together with the bag of food.

Laura watched them, and as they drew near, raised up on her knees to greet Rye as if he'd been gone a long time. "Come here." She held her arms open and he walked flush against her. She pressed her face against his lower belly, then against his flaccid manhood before backing away and looking up at his face, which was bent to watch her smilingly. "You're a beautiful man. I could watch you walk naked across the grass forever and never turn my eyes away." He touched her face. "I love you, Rye Dalton." Her arms tightened about his hips. His blue eyes smiled down at her with a fulfillment he hadn't known since his return.

"I love you, Laura Dalton."

Ship's cold, wet nose divided them as she thrust it against Laura's bare side. Laura jumped back, scolding and laughing.

Rye laughed and dropped to the grass with a rough, affectionate graze of his palm on the dog's head. "She's jealous."

Laura watched as he worked the bag open. "What do you have?" she asked.

His hand plunged inside. "Oranges!" Up flew an orange, high above her head. She caught it with a lilt of laughter. "For the lady who likes to share oranges with gentlemen in a most enticing way." His teasing grin brought a smirk to her lips.

"Oh, oranges. Perhaps you should have invited DeLaine Hussey today. I have the feeling Miss Hussey has wanted to get her hands on your oranges for years."

"I only share my oranges with you." The dimple in his cheek was thoroughly engaging as he raised his eyes. Then it grew even deeper when he looked up to find her sitting back on her heels, breasts thrust forward and hidden impudently behind a pair of concealing oranges.

"And I only share my oranges with you," she returned innocently.

His wide brown hands came up to squeeze the fruit. "Mmm

. . . you have nice, ripe, firm oranges. I'd love sharing them."
He dipped his head as if to sample with his teeth, but with one
orange she rapped his cheek aside.

"Where are your manners, Rye Dalton! You have to ask
politely first."

He lunged at her then, knocking her backward in the grass,
their laughter carrying over the meadow while Ship watched
their antics with a lazy eye.

"I'll show y' the proper way t' share an orange, y' little
minx!"

In their tussle one of the oranges went rolling, but he captured the other, subduing Laura finally until she ended up on
her back, and he knelt over her with one powerful and well-
placed knee pressing hard against her ribcage.

She pushed at it, laughing with utmost difficulty. "Rye, I
can't breathe."

"Good." He ripped off a piece of orange peel. It landed on
her cheek, and she twisted her head aside, laughing harder.
"First y' have t' peel the orange just so." Another piece of
peel fell to her closed eye.

"Rye Dalton, you overgrown bully!"

"But only halfway, so y' have somethin' t' hang on to."

Plop! This piece hit her on the nose, which she wrinkled as
she pushed at his knee. "Get off . . ."

He ignored her plea, letting her squirm away while calmly
completing his chore. "And when y' have the juiciest part exposed . . ." The conquerer let another chunk of peel hit the
vanquished on her upper lip. ". . . you're ready t' share y'r
orange."

She was still pushing at his knee with her hands, but she bit
her lip to keep from smiling. Lordly and lean, he held her
down and kept his blue eyes on her mouth as he lifted the
orange and sank his teeth into it. While he chewed, his lips all
wet and sweet, she grew increasingly aware of his bold pose
that left bare essentials hovering just above her. He tore into a
second bite and lazily savored it, then swallowed.

"Y' want some?" he asked, arching a brow at her.

"Yes."

"Some what?"

"Some of your orange."

"Where're y'r manners, Laura Dalton? Y' have t' ask politely first."

"May I please have some of your orange?"

His eyes raked her body, from one breast, half-flattened by his knee, to the white flesh of her stomach, the triangle of hair, the flare of hips, then slowly back up to her face again. "I guess so."

The orange came slowly toward Laura's mouth, and she opened her lips slowly until at last the succulent flesh was pressed against her teeth, and she tore off a chunk with a twist of her head, all the while keeping her burning gaze on his deceptively fierce blue eyes. The pressure from his knee relaxed, and he began brushing it against her breast until the nipple rose up to meet the rough texture of the hair on his leg.

She swallowed, licked her lips, but left them parted and glistening. "Mmm . . . sweet," she murmured.

"Aye, sweet," came his throaty reply, while his eyes did queer things to her stomach.

"It's your turn," she said softly.

"Aye, so it is." His knee was gone from her breast. His dark hand moved above her, holding the orange. Its power was evident in the wide wrist, the blue veins on its back, the muscles corded from coopering these many years. Her eyes were polarized by the sight of his fingers slowly clenching about the orange. She started only slightly as the first cold droplet landed on her breast. She watched in soaring anticipation as his lean fingers squeezed, squeezed, sending the juice in a cool line down the valley between her breasts, to her navel, along her stomach, and down one thigh.

Then his head was slowly bending to her, his tongue tracing the sweet path of the juice, licking it from her while her eyelids slid shut and her heart went on a Nantucket sleighride.

He'd been five years at sea with a whaleship full of lusty men who'd had nothing more than talk and memory to buoy them over the course of the voyage. Rye Dalton had learned from listening.

And as he'd done in a loft above a boathouse and in a cooperage before a warming fire, he taught Laura new things

about her own body. As he dipped his head to taste of her
orange sweetness, he brought her a splendor of which she'd
never dreamed. And later, he peeled a second orange and
handed it to her while her eyes grew wide and she stared at his
offering, then slowly, slowly reached to take it while he lay
back on the grass and took his turn at splendor.

Chapter 12

THE AFTERNOON WANED, and they were forced to regard the bell from the church tower as it chimed out each quarter hour. They lay on their backs, each with an ankle crossing an up-drawn knee, their bare soles touching. Rye held Laura's hand, rubbing his thumb absently in her palm.

"Do you know what I did the night before you sailed?" she asked, smiling at the memory.

"What did y' do?"

"I put a black cat under a tub."

He laughed and pillowed his head on his free wrist. "Don't tell me y' believe that old wive's tale!"

"Not anymore, I don't. But I was so desperate, I'd try anything to keep you from sailing. But even the cat under the tub didn't bring anything resembling a strong enough headwind to keep your ship from leaving the harbor the next day, like it was supposed to."

He turned to study her. "Did y' miss me like I missed you?"

"It was . . . awesome. Terrible." A solemn moment of memory passed.

He shifted his weight and rolled onto his side, laying a hand on her stomach. "Y'r stomach is rounder . . . and y'r hips're wider."

"I've had your baby since you've been away."

"Why didn't y' have one of Dan's?"

181

The magic spell was broken. She sat up, curling her back and hugging her knees. "I said I don't want to talk about him."

Rye braced up on an elbow, studying her back. "Y' didn't tell him last night, did y'?"

She dropped her forehead onto her knees. "I . . . I couldn't. I tried, but I just couldn't."

"Do y' love him more than me, then?"

"No . . . no!" She turned with a quick flash of fire in her eyes, then once more presented her back. "Next to you he's . . . oh, Rye, don't make me say things that will only cause us both to feel guiltier than we already are."

"I don't like playin' him false any more than you do. But I won't have y' sleepin' with him nights and me days and not tellin' him it's over between y'."

"Rye, I know I promised, but . . . but there're Josh's feelings to consider, too."

He sat up and jerked distractedly at a tuft of grass. "And what about y'r feelin's for me? Do they count for nothin'? Do y' want me—us—t' settle for this, sneakin' up into the hills to make love once every month or so while Dan keeps remindin' you y' have an *obligation* t' him and the boy?" Rye flung the grass away angrily.

"No," she answered in a tiny voice.

"What, then?"

Miserable, she had no answer. Rye stared at the ground, realizing he had the power to tell Dan the truth and be done with it, angry with himself for even having the thought because Laura trusted him not to do such a thing. His eyes moved down her bare spine, then to her arm as she reached for her clothing.

"Laura, if we keep on this way, it'll only get worse. I send y' home t' him, y' send me back t' my father, and everybody's miserable."

"I know."

As she slipped on the first article of clothing, the chimes rang again below. Rye, too, reached for his breeches. While donning them, he watched her reach for her chemise, pull it on, and begin lacing its ribbons. Standing behind her, he could not resist asking, "Laura, does he make love to y' often?"

She would not turn and face him. "No."

"Since I've been back?"

"Only a few times."

Rye drew a shaky breath and ran a hand through his hair. "I shouldn't have asked, I'm sorry," he said gruffly.

Her voice trembled, but her back remained turned upon him. "Rye, with him it's never been like it is with you . . ." She spun now to face him. "Never!" Her throat worked. "I guess it's because I . . . I love him out of gratitude, not passion, and there's a world of difference between the two."

"And y'll stay with him out o' gratitude, is that what y're sayin'?"

There were tears on her lashes now. "I . . . I . . ."

Rye Dalton then spoke the hardest words he'd ever said. "I won't string this out forever. Y'll have t' choose. And y'll have t' do it soon, else I'll be leavin' the island for good."

She'd guessed something like this would happen. Yet how could she tell Josh? How could she tell Dan?

"Promise!" Rye ordered, standing firmly before her, intensity in every rigid muscle of his body. "Promise y'll tell him tonight. Then we'll go t' the mainland and begin divorce proceedin's immediately." At her hesitation, his words grew harsh. "Woman, you tempt me in my dreams at night, when I walk the beaches with miles between us, and every wakin' hour of the day. T' me you're still my wife, and I've done what y' asked—I've given y' time t' break away from him. How much longer do y' think I can stand your livin' with him?"

Laura threw herself against Rye and their arms clung. "I will tell him. Tonight. I promise on my love for you. It's always been you, always, since we were old enough to know the difference between boys and girls. In my heart the vow between you and me has never been broken, Rye. I love you." She backed away, took his cheeks in her palms, and said into his sea-blue eyes, "I promise I will tell him tonight, and I'll meet you at the ferry tomorrow and we'll do as you said. We'll go to the mainland and begin divorce proceedings."

He grasped the back of her hand and his eyes closed as he fiercely kissed her palm. "I love y', Laura. God, how I love y'."

"And I love you, Rye."

"I'll meet y' at the ferry."

She kissed his lips lightly. "At the ferry."

The promise was still fresh on Laura's lips as she walked up the scallop-shell path with Josh an hour later. As the house came into view, she immediately sensed something was amiss, for sitting on her doorstep was Josh's best friend, Jimmy Ryerson. But instead of leaping to his feet at the sight of Laura and Josh, Jimmy hunkered quietly, watching them approach.

"Hi, Jimmy!" Josh broke into an excited gallop.

"Hi." But Jimmy was all six-year-old business as he reported, "We can't play. I gotta tell your ma something and then you're supposed to come home with me."

"What is it, Jimmy?" Laura questioned, alarmed now, clasping his shoulder.

"They couldn't find you, and they said I was s'posed to sit here and wait till you come home and tell you to go down to Straight Wharf right away."

Laura's eyes flew toward the bay. "Who?"

Jimmy shrugged. "Everybody. They're all down there— your pa, too, Josh. They said your grampa's boat, it tipped over comin' across the bar, and they can't find him."

Laura's heart did somersaults. "C . . . can't find him?"

Jimmy shook his head.

"Oh no." The words were a whispered lament, and Laura's fingers covered her lips as she again looked down over the bay. Reactions tumbled through her in a swift succession: there's got to be some mistake . . . Zachary Morgan couldn't possibly have capsized, he knows these waters too well . . . they've all been looking for me . . . they'll know Rye was gone, too . . . where is Dan?

"How long have they been out looking?" she asked.

"I don't know." Jimmy shrugged again. "I been waitin' here a long time. They says I wasn't s'posed to—"

But Laura cut him off with a firmer grasp on his shoulder. She turned both him and Josh toward the path, ordering, "You go down to Jimmy's house and stay, like they said. And, Josh, you wait until Papa or I come for you. I've got to hurry down to the wharf and find him.''

Josh's eyes widened. "Wh . . . what's the matter, Mama? Is Grampa all right?''

"I don't know, darling. I hope so.''

Sensing tragedy, Josh suddenly balked. "I don't wanna go to Jimmy's house. I wanna come with you to find Grampa and Papa.''

Though each passing second felt like an hour, Laura went down on one knee and brushed her son's hair back in a gesture of comfort. "I know you do, darling, but . . . it's best if you go with Jimmy. I'll try to come for you soon.'' She gave him a reassuring hug, forcing herself to appear calm for his sake while every muscle in her body was tensed to run.

At last Jimmy came to Laura's aid. "C'mon, Josh. My ma made poundcake and she said we could both have some when we got back.''

The mention of poundcake at last put Josh's skepticism to rout, and he turned down the path toward Jimmy's house. Laura stared unseeingly at their backs for a moment, suddenly reluctant to make the journey down the hill herself. She pressed a hand to her lips, shut her eyes, thinking, No! no! This is all some . . . some silly little boy's mistake!

But a moment later she hiked up her skirts and flew like a windjammer before a gale—down the scallop-shell path, along the sandy lanes, onto the cobblestones that echoed the alarm of her running feet as she crossed deserted Main Street Square and ran on toward the blue water of the bay, where masts had come to harbor for the night. The closer she came to the wharves, the greater grew her terror, for she saw a crowd gathered there, all faces turned toward the bar, where nets were stretched between bobbing dories. She realized, too, that the wind had switched to the north, pushing the ocean before it. The bar, always treacherous, was more so when the winds blew northerly. Yet it seemed impossible that the bar could have wreaked disaster, for from here, the breakers did not look high enough to pose a threat.

Laura shouldered her way through the crowd. Murmurous voices trailed after her, and eyes watched her progress.

"Here she is now.''

"They've found her.''

"It's Laura."

Somber expressions turned her way as she lifted her skirts and edged toward the end of the wharf. Laura flashed pleading glances to one person after another while moving woodenly through the group, seeking a single face that did not reflect disaster. Her breath fell in bellowlike heaves after her headlong run, and her eyes were wide and sparkling with fear.

"Wh . . . where's Dan? What happened?"

A sympathetic hand touched her arm, but it seemed they'd all lost their tongues. Laura wanted to scream, shake someone, force at least one voice to speak!

"Where is Dan?" The words sounded strange, for her throat was tight with rising hysteria.

At last someone answered.

"He's out lookin' with the others." It was old Cap'n Silas who spoke. He surveyed the knot of people at the end of the wharf—the family—while Laura's knees turned to water and she put off going to them.

She clutched Cap'n Silas's wiry arm. "H . . . How long have they been looking?"

"Near two hours now. Y' mustn't fret, girl. All y' can do is wait with th' rest of us."

"Wh . . . what happened?"

Silas clamped his teeth hard on his cherrywood pipestem, turned rheumy eyes toward the waters of the bar, and replied tersely, "Pitchpoled."

"Pitchpoled?" Laura repeated disbelievingly. "But how? Was he alone?"

"With his brother Tom, as usual. But Tom was thrown clear. He's out there lookin', too."

Again Laura's eyes were drawn toward the searchers. Tom was out there looking, too? Searching for his own brother after the two had fished these waters together all their lives?

"But how?" Laura repeated, raising pleading eyes to Cap'n Silas. "How could a thing like that happen when they know every whim of these waters?"

"Overloaded 'er bow," Cap'n Silas answered flatly. He'd been a whaler for forty years, and after those forty had taken up his station as guardian of these wharves. He had seen everything that could happen along them. With the grim acceptance of one older and wiser, he'd come to understand that life and death meant little to the sea. If a man worked by it, he knew he might die by it. A fickle bitch, the sea.

"Good catch today," he went on, scanning the horizon. His voice was like the crackle of an old salt-caked tarpaulin. "Stayed out t' bring in a few more barrels, Tom said. Knew she was yawin', so they shifted a little weight to 'er stern before they hit the bar. But not enough. Wave caught 'er and flipped 'er end over end like a clown doin' handsprings." He puffed once on his pipe. "Tom was the only one surfaced afterwards."

On the calmest day there were breakers over Nantucket Bar. When the wind came in behind them, as it did now, the waves grew steep. Laura pictured Zach and Tom heading in, happy with their day's catch, when they misjudged the speed with which they climbed a wave; the bow, plummeting hard down the forward face of the wave while its succeeding crest nudged the underbelly of the schooner and flipped it stern over bow.

And now Tom Morgan was out there searching for his brother, and Dan Morgan for his father.

At last Laura could put it off no longer. She looked toward the end of the wharf. There, staring out over the water, was Dan's mother, Hilda, with a black shawl clutched tightly around her shoulders, as if to hold herself together. Beside Hilda stood Tom Morgan's wife, Dorothy, in much the same pose. The two women's shoulders almost touched as they stared out to sea. What went through their minds as they watched the hungry waters where brother searched for brother and son searched for father?

Laura looked at the spot at which the two women stared. The scene on the bar appeared to be nothing more momentous than a few fishermen putting out seining nets for minnows. From here the figures of the searchers appeared very tiny, and she could not make out which one was Dan. What was going through his mind out there in the boats when time after time the nets came up empty? And, my God, how long has he been hauling on them? For two hours, while Rye and I lay naked in a meadow, deceiving him? The first wave of guilt washed over Laura, leaving her stomach churning.

She studied the squared shoulders of the two women at the

end of the wharf, thought of her afternoon with Rye, and silently cried, Dear God, what have I done?

Suddenly realizing she'd put off going to Hilda as long as she could, Laura approached her mother-in-law. Nantucket women had been schooled for generations to wait for their seafaring men with stiff backs, and as Laura lay her hand upon Hilda's shoulder, she felt that lesson incarnated: Hilda's back was as rigid as any whalebone.

"Hilda, I've just heard."

Hilda turned but seemed to maintain that same stoicism that Cap'n Silas managed. "Dan's out there, and Tom, too, with the others. All we can do now is wait." The stiff back turned away.

Laura found herself clutching her arms just as Hilda and Dorothy clutched theirs, and tremors ran through her flesh as she squinted over the water toward Dan, besieged by memories of receiving the news of Rye's death. Oh, that corpseless death. No, Dan, no. Not again.

Feet shuffled behind Laura, and she turned to find Dan's older sister, Ruth, standing there with two cups of steaming coffee in her hands. Asperity was written on every muscle of Ruth's face as she assessed Laura's white dimity dress and broad-brimmed bonnet. Her eyes were red-rimmed and her mouth pinched in much more than grief. Even as she stared balefully at Laura, Ruth's lips pursed tighter and a knowing expression arched her eyebrows.

She pushed past Laura, handing the cups to her mother and aunt, elbowing her way as if to make it clear that *she* would do the comforting here!

Laura stepped back, but Ruth turned to confront her with slate eyes. "We tried to find you. Dan was nearly out of his head."

Laura swallowed, sickened further by the need to lie. "I walked out to Jane's for the afternoon."

Ruth made no effort to disguise her opinion of Laura's dress, which was totally inappropriate for a walk across the moors. The critical eyes raked from neck to hem, then back up. "Well, you might have told Dan where you were going."

"I . . . I thought he knew. Josh wanted to go out and spend the day with his cousins."

But Ruth's expression told Laura she didn't believe a word of it.

Did they send someone out to Jane's looking for me? Would Jane have tried to cover for her?

Without another word, Ruth turned away, moving protectively to her mother's side, effectively shutting Laura out.

She knows! She knows! And if she knows, it won't be long before everyone on the island knows. Ruth will see to it. For the first time Laura scanned the faces on the wharf—DeLaine Hussey was there, and Ezra Merrill, and . . . and even Rye's cousin Charles! The whole town had seen her tardy arrival! Laura's insides trembled uncontrollably. She was shaken by guilt not only for the afternoon's act, but because she could stand here now more concerned with being found out than with the tragedy at hand.

No, that's not true, she told herself. You care about each of these people. Their sorrow is yours.

Yet Ruth Morgan had hit her mark. Laura felt tainted, outcast, and swamped by remorse. She stood removed from the trio of women, watching the pitiful spectacle on the water. Out near the bar, the searchers had pulled in their nets, hauled anchor, and were turning their bows toward shore. A muffled sound of despair came from Hilda Morgan's throat. She covered her mouth and watched the boats heading in and wept against Dorothy Morgan's shoulder.

Standing behind them, Laura felt helpless. She wanted to reach out and comfort Hilda, but Ruth and Dorothy still flanked her. Hilda, Hilda, I'm sorry. Have I been the cause of all this? I didn't mean to, I didn't mean to. Laura bit her lips to keep from crying as the boats came nearer and nearer. Let him be alive, she prayed, though she knew from the expressions of the approaching men that they had not found Dan's father, either dead or alive. Laura's eyes were dry as she picked out Dan's white face among the others. How will I answer when he asks where I was? With more lies?

As if she possessed some sixth sense, Ruth turned to pierce Laura with eyes that convicted and sentenced. But a moment later the reproachful stare moved to a point behind Laura's shoulder, where it remained fixed until at last Laura turned, too, to see what Ruth stared at.

There a few feet behind her stood Rye. He was still dressed in the clothes he'd worn this afternoon. His expression was somber as he looked from Laura to the approaching boat.

He found Dan among those on the water, and his gaze again returned to Laura. Already he sensed the direction her thoughts were taking, and he forced himself not to rush to her and say, Laura, Laura, it would have happened anyway. We are not to blame.

Suddenly aware that Ruth studied their silent exchange, Laura pulled her gaze away from Rye. But as she turned to await the search boats, Ruth's censuring eyes remained coldly assessing, until Laura felt transparent.

The dories drew nigh and Laura again found Dan's stricken face, the eyes empty and sunken, the skin deathly pale. He still wore the wool suit he'd donned that morning before leaving for the countinghouse, and the sight of it there among the ruggedly dressed men intensified Laura's feeling of guilt. She stared at his sleeves, wet to the elbows, and the wrinkled, ruined trousers, imagining Dan sitting at his desk on the high stool, looking up as someone approached with the horrifying news, then running home to tell her but finding the house empty. Had he paced the rooms in a frenzy, wondering where she was? Had he set out with the search party doubly forlorn because she wasn't there when he needed her? Had he tugged at those nets all afternoon with his suspicions of Laura and Rye adding weight to his grief?

The dejected men clumped tiredly onto the wharf only to face the next heart-rending task, consoling the grief-stricken women. Dan lunged to his mother, taking her in his arms, pressing his cheek against her hair while she cried against him. Laura watched the mother seek strength from her son, the son sprung from the man the sea had claimed—father, husband, lost to both of them in life's inexorable cycle.

Laura hovered, tristful and uncertain, waiting for Dan to see her. When he did, he gave his mother over to the arms of his uncle, aunt, and sister and came to her. She saw his gaze move momentarily to Rye, still standing behind her, then she was clasped against his chest. She held him hard, awash with emotions—pity, shame, guilt, and love. Laura grasped him tightly while over the wharf drifted the awful sound of Hilda and Tom Dalton's weeping, though Dan made not a sound, only swallowed convulsively beside Laura's temple. He clung, arms trapping her in a crushing grip, while the town and Rye Dalton looked on.

At last Dan choked, "He's b . . . been sailing over that b . . . bar all his life," as if unable to comprehend how an incredible thing like this could have happened.

"I know, I know," was all Laura could manage. He rocked her back and forth while tears flooded her eyes.

"Where were you? I looked everywhere."

His question was like a thorn piercing her heart as she was forced to answer in a half truth. "I took Josh to Jane's."

"I was so . . ." He gulped to a stop, and she felt his body tremble. "I needed you." His eyes were pinched tightly closed, his cheek pressed against her hair.

"I'm here, I'm here," she reassured him, though half her heart was with the man who watched from a few paces away.

Dan opened his eyes to find Rye watching them. But friendships don't die as easily as Nantucket fishermen . . . and the gazes of the two men locked together with the joys of a thousand happy yesterdays come to revisit this sad today. Each felt the need to comfort and be comforted by those most familiar, those longest loved. And they were moved by forces quite beyond their control.

Dan released his hold on Laura. His heart thudded hard and heavy while the eyes of Rye Dalton remained burdened with deep sadness. They stood before each other, taut and straining, and it was Rye who took the first long step.

They met with a pining, silent agony, chest to chest, heart to heart, their competition for the woman who looked on arrested temporarily by the far greater importance of death. Clasping Dan tightly, Rye knew a confusion of emotions such as he'd never felt before: love and pity for this man, the need to solace him, and guilt for what he and Laura had done.

"Dan," he said thickly.

"Rye, I'm glad you're here."

The two separated. Rye placed a wide hand on Dan's shoulder. The wool of his jacket felt damp. "I'll wait with y' if y' want. He . . . he was good t' me . . . a good man."

Dan clamped a hand on Rye's hard forearm, pulling the

comforting palm more firmly against his shoulder for a moment. "Yes, please. I think Mother would like it if you did . . . and . . . and Laura, too."

The onlookers shuffled their feet and glanced at each other self-consciously. They looked from Rye to Dan to the woman beside them. The face of Laura Dalton was a study in torment. Her hands were tightly clasped between her breasts. Tears trembled on her eyelids, then rolled down her cheeks as she watched the emotional exchange.

They turned then, Dan to Laura's side, and Rye to Hilda's. As Rye's arms went about Dan's mother, she wept against him. "R . . . Rye . . ."

"Hilda," was all he could manage as he spread a large brown hand on the gray knot of hair at the back of her head and held her firmly, silently, letting her weep.

The days turned back and Rye was a boy again, slamming in and out of Hilda's house on Dan's heels. He was fishing with Zachary, presenting Hilda with a fresh catch, and staying for supper when she'd cooked it. Then he and Dan were fetching water for dishes, at Hilda's orders, and being scolded equally when they spilled some on her clean floor. In those days Rye had only reached Hilda's shoulder; now she barely reached his. He swallowed and held her tight.

An awesome welling filled Laura's throat as she looked on. To the best of her knowledge, it was the first time Rye had spoken to Hilda since his return. Laura remembered Hilda offering comfort at the news that Rye had been drowned without a trace. How ironic that it should now be he offering comfort to her when it appeared her husband had met the same fate.

Laura glanced at Dan to find him watching Rye and his mother with glistening eyes, his throat working convulsively.

At last Hilda moved out of Rye's arms, and the voice of Cap'n Silas seemed the only one to have a calming effect, perhaps because he had lived through scenes like this before and had learned to accept them.

"Tide'll turn in a couple hours or so. Y' can all go home till then. No sense waitin' here. Go home, have y'r supper."

The crowd parted to make way for Tom and Dorothy Morgan, who turned to do as Silas suggested. They were followed by Ruth and Hilda. Behind them came Dan, flanked by Rye and Laura. The rest of the crowd dispersed, but when the trio came to the old worn benches on either side of the bait shack door, Dan turned to Cap'n Silas. "Do you mind if we wait here? I'd rather."

Seating himself on one of the benches, Cap'n Silas pointed toward the other one with his pipestem. "Set yerself down."

The three of them sat on the bench: Rye, Dan, and Laura. Their order had at last changed. For Laura there seemed some bizarre form of justice at work, that on this day when she and Rye had willfully betrayed Dan, they should now end up on either side of him, offering their united support and comfort. She held Dan's hand and rested her head wearily against the silvered boards of the bait shack wall while guilt made her dizzy and sick. If Zachary was dead, most certainly it was the great hand of justice reaching out to mete swift retribution and teach her a lesson. She squeezed Dan's hand tighter and waited for the tide to turn.

Sunset spilled over the island and bay. The sandpipers came in to nest while the piping plovers, with their dreary peeps, played their last evening song. The incessant carp of the gulls quieted at last as they settled on wharf piling and spar, fat-breasted and content. The wind disappeared, and the gentle lap of the water under the wharf seemed the world's only sound until the solemn notes of the vespers rang out from the Congregational bell tower.

Soon the tide would turn, but it would be grim either way —whether the body was borne in upon it or if it was not.

Laura's eyelids slid closed and she relived the horror of those days right after news of Rye's death had reached the island. Against her arm she felt the touch of Dan's sleeve. He sat utterly still, resigned. Now she would be the one to comfort him as he'd once comforted her. She opened her eyes to study his melancholy posture, hunched forward, elbows to knees, and Rye, too, came into view. Laura closed her eyes again and resigned herself to remaining with Dan as his wife.

When she lifted her eyelids it was to feel Rye's gaze on her, and she turned to find his head rested tiredly against the wall, his face turned her way. His arms were crossed on his chest, feet flat on the floor, and knees widespread while his somber blue eyes studied her. She read in those eyes the memories of

the afternoon that came back with a haunting beauty. But
there was hopelessness, too, in the mournful yet loving expression, and for long minutes she was unable to tear her gaze
away. But then, of one accord, they turned their heads to face
the bay again.

Just then Dan sighed. His shoulders lifted, then slumped,
and he stared at the boards between his feet. Laura rested a
palm on his back. Rye's eyes followed it. Dan looked back
over his shoulder at Laura, then at the harbor again. As if
seeking the comforting assurance that life still went on, he
asked, "Where's Josh?"

Laura felt Rye's gaze move to her again as she answered,
"He's at Jimmy's house."

"Did he have a good time at Jane's?"

It was all Laura could do to answer, "Yes . . . yes, he loves
it there."

"What did they do today?"

Guiltily, Laura scoured her brain for a shred of the prattle
that had hardly infiltrated her mind while she and Josh had
walked home. She sensed Rye holding his breath, waiting for
her answer, and suddenly remembered what Josh had said.
"They made salt-water taffy."

From the corner of her eyes she saw Rye's shoulders wilt
with relief as his eyelids drifted shut. Laura experienced a new
agony at the duplicity she and Rye were practicing. Then, to
her horror, Dan stretched, rubbed the back of his neck, and
commented, "I don't know if it's the mention of something to
eat or what, but I keep thinking I smell oranges."

Rye shot up off the bench while Laura's face burned, but
Dan didn't turn around.

"Are you hungry, Dan?" Rye asked.

"No, I don't think I could eat if I tried."

But Rye went away just the same and returned with coffee,
again taking up his place on the far side of Dan and keeping
his eyes off Laura with an effort.

Twilight came on. They finished their coffee. Someone
brought sandwiches, but nobody ate. Dan sighed again, rose
from the hard bench, and walked aimlessly up the wharf to
stare out over the water, his back to Rye and Laura while only
the width of his absent shoulders separated them.

Soon he returned, took his place between them, and leaned back tiredly, then began speaking quietly. "I remember when the news came in that you were dead, Rye. Has Laura ever told you what a sea widow goes through?"

"Aye, a little. She said y'd got her through it."

A sound came from Dan's throat, a rueful half chuckle, while he shook his head tiredly, as if the memory must be cleared. Then he bent forward, again presenting a forlorn curve of shoulders to the two behind him while he went on in a heavy voice that seemed dredged up from the depths of despair.

"I was the one who got the job of going up to . . . to your house to tell Laura your ship had gone down. They sent me because the news came into the countinghouse and I was there working. And they knew, of course, that we were . . . we were best friends. I'll never forget how she looked that day when she opened the door." He paused, dropping his chin to his chest momentarily before he lifted it and stared vacantly across the harbor.

Laura wished Dan would lean back and cut off her view of Rye, but he didn't. Rye sat tensely, frowning at the back of Dan's neck.

"Do you know what Laura did when I broke the news to her?" When Rye remained silent, Dan glanced back over his shoulder briefly before facing away again. "She laughed," he said sadly. "She laughed and said, 'Don't be silly, Dan, Rye can't be dead. Why, he promised me he'd come back.' It would have been so much easier if she'd broken down and cried then and there, but she didn't. Not till months later. I suppose it was natural—her denial, I mean—especially since she had no corpse for proof."

Laura's palms were damp. Her stomach felt cramped. She wanted to leap to her feet and escape, but she was forced to sit and listen while Dan went on.

"After that, every time a sail was sighted, she'd run to the wharves to wait, certain that the ship was bringing you back, still claiming there'd been some mistake. I can see her yet, hurrying down the square with that awful, too-bright smile pasted on her face, and me wondering what to do to get her to admit the truth and go on from there. I remember one evening when there were no sails at all, the first time I caught her haunting an empty harbor as if willing you to appear. I told her there were no sails, that she was deluding herself, that you were never coming back, that people were beginning to titter about poor, odd Laura Dalton who hounded the wharves waiting for her ghost husband. She slapped me . . . hard. But afterwards she burst into tears . . . for the first time.''

Stop, Dan, stop! Laura begged silently. Why are you doing this? To punish us? But again he went on.

''She stood there facing me defiantly with the tears running down her face, and she said, 'But don't you see, Dan, he's got to come back because . . . because I'm carrying his baby.' That's when I first understood why she'd continued to deny your death as long as she had.''

Laura stared at the harbor now, dry-eyed, recalling the vigils she'd spent here while willing the sea to return Rye to her. And it had . . . but too late. He sat now only a body's width away from her, but separated by a chasm as deep and wide as hell's while the soliloquy went on.

''I followed her one day—it was November, I think, with the beginning of a sleet storm coming out of the northeast. When I caught up to her, she was standing at the top of the cliffs, staring at the ocean as usual. But this time I could see she was resigned. God, she made a pitiful sight with the rain pouring down on her face and her not moving, as if she didn't know or didn't care it was there. She'd . . .'' Dan swallowed loudly. ''She was rounded out already, and when I told her she shouldn't be out there in that wind and rain, that she had to think about the baby, she said she didn't give a damn about the baby.''

Not one of the three moved so much as a muscle. Dan's back might have been carved of stone while the eyes of Rye and Laura remained riveted on it. His voice dropped to a scarcely audible murmur.

''This time I slapped *her*. It nearly killed me to do it. I . . . I thought she'd been standing there thinking about . . . about killing herself, and the baby with her.'' Dan dropped his face into his palms. ''Oh God,'' he muttered against his hands, and the silence grew crushing before he finally raised his face, drew a deep breath, and went on. ''That was weeks after the news of your death, but it was the first time she cried, I mean really broke down and cried like I knew she hadn't before. She said her heart had drowned with you. That was exactly how she said it—'my heart drowned with Rye'—but at least she'd finally admitted you had drowned.

"After that, she finally agreed we should have a funeral." At last Dan rested his shoulders and head against the building again. He closed his eyes, and he rolled his head tiredly from side to side. "I never want to go through a thing like that again. There we were, praying for . . . for . . ." But he seemed unable to go on.

After a long pause he cleared his throat. "A funeral like that is hard on a woman. I don't want my mother to have to go through that." Then, abruptly, he rose, clumped down the echoing wharf, and stood staring out at Nantucket Bay, leaving the two behind him to wonder at his reason for delivering the painful recital.

At times it had sounded as if he were preparing himself to relinquish Laura to Rye, admitting he'd won her only by default. Yet at other times he seemed to be making it clear he was maintaining his claim on both her and Josh.

Rye Dalton interlaced his fingers across his belly. Inside, it fluttered from the vivid pictures Dan had drawn. Though his eyes were on the woeful figure before him, he was ever aware of Laura. He wanted to reach across the space that separated them and take her into his arms, kiss her eyelids, and soothe her for all she'd suffered over him. He needed very badly to touch her in an affirmation of life while they waited together for the verification of death. He loved her; she was the one he longed for, quite naturally, in this time of tragedy. Yet he could only sit with his hands pressed hard against his belly to keep them from reaching.

The mists came up, eerie fog fingers lending a ghostlike effect to the scene as the townspeople returned to the wharf with the uncanny timing of those who live by the tides. It was neap tide, that time of the lunar month when the difference between high and low tides is smallest. Did that mean the chance of a body washing in was better? Laura wondered. How odd that after living on the island all her life she didn't know the answer to that question. Would a body be bloated after being in the water for four or five hours? As she watched Hilda return with the others, Laura relived the dread she had borne once before while imagining Rye's body, claimed by the sea, fed upon by fishes. She wanted to go to Hilda and comfort her, but there was no consoling this anguish. If a wife was spared the uncertainty of a bodyless death, she must then suffer the nightmare of viewing the unsightly, distorted corpse, or worse, a portion of it, should the fish have been hungry.

As the search party formed, their voices were hushed and respectful. They carried lanterns, now, that burned their precious whale oil—for such an occasion it could be spared. The hazy haloes of light refracting off the thick salt air seemed to bear witness to the fact that Nantucketers did indeed live *and die* by the whales.

Cap'n Silas dispersed them in parties of two and three to comb the length of the inner harbor. Again, Laura, Dan, and Rye moved together, paralleling the whispering waves as they'd done countless times in years past. The gulf stream had warmed the summer waters to a balmy seventy-two degrees, yet Rye was chilled by dread as he moved to his grisly task, wading barefoot through the shallows, wondering when his foot might strike a soft, inert lump. Dan and Laura were shuffling through the wet-packed sand of the tide wrack.

Rye carried the lantern as the three inched along, more slowly than any of the other searchers, for fear of being the ones to stumble upon the corpse. The lantern revealed a black shape ahead and the three halted, their eyes instinctively seeking one another. In the glow of the burning whale oil and surrounded by fog, their faces were mere glimmers.

"I'll check it," Rye said, clamping his jaw and moving ahead. When the wavering light fell on the dark mass, he sighed with relief and turned back to Dan and Laura. "It's just a log."

They advanced again through the fog-thwarted night, the two men and the woman who seemed, by tradition, both of theirs. And during the hours of the search they shared her equally, and she them, without thought of possessing or belonging. All enmity was, for the time, gone, displaced by the need to remain close, to support one another and draw sustenance for what lay ahead.

The body was found shortly after midnight, "neaped" on the shore after the tide had turned back to sea. The church bell signaled the message. At the sound of its muffled knell in the distance, three heads snapped up. Nobody moved. Rye stood yet in the water. Laura, still in her white dress with its hem gray and ruined, looked like a ghost beside Dan in his dark, shrunken suit.

Rye broke the silence. "They must have found him. We'd better go."

Yet they were reluctant to turn back. Waves slapped softly at Rye's ankles. The night air was thick and blanketing. The eerie bonging of the bell sent shivers up their spines.

Finally, Rye moved to Dan's side, placed a hand on his arm, and felt shudders there. "Are you all right?"

Dan seemed to be staring at nothing. "Let's just hope the sea returned a whole body."

Rye moved his hand to the side of Dan's neck and let the pressure of his palm speak a message too poignant for words. He turned, the lantern swinging squeakily on its hinges, and as if by some silent signal, Rye and Laura moved to flank Dan as together they made their way back, trudging desultorily through the fog, with shoulders often touching.

The sea had been generous. It had returned Zachary Morgan whole, undistorted. It was the living who felt distorted by the events of that day and that night, for in the moment just before parting, when Dan stood hollow-eyed, weaving as if ready to collapse, he reached a hand to Rye in thanks. As their palms touched and then clutched, they found themselves again roughly clinging while Laura stood in the shifting mists, watching.

Separating from Dan, Rye turned to her and ordered softly, "Take him home to bed. He needs some sleep." Speaking the words, Rye felt as if he, too, were drowning.

Laura's eyes were incredibly weary as she looked up at Rye. The tracks of tears painted colorless lines down her cheeks, reflecting the light from the lantern. Then suddenly she moved close, swirling about Rye like the night mists, her arms momentarily easing his pain as she pressed her cheek against his.

"Thank you, Rye."

Over her shoulder, Rye saw Dan looking on while a single, raspy word came to his own throat. "Aye." His hand touched the small of Laura's back for only a brief second, then she and Dan were gone, into the eerie fog that shut them away and left Rye isolated, alone.

Heaving his tired legs up the lonely steps to the loft above the cooperage, he pictured Laura and Dan going to bed together, comforting each other. He fell onto his own bed with a weary sigh, eyes sinking shut, wishing for arms to comfort him, too. The day's events passed before him in hazy review, and he rolled over, curling his body toward the wall.

Then without warning, Rye Dalton wept, anguished sobs of hopelessness and grief such as he had not known since he was a boy. Ship heard and came ambling across the dark loft to stand beside the bunk uncertainly, emitting a sorrowful whine of compassion. While her nostrils dilated, the dog turned questioningly toward the place where the old man lay. But there was no answer. Ship whined pitifully again, but the sounds from the bed continued and no loving hand reached out to assure. So she laid her chin on the warm back and whimpered while shudders lifted the ribs of her master, even after he at last slept in exhaustion.

Chapter 13

ZACHARY MORGAN'S FUNERAL was held two days later. It was a flawlessly clear day, and gulls scolded from an azure sky while mourners pressed in a wide, deep circle around the grave. Laura's mother was there, along with Jane and John Durning and all their children. So was Josiah, as well as aunts, uncles, and cousins of both Dan and Rye—so many on the island were related. Friends, too, had come to pay last respects, among them DeLaine Hussey, the Starbucks, and everyone who worked at the countinghouse, which was closed for the afternoon.

Laura wore a black bombazine dress and a coal scuttle hat with a nubby veil that covered her face to the chin. She stood beside Dan and his family while Rye faced her from the opposite side of the grave. He stood in the traditional pose of funereal respect—feet spraddled, the palm of one hand clasping the back of the other over his lower abdomen. From behind her black veil, Laura studied his somber face while the rector's monotone drifted above the silent gathering. Then it, too, fell still, and the bombazine crackled as Josh shifted restlessly and pressed against Laura's legs. He jerked on her hand and she looked down.

"Are they gonna bury Grampa in the dirt?" Josh asked plaintively, his voice carrying clearly across the silent graveside. "I don't want Grampa to get buried in the dirt." Laura smoothed Josh's hair with a black-gloved hand, leaning over his head to whisper comforting words as the muffled sound of weeping increased upon the heels of his innocent question.

Straightening, Laura found Rye's gaze on her from across the grave. Josh started whimpering, and Rye looked at him with an expression of helplessness.

Beside Laura, Dan bent and picked up Josh in his arms, whispering something, while again Rye's gaze followed, fixing on the child's palm, which rested on Dan's cheek as the two exchanged words too soft to be heard across the grave. Laura leaned near them, her head close to Dan's as she rested a hand on Josh's small back, and they whispered. When she turned to attend the proceedings again, she found Rye still watching the three of them with the same wounded look. But she sensed Ruth observing every exchange of glances, so she dropped her eyes to the black-draped coffin with its spray of summer gladiolas and chrysanthemums from somebody's island garden.

The final prayers were intoned and the last hymn was sung. At a soft word from the minister, Rye and three others leaned to grasp the ropes while the weight of the coffin was released from wooden slats across the grave. Then the ropes creaked and the coffin swung slightly as it was lowered and finally touched the earth. Rye went down on one knee, pulling his rope up hand over hand, while Laura trained her eyes on that knee, battling against a new freshet of tears. As Rye again stood up, she blinked and saw the black fabric of his trouser leg now covered with a pale dusting of sand. The sight of it clinging there created a new surge of sorrow within Laura. She lifted her eyes behind the black veil with a look of desolation while the silence was broken by the soft sound of weeping, and Laura longed to go to Rye, to brush the sand from his knee and the agony from his brow. His eyes said a hundred things, but she understood one above all others: when? Now that this has happened—when?

She turned away, unable to offer even a reassuring glance, no matter how badly she wanted to. There was Hilda weeping as the first spadeful of dirt fell, and Dan with his eyes filled, too, and Josh, too young to understand, but forced to be here by rigid religious custom that Laura was helpless to change.

It was past midafternoon when the funeral party repaired to the home of Tom and Dorothy Morgan to share foods provided by friends and neighbors from all over the island. Black-clad matrons tended to setting out meats, pies, and breads on the trestle table in the keeping room, replenishing bowls, and constantly washing dishes and pewterware. Beer was abundant, for here on Nantucket it was as common a drink as water, being taken on every whaling voyage as a preventative for scurvy.

Tom Morgan's house was a saltbox like most on the island, consisting of a keeping room with two linters and a loft, scarcely enough room to hold the many who came to offer condolences. Rye stood in the yard with an overflow of men who drank beer, smoked pipes, and discussed news of the day. A Harvard graduate named Henry Thoreau had perfected a new gimmick called a lead pencil . . . some were saying there was danger of depleting the ocean of whales while others said such an idea was crazy . . . talk moved on to a discussion of the profits to be had by converting whaleships to haul ice from New England to the tropics.

But Rye's interest in the conversation died when he saw Laura step from the back linter, carrying a bucket. She crossed the yard to the sweep well and leaned over the rock coping to hook the rope handle in place. Rye quickly scanned the yard, looking for Dan, but finding him nowhere in sight, he excused himself and crossed to the sweep. It consisted of a long post, offset on a forked support that was anchored in the ground. It was weighted on its short end by a stone cradle, while the longer end of the pole hovered above the mouth of the well, making it easy to bring a full bucket up, but a struggle to get the empty bucket down. As Rye approached, Laura was leaning over the coping, straining on the rope.

"Let me help y' with that."

"Oh, Rye!" At the sound of his voice, Laura straightened with a snap. The rope slipped from her palms and the sweep pole flew into the air. She pressed a hand to her heart and quickly scanned the yard. Her coal scuttle hat was gone, the veil no longer shielding her face.

"Y' look tired, darlin'. Has it been bad?" One of Rye's

hands closed on the rope, but he made no further move to lower it, looking instead into Laura's distressed eyes.

"I think you must not call me darling anymore."

"Laura—" He seemed about to drop the rope and take a step toward her.

"Rye, lower the bucket. People are watching us."

A quick glance confirmed it, so Rye tended to the task, forcing the pail down, hand over hand, until they heard it splash below.

"Laura, this doesn't change anything."

"How can you say that?"

"I still love y'. I'm still Josh's father."

"Rye, someone will hear."

The pail was back up. He rested a hand on its rope handle while it hung, dripping, above the mouth of the well, the sound echoing up to them in faraway musical blips while he filled his eyes with her. "Let them hear. There isn't a soul in this yard who doesn't know how I feel about y' and that y' were mine first."

The shadows beneath her eyes seemed to darken as she cast a furtive glance at the curious people who studied them. "Please, Rye," she whispered. "Give me the pail."

He reached above the well coping, and her eyes followed the strong muscles beneath the black suit jacket while his shoulders turned away and he hefted the pail. When he swung around he disregarded the hand that reached for the pail, turning toward the back linter, giving Laura no recourse but to follow at his side. He paused to let her move ahead of him, then followed into the cramped space containing ranks of wood and an assortment of wooden pails and tubs hanging on the wall. Inside, they were momentarily out of sight of either yard or house.

Laura glanced nervously toward the door leading into the keeping room from the rear, but it remained closed. "Rye, I can't—"

"Shh." His fingers touched her lips.

Their eyes met—troubled blue eyes fixed on worried brown ones.

The touch of his fingers on her flesh was like balm, but she forced herself to pull back. "Rye, don't touch me. It only makes it harder."

"Laura, I love y'."

"And don't say that . . . not now. Everything is changed, don't you see?"

His gaze roved over her face, studying the depths of her eyes, where he read things he did not want to read. "Why did this have t' happen now?" he asked miserably.

"Maybe it was a message to us."

His expression grew stern, and his voice was a hiss. "Don't say that—don't even think it! Zachary's death had nothin' to do with us, nothing!"

"Didn't it?" She studied him levelly.

"No!"

"Then why do I feel like I personally sent that boat bow over stern?"

"Laura, I knew that's what y' were thinkin' while we sat on the wharf beside Dan that night, but I won't have y' believin' such a thing." He still held the bucket in one hand while with his other he squeezed her upper arm, making the bombazine sleeve crackle in the confines of the linter.

"Don't you?"

Her eyes remained steadfastly on him, forcing him to admit the awful possibility. He wanted to answer no, but could not. The evening light bounced off the white shells outside the doorway, reflecting inside and lighting her face from below, giving her an ethereal glow, like an angel of judgment. She reached for the handle of the pail, but he refused to relinquish it. He studied her face, wanting her back worse than ever, now that he'd again had a taste of her body. Yet it was not her body alone he craved. He craved a return to things as they used to be, contentment, peace, sharing their home. And now their son. Yet Rye Dalton, even in the depths of his want, could not deny her words or force her to come back to him any sooner than she was ready. Their hands slipped close together on the rope, and he raised his free hand to touch her jaw.

"Is it so wrong for us t' want t' be together when we love each other?"

"What we did was wrong, Rye, yes."

His eyes took on a new pain. "How can y' call it wrong, Laura, knowing what it was like—what it always was like between us? How can y' walk away and st—"

The kitchen door suddenly opened.

"Oh, excuse me." Ruth Morgan confronted them with reproof in every unsmiling muscle of her face. "We were beginning to wonder if Laura dropped down the well, but I can see what's taken so long."

Rye flashed Dan's sister a look of sheer loathing, thinking that if she'd ever gone out and gotten herself frenzied with a man, she wouldn't have such a burr under her corsets when somebody else did. Ruth Morgan was nothing but a dried-up old maid who wouldn't know what to do with a man if she had one, Rye thought as he strode angrily into the keeping room and clapped the pail down.

The remainder of the day found Laura growing increasingly uncomfortable as Ruth Morgan's censure became more evident. At times she ostentatiously held her skirts from brushing Laura's hem as they moved about in the keeping room, clearing away dishes and foods. Rye did not leave, as Laura hoped he would. Instead, he was one of those who remained as night drew on and the men moved inside to continue drinking the everlasting beer. But Dan had already overindulged and had reached that maudlin stage of drunkenness accompanied by depression and self-pitying gibberish.

He sat at the trestle table in the keeping room, elbow to elbow with a group of others, his head slung low while his arms sometimes slipped clumsily off the table edge.

"The old man was always after me to be a fisherman." He swayed toward the companion at his left and looked blearily into the man's eyes. "Never liked the stink of fish, did I, Laura? Not like you and Rye." He twisted to pick her out where she sat with the women while Rye stood near the fireplace, looking on silently from behind Dan's back.

Laura rose. "Come, Dan, let's go home."

"Whatsa matter? Did Rye have t' leave?" Dan turned a loose, inebriated smile to the circle of men at the table, and brandished a floppy hand. "Party's over for my wife once Rye Dalton's not around anymore. Did I ever tell you—"

"You're drunk, Dan." Rye interrupted as he moved behind the slouched form. "Time to put your glass down and go home with Laura." He took the mug from Dan's hand and set it on the table with a decisive thud.

Dan twisted at the waist, turning watery eyes up at the man looming behind him. "Well, if it isn't my friend Rye Dalton, the one I share a wife with." He smiled crookedly.

Horrified, Laura saw everyone in the room look away uncomfortably. Feet shifted, sounding like thunder, then an awful silence hovered in the tense air.

"That's enough, Dan!" Rye spoke sharply, skewering the drunk man with a look of warning, ever aware of Laura waiting uncertainly behind them with Josh at her side, and of Ruth, standing in the dark corner of the room, her eyes snapping.

"I just wanted to tell the story of the three musketeers who grew up sharing everything. But I guess they all know it anyway." Dan's eyes went from man to man around the table, finally coming back to rest on Rye. "Yup! Guess they all know about it. No sense tellin' 'em what they already know. Where's that wife of ours, eh, Rye?"

Laura's face was poppy-red while Rye's looked thunderous. He stood stern and unmoving, scarcely holding himself back from plucking Dan to his feet and slamming a fist into him to shut him up.

"She's *your* wife, and she's waitin' for y' to gather yer wits and go home with 'er. Now put down the mug and stop makin' an ass o' yerself."

Murky eyes appealed to the circle of faces. "Am I making an ass of myself?"

Finally, one of the men suggested, "Why don't you do what Rye says? Go on home with Laura now."

Dan smiled stupidly at the tabletop, then nodded at it. "Yup, I guess you're right. 'Cause if I don't, my friend here will."

"Dan! Have y' forgotten y'r son is in the room?" Rye snapped, the anger growing more evident in each word.

"*My* son . . . now there's a subject I'd like to take up, too."

Rye waited no longer. With power spawned by rage, he

clutched the shoulders of Dan's jacket and jerked him to his feet, sending the table screeching back as Dan's body jarred against it. Rye spun the limp form around and clutched Dan's lapels roughly, then ground out his next words through nearly clenched teeth. "Y'r *wife* is waiting for y' t' straighten up and take her and Josh home. Now are y' going t' do it, or do I have t' crack y' one to bring y' to your senses!"

Sobered somewhat, Dan yanked himself free of Rye's grip, shrugging his jacket back into place, then wavering a moment while trying to gather dignity that could not be restored in one so far gone.

"You always did have your way with her, Rye, starting when the two of you were—"

That was the last word Dan uttered. Rye's fist whistled out of nowhere and settled into Dan's stomach with a thud. A single grunt swooshed from Dan before he folded in half and slumped into Rye's arms.

Laura's hands flew to her mouth as Josh came to life, racing across the room, crying, "You hit my papa! You hit my papa! Put him down! Papa . . . Papa!" The pitiful little creature rushed to Dan's defense, but Rye bent down, put a shoulder to the inert stomach, and lifted the man onto his broad shoulder like a sack of potatoes. Before Laura could stop Josh, he'd fallen against Rye's stomach, punching him and yelling, "I hate you! I hate you! You hit my papa!"

It had happened so fast, Laura was stunned. But she finally moved, lurching forward to pull Josh away from Rye and calm him, then finally turn him toward the door.

Rye bounced Dan more comfortably onto his shoulder and spoke to a shocked Tom and Dorothy Morgan. "I apologize for the scene, but it's been a rough day for Dan. My condolences on the death of y'r brother." Then, turning to Laura, he ignored the curious onlookers, and ordered, "Come on, let's get him and the boy home."

They left the house without looking back, realizing that behind them speculation billowed. Rye's long legs strode along the cobblestones while Laura hurried to keep up. Josh was still crying, but she tugged him along by the hand.

"Why did he hit Papa?" Josh whimpered.

Rye stalked along without slowing or glancing at either Laura or Josh.

"Papa had too much beer," was all Laura could think of as explanation.

"But he hit him!"

"Hush, Joshua."

The heavy clump of Rye's heels led the way while Laura followed with her heart breaking and her son too young to comprehend any of it.

"And he put Grampa in that hole so they could bury him in the dirt."

"Joshua, I said hush!"

She yanked at Josh's hand and his head snapped. But when his accusations subsided into sniffling, tears brimmed in Laura's eyes and guilt tore at her insides. She leaned to scoop Josh into her arms and carry him the rest of the way home while he buried his wet face against her neck, clinging and confused.

When they reached the *Y* in the path, Rye stalked on ahead and she followed the sound of his footsteps up the scallop shells in the dark. At the door of the saltbox, Rye paused, letting her enter first. He stood with Dan's dead weight now creating an unbearable ache on his shoulder, listening as Laura found the tinderbox and lit the candles. As the light blossomed around them, her dark eyes sought Rye, then immediately she ordered Josh, "Get your nightshirt on, and I'll tuck you in in a minute."

She left him standing in the middle of the keeping room, watching as she led the way into the bedroom linter with a candle. Standing back, she watched Rye dump Dan's inert body on the bed. When he straightened, his eyes moved around the room from the bed to the partially opened door of the chifforobe where Laura's and Dan's clothing hung, to the small commode where her whalebone comb rested beside a pitcher and bowl. When his eyes at last came back to her, standing in the doorway with her hands clasped tightly against her bosom, Rye's expression was closed and stiff.

"You'd better take his clothes off."

Laura swallowed the lump in her throat and moved farther

into the room. But there was little space, and as she neared the bed Rye was forced to step around her. He moved to the door as she bent over Dan and began removing his shoes.

From the doorway, Rye watched her lift one foot, then the other, and set Dan's shoes quietly on the floor beside the bed. She loosened his tie, then slipped it free and laid it on the commode. She freed the button at Dan's throat while Rye remembered those hands removing his own clothing such a short time ago in the meadow. He scowled as Laura sat on the edge of the bed and struggled to remove Dan's jacket, but his limp body refused to comply, and at last Rye ordered, "Leave him to me and go see to the boy."

She stood to face him again, and he saw tear-filled eyes and quivering lips. Then she brushed around him, holding her skirts well aside as she hurried out.

Rye removed Dan's coat, trousers, and shirt and managed to roll him beneath the covers into an unconscious, snoring heap. He studied Dan for a long minute, then—more slowly this time—he looked across the room. He stepped to the commode, picked up Laura's comb, and ran his thumbnail along its teeth. He brushed the back of his fingers along a towel hanging on a mirrored rack on the wall behind the pitcher. Swiveling slowly around, Rye confronted the chifforobe. With a single finger he slowly opened the carved mahogany door. It widened silently, and he removed his finger and slipped it inside his waistcoat pocket while his gaze glided over the contents of the chifforobe where her dresses hung beside Dan's shirts and suits. He reached out to finger the sleeve of the yellow dress she'd worn that first day he'd seen her in the market. He worked the fabric lightly between his fingertips, then wearily dropped his hand and sighed, deep and long. Glancing over his shoulder at the man sleeping behind him, Rye silently closed the chifforobe door before blowing out the candle and returning to the keeping room.

Laura was sitting on the edge of the alcove bed, tucking Josh in for the night. Rye told his feet to remain where they were, but the temptation was too great. With slow steps, he crossed to stand beside the bed and look down at Josh over Laura's shoulder. She leaned to kiss the child's face, which was still puffy and red from crying.

"Good night, darling."

But Josh's lip trembled, and he had eyes only for the man who hovered behind his mother. The accusing stare scored Rye's heart, but he submerged the hurt and moved a step nearer. As he did, his hips and stomach came lightly against Laura's back. He reached a hand over her shoulder and touched the boy's fine, soft bangs with a calloused finger while Josh's eyes remained wary and defensive.

"I'm sorry I hit your papa."

"You said you was his friend," the quavery little voice accused.

"Aye, and I am."

Laura watched the long, tanned finger slide away from the blond hair and retreat somewhere behind her, but she felt the warmth of Rye's body still pressing comfortingly against her back.

"I don't believe you." The little chin trembled. "And . . . and you put that box in the ground with my grampa in it."

"He's the one taught me t' fish when I wasn't much older than you. I loved him, too, but he's dead now. That's why we had t' put him in the ground."

"And I'll never see him again?"

Sadly, silently, Rye shook his head, assuming the role of father now, but with a pain he'd never imagined it might bring.

Josh dropped his gaze to the blanket over his chest, picking at it with an index finger. "I didn't think so, but nobody'd tell me for sure."

Rye felt a tremor run through Laura and lightly rested his palm on her shoulder. "That's because they didn't want t' hurt y' or make y' cry. They didn't think y'd understand, bein' y're only four."

"I'm almost five."

"Aye, I know. And that's old enough t' understand that y'r . . . y'r papa is going t' be very lonesome for his papa for a while. He's goin' t' need lots o' cheerin' up." Rye looked down at the top of Laura's head. "And y'r mama, too," he added with great tenderness.

Unable to stay there between the two of them and contain her tears a moment longer, Laura again leaned to kiss Josh.

"Go to sleep now, darling. I'll be right here."

He turned over on his side, facing the wall, curling up into a little ball. But when he felt Laura's weight shift off his bed, he looked back over his shoulder. "Don't shut my doors, Mama."

"N . . . no, Josh, I won't."

She left the hinged doors wide and turned, wiping tears from her eyes. When she'd crossed to the far side of the room beyond Josh's range of vision, Rye remained where he was, studying the boy. From the bedroom came the sound of Dan's sonorous breathing, his repetitive soft snore the only sound in the dusky room. Rye looked at Laura's back, then tiredly crossed to stand behind her, studying the intricate coil of hair at the back of her neck, the tight stricture of her black mourning dress across her slumping shoulders. From behind, he covered her upper arms, chafing them gently, watching the tender hollow at the back of her neck as she dropped her face into her hands and wept softly.

"Aw, Laura-love," he uttered in a shaken whisper, pulling her back against his chest, feeling her shoulders shaking. She stifled her sobs into her palms, and he drew a handkerchief from his pocket and pressed it into her hands. He let her weep, feeling so much like weeping himself, but swallowing thickly, closing his eyes and rubbing her arms once again.

"Oh R . . . Rye, I feel so guilty, and I'm even more ashamed because I've been mourning as much for us as for Zachary."

He spun her around and crushed her against him. Her arms clung to his back as his head dropped down to her shoulder and they rocked together, solacing each other.

Josh heard his mother's sobs and slipped his feet over the edge of his alcove bed to stand beside it uncertainly, one hand still under the blankets while he watched the wide back of the man curving to hold her. He saw his mother's arms come up around Rye's neck, then the big man rocked her, the way she sometimes rocked Josh when he felt bad and cried. Josh studied them silently, perplexed, wondering whether or not he should be mad at Rye for hitting Papa like he had. It seemed like Mama would be mad at Rye . . . but she wasn't. Instead, she was hugging him and had buried her face in his neck just as Josh had buried his face against her when Laura carried

him home tonight. Again he heard his mother's muffled sobs,
and while the two rocked from side to side, the boy caught a
glimpse of Rye's wide hand holding the back of his mother's
head tight against him. He watched a moment longer, remembering how Rye had said his mother, too, would need cheering
up. Then, silently, Josh lifted a knee to climb back into his bed
again, to listen and wonder and decide that mamas, too, liked
to be hugged.

Laura wept bitterly, allowing the full flood of grief to
escape as it hadn't during the past three days.

"Laura . . . Laura . . ." Rye said against her hair.

"Hold me, Rye, oh hold me. Oh my darling, what you must
have suffered through these last three days."

"Shh . . . hush, love," he intoned softly.

But she went on. "My heart broke for you when I saw you
facing Dan at the end of the wharf, and . . . and when I saw
you hold him in your arms and comfort him. And again along
the beach while we were searching. Oh, Rye, I wanted to rush
to you and hold you and tell you I loved you for what you
were doing for him. He . . . he needed you so badly then. I
sometimes think that fate keeps throwing the three of us
together, knowing we all need each other."

"Damn fate, then. I've had all of it I can stand!" His voice
shook as he held her near, running a hand along her back.

"Rye, I'm so sorry about Josh tonight. But he'll get over it
and stop blaming you."

Rye backed away abruptly, gripping the sides of her head.
"It's not them I care about. It's not them I need. It's you!"
He gave her head one emphatic shake and their eyes delved
deeply into each other's. Then he took her roughly against him
again, breathing in the scent of her hair and skin, his voice a
murmur of despair at her ear. "Why did this have t' happen
now? Why now?"

"Maybe we've been made to pay for our sins."

"We did *not* sin! We are victims of circumstance, just like
the others are. Yet we're the ones made t' suffer, t' stay apart,
when it's none of our doing. We belong together, Laura, so
much more than you and Dan do."

Her tears flowed afresh. "I know. But . . . but I can't leave
him now, don't you see? How can I leave him at the worst

time of his life, when he supported me through the worst time of mine? What would people say?"

"I don't give a damn what they'll say. I want y' back, and Josh along with y'."

"You know that's not possible, not now . . . not for a while."

Again he backed away. "How long?" His blue eyes were beginning to show anger.

"Until a decent period of mourning has passed."

"The mourning be damned! Zachary Morgan is dead, but must we pretend we died with him? We're alive, and we've wasted five years already."

"Please, Rye, please understand. I want to be with you. I . . . I love you so."

Suddenly Rye grew still. He studied her face in the dim light from the candle across the room. "But y' love him, too, don't y'?"

Her eyes dropped to Rye's chest, and when after a long silence she neither looked up nor answered, he moved his hands to span her throat, pressing his thumbs up against the underside of her jaw, forcing her to meet his gaze.

"Y' love him, too," he reiterated painfully.

"We both do, Rye, don't we?"

"Is that what it is?" He searched her brown eyes with their spiky, wet lashes while from the bedroom came the steady sound of Dan's snoring.

"Yes, that's why it hurts both of us so much to see him this way."

"Does he drink this much often?"

"More and more often lately, it seems. He knows how I feel about you, and he . . . he drinks to forget it."

"And so either way his turnin' to alcohol will bind y' t' him with guilt. If y' stay, he drinks because he knows y' want t' leave. And if y' leave, he drinks because y' did not stay."

"Oh, Rye, you sound so bitter. He's a far weaker man than you. Can't you take pity on him?"

"Don't ask me t' pity him, Laura. It's enough that I love him, God help my soul, but I will not pity him for usin' his weakness t' hold y'."

"It's not just that, Rye. This island is so small. What would people say if I walked away from him now? You saw the looks we got from Ruth today."

"Ruth!" Rye exclaimed in an exasperated whisper. "Ruth'd do well t' go out and spread her legs under a man so she'd know what hell you're goin' through!"

"Rye, please, you must not—"

He gripped her jaw and kissed her mouth with a battering assault of his own until he became aware of her working to free herself from the pressure of his thumbs. Then he hugged her to him, immediately repentant.

"Oh God, I'm sorry, Laura. It's just that I can't bear t' walk out of here and think of y' in that bed beside him when it should be you and me sharin' it as we used to."

"Six months," she said. "Can you bear it for six months?"

"Six months?" The words fell cold from his lips. "Y' may as well ask me t' bear it for six years. It would be as easy."

"It'll be no easier for me, Rye, you have to know that."

His thumbs brushed her cheeks, softly now, lovingly. "Tell me, is it possible you could be carryin' my baby now? Because I won't let y' stay with him if there's any chance of it whatsoever."

"No. It's the wrong time of month."

His haunted eyes roved her face. "Will y' let him make love to y'?"

She pulled away and turned her back on him. "Rye, why do you torture—"

"Why?" He spun her around by an arm. His eyes were blazing. "Y' do love him or, by God, you, too, would be tortured by the thought!"

She clutched his forearms. "I pity him. I've betrayed him, and I owe him something for that."

"And while y're payin' y'r debt, what if y' become pregnant with his child? What will y' do then? Plead for more time while y' decide which of the two fathers y'll grant y'r favors to next time?"

She struck at him then, but he backed away just before her hand hit its mark.

Chagrined, she reached to touch his chest. "Oh, Rye, I'm

sorry. Don't you see, we're angry at what we're forced to do, not at each other? We strike out this way because we can't strike out at the true cause of our trouble.''

"The true cause of our trouble is y'r obstinance, and y' can end it with a single word—yes! Yet y' choose not to.''

He stalked toward the door.

"Rye, where are you going?''

He turned, lowering his voice when he caught sight of the alcove bed in the shadows behind her. "I'm leaving y' to your drunken husband, who is not worthy of y' yet somehow manages to keep y' loyal even while he snores in that besotted state. Six months y' ask for? All right, I'll give y' six months. But during that time, keep out of my sight, woman, or I'll see t' it y' betray y'r husband again, and I won't be fussy about where or when or who knows about it. The whole island can watch for all I care, and Ruth Morgan and her ilk can take lessons!''

Chapter 14

DAN MORGAN AWAKENED the following morning to the sight of Laura lying beside him, still in her whalebone corsets. He groaned, remembering, and rolled to the side of the bed, where he sat clutching his head. He dug the heels of his hands into his eye sockets, then straightened gingerly, holding his stomach while he unfolded one muscle at a time. As he eased to his feet, the power of Rye Dalton's fist made itself felt in every muscle of his torso.

At Dan's soft groan, Laura awakened, bracing up on an elbow to ask sleepily, "Dan, are you all right?"

He was ashamed to face his wife after the public insinuations he'd made yesterday. Glancing over his shoulder, Dan's shame redoubled at the realization that he hadn't even remained sober enough to help her out of her stays, but instead had left her to sleep in them like a freshly wrapped mummy.

He sank to the edge of the bed, again clutching the sides of his head and staring at the floor between his bare feet. "Laura, I'm sorry."

She touched his shoulder. "Dan, this drinking has got to stop. It won't solve anything."

"I know," he mumbled forlornly. "I know."

The back of his hair was mussed and flattened. She touched it reassuringly. "Promise me you'll come home for supper tonight."

He dropped his head farther forward and rubbed the back

of it, brushing her touch away. Then his shoulders lifted as he sighed deeply. "I promise."

He got to his feet slowly, stretching his ribs and breathing carefully, then clumped out of the room to begin getting ready for work. They spoke little, but when he was ready to leave for the countinghouse, wearing the black armband of mourning on his left sleeve, Laura stepped up behind him and rested a hand on his shoulder.

"Don't forget . . . you promised."

But all day long as Dan worked over his ledgers, the figures on the pages seemed to twine themselves into the shapes of Rye and Laura, and when he left work at the end of the day, Dan knew he could not go home without fortification.

So he turned back toward Water Street and entered the Blue Anchor Pub. The place was adorned with quarter boards bearing the names of old vessels, the most prominent from a long-gone ship called *The Blue Lady*. Whaling paraphernalia hung from the walls and from the open beams of the ceiling: harpoons, flensing knives, macrame, and scrimshaw. But best of all, kegs of beer and ale rested on their cradles at the rear of the room. Behind the kegs hung the personal tankards of the clientele who frequented the place, but since there was none with Dan's name, the alekeeper produced one of his own, offering his condolences by way of a free round of "flip"—a powerful mixture of apple cider and rum. By the time Dan left for home, it was dark and long past the supper hour.

Laura looked up when Dan entered the keeping room. It took little more than a glance to know what had detained him. His movements were slow and deliberate as he hung up his beaver hat, then turned to stare at the table, where a single plate waited.

"I'm sorry, Laura." He slurred the words, weaving slightly, but making no move toward the trestle.

Laura stood behind a ladderback chair, clutching its top rung. "Dan, I was so worried."

"Were you?" Silence fell heavily while he studied her with bleary eyes. "Were you?" he repeated, more quietly.

"Of course. You promised me this morning—"

He waved a hand as if shooing away a fly, tucked two

fingers into his watch pocket, gazed at the ceiling, and swayed silently.

"Dan, you have to eat something."

He gestured vaguely toward the table. "Don't bother with supper for me. I'll just—" His words trailed away listlessly, and he sighed. His chin dropped to his chest as if he'd fallen asleep on his feet.

Dear God, what have I done to him? Laura asked herself.

But the days that followed were to answer her tortured question only too plainly, for Dan Morgan was a wretched and torn man. And though he had promised to end his intemperance, his own personal tankard soon came to hang on the wall pegs behind the barrels at the Blue Anchor. Before long, his wife, waiting in the candlelit house on Crooked Record Lane, set aside her whalebone corsets and returned to the unbound freedom of only a chemise, for too many nights there was no one to help with her laces.

Summer drew to a close, and Laura filled her days with countless preparations for winter. The wild beach plums came ripe, and Laura took Josh with her to gather the fruit in baleen—whalebone—baskets, haul them home, and make mincemeat and preserves. But as she hurried back from her day on the moors, it was with a heartful of memories of Rye and to face an empty supper table, a lonely house, for Dan continued his late nights at the Blue Anchor.

Josh begged to go picking grapes next, and though Laura knew they hung in royal purple splendor in the best arbor on the island, she was reluctant to go there again and face more poignant memories. But the grapes were a ready source of provender for the making of jam, juice, and the dried, sugared sweetmeats called comfits, Josh's favorites, so at last Laura went. The sight of the arbor brought back a renewed surge of longing for Rye, but these thoughts were immediately followed by the now-familiar guilt that always came in their wake, especially that particular night, when Dan again appeared at supper and stayed home in the evening, lavishing time on Josh. Laura's spirits buoyed as Dan remained punctual and sober for several days. She put thoughts of Rye from her mind and strove to make their home the happy place it had once been.

But then one morning when Dan reached into the chifforobe for a fresh shirt, something fell to the floor—Laura's corset. He leaned to pick it up and held it in hands that were always slightly shaky these days. He stared disconsolately as he rubbed a thumb absently on a whalebone, then closed his eyes for a moment, wondering what was to become of his marriage. When he opened them, he saw part of a stay projecting from its cotton sheath. Haltingly, he reached to touch its smooth, rounded end, only to realize it was not just any whalebone but a busk. With growing dread he slipped it up until, word by word, the carving was revealed.

He stood a long time, head and shoulders drooping, as he read and reread the scrimshawed poem beneath his thumb. After some minutes he swallowed hard, then reeled on his feet as if Rye Dalton's fist had again leveled him. He pictured himself helping Laura cinch up the strings that had pressed Rye's words of love against her skin, and Dan suffered afresh the rending truth: Laura had never stopped loving Rye. Rye had always been and would always be her first choice.

"Dan, your breakfast is ready," Laura announced from behind him.

He dropped the corset, shut the chifforobe door, and spun around.

"Dan, what's wrong?" she said. He looked stricken and slightly ill. She glanced down to see what he held, but in his hands was only a clean shirt, and as he shrugged it on, he insisted nothing was amiss.

But after that, it was later than ever when Dan returned home at night.

September arrived. Dame school would soon open in the parlors across the island, thus several mothers planned a last squantum on the beach for a group of island children. Though it would be another year yet before Josh started school, he was included and went off exuberantly with Jimmy.

When the picnicking and games were over, the two boys went off by themselves. On their knees, they dug frantically after sandcrabs, which could bury themselves faster than any boy could dig them up. They laughed and sent sand flying behind them, knowing it was useless, but enjoying the pursuit for itself. Finally, Jimmy gave up, dropped back onto his haunches, and said, "I heard somethin' at your grampa's funeral that I bet you don't know."

"What?" Josh went on digging.

"I ain't supposed to tell you, 'cause when Mama found me standin' there listening to them ladies, she made me promise not to, and then she scooted me out so I couldn't hear no more."

Josh's interest was immediately diverted and he turned to his friend, bright with curiosity. "Yeah? What'd she say?"

Jimmy made a pretense of sifting sand through his fingers in search of small shells. "I wasn't gonna tell you, but then . . ." He squinted up at the younger boy, suddenly unsure of the wisdom of divulging the secret. But finally he went on. "Well, I got to thinkin', and if it's true what they said, well, you and me, we're cousins."

"Cousins?" Josh's eyes were round with surprise. "You mean like me and all of Aunt Jane's kids?"

"Uh-huh."

"You heard your mama say *that*?"

"Well, no, not exactly. She was talking to my Aunt Elspeth and they said your real pa ain't . . . well, the one you got, but that other man, Rye Dalton."

Josh was silent for a moment, then said disbelievingly, "They din't neither."

"They did too! They said Rye Dalton was your real pa, and if he is, then you and me are cousins, 'cause—"

"He ain't my pa!" Josh was on his feet now. "He can't be or my mama would know."

"He is too!"

"You liar!"

"What're you so mad about—gosh, I thought you'd like bein' my cousint!"

Josh was having a hard time keeping from crying. "It ain't true, you . . . you . . ." He searched for the worst word he knew. "You liar! Dummy! Poop!"

"I ain't no liar. Mr. Dalton, he's some cousint of my pa's,

and that's why his name's even Rye, 'cause it's our last name, if you don't believe me!''

"Liar!" Josh scooped up a handful of sand and threw it in Jimmy's face, then spun and took off running.

"I'm gonna tell your ma you called me a poop, Josh Morgan! And anyway, I don't want to be your dumb old cousint!''

After the day of the picnic, Laura noticed an unusual reticence in Josh but attributed it to the fact that school had started and he was lost without his best friend, Jimmy. She knew, too, that he missed Dan's company in the evenings, and though she tried to make up for his absence, her heart was not totally in it, and Josh could not be cheered. He remained withdrawn and distant, at times almost angry. She tried to interest him in helping her with some of his favorite chores, but he showed no enthusiasm. When she finally invited him to go bayberrying and he refused this, too, Laura's concern grew. She waited for Dan one evening in hopes that he'd be sober enough to discuss the problem and offer some insight.

Dan was surprised to find her up when he came in. She was dressed in her nightgown and wrapper and came immediately to stand before him, working her hands together, her eyes sad and troubled. Her image grew fuzzy, then cleared, while through an alcoholic haze Dan thought, Why don't you just tell her she's free, Morgan? Why don't you just send her to Rye and be done with it? His eyes found hers and he knew the answer: because he loved her in a way she'd never fathom, and to give her up would be to give up his reason for living.

"Let me help you." Laura stepped close and reached to help Dan remove his jacket, but he brushed her hands aside.

"I c'n do it."

"Let me—"

"Get y'r goddamn hands off me!" he shouted, backing away, almost falling down.

She stiffened as if he'd slapped her. Her lips dropped open on a surprised breath, and tears glimmered in her eyes while she clutched her hands and backed a step away. "Dan, please—"

"Don't say it! Don't say anything, just leave me alone. I'm drunk. I j'st wanna go to bed. I j'st . . ." His knees were stiff as he swayed like a poplar in a summer breeze, staring at the floor between his feet.

For a horrifying moment Laura thought he was going to start crying, but suddenly he scooped her into his arms and held her tightly, clutching the back of her head while trying to maintain his balance.

"Oh God, how I love you." His eyes were squeezed tightly shut. His voice was wracked with emotion. "God help me, Laura, I wish Rye *had* been on that ship when it went down."

"Dan, you don't know what you're saying." His hold was unbreakable, and she was forced to remain where she was.

"I do. I'm drunk, but not so drunk I don't know what I've been thinking for weeks and weeks. Why did he have to come back? Why!"

But his cry became a maudlin appeal, and she remembered Dan turning to Rye at the end of the wharf, seeking his strength and comfort, and she understood his torture at the words he'd just spoken. "Go to bed, Dan. I'll blow out the candles and be in in a minute."

He released her and turned docilely toward the bedroom, deluged with shame at having put voice to such a heathen wish.

As she did every night, Laura went to peek in at Josh one last time before turning in. When he saw the flickering light approaching through the half-closed doors of his alcove, Josh shut his eyes and pretended to be asleep. But when she was gone, he lay in the dark, thinking about what he'd just heard, remembering the day he'd first seen Rye Dalton hugging Mama. Rye had said then that his name was Rye because his mother's name was Ryerson before she got married, and Jimmy had said the same thing. So could Jimmy be right? Josh remembered Rye hitting Papa . . . Rye hugging Mama . . . Rye making Mama smile on the hill by Mr. Pond's mill. He heard again the words his papa had just said. Papa wished Rye was dead! Dead . . . like Grampa. He tried to piece things together, but nothing fell into place. All Josh knew was that nothing had been the same since Rye came here. Papa never came home anymore, and Mama was sad all the time, and . . . and . . .

Josh could not understand any of it. So he cried himself to sleep.

It was a mellow day in mid-September when Laura invited Josh to join her in measuring and mixing the ingredients for potpourri, which the two of them had been carefully gathering and drying all summer.

Though he wistfully eyed the rose petals, citrus rinds, and spices, he jammed his hands into his pockets and hung his head. "Don't wanna."

Oh, Josh, Josh, what is it, darling?

"But you helped me last year, and we had such fun."

"Gonna go outside and play."

"But if you don't help me, the moths will eat holes in our things this winter." But Laura's effort at cajolery fell flat, for Josh only shrugged and reached for the latch.

Laura stared at the door a long time after he'd left, wondering how to bring him out of this uncharacteristic standoffishness. Her eyes wandered back to the fragrant collection on the table and the rose petals seemed to swim before her eyes. Leaning her forehead on her knuckles, she battled tears. As they often did at times like this, her thoughts turned to Rye, and she wished she could talk to him about Josh. The sight of the curled bits of orange and lemon rind and the perfume of the pungent collection mingled to remind her that each year at this time she was in the habit of walking down to the cooperage to fetch a bag of fragrant cedar chips to add to her potpourri, but this year she'd have to do without it.

Outside, Josh hunkered in the sun, poking listlessly at the scallop shells, wanting to go back in and join his mother, because mixing was the most fun—way more fun than scraping rind and plucking petals and all the hard stuff they'd done all summer. He looked toward the bay and his boyish lips tightened. Down there somewhere was Rye, and if it hadn't been for Rye, Josh would be inside right now doing one of his favorite things with his mother.

Rye was teaching his cousin, the apprentice, how to make the slats of a pail uniform when a small figure stopped in the doorway of the cooperage. Josh! Rye turned back to the task at hand, assuming Laura would appear next. But a full minute went by, and nobody joined the boy. He remained in the doorway, studying the interior of the cooperage and, more specifically, Rye himself. The cooper could feel the lad's eyes following each motion he made. Glancing up, he saw Josh's mouth drawn tight and a belligerent expression around his blue eyes.

"Hello, Josh," Rye greeted at last. When no reply came, he asked, "Y' down here all alone?"

Josh neither answered nor moved, but stood as before, antagonism written on every muscle of his face. Rye ambled toward the doorway, nonchalantly lifting two staves and comparing them. As he neared Josh, the boy defiantly stepped back. Outside, Rye glanced in both directions, but Laura was not in sight.

"Y'r mother know y're down here all alone?"

"She don't care."

"Aw, lad, y're wrong there. Y'd better get back up home. She'll be worried about y'."

Josh's small chin grew even more defiant. "You can't tell me what to do. You . . . you ain't my papa." Before Rye could move, Josh rushed him, tears on his cheeks now. He hit Rye with his boyish fists, crying, "You ain't neither my papa! You ain't! My papa is my papa, not you!" And before Rye could recover from his stunned surprise, Josh wheeled and ran off up the street.

"Joshua!" Rye called after him, but the child was gone.

"Damn!" Rye stalked back into the cooperage and flung the pair of staves down with a clatter. His heart pounded and a film of perspiration sprang to his palms as he stood before the tool bench pondering what to do. Josh had been so angry, so hurt. He must have just found out, but if Laura was the one who'd told him, Rye was certain she'd have explained in a way that wouldn't have set the boy off this way. Suppose he didn't return home? He was disillusioned and upset right now, and Laura should know about it. But the last place on the island Rye should go was up to the house. Suddenly he spun around.

"Chad, I want y' to run an errand for me."

"Yessir."

Rye glanced around for paper, found none, and instead grabbed the first thing he could find: a flat clean scrap of cedar from the pail he'd been working. With a chunk of charcoal, he wrote, "Josh knows," and signed it simply, "R."

"Y' know the house where Dan Morgan lives, up on Crooked Record Lane?" Chad nodded. "I want y' to run this up there and give it t' Mrs. Morgan. Nobody else, y' understand?" Rye scowled.

"Yessir," Chad replied smartly.

"Good. Now be off with y'."

Rye watched the boy head away, and a frown deepened between his eyebrows. He thought of the day he'd met Laura and Josh coming from the hill. *I like you*, the boyish voice came back. Rye stared into space, hearing the words again as he rubbed his stomach where Josh's fist had struck out against the truth. Rye's head dropped forward and a long sigh escaped. Would life ever be simple again? He wanted so little. The wife he loved, the son he'd lost out on, the home on the hill. He wanted only what was his.

Josiah watched his son's forlorn pose, then moved up behind Rye and clapped a hearty hand on his shoulder. "Boy's not yet five years old. Too young t' reason things out. When he can, he'll judge y' for y'rself, not as the man who stole his father. Been a bit of a shock to him, I'd say. Give the lad some time."

Though Rye seldom burdened Josiah with his cares, he now found himself somewhat shaken and very depressed. Still facing the door, still with his hand on his stomach, he said, "There're days when I wish I'd never've been put off the *Massachusetts*."

Josiah squeezed Rye's sturdy shoulder. "Naw, son, don't say that."

Rye looked back at his father and shrugged away his apathy. "Y're right. I'm sorry, old man. Forget I said it." Then he turned back to work, forcing a cheerfulness he didn't feel.

When Josh burst into the house, Laura was unaware that he'd been gone from the yard. She straightened in surprise as the door slammed and Josh barreled across the room to fling himself, belly down, on his bed. Immediately, Laura was on her feet, scattering airy rose petals as she crossed to sit on the edge of the bed and smooth Josh's hair.

"Darling, what is it?"

But he only burrowed deeper into the pillow, weeping harder. When she attempted to turn him over, the boy pulled away. "Josh, is it something I've done? Please tell Mama what's made you so unhappy."

A muffled response came from the pillow while Josh's shoulders jerked pitifully.

Laura leaned low over him. "You what? Josh, come, darling, turn around here."

He lifted his head and sobbed, "I h . . . hate Jimmy!"

"But he's your best friend."

"I hate h . . . him anyway. He s . . . said all kind of st . . . stuff that ain't true!"

"Tell me what Ji—"

Just then Chad's knock interrupted, and Laura frowned in the direction of the door, brushed a staying hand across her son's shoulders, and went to answer. No sooner had she opened the door than Chad spit out, "Your little boy, he was down at th' cooperage, ma'am. Mr. Dalton, he says to give you this." Before Laura could say thank you, Chad had thrust the cedar scrap into her hand and was gone. She quickly read the message on the thin band of wood, then pressed it to her heart, glancing back at Josh, still crying on his bed. Oh, Josh, so this is what's been troubling you. Again she read the message, then, as tears burned her eyes, she pressed her nose against the pungent piece of cedar, searching for the right words. She closed her eyes, gathering composure. The piece of wood smelled like Rye, the clean, woodsy aroma that always clung to him. It seemed to drift to Laura now in a message of support while her heart throbbed with uncertainty.

Our son, she thought, swallowing the lump of love in her throat. Slowly, she moved to sit again beside the child, whose muffled sobs filled the alcove.

"Joshua—" She smoothed the blond locks on the back of his head, wondering what had taken place at the cooperage, wishing more than ever that Rye were here at this moment. "Darling, I'm so sorry. Please . . ." She forcibly turned the narrow shoulders over, and though Josh struggled to remain on his stomach, once she'd managed to get him turned, he flung his arms around her and clung. She pressed him close, resting her chin on his head. "Oh, Josh, don't cry."

"B . . . but Jimmy says Papa ain't m . . . my real papa."

"We'll talk about it, dear. Is that why you've been so quiet and upset with me lately?"

Josh's only answer was his continued sobbing, for he no longer knew who he should be angry at.

Laura sifted her fingers through Josh's angel-fine hair. "Your papa . . . Dan loves you very much. You know that, don't you?"

"B . . . but, Jimmy says R . . . Rye is my real papa, and he ain't! He ain't!" Josh sat back and tried to look defiant, though his chin quivered and tears streamed everywhere.

Laura searched his watery blue eyes, groping through her mind for the least painful way to make Josh understand and believe the truth. "Did you go to the cooperage to ask him?"

"N . . . no."

"Then why?"

Josh's chin dropped and he shrugged.

Laura searched into her apron pocket, leaving the cedar piece in it, coming up with a handkerchief to dry her son's streaming eyes. "I'll tell you why Jimmy told you that, but you must promise to remember that I love you, and Dan does, too. Promise?" She tipped up his quivering chin.

After an uncertain nod, Josh let himself be gathered back against his mother while her voice went on comfortingly.

"Do you remember the first day you saw Rye? When you came home for dinner and found him kissing me? Well, that was . . . I don't even know how to tell you how important that moment was for me. You see, I had thought for a long time that Rye was dead, and because he was my . . . my friend since I was a child not much older than you are now, I was so, *so* happy to find him alive. You already know that all three of us were friends when we were little, your papa and Rye and me. We went to school together and pretty soon we were just like . . . oh, like three children playing follow the leader. Everywhere one of us went, the other two followed. Like you and Jimmy."

Laura pulled back to give her son a brief smile of reassurance, then tucked him where he'd been before. "Well, I was about fifteen years old when I discovered that I liked Rye in a different way than I liked Dan. And by the time I was sixteen, I understood that I loved Rye and he felt the same way about me. We got married as soon as we were old enough, and not long after that, Rye decided to go out whaling. I . . . I was very sad when he went, but he did it to earn money for both of us, and we planned that when he came back home, he'd never have to sail away again. But then the ship that Rye sailed on was sunk, and the news came back to Nantucket, and we all believed he'd drowned with the other men on the ship."

Josh pulled back and gazed up at his mother with wide, glistening eyes. "Drowned? You mean like . . . like Grampa?"

Laura nodded solemnly. "Yes, except we thought Rye was buried in the sea. We were very sad, Dan and I, because we both . . . well, we missed Rye very much."

Josh now centered his rapt attention on each word his mother said as she went on quietly.

"It was after I thought Rye was dead that I learned I was going to have a baby—that was you, of course." Laura held Josh's hand, gently rubbing the backs of his fingers. She looked directly into his blue eyes, which were so very much like Rye's. "Yes, darling, Rye is your real papa. But he went away not knowing you were going to be born, because you were still inside my stomach then. I felt sad when I thought he was dead, because he would never know about you, and you would never get to know him." Josh stared at her, showing no reaction for the moment. She pressed his hand between both of hers, continuing to caress it lovingly.

"Jimmy told you the truth. Rye *is* your real papa, but he's only one of them, because Dan was always there, taking care of you and me from the time you were born. He *chose* to be your papa, Josh, and you must always remember that. He knew you'd need one, and . . . and Rye wasn't here to take care of you and me, so we were . . . we were very lucky to have Dan, don't you think?" Laura tipped her head aside and touched Josh's cheek, but he dropped his eyes in confusion. "Nothing can ever change how much Dan loves you, do you understand, dear? That's the important thing. He was the only father you had until that day when Rye came back, and we found out he wasn't dead after all. But we all knew you would be confused and hurt if we told you, so we decided not to for a while. I . . . I'm sorry now that I put it off. It should have been me telling you, not Jimmy. And, darling, you mustn't blame Jimmy for any of this.''

Josh looked up guiltily. ''I . . . I called Jimmy a liar and a . . . a poop.''

Laura stopped a tremulous smile before it could form. ''You must have been very upset with him. But you must be sure to tell Jimmy you're sorry. It's not nice to call others bad names.''

''So I . . . I got two papas?'' Josh asked, trying to puzzle it out.

''I'd say so. And they both love you, too.''

Josh seemed to digest that novel idea for a moment while staring at his knee. Then he looked up. ''Do they love you, too?'' he asked.

It was all Laura could do to keep her voice from trembling. ''Yes, Josh, they do.''

''Then are you married to both of 'em?''

''No, just to Dan.'' From her apron pocket, the scent of cedar drifted to Laura's nostrils as she battled emotions the story had managed to arouse within her.

''Oh.'' Again Josh seemed to mull, and soon he asked, ''Did Rye know Papa helped me and you while he was gone?''

''Yes, he found out that day he came back and you saw him here.''

''Then he shouldn't have hit Papa,'' Josh declared, as if coming to a firm decision.

Laura sighed, not knowing how to straighten out all the mistaken thoughts in Josh's young mind even as the child went on.

''And besides, after Rye came back, Papa started not coming home at night. I . . . I wish he'd come home for supper like he used to.''

Unable to keep tears from forming, Laura hugged Josh close again to keep him from seeing her distress. ''I know. So do I. But we have to be patient with him, and . . . and extra nice, too. Remember what Rye said? Papa needs an extra lot of cheering up, because it's a bad time for him right now, and we . . . we have to understand, that's all.'' What a large order for a child of four, thought Laura. How could he be expected to understand what she herself at times could not?

Yet there was a new peace within Laura now that Josh knew the truth about Rye. And later, as she and her son carefully measured and mixed the potpourri, Laura took the piece of cedar from her pocket and cut it into tiny pieces, which she added lovingly to the recipe. It seemed like a message of hope from Rye, one that would lie in her bureau drawer through the long winter ahead.

Chapter 15

IT WAS OFTEN said that the commerce of the world would have come to a complete standstill without the lowly barrel stave. On a day in late September, there appeared at the cooperage a dapper little gentleman who knew well how highly honored the coopering craft was and understood that coopers were among the most respected and sought-after of tradesmen. As the visitor paused in the doorway, he produced a fine lawn handkerchief and wiped his nose, upon which perched a pair of oval wire-rimmed spectacles.

"G'dday," Josiah muttered around his pipestem, eyeing the stranger.

"Good day," came the nasal reply. "I'm looking for the cooper, Rye Dalton."

"That'd be m' son there." Josiah indicated Rye with the stem of his pipe.

"Ah, Mr. Dalton. Dunley Throckmorton is my name." He moved toward the rear of the cooperage, where Rye turned to meet the congenial handshake with a firm one of his own.

"G'dday, sir. Rye Dalton, and this is m' father, Josiah. What can we do for y'?"

"Don't let me stop you from your work. This world needs barrels, and I'd hate to be guilty of slowing down production for a moment." Throckmorton sniffed and burst out with a sneeze, after which he apologized. "The weather on the sea-coast doesn't agree with me, I'm afraid." He dabbed his nose. "Please, Mr. Dalton, please go on with what you were do-ing."

Throckmorton watched as Rye went back to work on a par-tially constructed barrel, which had already been hooped and had its uneven ends trimmed off with a hand adz. Rye now set to work smoothing them with a sunplane. Throckmorton watched his powerful shoulders curve into his planing. The man had arms and hands of enviable strength, the kind Amer-ica needed as its borders pushed westward.

"Tell me, Dalton, have you ever heard of the Michigan Ter-ritory?"

"Aye, I've heard of it."

"A beautiful place, the Michigan Territory, a lot like here, with its snowy winters and mild summers, only without the ocean, of course. But it has the great Lake Michigan instead."

"Aye?" Dalton grunted almost indifferently, never missing a beat.

Throckmorton cleared his throat. "Yes, a beautiful place, and all its land free for the taking." The visitor sensed Dal-ton's complacency and wondered what it would take to con-vince this young man to follow him into the frontier. He was of prime, child-producing age, which was vital to the future growth of newly established towns. And he knew his craft well, so could pass it on to others. A hearty, healthy, skilled young buck—Rye Dalton was exactly the kind of man Throck-morton sought. But competition for skilled coopers was keen.

"How's business, Dalton?"

Rye chuckled. "Y' come askin' that of a barrel maker in a whalin' town? What do y' think those outgoin' whaleships put water and beer and flour and salt beef and herring in? And what do y' think they bring back blubber and oil in? How's business?" He couldn't resist a second chuckle, for he had already guessed why Throckmorton was nosing around. "We could turn off the lights o' the world if we stopped makin' bar-rels, Throckmorton. Business is boomin', as y've already guessed."

Throckmorton knew it was true. Whale oil alone made up a

large share of the commodities shipped to world markets in barrels. Still, he asked, "Have you ever thought about leaving here?"

"Leave Nantucket?" Rye only laughed in reply, and the visitor now employed his most convincing voice.

"Well, why not? There are other parts of the country where barrels are needed just as badly."

Rye's muscles continued flexing as he laughed a second time. "Somebody's got y' misinformed, man. Or haven't y' heard it's Yankee factories supplyin' the rest o' the country with everythin' from nails t' gunpowder? T' say nothin' of the Boston and Newport distilleries—and all shipped in barrels. Why, we could shut out more than the lights o' the world. We could keep it sober, and bring the triangle trade to a complete standstill."

What Dalton said was true. Canary and Madeira—the "wine islands"—shipped raw sugar and molasses to New England distilleries, which in turn shipped their rum and whiskey to Africa, whose slaves supplied labor to the Caribbean plantations, completing the triangle. And it all hinged on barrels produced along the northern seaboard, since the wood supplies of Europe were sorely depleted.

Throckmorton shook his head in surrender. "I can't deny it, Dalton. What you say is true. Let me lay my cards on the table. It takes barrels to build new towns, and I've got a group of men and women who believe Michigan's the place to do it." Throckmorton paused for effect, then went on. "We're forming up a group to leave Albany for the Michigan Territory in the spring, as soon as the Great Lakes open up, but we need a cooper."

Rye's hands fell still on his work while he peered at the man from beneath lowered brows. "Y' askin' me t' go to Michigan t' start up a town with y'?"

"I am." The dapper man gestured earnestly. "We can't survive out there without barrels for flour, cornmeal, threshed grain, maple syrup, cider, soaking hams, and . . . and . . ." Throckmorton released a distressed sigh. "Even housewives need you for washtubs, pails, churns, dashers . . . why, you could be a rich man in no time, Dalton, and highly respected at that."

Again Rye hunched over his work. "I'm respected where I am, Throckmorton, and I have no hostile Indians t' contend with. If I wanted a change o' scenery bad enough t' leave Nantucket, why go to that godforsaken land? I could go t' the South and sell m' barrels for transportin' rice, indigo, tar, turpentine, rosin, sourghum—why, the list goes on and on. Why go with y' when the South's already civilized? I wouldn't have t' do without convenien—"

"Bah! The South!" The small man clasped his hands behind his back and took up pacing like an incensed headmaster. "What would you want in that wretched part of the country? No man accustomed to the . . . the healthy rigors of a brisk northern winter would be content in that hot, miserable climate!" He gestured theatrically.

Rye smirked, erasing the expression when Throckmorton looked back at him. "I didn't say I wanted t' live there. I was just pointin' out the fact that I can earn my livin' anywhere. I didn't spend seven years as an apprentice t' risk life and limb followin' a bunch of strangers into the wilderness. Besides, I'm content where I am."

"Ah, but there's little challenge in this easy life, my boy. Think about having a hand in shaping America, extending its perimeter!"

The man was well chosen for his errand, thought Rye, who was enjoying this stimulating exchange more than he let on. Throckmorton was glib, and earnest to boot—a quite likable fellow, who aroused Rye's penchant for debate. The cooper found himself happily immersed in discussing the merits of the frontier versus civilization.

Still clasping his hands against his lower spine. Throckmorton studied him from beneath lowered brows. "Tell me, Dalton, they say you've gone whaling. Is that true?"

"Aye, one voyage."

"Ah! So you're the kind of man who seeks adventure and knows how to rough it, if need be."

"Five years on a whaleship was enough roughin' it t' last me a lifetime, Throckmorton. Y're barkin' up the wrong tree."

The visitor's spectacles turned toward the arresting sight of the cooper riding a croze cutter around the inner edge of the staves, beveling out the deep groove, called the chines, into which the barrel cap would be seated. Damn, the man knew his craft too well to let him slip away!

"How's your wood supply here, Dalton?"

"Y' know perfectly well we barter for our rough staves with the mainlanders."

"Exactly!" An index finger pointed to heaven for emphasis. "Imagine, if you will, not this windblown island where the sea prunes every struggling tree to the height of the nearest hill, but a forest so thick and high you could make barrels until your hundredth year and never make a dent in your raw supplies."

Rye could not restrain the grin that appeared on his face as the man looked upward and raised a hand, gesturing toward the ceiling beams as if he were standing in a verdant forest. Rye nodded and gave the shrewd man a point. "Aye, y've got me there, Throckmorton. That'd be somethin', all right."

As the cooper continued gouging out the chines, the other man pressed his advantage. "The blacksmith we've found to go with us will have none of your advantage when it comes to raw materials. He'll have to have every ounce of iron shipped in from the East. Yet he's willing to take the risk."

Rye looked up, surprised. "Y've found a smithy?"

Throckmorton looked pleased. "And a good one." Now his expression became the slightest bit smug.

Almost to himself, Rye muttered, "I'd need a smithy." Then, remembering that Josiah was listening, he glanced in the old man's direction with almost a guilty cast to his eyes. Josiah gave no indication he'd heard Rye's remark, yet Rye knew he was taking in every word.

"We've found some fifty-odd people so far, among them all the necessary tradesmen the town will need to survive, except a cooper and a doctor. And I've no doubt I'll yet come up with a doctor this winter in Boston. As I said, the party is set to leave just after the spring thaws, as soon as the inland rivers open up."

For just a moment the thought of making a fresh start in such a place as the Michigan Territory excited Rye's spirit of adventure. He was—it was true—a man who'd gone whaling, one of the greatest adventures a man could make. Yet the thought of leaving Nantucket gave him a sharp twinge of homesickness. He glanced again at Josiah, busy banding a hogshead, adjusting the pins through the holes of a temporary leather hoop like a man adjusts his belt. A puff of smoke drifted above the old man's head. The young cooper turned back to meet the earnest eyes behind the oval spectacles. "I'm not for y', Throckmorton, though I appreciate the invitation. I have . . . family I wouldn't care t' leave behind."

"Bring your father along," the agent said heartily. "His knowledge would be as invaluable as yours. He could teach the young people far more than just coopering, I'll be bound. The West is a place where all ages are necessary—the old to bring experience, and the young to bring children. Tell me, Dalton," Throckmorton said, glancing around. "Are you married? Have you a family?"

Dalton now stood erect, his croze forgotten in his left hand. The agent's eyes traveled down to check it and found there a gold wedding ring.

But Dalton's answer was, "I'm . . . I'm not, sir, no."

"Ah, well . . . a pity, a pity." But then the man gave a wily smile as he patted his waistcoat buttons as if preparatory to taking his leave. "But then, there'll be young women making the trip, too."

"Aye . . ." the cooper said tonelessly.

Suddenly Josiah tipped the hogshead up on end and abandoned it to shamble across the dirt floor in his usual unhurried fashion, squinting and drawing on his pipe.

"Young man, if I was y'r age, y' could talk me inta goin' with y'. Specially on a day like this when the Little Gray Lady gits to givin' me twinges of the rheumatis'." He took the pipe from his mouth and rubbed its bowl thoughtfully. "But m' son now—well, he ain't got no rheumatis' t' spur him on t' such *hiiigh* adventure." He drew the word out drolly as only a crusty New Englander can.

Rye's head snapped around. It sounded as though Josiah was issuing a challenge, though his eyes never touched his son as he went on with dry perspicacity.

"If y' was t' come back when his bones're creakin' and his hands gnarled and he's not good fer much anymore, y' might get him to take y' up on it then."

Almost as if on cue, Throckmorton sneezed, reminding

them how inclement the weather of Nantucket could be. When he'd dabbed his nose and tucked away his handkerchief, he shook hands with both men, first Josiah, then Rye, whose hand he clasped while delivering his final appeal.

"I ask you to think about it, Dalton. You have all winter to do so, and if you should decide to come along with us, I can be reached at the Astor in Boston. The party sets out from Albany on April fifteenth."

"Y'd better keep lookin', sir. I'm sorry." After a last hearty shake, Rye released the man's hand and a moment later he was gone.

Josiah buried his hands between his britches and his back shirttails, clasping his waistband and rocking back on his heels while air hissed softly into his pipestem. He concentrated on the doorway through which Throckmorton had just disappeared. "Notion's got some merit to it. Specially for a man caught in a sticky triangle's got him achin' like a horse 'ts thrown a shoe."

Rye scowled at his father. "Y're sayin' y'd have me go?"

"Ain't sayin' I would . . . ain't sayin' I wouldn't. I'm sayin' it's gettin' t' feel a mite crowded on this island, what with you and Dan Morgan both livin' on it full grown."

The old man's curious comments settled like a burr in Rye's thoughts as September gave way to October. Josiah was old; Rye couldn't leave him. But had the old man meant he'd actually consider going along? Though Rye puzzled over the conversation, he resisted bringing up the subject again, for talking about it lent the idea credence, and Rye wasn't at all sure he was prepared for that. There was Laura to consider, and Josh. But the thought of them presented the dizzying possibility of taking them along.

The first frosts came, and with them the most beautiful season on the island. The moors lit up with their autumn array of colors as out along Milestone Road vast patches of huckleberry turned bright red, then began softening to rust. Skeins of poison ivy thrilled the eye with their new hues of red and yellow. The scrub oaks turned the color of bright copper pennies and the bayberries turned gray, their skins like the texture of oranges. Ready for picking now, their fragrance was as spicy as any apothecary shop.

In the dooryards, mulberry bushes took fire and chrysanthemums put on their final show of the year, while the deepening frosts brought appropriate blushes to the cheeks of the island's apples.

Then the whole island took on a delicious fragrance, until it seemed the very ocean itself must be made of apple juice as wooden apple presses were brought into yards for cidering. The scent was everywhere, redolent and sweet. Cauldrons of peeled apples were boiled down into apple butter and jelly. Circles of white apple meat were strung up to dry until it seemed the ceiling beams in the keeping rooms of Nantucket would collapse beneath their weight.

In the house on Crooked Record Lane, baskets of bayberries waited for the cold days of December, when Laura would begin candle making. Overhead, the apple slices drooped like garlands between cheesecloth sacks filled with drying herbs—sage, thyme, marjoram, mint—filling the keeping room with an almost overwhelming essence.

Laura had delayed making apple butter until last. It was midafternoon when she hammered a scarred wooden lid onto the last wide-mouthed crock. Suddenly the cover cracked in half and one of the broken pieces dropped into her clean yellow fruit.

Tossing the hammer aside, she muttered an oath and fished the broken piece out, then licked it off before tossing it into the fire. Laura searched through her remaining wooden covers only to find that none fit the crock.

She glanced out the window at the bay, visible in the distance, and the forbidden thought crossed her mind. There was nothing to stop her—Josh was at Jane's for their annual pumpkin carving. Resolutely, Laura knelt down to try each wooden lid again. But still, none fit—no matter how she pushed, maneuvered, and jiggled.

Suddenly her hands fell still. She looked up at the window again. Scudding gray clouds with dark underbellies galloped across the skies like wild mustangs while the wind lifted loose mulberry leaves and threw them impatiently against the glass.

Laura squeezed her eyes shut, slumped forward, and clasped her thighs as she sat on her haunches before the burning wooden cover. I must not go near him. I can put a plate over the crock.

But a minute later she was measuring the diameter of the container with a length of tatting string, then her apron was flying off to fall forgotten across a chair, and she was hurrying down the scallop-shell path toward the cooperage.

Its doors were closed now. She hesitated before opening them, to glance off down the street toward the quayside, where the large blue anchor hung over the door of the pub where she'd heard Dan spent most of his evenings. She shivered, drew her cape together, and stepped through the cross-buck doors into a place of bittersweet memory. It was shadowy, and fragrant with the smell of fresh-worked cedar, and warm from the fire blazing a welcome on the hearth.

Josiah was there, straddling his shaving horse, a curl of smoke twining through his grizzled gray eyebrows. He raised his head, relaxed his grip on the drawknife, then slowly leaned over to rest it against the horse. His benevolent gaze never left Laura as he swung to his feet and reached for his pipe, intoning in his familiar voice, "Well hello, daughter."

Always he had called her daughter that way, and the term now raised a wellspring of affection in Laura's breast as Josiah offered open arms.

She went against his woodsy-smelling flannel shirt, closing her eyes as the stubble on his chin abraded her temple. "Hello, Josiah."

He backed her away and smiled indulgently. "I was beginnin' t' think this old cooperage'd never see y'r smile again."

She turned to take it in. "Ah, yes, it's been a long time, Josiah. It looks the same and smells just as good as ever." Her eyes fell to the other shaving horse and found it empty. A stab of disappointment knifed through her.

"Undoubtedly y're lookin' for my son."

She turned quickly and assured Josiah a little too brightly, "No . . . no . . . I . . . I've only come to order a lid for a crock."

Josiah squinted, replaced the pipe between his teeth, and went on as if she hadn't spoken. "He's stepped out for a minute, gone down t' Old North Wharf t' see about some hogs-heads that's bein' packed aboard the *Martha Hammond*."

Laura took refuge in the unoccupied shaving horse, turning to study it again, but she gave up her pretense to ask softly, "How is he?" Behind her she heard the soft sibilance of Josiah drawing on his pipe.

"Fair to middlin'. Better'n Dan, from what I hear."

Laura swung around, her face now drawn and pale. "I . . . I guess everybody on the island must know how Dan has been drinking since . . . since his father's death."

"Ayup." Josiah picked up a side ax and intently tested its edge with a horny thumb. "They're talkin', all right." Then he dropped the tool and swung onto his shaving horse again, turning his back to her and bending to work. "Been talkin' some about how that woman DeLaine Hussey finds excuses t' come pokin' around the cooperage every other day or so, too."

Laura spun around to gape at Josiah's flexing shoulders. "DeLaine Hussey?"

"Ayup."

"What does *she* want?"

Josiah smiled secretly at Laura's sudden, vitriolic response. "What does any woman want who dreams up excuses t' put herself in a man's vicinity?" Josiah let that sink in while he drew his knife toward his knees, shaving a wide white wood curl from the stave, then another and another. Next, he tested the concave curve with his fingers, running them time and again along the piece until he deemed it fit, and released it from the wooden jaws of the footclamp. "She came in t' buy a piggin for her mother, then she brought a basket of beach plums, then a batch of orange cookies."

"Orange cookies!"

Again Josiah smiled, though Laura could not see, for he'd kept his back to her. "Ayup. Tasty they was, too."

"O . . . orange cookies? She brought Rye orange cookies?"

"Ayup."

"What did he think about that?"

"Why, as I recall, he said he thought they was tasty, too. Seemed t' enjoy 'em tremendously. Then after that, I guess it was the cinnamon apples, then—let's see—oh, o' course. Then she came t' ask if he was goin' t' the clambake.''

"What clambake?"

"Starbuck's annual clambake. Last o' the season. Whole island's bound t' be there. Didn't Dan tell y' about it?''

"He . . . he must've forgotten to mention it.''

"Forgets a lot these days, Dan does. Even forgets t' go home at night and eat his supper, the way I've heard tell.''

From the doorway a voice boomed. "Old man, y'r jaws're flappin'!"

Rye stood tall and stiff-shouldered at the entrance, dressed in high black boots, tight gray breeches, and a thick sweater that hugged his neck and emphasized the breadth of his shoulders. Laura felt her heart leap at the sight of him.

Rye glowered darkly at his father while Josiah, unflustered, only agreed amiably, "Ayup.''

"I'd suggest y' put a lock on 'em!" his son returned none too gently, while Laura wondered how long he'd been listening.

The unflappable Josiah only inquired, "What took y' so long? Customer's waitin'.''

Rye at last looked directly at Laura, but when his gaze drifted from her face down her arm, she realized she was standing beside his shaving horse, her fingers resting caressingly on the high arm of its clamp. She jumped and jerked her hand away, then crossed to Josiah's side, pulling the piece of tatting string from the pocket of her cape. "I told you it wasn't necessary for me to see Rye. You can do the work as well. All I need is a . . . a cover for a crock. This long.''

Josiah squinted one blue-gray eye at the string in her palm, puffed once, twice, then turned away uninterestedly. "I don't do covers. He does." He gave a backward nod at Rye.

Helplessly, she stared at the string, thinking of DeLaine Hussey and Rye and a clambake. Laura was now utterly embarrassed for having come to the cooperage at all. But just then she sensed Rye at her elbow.

"When do y' need it?''

His voice was unemotional as a wide, familiar, callused palm came into Laura's range of vision, outstretched for the string. She handed it over, making certain not to touch him. "Whenever you get around to it.''

"Will the end o' the week be soon enough?"

"Oh . . . certainly, but there's no need to rush."

He strode across the room and tossed the string onto the waist-high workbench, then stood with his back to the room, palms braced hard against the edge of the bench, far away from his sides. "Will y' come t' pick it up?" He stared out the window above the bench.

"I . . . yes, yes, of course."

"It'll be done."

His back was rigid. He neither turned nor spoke again, and Laura felt tears prickling at the backs of her eyelids. She presented a false, wavering smile to Josiah. "Well . . . it's been nice seeing you again, Josiah. And you, too, Rye."

The wide-held arms and stubborn shoulders didn't move. Her tears were now stinging, closer to overflowing, so Laura whirled and ran for the door.

"Laura!"

At Rye's bark, her feet didn't even slow. She jerked the door open while from behind her came a muffled curse, then, "Laura, wait!" But she swept outside and onto the street, leaving Rye to give chase in a long-legged stride. He shouldered through the door into the wind-wild day.

"Hove to, woman!" he ordered, grasping her elbow and forcing her to stop.

She swung around and yanked her elbow free. "Don't speak to me as if I'm the . . . the miserable whaleship that took you out to sea!"

"Why'd y' come here? Isn't it hard enough?" His eyes blazed down into hers.

"I needed a lid for a crock. This is the cooperage where one gets such things!"

"Y' could have got one at the chandlery as well."

"Next time I will!"

"I told y' t' keep out of my sight."

"Forgive me, Mr. Dalton, I had a temporary lapse of memory. You can be assured it won't happen again, unless, of course, it's absolutely unavoidable. In which case I would make sure I came with a basket full of *orange cookies* to pay for my wares."

His eyes took on a hooded look and he backed a step away

from her, hooking his thumbs into his belt. "The old man doesn't know when t' shut his trap."

"I disagree. I found his conversation very . . . enlightening."

Rye pointed a finger up the street, scowling angrily. "It's all right for you t' live up there on the hill with him, but when it comes t' me and DeLaine Hussey, it's a different matter, is that it?"

"You may do exactly what you want with Miss DeLaine Hussey!" She spat the words.

"Thank you, madam, I will!"

She had expected him to deny spending time with DeLaine. When instead he confirmed it, the pain seemed too great to bear. Haughtily, she looked down her nose, then lifted cold eyes to his and arched a single eyebrow. "Have you taught her how to employ the shaving bench yet? I'm sure she'd find it delightful."

For a moment Rye looked as though he wanted to strike her. His fingers bit into her arm, then he let her go, and a moment later he spun and strode angrily back to the cooperage, slamming the door behind him.

Immediately, Laura felt remorseful and wanted to run after him. But her angry words could not be recalled.

They were still echoing through her mind that night as she lay in bed, crying. *Why did I say such a thing, oh why? He's right—I have no call to fault him for seeing DeLaine Hussey when I'm still living with Dan.*

But there existed the very real possibility that DeLaine might eventually succeed in charming Rye, and it filled Laura with fear. Rye was lonely and miserable and more vulnerable than ever to a woman's advances. Laura remembered very clearly the night of the supper at the Starbucks' and DeLaine's flirtatious glances, as well as all that business about the Female Freemasons. There could be no doubt the woman had her sails set for Rye. In his forsaken state, how long could he resist the invitation of affection . . . and perhaps much more?

Chapter 16

THE FOLLOWING DAY Laura's face looked as grim as the Nantucket skies as she set out for Jane's house to fetch Josh home. The open heathland was no longer a magic carpet of color. The sweet fern, Virginia creeper, and highbush blueberry had all succumbed to the ravages of frost, their golds and rusts now put aside. The huckleberry branches were no more than skeletal black fingers reaching bleakly toward the sky. The grapes that had formed a wall of green now shrouded the split-rail fences in barren tangles from which came the sharp, lonely bark of a pheasant who searched there for any last clinging berries. The double cart track of white sand wound through the hills before Laura with a singular loneliness common to late October. The sky was leaden and low, so heavy in places that it reached downward to lick at the barren moors that shivered as the wind picked up and moaned a lament for the passing of autumn. Soon the northers would bluster and blow, and the island would be battered by strong seas, then sealed off by ice and snow.

It seemed the world had taken on a brooding sadness to complement Laura's own. Her heart felt heavy, and she shuddered inside her woolen cape, drew the hood together tightly beneath her chin, and hurried on.

* * *

Jane took one look at her sister and said, "I'd better put on the tea. I think you can use it."

Half of Jane's brood had gone to school, leaving the house, for once, almost peaceful. A warm fire burned beneath the crane, and Josh came running with a welcome hug before Jane wisely bustled him and his cousins off into another room with a bowl of crisp-baked pumpkin seeds to nibble on. Then the two sisters settled across the table from each other, sipping strong mint-flavored tea.

"You look terrible," Jane opened frankly. "Your eyes are all swollen and your face is puffy."

"I had myself a good cry last night, that's why."

"Caused by which of the two men in your life?"

"The one I'm trying to avoid—Rye."

"Ah, Rye. I take it you've heard about DeLaine Hussey, then."

Laura's head snapped up in surprise. "Y . . . you know about it, too?"

Jane met her gaze steadily. "The whole island knows about DeLaine Hussey's unabashed pursuit of Rye. It shouldn't come as such a surprise to you that I've heard about it, too."

"Why didn't you tell me?"

"I haven't seen much of you. You've been hiding away down there, I suspect, so you wouldn't run into Rye."

Laura sighed. "You're right, I have been hiding away— scared to death of running into him someplace."

The room grew silent for a moment while Jane studied her sister's eyes. Beneath them were small swollen pillows of purple. "It's that strong between you two, is it?"

The truth was printed on each tired line of her face. "Yes, Jane, it is. I . . . we . . ." And without warning the tears came again. She covered her face with both hands and braced her elbows on the table. "Oh, Jane, I've met Rye alone, I've . . . I've *been* with him again, and it's made my life a living hell."

Jane placed a comforting hand on Laura's forearm, stroking it lightly with a thumb. "*Been* with him as a man and woman, you mean, in the fullest sense of the word." It was not really a question.

Behind her hands, Laura nodded her head wretchedly. Jane

patiently waited for the fit of weeping to pass. When it had, she pressed a handkerchief into Laura's hands, and while Laura blew her nose, the two shared quavering smiles.

"Oh, Jane, you must think I'm terribly wicked, admitting that."

"No, dear, I don't. Not at all. I've told you before, I always knew how it was between you and Rye. Do you think I've been blind during all these years you've been married to Dan? I knew there was . . . well, something missing between you two. I only wondered when you'd admit it. Apparently, it took Rye's return for that to happen."

"I tried to stay away from Rye, believe me, Jane, I did." Laura's haunted eyes pleaded for understanding. "But I met him one day up in the hills when I'd gone to the mill to order flour. Josh was with me and . . . and seeing the two of them together, looking so much alike . . . I . . . well, he asked me to meet him and I did. The following day. That's the day I brought Josh here, the day when . . . when Zachary died."

The full implication of Laura's words struck her sister, and Jane crooned sympathetically, "Oh, Laura, no."

Laura swallowed hard and nodded. She took a fortifying gulp of tea, then warmed her palms around the cup. "I thought perhaps you'd guessed."

"I suppose I did, about how difficult it was for you and Rye. But I had no idea it had happened that particular day."

Laura studied her cup, remembering. "Fateful, isn't it, that while Rye and I met and . . . and deceived Dan, he was out searching for his father on the bar."

"Oh, Laura, you aren't saying you blame yourself for Zachary's death?"

Laura's eyes were etched with pain as she fixed them on her sister. "Don't you understand? We were out there together, and when we returned to town, it was to the news that Zach was missing. The next time Rye and I saw each other was . . . was down at the wharf. But Dan was there, too, and . . . oh, Jane, I'll never forget the sight of Dan turning to Rye when he came in with the search party. He tried to . . . to resist going to him, but he couldn't. He needed comfort, and right there before the whole town, the two of them flung their arms

around each other right after Rye and I had . . . oh, everything
is so mixed up.'' Again Laura dropped her face into her
hands. "I feel so guilty!"

"I suppose that's natural, but to blame yourself for Zach's
death is foolish. You're no more responsible for the fact that
Zach drowned than you are for the fact that Rye Dalton
didn't! I'll grant you the timing was unfortunate, but that's all
I'll concede!"

"But you weren't there the night of the funeral when Dan
was so drunk."

"I wasn't there, but I heard about it."

"Oh, Jane, it was dreadful. But it was true, everything he
accused me of. I'm the one who's driven Dan to drink, and
there's no way to cover up my feelings for Rye. I've vowed to
stay away from him for six months, at least during the period
of mourning. But Dan has guessed how I feel. He never comes
home until late at night, then he stumbles in, too inebriated
for us even to talk. And all the time I keep wondering, even
after six months—if I divorce Dan and go to Rye, how can we
face Dan then?"

Suddenly, Jane jumped to her feet, going to fetch more hot
water for tea. "You know the answer to that, Laura. You've
always known. This island is not big enough for all three of
you. It never has been."

"N . . . not big enough?"

Jane replaced the kettle on the hearth, then turned and impaled her sister with a look that would force Laura to admit
the truth. "Hardly. It wouldn't matter which of the two
you're married to. There's bound to be conjecture about the
other, and you're bound to confront each other time and
again and dredge up the past. Somebody will have to leave
sooner or later."

"But Nantucket is our home, all three of ours!" Laura
wailed.

Jane moved briskly back to her chair, but suddenly she
looked ill at ease. Lifting her cup, she fixed her eyes on it as if
reading its tea leaves. "There's been talk, Laura."

"Talk?" Laura looked puzzled.

"I can see you haven't heard."

"Heard what?"

"There's been a man visiting the island, named Throckmorton. He's an agent for a land company that's organizing a group of families to go to the Michigan Territory, come spring."

"M . . . Michigan?" Laura's brown eyes widened.

"Michigan." Jane swallowed a mouthful of tea. "To settle a new town there. And as you know, no town can survive without a . . . a cooper."

Laura's lips dropped open as realization dawned. "Oh no," she whispered.

"This man, this Mr. Throckmorton, has been seen at the cooperage more than once."

Foolishly, Laura looked toward the door, as if she could see the cooperage from where she sat. "Rye? Rye is planning to go to the frontier?" Laura's eyes again sought Jane's, hoping for denial.

"I don't know. I haven't heard that. All I've heard is that this Mr. Throckmorton has been sent to New England to drum up excitement, to seek skilled men, the kind of men necessary to carve out a living in the wilderness. They say a man can have all the land he wants. It's free for the taking. All he has to do is live on it and clear it and farm it for a year."

"But Rye is no farmer."

"Of course he isn't. I doubt that he'd homestead. He'd be going where his skill as a barrel maker would make him far more successful than farming."

"Oh, Jane!" Laura fairly wailed.

"I'm not saying it's true that Rye's going. I'm only saying what I've heard. I thought you should know."

Laura remembered Rye's stiff, forbidding pose the day before, how he'd turned his back on her, and her own impetuous words on the street. Could he be thinking of escaping Nantucket and its triangle of tension by simply turning to DeLaine Hussey and the frontier, accepting the challenge of both?

The thought haunted Laura continuously until the day when she returned to the cooperage to collect the lid she'd ordered. She fully intended to confront Rye and question him about his intentions for the future. But she was not to be given the chance, for when she arrived, it was to find only Josiah there. She had the distinct impression, though, that Rye had been on the watch for her and had hurriedly escaped to the lodgings overhead, for when she entered, Josiah was standing near the foot of the steps, looking up.

"Good morning, Josiah."

He nodded. "Daughter."

"I've come for my cover."

"Ayup. And it's ready."

He fetched it, handed it to her, then watched while she held it almost caressingly. She looked up directly. "I . . . I wanted to talk to Rye. Is he here?"

The shrewd blue-gray eyes roved about the cooperage, but Josiah answered with deliberate evasiveness. "Y' don't see him about anyplace, do y'?"

"No, Josiah, I don't *see* him," she replied pointedly.

"Then it'll be a bit difficult t' talk to him, won't it?"

"Is he deliberately avoiding me?" she asked.

Josiah turned his back. "Now, that I can't answer. Y'll have t' ask him next time y' see him."

"Josiah, has there been a man named Throckmorton around here talking to Rye?"

"Throckmorton—well now, let's see . . ." He scratched his chin thoughtfully. "Throckmorton . . . mmm . . ."

"Josiah!" she said with strained patience.

"Ayup. Come t' think of it, there has been."

"What did he want?"

Josiah pretended to be busy cleaning the top of the tool bench, making a lot of racket as he rearranged tools. "I don't listen to all the prattle of everybody who comes drifting in here t' talk t' that son o' mine. If I did, I wouldn't get a lick o' work done."

"Where was Mr. Throckmorton from?"

"From? What do y' mean, from?"

"Was he from the Michigan Territory?"

Again Josiah scratched his grizzled chin, finally turning to face her, but assuming an expression of little concern. "Well now, seems t' me I did hear him mention Michigan, not that I paid much attention."

Laura's heart seemed to rattle against her ribcage. "Thank you, Josiah. What do I owe you for the lid?"

"Owe me? Don't be silly, girl. Rye'd tar 'n' feather me if I tried t' take any money for it."

Momentarily, her heart lifted, then she could not help asking as she looked down at the newly hewn cover. "Did he make it or did you?"

Again the old one turned away. "He did." At that moment Laura heard a floorboard creak overhead. She looked up at the ceiling and said loudly, "Tell him thank you, Josiah, will you?"

"Ayup, I'll do that. I'll be sure t' do that."

Several minutes later, Rye came down the steps and paused with his foot on the last riser, his palm resting on the upright post there.

"She's gone," Josiah grunted. "No need for y' to skulk any longer. Y' weren't foolin' her, though. She knew y' was up there."

"Aye, I heard her thankin' me."

"Things've come to a fine pass when y' leave an old man t' tell lies to y'r woman," Josiah grumbled, "and all the time y' hidin' over m' head like some sneak-thief."

"If she were really my woman and mine alone, there'd be no need."

"News of Throckmorton and his business here's got her scuttled."

"Not enough to leave Dan, though."

"How do y' know when y' wouldn't let her have her say?"

"If she'd decided, she'd have come up those steps and nothin' would have stopped her. I know Laura."

"Aye, I suspect y' do, though y' didn't see the look on her face when she mentioned Throckmorton. Who d' you suppose told 'er about him?"

"I haven't any idea, but the man's been talkin' to others besides me. Plenty on the island know his business here."

"And have y' been considerin' his offer?"

Rye's eyebrows drew together until they almost touched, but he didn't answer.

Josiah picked up a tool, turned his back and stepped to the

grindstone, testing the dull blade with a thumb while asking nonchalantly, "Well, then have y' been considerin' the offer of that *hussy*?"

Rye jerked around to stare at his father's back. The way Josiah pronounced the word, it was questionable whether he meant it as a surname or a slur. "Aye, I'm takin' her up on it."

Josiah peered back over his shoulder to see Rye with a caustic smirk twisting one corner of his mouth.

"She makes a damn fine orange cookie."

"Humph!" The whine of the grindstone against steel cut off further conversation.

The final clambake of the season was held each year when the last of the winter stores had been put up and the beaches were not yet frozen. Cap'n Silas was the perennial tender of the firepit and could be seen each year on the day before the bake, gathering the indispensable rockweed from the stones and mussels on which it grew. Patiently, he filled burlap bags, each with nearly a hundred pounds of the yellowish-brown weed that contained small air sacs that flavored the food as the sacs burst. Bag after bag he dragged to the location of the clambake, heedless of the winds that gusted up to forty miles per hour—normal for this time of year. "We'll find a lee," he said, and they always did.

The hearty islanders thought little of braving the elements for a squantum such as this, the reward being the succulent scallops and clams that had been dug along Polpis Harbor and waited in baskets along with potatoes, squash, and cheesecloth bags stuffed with sausage, which would all be steamed along with the seafood.

On the day of this year's clambake, Rye and DeLaine Hussey arrived at the dunes in the late afternoon to find a large gathering already there and old Silas reigning over the building of the fire, ruling each step of the procedure like a despot. A shallow depression had been dug in the sand and was being lined with wood, then filled with rocks. "This is the tricky part," old Silas preached, as he did every year. "Got t' build y'r mound so's air c'n filter around every rock, else y'll get no draw t' heat 'em proper!"

DeLaine leaned close to Rye and whispered behind her hand. "Oh, thank heavens he told us!"

Rye chuckled silently, then drew his brows together in a mock scowl. "Got t' have good draw," he whispered back.

Rye Dalton had not been particularly anxious to spend the day with DeLaine Hussey, but her humorous remark seemed to loosen him up. She wasn't a bad-looking woman, and he realized he'd never spent enough time with her to know whether she had a sense of humor or not. It suddenly dawned on him that he knew very little about her. Standing now beside the pit in the buffeting winds, he made up his mind to enjoy the day as best he could. He was thankful the Morgan family, still in mourning, would not be joining the group.

Silas lit the fire, and true to his word, he'd laid it skillfully. Soon it spread and grew. Tankards of apple cider were warmed over it while the picnickers waited for Silas's final word that it was time to proceed. When the rocks began to crack and flake, he carefully spread them out and covered them with a layer of rockweed. On top of that went the food, then another layer of weed. Rye lent a hand as several men threw a tarpaulin over the mound, but this was the only role Silas assigned to anyone but himself. He took over again to weight the tarp with sand, sealing in the heat. At last the pit was steaming, and the crowd dispersed for the kite flying that had become traditional on this day.

As DeLaine and Rye ambled away from the fire, he studied her from the corner of his eye. She wore a simple bonnet of stiff blue silk that covered her to the ears. A caped woolen coat was buttoned high beneath her chin, and her hands were warmed by gray gloves. Rye turned up the collar of his pea jacket and resolved once again to enjoy himself.

They stood on a bluff with the wind at their backs and let out the kite to join the others that soared above the turgid ocean below. The breakers came pounding in, sending spray up toward the kite tails, which dipped and waggled, as if teasing the waves.

It had been years since Rye had flown a kite, and it brought a sharp smack of freedom as he watched the colorful triangle battle the wind, then crack smartly like a sail beneath a halyard. He looked up and watched the kite grow smaller. Suddenly, beside him, DeLaine laughed. He turned sharply to find her face tilted skyward as she held the string and felt it tug against her gloved hands.

"Did you know that when we were children I used to dream of doing this with you?"

"No," he answered, surprised.

She glanced at him. "I did. But you know what they say." Again she turned toward the kite. "Better late than never."

Rye could not think of a single thing to say, so he stood with his hands in his pockets, studying the kite.

DeLaine's voice was a deep contralto. "I used to envy Laura Traherne more than any other girl I knew."

Rye felt himself coloring, but DeLaine concentrated on the kite.

"She had you to follow everywhere, and such . . . such freedom, for a girl. I always envied her that freedom. While the rest of us were tucked away in our keeping rooms learning to tat and embroider, she was off running barefoot on the beaches." Now DeLaine turned and looked up at Rye's crisp jaw, outlined by the side-whiskers she'd longed to touch ever since she'd first seen them. "Am I embarrassing you, Rye? I don't mean to. It's all right, you know, that you love Laura."

His eyes flew to her face and found hers steady and assured.

"Everyone on this island knows how the two of you feel about each other. I just want you to know that I know, too, and it makes no difference to me. I intend to enjoy being with you because it's something I've wanted for a long, long time."

Again Rye was speechless, his lips open in surprise.

Abruptly, Delaine became gay and lilting again. "Tell me, Rye, have you seen Portugal?"

"Aye, of course."

DeLaine pulled in a deep draft of air through flared nostrils and studied the faraway horizon. "I've always wanted to see Portugal. It's out there—just imagine—I'm looking at it right now. I'd give anything to see it, or to see anyplace besides this stifling little island. I'm sick to death of it, and of the smell of whale oil and tar."

"That's not the impression y' gave me the night y' brought up the Female Freemasons. Y' talked as if y' were proud of

Nantucket and its . . . whalers.''

"Oh, that." She gave a self-deprecating grin. "I was just saying that to see if I could get your attention, you know that. I couldn't care less if a man's killed a whale or not." The wind caught a wisp of her hair and blew it across her lips, and Rye quickly looked away. "Tell me, Rye, is it true what they say, that you've been asked to go to the Michigan Territory, where they're settling a new town?"

He cast her a sidelong look, but she was studying him, so he quickly turned his attention to the waves below. "I've been asked."

"Oh how I envy you, *too*, being a man! Men have the freedom to make so many choices."

"I haven't chosen t' leave Nantucket."

"No, but you can if you want to. Just like you could choose to go whaling. I've been thinking about it a lot lately, about how women have to stand by idly and let the years march along while waiting for something to change the course of their lives. I thought about Laura and how different she was, flaunting convention and doing what she pleased, and I thought, DeLaine Hussey, it's time for you to do as *you* please! And so here I am, telling you things that no lady ought to tell a man. But I don't care anymore—I'm not getting any younger, and I'm still single, and . . . and I . . . I don't want to be." DeLaine's voice had grown soft, as if she were making wishes to herself. "And I would give anything to be given the choice of starting a new life in a place like . . . like the Michigan Territory."

Rye studied her profile while she studied the kite. My God, the woman was proposing marriage! "DeLaine, I—"

"Oh, don't look so stricken, Rye, and don't bother saying anything. Let's just have a wonderful day and eat buckets of clams!" She smiled brightly while he realized she was probably feeling quite chagrined at what she had just admitted. He had never before pondered the plight of a woman who wishes to marry but is never asked.

Without warning, the kite broke loose and soared away above the Atlantic.

"Oh look!" DeLaine lifted a hand to touch the brim of her

hat, which fluttered in the brisk wind. She laughed again and the sound was carried eastward, where a quartet of gulls swooped and called. "It's heading for Portugal." The front of her coat lifted, too, and flapped against his trouser legs.

He smiled and took her arm, swinging back toward the fire. "Portugal's got nothin' as good as Nantucket clams. Come on."

They trudged back to the sunken pit, their moods once again carefree.

Cap'n Silas reversed the process he'd carefully overseen an hour before, removing the canvas in a great billow of steam, then pitching aside the limp seaweed whose tangy flavor lifted through the salt air.

Rye and DeLaine sat side by side on a blanket, eating succulent clams and scallops, tender vegetables, and spicy island sausage that never tasted quite as good when prepared in a roasting oven. They licked their lips and laughed and ran the backs of their hands across their chins and found themselves more at ease with each other as the evening wore on. When the meal was finished, nearly every man in the circle lit a pipe or a cigar.

"You don't smoke," DeLaine noted.

"Never had t', I just breathed the air m' father left behind."

Again they chuckled, and Rye clamped his arms around his crossed and updrawn legs while DeLaine thought of how many years she had waited for this night.

It was dark by the time the charcoal had cooled, sending the islanders straggling back home along the beach. Though the wind had died with the coming of night, it was still cold, and now the damps crept in from the ocean to sneak down inside collars and up beneath petticoats.

Rye and DeLaine made their way back toward town silently. Now and then their shoulders bumped. She clutched the neck of her coat while watching the dark flare of her skirt on each step.

"Are y' cold?" he asked, seeing her shiver.

"Isn't everyone on this island at this time of year?"

"Aye, and the worst is yet t' come." He had never touched

DeLaine in a personal way before, but he draped an arm around her shoulders now, chafing her coat sleeve while their breaths created white clouds of mist on the night air.

They came to the streets of town, where an occasional lantern created a puddle of light in the murky darkness. DeLaine lived in a silvery clapboard house near the square, and as they reached its picket fence, Rye dropped his arm, opened the gate, and let her pass through before him. Her steps slowed as they neared the door, then she turned to face him.

"Rye, I've enjoyed every minute of it, and I'm sorry if—"

"There's no need t' be sorry about anything, Delaine." He studied her upturned face in the shadows. She was smaller than Laura, and her scent was different, spicy instead of floral. With a small jolt, he realized it was the first time he'd thought of Laura all evening.

DeLaine studied his face; he stood so near that her hem brushed his pantlegs. "Rye, there is something I have wanted to do ever since that night at the Starbucks' dinner party. Would you mind very much if I . . . indulge myself?"

He wasn't at all sure he wanted to kiss DeLaine Hussey, but there was no way to avoid it gracefully. "By all means," he replied quietly. But instead of rising up on tiptoe, she carefully removed one glove and raised her bare hand to embrace his cheek and the swooping side-whiskers.

"Why, they're soft!" she exclaimed.

He chuckled as she ran the backs of her fingers over the opposite jaw, then tested the first one again, toying with the facial hair, running her fingertips over it.

"Of course they're soft. What did y' expect?"

"I . . . I don't know. They make your jaw look as hard as an anvil, and I just expected the whiskers would be . . . well, sharp."

Her palm had fallen still, but she did not withdraw it. It was very warm on Rye's cheek in the cool, damp night. "Have y' always been such an impetuous woman, DeLaine Hussey?"

"No, not always. I was taught, like all well-bred young misses, never to let my feelings show." But her fingertips trailed to the hollow of his cheek while her words died away into a whisper. The night was thick around them, while from the windows of the house candlelight painted their profiles a dim orange.

"DeLaine, what y' said today . . . I've no way of knowing what—"

"Shh." She placed a single fingertip over his lips.

It, too, was warm and lingering, and the invitation was unmistakable in her touch and her eyes. He'd had no desire ever to kiss another woman except Laura. He had no intention of taking DeLaine Hussey to the Michigan Territory. But she was female, and yearning, and the finger on his lower lip gently glided across its width, and without warning Rye's blood set up a wild coursing through his loins.

What the hell, he thought. Try her.

He gently bit the tip of her index finger and reached for her waist with both hands. As he bent to press his mouth over hers, she raised up and lifted her arms, twining the fingers of the gloveless hand into the thick hair at the back of his head.

He had been manipulated by her all day long and Rye Dalton knew it, but for the moment it didn't matter. He was lonely and vulnerable and she tasted faintly of butter and smelled of sandalwood, and her mouth opened so willingly it surprised his own into doing the same. She made a soft sound in her throat and pressed herself close, until the front of her coat met the sturdy wool of his peajacket. DeLaine Hussey, he thought. Who ever would have guessed this would happen with her? She moved her mouth and head in gestures of invitation, slipping her palm into the warm recesses of his collar, and natural curiosity took over in Rye. He ran his hand up the bulky side of her coat to the place where her breast swelled beneath it, and she brought her midsection firmly against his. Again came a throaty sound of ardor, and his hand moved between them to unbutton first his own jacket, then her coat, before slipping both arms inside against her warm back.

Their bodies molded tightly together, and DeLaine Hussey felt the male hardness of the man she had coveted for years and years. Rye's palm slid to her breast and a shudder ran through her.

He felt it, and knew a small surge of satisfaction, remembering what she'd said this afternoon, how long she had had feelings for him. The breast was fuller than Laura's, and the feel of the mouth beneath his was different. But when her hips writhed once, he realized what he was doing. Comparing.

He broke the kiss and lifted his head, squeezing her waist inside the coat while pushing her slightly away. "DeLaine . . . I . . . listen, I'm sorry. I shouldn't have started this."

"Rye, I told you. It doesn't matter if Laura comes first with you—"

"Hey, hey," he said softly, drawing out the words, releasing her, and moving back a step. "Let's just leave it here for tonight, all right? My life is in a mess right now, and I have no business imposin' complications on y'."

"Imposing? Rye, you don't understand—"

"I do, but I'm not free t' . . ." He sighed and ran a hand through his hair while backing even farther away.

She suddenly looked down at her hands while pulling the glove back on. "I'm sorry I pushed, Rye." She looked up imploringly. "Forgive me?"

He relented and covered her upper arms with his palms. "There's nothin' t' forgive, DeLaine. I've enjoyed the day, too." He gave her a brief parting kiss, squeezed her arms, and said, "Good night, DeLaine."

"Good night, Rye."

He turned down the walk, and she heard the squeak of the picket gate before his footsteps echoed away into the blackness. Damn you, Laura Dalton Morgan! she thought. Isn't one man enough for you?

Chapter 17

NOVEMBER DEEPENED, shrouding Nantucket with fog that seemed never ending. When it lifted, it was never for long: soon the wind would blow steadily from the southwest, and again the fog would appear as a gray line on the horizon, then race across the water to engulf the island like a windy cloak, and within ten minutes no one could see beyond twenty yards. The damp, frigid air sought a man's marrow, making fishermen bundle up like arctic whalers. But the fog was as much a part of life on Nantucket as was fishing itself, and those who gathered the provender of the Atlantic only dressed warmer and whistled softly between their teeth as they went about their work, accepting the whims of the weather.

Bass and bluefish were feeding off Rip Point, where the tides surged over the shoals, gouging and sucking at the shore in a froth of white water. John Durning, Tom Morgan, and others like them braved the elements daily, toiling at the nets until their chilled hands became bluer than the blues they caught.

Their boats, coming into the slips at the end of day, often appeared like spectral visions, gliding through the fog like silent ghost vessels. Then a voice would be heard calling hello, and another in answer, but it seemed no man ever stood in the spot from which a voice came, for the fog distorted the sounds and made them reverberate hollowly through the murky whiteness, like the disembodied utterances of wraiths.

During these bleak days, which Rye shared with Josiah, he thought about the coming of spring and the possibilities presented by the Michigan Territory. More and more he contemplated starting a new life there with Laura and Josh at his side. But would she truly leave Dan as she'd promised? And if so, could she possibly be legally divorced by that time? Perhaps she wouldn't consider leaving the island where she'd been born. There was no doubt in Rye's mind, however, that DeLaine Hussey would venture forth as his wife. Did he want her, though? Rye had the entire winter to answer that question for himself, but supposing he courted DeLaine and decided to marry her, there was the question of his father, who'd overtly demonstrated his distaste for her. Could the old man be persuaded to go to Michigan even if it were DeLaine going along as Rye's wife instead of Laura?

Rye and Ship took a walk one day to the house on Crooked Record Lane, but as they stood on the scallop-shell path, he knew it would be imprudent to knock on the door. He studied it, his hands buried deep, his hair covered by a woolen knit cap. Laura was inside, he knew, for the windows glowed through the gray day. But Josh was undoubtedly there, too, and as Rye studied the house that had once been his home, he felt again the pain he'd known that day the boy had flown at him, pummeling, crying, "You ain't neither my papa!" How many times since then had Rye wondered if Josh had accepted the truth yet? Countless times he'd cursed his own temper for flaring on that day Laura had come to order the lid, for he'd been so incensed, he hadn't even asked after the boy's wellbeing.

The wind shuddered through the barren leaves of the apple trees and sent the tall arborvitaes swaying against the linter, scraping the edge of the shingles with an eerie screech. Rye shivered.

Suddenly, he realized the foundation of the house had not been ballasted for the winter. So Dan's drinking was now affecting the way he carried out his responsibilities. Every house on the island was fortified against the drafts that seemed to creep and seep into every available crack during the cold months, and he was sure Dan had seen to it every winter during his absence. What an irony that it was Rye's turn to see to it in Dan's "absence."

With another glance at the window, Rye turned on his heel and made his way down to search out Cap'n Silas and ask if he knew someone who'd do the job.

The first snows fell; sleighs and bobsleds came to replace carriages and wagons. Across the undulating heathlands, ponds froze and small children skated with wooden runners strapped to their boots. Sometimes at night, fires could be seen near the frozen ponds where young people held skating parties. In keeping rooms, knitting needles clicked, turning out warm wool stockings.

A horse and bobsled delivered a load of kelp one day, much to Laura's relief, for though she'd piled the beds high with feather ticks, by morning the drafts had frozen the water in the bowl and left noses in nearly as bad a shape.

There came a day in early December when the fog rolled off across the Atlantic, leaving behind a churlish sky of clouds so gray they seemed to make dusk of day. The winds keened out of the northwest, delivering a stinging slap to the island.

Laura had set aside her bayberry-candle making until just such a day as this. When she rose that morning to the lowered clouds and blustering winds, she thrilled Josh by announcing that this was the day they would begin the task. Since Josh had patched up his friendship with Jimmy, he had softened toward Laura, too, and was now under foot, "helping" with the candle making. He sat at the trestle table with his mother, sorting through the first batch of berries, picking out twigs.

When they had enough, he begged, "Can I scoop 'em in the kettle, Mama?"

In the process, bayberries dropped to the floor and rolled into hiding, followed by Josh, who scrambled on hands and knees to find them.

It was a slow, time-consuming process, making candles, and as Laura stirred the kettle over the fire, she was grateful for Josh's chatter.

"Will Papa be home tonight?" he asked from his perch on a sturdy stool beside the crane.

"Of course Papa will be home. He comes home every night."

"But I mean for supper."

"I don't know, Josh."

"He promised me I could have skates this year, and he said he'd teach me how to use 'em."

"He did? When?"

Josh shrugged and looked into the brilliant coals beneath the kettle. "Long time ago."

Laura studied him. Poor darling Josh, she thought. Dan doesn't mean to disappoint you, and neither do I, but I'm running out of excuses for him.

"Maybe you should ask for skates for Christmas."

But Josh's expression was forlorn. "Christmas is so long to wait! Jimmy, he's already been skating twicet. He says I could go with him if I had skates."

But Laura had no answer for her son. "Come, would you like to stir the berries for a while?" she suggested brightly.

"Could I!" His eyes widened into blue pools of excitement.

"Pull your stool over here."

He stood on the high stool with Laura's arm around his waist, ineptly stirring the gray-green nuggets that were already beginning to separate, sending a heady evergreen scent throughout the house. As the dark, blackish tallow rose to the surface, wax formed. This first rendering of tallow had to be cooled, skimmed off, strained, then melted down a second time, yielding an almost transparent wax ready for pouring into the molds. But long before the refining process was completed, Josh had tired of the activity, and lolled on his belly along one of the trestle benches.

At noon a driving rain began, and Laura looked up from her task of measuring and cutting wicks for the molds as the first droplets hit the window panes.

"A nor'wester," she remarked idly, happy to be inside in the warm house.

After the wicks were strung and the molds filled for the first time, Laura made a cup of hot tea and took a break before starting with the next batch of berries. Josh stood on a chair, peering out the window, and she wandered across the room to stand behind him. The rain had turned to sleet, glazing the surface of the snow and freezing on the limbs of the apple trees until they trebled in size and shimmered like ice-covered fingers.

"I wanna go skating," Josh lamented, pressing his nose against the window.

She ruffled his hair and watched the frosted limbs quake with the wind. "Nobody's skating today." Josh looked dejected and lonely, and for a moment Laura wished there was another child to keep him company. She wondered, if she'd been married to Rye all these years, how many there would be. "Come, Josh, you can help me sort through the next batch of berries for twigs."

"I don't like pickin' twigs," he decided now. "I wanna go skating."

"Joshua! Do you have your tongue on that window?"

He looked over his shoulder guiltily, and though he didn't answer, there were two melted spots in the ice on the pane. Laura couldn't help smiling. "Come on down from there. Let's make another batch of candles."

The weather worsened as the day wore on. The sleet covered everything with a dangerous sheet of ice before giving way to hard, dry snow that snaked ahead of the gale in undulating patterns across the slippery cobblestone streets.

Down in the harbor, not a boat moved. The rigging was draped with icicles that hung aslant, frozen by the winds at an odd angle, as if the earth's kilter had slipped awry. Gulls huddled beneath the piers, their feathers lifting as the wind buffeted their backs. Shopkeepers hunkered low, gripping their collars as they headed home at day's end.

Dan Morgan left the countinghouse, turning his collar high, too, and clamping a hand on his beaver hat as the wind threatened to carry if off to Spain. He bent low, making his way toward the Blue Anchor, already anticipating the warming effect of a hot rum toddy on this devil's day. Down below, the mainmasts of the windjammers rocked wildly as the water churned and billowed. Dan slipped once, caught himself, and shuffled more carefully toward his destination.

Inside the Blue Anchor, the fire roared and the smell of boiling shellfish permeated the air. But Dan disdained an offer of hot chowder, ordering the toddy instead and hunkering over the tankard after savoring the first taste of its welcome contents.

The tankard was emptied and refilled, and the usual gathering of indulgers clustered about the fire, reluctant to budge from their comfortable seats and face the snowy gale outside.

Ephraim Biddle came in, ordered himself a stiff one, and ambled over to Dan, commenting, "Got that load o' kelp around y'r house, just like y' ordered."

It was the first time it had occurred to Dan that he'd neglected to see about the kelp. "You did?"

"Well, didn't y' see it there, man?"

"Oh yes, of course."

Ephraim lifted his drink, swallowed heartily, then backhanded his lips. "Wull, I sh'd hope so. Cap'n Silas, he come on down by the shack and says he had two dollar f'r anybody'd do the kelpin' around y'r foundation, so I took th' two and did it."

"Rye," Dan muttered into his tankard, then added under his breath, "Rye Dalton . . . damn the man." He took a deep draft of his toddy, clapped it down, and ordered, "Another!"

The night settled in, and the elbows at the Blue Anchor pressed more heavily against the trestle tables. Outside, the anchor above the door complained as the wind buffeted and sent it creaking. The snow began gathering on the leeward sides of picket fences, leaving swales of exposed earth to the windward. In protected corners it clung to shingled walls, climbing high, inching up slowly until it rose in delicate spears of white that were oddly anomalous to the raging winds that sculpted such beauty. On the streets outside the pub, snow inched across the cobbles until its white shroud covered the dangerous ice hidden beneath it. In the belfry of the Congregational church, the wind pushed at the bell, sending out a dreary offbeat *clon-n-ng* that shivered away toward the bobbing boats on the harbor, where it mingled with the whistle of wind in the rigging.

The hour was half-past ten when Dan Morgan at last stumbled from his bench at the Blue Anchor and went weaving toward the door. Behind him only the alekeeper, Hector Gorham, and Ephraim Biddle wished Dan good night. With his back to the pair, Dan lifted a hand in a gesture of farewell, then stepped through the door into the howling night. He had not negotiated the first step along the street before his beaver hat was torn from his head and went sailing off toward Nantucket Harbor, first in the air, then spinning to earth and bouncing along on its brim as it went.

"Damnash'n," Dan mumbled as he turned to follow it, trying to focus on the black object that immediately tumbled beyond his range of vision. Giving the hat up for lost, he turned back toward home, battling his way against the wind that clawed at his coat front and sent it flapping open, though he clutched it time and again with one bare hand. "Sh'd've brought m' gloves," he muttered to himself as he teetered along the streets, where the gale had managed to put out all the street lanterns, leaving the way black except for the shifting patterns of snow that whirled beneath Dan's feet.

Somewhere through his bleary mind came the realization that he had not buttoned his coat, and he was struggling to do just that when a fresh wall of wind struck him like a battering ram. His feet skidded, and he tried to regain his balance, but the force seemed to lift him as if by magic, flipping his body up, then dropping it to the cobblestones with the carelessness of a child examining a toy, then tossing it aside as if it were worthless after all. His head struck the bricks with a dull crack that made but the merest sound in the stormy night. The greatcoat he'd been attempting to button as he went down was opened by the wind and left to flap against Dan's thighs, which were sprawled on the icy street. The hands without gloves rested palm up on the ice-covered bricks while snow gathered around his hair and covered the warm splotch of blood that quickly froze into a pool of red ice. Heedless of what it had done, the nor'wester meted out its wrath on the unconscious man and his island home, which had taught him well, through all his growing years, the bitterness of its merciless winters. He lay now supine and exposed, his breathing shallow as the snow hit his face and built up, as it had around the fences, drifting on his leeward side, swaling to the wind-ward.

More than an hour later, Ephraim Biddle swallowed his last gulp, made a sound of resignation deep in his throat, and pushed himself off his cozy perch, reaching for the buttons of his jacket. "There's no help f'r 'it but t' face th' long walk 'ome," he slurred. "G'night, Hector," he mumbled to the alekeeper.

"G'night, Eph." Hector followed his last patron to the door gratefully, lowering the bar behind him.

Outside, Ephraim slogged up the street, muttering oaths as he bent low and balanced precariously on footing made all the more doubtful by his own inebriated state. The wind and snow drove down with a fury, and he clutched his collar, stooping even lower to protect his face from its wrath. When he stumbled against the inert body of Dan Morgan, he backed a step away, scanned the unmoving lump at his feet, and mumbled, "Wh . . . what's this?" A closer look revealed the shape of a man, and Ephraim bent on one knee, trying to clear his befuddled vision. "Morgan? 'zat choo?" He shook the limp arm. " 'ey, Morgan, git up!" But suddenly Ephraim sobered. "Morgan?" he said with a note of alarm. "Morgan!" He shook Dan harder, but to no avail. The man lay unmoving, unspeaking, while around him the snow already lay in drifts. "Aw Jesus, no . . ." Then Ephraim was on his feet again, running back toward the Blue Anchor, managing somehow to retain his footing on the icy cobbles, desperation keeping him upright.

Hector had already slipped the suspenders from his shoulders when a pounding came from below. "Goddamn," he cursed, raising the suspenders once again and grudgingly taking the candle to light his way down the steps. "I'm coming! I'm coming!"

"Hector! Hector!" he heard through the door, as the pounding continued, harder. "Hector, open up!"

The door swung open on a panic-stricken Ephraim Biddle. "Hector, y've got t' come! I found Dan Morgan layin' dead in the street!"

"Oh God, no! I'll get my coat!"

Biddle waited by the door, shivering, afraid to make a move
on his own now. When Hector returned, they leaned into the
storm together, retracing Biddle's ever-fainter footprints to
the motionless form lying in the snow. Without the slightest
hesitation, Hector leaned and slipped his strong arms beneath
the shoulders and knees of Dan Morgan, carried him back to
the Blue Anchor, and lay him flat on a trestle table before the
fireplace, where the coals had already been banked for the
night.

"Is 'e dead?" Biddle's eyes looked like those of an unfinished marble sculpture, two wide, deep, fearful depressions in
his face.

Hector pressed his fingertips just below Dan's jaw. "I can
feel a pulse yet."

"Wh . . . what we gonna do with 'im?"

"I don't know. I don't want him dyin' here, givin' the place
a bad reputation." The alekeeper thought for a moment—
Morgan's father was dead, and what could his mother or wife
do? "I'll get a quilt and stoke up the fire and you go down to
the cooperage and get Rye Dalton. Tell him what's happened.
He'll know what t' do."

Biddle nodded as he made for the door with a wild look on
his face. Never in his life had he had such a scare. He'd been
spending evening after evening swilling with Morgan, and it
was sobering in more ways than one to find his cohort brought
so low by alcohol. Why—by the saints!—it coulda been me,
Biddle thought.

Rye and Josiah were both in bed asleep when they were
roused by a hammering from below.

"What the hell . . ." Rye muttered as he braced up on an
elbow and ran a hand through his hair in the dark.

Josiah's voice came from the opposite side of the room.
"Sounds like somebody's in a hurry f'r somethin'."

"I'll go," Rye said, rolling to the edge of the bed, searching
for the flint. When the wick caught, he quickly slipped on his
pants, then made his way down the rough-hewn steps to the
dark cavern of the cooperage below.

"Dalton, git up!"

"I'm comin'! I'm comin'!" The door opened and Rye unceremoniously hauled Ephraim Biddle inside. "Biddle, what the hell do y' want at this hour o' the night?" Biddle's eyes looked like he'd been on more than a bad drunk.

"It's y'r friend Dan Morgan. He got drunk and fell down on the street, and we found him layin' there, all sprawled out and half froze to death."

"Oh Jesus, no!"

"Hector says he's still got a pulse beatin', but—"

"Where is he?" Already Rye was taking the steps two at a time, shouting back over his shoulder.

"Hector's got 'im layin' on a table at the Blue Anchor, but he don't know what t' do with 'im. Said t' come and fetch you and you'd know what we oughter do."

"What is it?" Josiah asked from his bed. Rye lunged across the room, yanking a sweater over his head, reaching for his pea jacket, mittens, and warm cap. "Dan's been found out cold, in the storm someplace."

Josiah, too, reached for his clothes now. "Y' want me t' come?"

Ship whined and stood watching every motion of Rye, who roughly yanked on boots, then turned toward the stairs again.

"No, y' stay here and keep out o' the storm. I'll need a warm fire when I get back." Ship followed on the heels of his master, who ordered, "Come on, Biddle," as he led the way out the door too hurriedly to take time to send the dog back inside.

Rye Dalton had rounded the Horn on a schooner. He knew the perils of an icy deck that tilted and pitched and threatened to toss men into the turbulent sea. Running across a flat cobblestone street was nothing for such a man. He hit the door of the Blue Anchor before Ephraim Biddle had scarcely found his footing. He stalked across the dim room toward the motionless form on the trestle table.

"Get 'im away from the fire!" Dalton roared. "Are y' daft, man?" Without a pause, Rye pressed his weight against the edge of the trestle, sending it skittering away from the heat, then he reached to yank down the quilt with which the well-meaning Hector had covered Dan. "Bring a candle!"

Hector jumped to follow the brisk order while Rye searched for one of Dan's hands. In the wavering candlelight, he immediately saw that Dan's fingers were frozen. With a quick snap he settled the quilt on the floor, then lifted Dan and lay him on it while he gave further orders.

"How long do y' think he was there?"

"An hour maybe, judging from when he left here."

"Y' can't thaw out frozen flesh that fast or a man'll lose it, Hector!"

"I didn't—"

"Get over t' Doc Foulger and tell him t' meet me at my house—Dan's house, I mean—immediately. Dan'll need attention that only his wife can give him once the doc takes a look at these hands." Then Rye placed his own mittens on Dan's hands, his cap on Dan's head, wrapped the quilt around him as if he were an infant, hefted him off the floor, and strode toward the door. "And send along a pint of the strongest brandy y' got with the doc. Now git y'r feet movin', Hector!" Dalton didn't even pause to kick the door shut behind him as he shouldered through into the snow-swept night.

Laura was aroused from sleep by the sound of someone kicking the door. Thinking it was Dan, she swung her bare feet to the icy floor and hurried to the keeping room, where the mighty racket continued, as if Dan were trying to break the door down.

"Laura, open up!"

She realized it was Rye's voice in the same moment the wind knocked the door from her hand and sent it against the wall with a sound thud.

"Rye? What is it?" He swept inside carrying something in his arms.

"Shut the door and light a candle, Laura."

Even before she could move to obey his orders, Rye was clumping across the floor toward the bedroom doorway. The bulky shadow of Ship slipped inside, then the door cut off the wind and Laura groped her way toward the flint. In the dark she kicked over a basket of bayberries and heard them roll across the floor, but paid little heed as she called into the blackness, "Rye, what happened?"

"Bring the candle in here. I need y'r help."

"Rye, is it Dan?" Laura's voice shook.

"Aye."

The candle flared at last, and she moved toward the doorway with growing dread. Inside the bedroom, Rye had already placed Dan on the bed and was leaning over him, pressing his fingers to Dan's neck. Laura's stomach went weightless with alarm, then just as swiftly felt as if a lead ball were lying in it. Fear sent moisture to her palms as she hurried to the opposite side of the bed to lean over the unconscious man.

Josh came awake at the commotion and slipped over the edge of his bed to follow his mother to the doorway of the linter and observe the two, who were unaware of his presence.

"Oh, dear God, what's happened to him?"

"He got drunk at the Blue Anchor and fell down on his way home. Apparently he was lyin' there for an hour before Ephraim Biddle stumbled on him."

"Is he alive?"

"Aye, but his fingers're frozen, and I don't know what else."

Josh read the fear in his mother's face and sensed a great urgency in Rye as the two leaned across Dan from opposite sides of the bed. They hardly looked at each other. Instead, they both touched Dan as if they wanted him to wake up. Then Rye started taking off one of Dan's shoes like he was in a real hurry.

Laura pressed a palm to Dan's temple and forehead, trying to control the fear that made her hand tremble and tightened the muscles in her chest. She bit her lips and felt tears begin to swell as the fear of helplessness began to take hold. Laura Morgan, don't you go to pieces now! She dashed away the useless tears with the side of her hand, turned to Rye, and took command of her emotions. "What do you want me to do?" she asked with brisk intensity.

"Take off his socks. We have t' see if his toes are frozen, too."

She peeled off the first sock to find the toes red but pliant.

"Thank God, they're not," Rye breathed, scanning the room now with an unemotional eye, his mind racing ahead. "Doc Foulger is coming. We'll need a hammer and an awl, and y' can build up the fire out there a little at a time." Rye flung his jacket off and dropped it on the floor, then turned back to Dan. "And bring an absorbent cloth and a small pitcher." Only then did Rye see the child, in his nightshirt, clinging to the doorframe, eyes wide with uncertainty and fear. As Laura headed for the keeping room, Rye issued one more order, but more gently. "And keep the boy out there."

"Josh, come. Do as Rye says."

"Is Papa dead?"

"No, but he's very sick. Now you get back into your bed where it's warm and I'll—"

"But I wanna see Papa. Is he gonna die like Grampa?"

"Rye is taking care of Papa. Now please, Josh, just stay out of the way."

Laura had little time to concern herself with Josh as she found the things Rye wanted. Neither had she time to wonder exactly what he wanted them for.

His voice came firmly from around the bedroom doorway. "Laura, have y' got a small breadboard?"

"Yes."

"Bring it!"

While she was reaching for it, Ship let out a single sharp bark, making Laura aware for the first time that the Lab lay on the rug at the door. Scarcely had she looked up before an impatient knock sounded, and the door was opened not by Dr. Foulger, but by the apothecary, Nathan McColl, carrying an alligator satchel.

McColl swept inside without a moment's pause. "Where is he?"

"In there." Laura nodded toward the linter room, then followed McColl's black-caped shoulders through the doorway, her hands full of the items Rye had requested.

Rye straightened at the man's entrance, a deep frown lining his face. "Where's the doc?"

"Stranded on the other side of the island. When Biddle couldn't find him, he had enough sense to come for me."

Though doctors and apothecaries were authorized to practice almost identical methods, Rye had never trusted or liked McColl. But he had little choice now as the man stepped forward self-importantly.

McColl felt for a pulse, then examined one of Dan's hands. "Frozen."

"Aye, and not a minute t' waste before it thaws," Rye declared impatiently, reaching for the things Laura had brought.

"They can't be saved. We're better off concentrating on preventing the man from getting pneumonia."

Rye glared at McColl. "Can't be saved! Why, man, y're crazy! They can and *will* be saved if we act before they thaw!"

McColl allowed a smug expression to cross his face before glancing at the breadboard, hammer, and awl. "I take that to mean you know more about medicine than I do."

"Take it t' mean what y' will, McColl. Y've never been on a whaleship and seen a sailor's hands when he's pulled on the shrouds all night in an ice storm. What do y' think the captain does with frozen fingers? Chops 'em off?" Rye's face was stormy. "I'm not lettin' those fingers thaw without tryin' t' do what I can for 'em. If I can't save 'em, the pain'll be no worse either way. I could use a hand here." Rye moved toward the bed as if to place the equipment there, but McColl stepped forward to bar the way.

"If you're going to do what I think you're going to do, I'll have no part in it. I won't be held responsible for broken bones and infections that—"

"Out of the way, McColl! We're wastin' time!" Rye's expression was hard and angry as he counted precious seconds slip by.

"Dalton, I warn you—"

"Goddamnit, McColl, this man is my friend, and he earns his pay as an accountant—writin'! How can he do that without fingers? Now either lend me a hand or get the hell out of my way!" The order was issued at a near roar as Rye roughly shouldered the man aside and bent over the bed. "Laura?"

"Yes?" She stepped forward without hesitation.

Rye placed the breadboard on Dan's chest, then laid one

hand on it, and at last met Laura's eyes. "Since McColl chooses not t' help me, I'll have t' ask you t'."

She nodded silently, suddenly dreading the task, for whatever Rye was planning seemed something hard to stomach. "Just tell me what to do, Rye."

He took a moment to give her a reassuring glance, then snapped at McColl, "Did y' bring the brandy?"

The man handed over the flask and looked down his nose superciliously. "I assumed it was meant to fortify you and Mrs. Morgan."

Rye ignored him. "Here, Laura, take the cork out and pour some into the pitcher. Then come and sit on the bed and hold Dan's hand steady." He covered the board with the absorbent cloth, and arranged Dan's hand on it, shifting the entire arrangement around until the fingers could lie flat.

"You'll end up breaking his bones, Dalton, I warn you."

Rye thought that if time were not of the essence, he'd take several seconds to wrap McColl's jaw around his knuckles! "Better a broken bone than a lost finger. The bones'll mend."

Laura held the pitcher ready now, but her face blanched and her eyes grew wide with apprehension. Rye paused and looked directly into them. "Y've got t' hold his fingers flat while I puncture 'em, then pour the brandy into the holes when I say. Can y' do that, darlin'?"

For a moment her eyes flickered, and she looked as if she might be sick. She swallowed, willing herself to take strength from Rye, to trust his decision, and finally she nodded.

"All right, sit down there. We've wasted too much time as it is."

She moved to the opposite side of the bed and sat down, watching as Rye carefully arranged the first of Dan's fingers flat on the surface of the board and looked up at her. "Hold it just like this." She pressed the finger onto the cloth, horrified at how stiff and cold it was. Nausea crept through her as she saw Rye take up the hammer and awl—a wooden-handled tool with a short point like an ice pick. He rested the sharp prick on Dan's fingertip and tapped the hammer once, twice. Laura felt the gorge rise in her throat as the tip sank into the frozen flesh.

"Damnit, Laura-love, don't y' faint on me now."

Her eyes flew up at the half-gentle, half-harsh words, and she found Rye sending his encouragement to her once again. "I won't. Just hurry."

The awl pierced the first finger three times, once on each of its inner pads, before Rye gave the order, "Pour."

The brandy ran into the holes and drizzled onto the white cloth, staining it a pale brown. Though McColl refused to help, he nevertheless stood by watching, fascinated by the process and by the endearments that passed from Rye Dalton to Laura Morgan. Behind him, a child stood in the doorway, watching too. Beside the child sat a dog, both of them so quiet nobody took notice as the tap of the hammer on the awl fell into the still room again and again, followed by the firm but quiet order, "Pour." The man on the bed remained blessedly unconscious, the alcohol in his bloodstream serving a totally useful purpose for the first time in his life: not only did it keep him from rousing, but it made it necessary for Rye to puncture the fingers fewer times than he'd otherwise have had to.

It was with great difficulty that Laura assisted Rye. Time and again she swallowed the clot of nausea that threatened. Tears made Rye's and Dan's hands swim before her, and she hunched a shoulder and blotted her eyes on her sleeve, took a firmer grip on her emotions, and steeled herself to hold the next finger.

Never once did Rye falter. His movements were steady and efficient with the tools as he tapped delicately, gauging the depth of each hole with great care. Not until the last finger had been bathed with brandy did Laura look up at Rye again. She was stricken to find his face ashen as he stared down at Dan. He opened his mouth and drew in a deep draft of air, as if battling for equilibrium, and suddenly he threw down the hammer and awl and spun from the room. A moment later, the outside door slammed.

Laura's eyes met McColl's, and suddenly she remembered how Rye had called her Laura-love. Then she saw Josh, whose chin was quivering as tears ran down his face. She scooped him up and hugged him close, kissing his hair, and comforting, "Shh, Joshua. Papa's going to be just fine. You'll see. There's no need to cry. We're going to take good care of Papa

and make him teach you how to skate as soon as he's well
again." She deposited Josh back in his own bed, then tucked
him in, and whispered, "You try to sleep, darling. I . . . I've
got to go to Rye."

She turned to grab a woolen shawl and stepped out into the
howling night. Rye was sitting on the wooden step, slumped
forward with his head on his crossed arms. Ship was there
before him, whimpering softly, pacing back and forth and trying to nuzzle beyond his master's arms to his face.

"Rye, you must come back inside. You don't even have a
jacket on."

"In a minute."

The wind lifted the fringe of Laura's shawl and slapped it
across her face while snow streaked down and bit at her exposed skin. She hunkered down beside him and put her arm
across his shoulders. He was shaking uncontrollably, though
she realized it was not solely from the weather.

"Shh," she comforted as if he, too, were a child. "It's over
now, and you were magnificent."

"Magnificent!" he flung back. "I'm shakin' like a damn
baby."

"You have a right to shake. What you did was hardly easy.
Why, not even McColl had the nerve to do it. And me—why,
if you hadn't been so sure and confident, I'd have fallen to
pieces."

He raised his head, wiping his cheeks with long palms as if
exhausted. "I've never done anythin' like that before in my
life."

His shudders continued beneath her arm, and she gently
kissed the top of his head, tasting icy snow on his hair. "Come
on now. It won't do us any good if you catch pneumonia,
too."

With a shaky sigh he stood up, and she along with him.
"Just give me a minute, Laura. I'll be all right now. You go
back in."

She turned back toward the door, but his voice stopped her.

"Thank you for helpin'. I couldn't've done it alone."

The wind moaned through the black dome of night sky as
they were both stricken with the enormity of what they'd

done. There had been no second thoughts. They had not *acted* so much as *reacted* when they saw that Dan needed them. It was like the day of Zach's death all over again. The three of them forever caught in a tapestry, woven into it like figures unable to change the course of their intertwined lives.

Chapter 18

WHEN RYE DALTON stepped back inside, McColl was nowhere in sight. Laura had built up the fire and was heating water for tea. He stopped in the shadows near the door, and at the sound of his entry, Laura looked up, a teapot in her hands. During his preoccupation with Dan, Rye had scarcely noticed how Laura was dressed. But he paused now to note her wrapper of soft pink flannel, buttoned demurely from hem to high neck and belted around her middle, disguising her shape. On her feet were thick gray knit stockings. The fire danced and flickered, backlighting the outline of her hair, which was loosely braided in a single plait, with wisps flying free around her face. Their ends took on sparks of fire themselves as she stared into the shadows at Rye.

He shuddered and slipped his chilled fingers into the waist of his britches to warm them against his belly, but in that instant, while Laura poised and their eyes met, his body quivered from memory. It was the first time he'd been exposed to her, the Laura he remembered, moving about, doing familiar things, dressed in an intimate way. Almost as if she sensed his thoughts, she set the teapot on the table and turned to face the fireplace once again, the single braid swinging between her shoulder blades as she bent forward.

With a deep sigh, Rye pulled his errant thoughts back to the problem at hand; this was not the appropriate time for either memories or wishes.

He crossed the keeping room, but as he passed the alcove bed, he made out Josh, lying wide-eyed in the dimness, staring up at him. Still with his hands tucked against his belly, Rye paused, meeting the blue eyes of the child with an earnest gaze. Enough light slipped into the cavern above the bed that Rye could see fear and questions in the child's expression. He leaned sideways from the hip, lightly running a forefinger along the edge of the patchwork quilt covering the boy. "Your pa . . ." But the boy knew the truth now—there was no sense in trying to disguise it. Rye's voice was very low yet curiously rough as he began again. "Dan is going t' get better, I promise y', son. Y'r mother and I'll see to it."

The small chin quivered and tears suddenly glimmered on Josh's fair lashes as he tried not to cry. Then his childish voice trembled. "H . . . he's got to, 'cause he . . . he promised t' teach m . . . me to skate."

For the first time Rye, too, felt like crying. His chest went tight. His heart felt swollen. He dropped to one knee, adjusted the quilts beneath the boy's chin, and let his hand linger just a moment on the small chest. Through the layers of bedding he could feel shaken breaths being held tenuously. A surge of love welled up in Rye as he leaned to do what he had so often dreamed of doing. He placed a gentle kiss on his son's forehead. "It's a promise, Joshua," he vowed against the warm skin that smelled different from any the man had ever been near—a child's scent, milky and mellow, and touched with the aroma of bayberry that clung to the room. "But in the meantime, it's perfectly all right t' cry," Rye whispered. "It'll make y' feel better and help y' get t' sleep." Even before Rye's words were out, Josh's tears spilled and his breath caught on a first sob. Realizing that Josh was chagrined at breaking down this way, Rye secretly added, "I've cried plenty o' times m'self."

"Y . . . you h . . . have?" Josh tugged the quilts up to dry his eyes.

"Aye. I cried when I heard m' mother had died while I was out t' sea. And I cried when . . . ah well, there've been plenty o' times. Why, I nearly cried out on the step just now, but I figured if I did, the tears'd freeze and I'd be in a fix.''

Somehow during this conversation Josh's tears had abated. Rye touched the blond hair on his son's forehead. "G'night now, son."

"G'night."

When Rye straightened and turned, he found Laura had been watching all the time. Her hands were clasped tightly together and her lower lip was caught in her teeth. She, too, appeared to be holding emotions in check, for her face reflected both tenderness and pain. Rye looked from her to the linter room doorway, from where McColl now watched them both. When Rye's glance shifted, Laura's did, too.

Flustered to find McColl observing something that was none of his business, Laura immediately sought to divert him. She crossed to pluck three mugs from their hooks on the wall and set them on the trestle.

At that moment Josh's voice came from behind Rye again. "Where's Ship?"

Rye turned. "Why, she's right here on the rug by the door."

"Could she come over here by me?"

Without hesitation, Rye ordered quietly, "Here, girl," and the dog ambled across the puncheon floor with clicking toenails. "Down," Rye ordered, and the Lab dropped to her stomach obediently.

Josh hung over the side of the bed to pet Ship's head, then looked up appealingly at his mother. "Couldn't she come up here with me, Mama, please?"

Rye could see the idea didn't agree with Laura, and put in quickly, "She's been trained that her place is beside the bed, not in it, Josh. But she'll stay right there and keep y' company."

"Will she be there when I wake up?"

Rye's blue eyes met Laura's brown ones across the firelit room. Then he turned back to his son. "Aye, she'll be there."

Again they both grew uncomfortably aware of the apothecary observing their every exchange. But then McColl cleared his throat and announced, "I'll need some boiling water."

Laura filled the teapot, then handed the simmering teakettle to him. "If you need more, I'll fill it again."

The apothecary answered with little more than a grunt before disappearing into the bedroom again. Laura and Rye sat down across from each other at the table, and she poured tea into two mugs. The fire snapped, and the wind howled around the windows, and from inside the bedroom came the sound of water being poured.

Rye had raised his cup to his mouth for the second time before some sixth sense warned him. He lurched to his feet, sending the bench scraping backward as he strode purposefully to the bedroom doorway, where he stopped short, his fists clenched.

"What the goddamn hell do y' think y're doin', McColl!"

His rage seemed to rival the force of the blizzard outside. Laura was beside Rye in a flash. She gaped in horror at the steam-heated glass cup McColl had placed upside down on Dan's exposed chest.

"We must restore his circulation . . ." McColl was lifting a second dome-shaped glass from the interior of the hot tea-kettle with metal tongs when both tongs and cup were suddenly smacked out of his hand and went flying across the room.

"Get the hell out, McColl!" Dalton roared, "and take y'r goddamn cuppin' with y'!"

Immediately, Rye spun toward the bed, searching for something to slip beneath the rounded lip of the cup to break the suction. He caught sight of the awl and quickly inserted its point beneath the thick-domed piece that was about the size of half a walnut shell, and handleless. Grabbing up the brandy-stained rag, he took the cup from Dan's skin, and as he did a little puff of steam came from beneath it. At the sight of the burn it had caused, Rye cursed, "Goddamn y', fool!"

"Fool!" The outraged apothecary glared at Dalton. "*You* call *me* the fool?" Cupping was as common a practice as pill-rolling, for the vacuum created beneath the steam-heated cups was believed to have the power to induce bad blood from incisions and cure respiratory ailments by stimulating the skin and drawing the blood to its surface. Thus, McColl's voice held a note of disdainful superiority as he scoffed, "People like you think you know more than trained men of medicine, Dalton. Well, I for one—"

"Trained men o' medicine! Y've burned him, man! *Needlessly burned him!*" Rye's face was a distorted mask of rage, and the power of his voice fairly shook the rafters.

"I did not invent the cure, Dalton, I only apply it."

"And enjoy every minute of it!" Rye's anger billowed afresh, for he knew that had he not stepped to the doorway when he did, McColl undoubtedly would have covered Dan's entire chest with the painful "cure-alls." Had the man shown any sign of compassion for the plight of his patient, Rye might have relented in his anger.

Instead, McColl only crossed to retrieve the cup from the floor, using his hanky to hold it as he headed toward Dalton to collect his bag. "The burns are an unfortunate side effect, but it's for the good of the patient in the long run," the apothecary stated smugly.

The sheer stupidity and pitilessness of such views was more than Rye could tolerate. Turning swiftly as McColl passed, the cooper suddenly pressed the hot cup he still held to McColl's cheek.

McColl jerked back, nursing the spot tenderly with his fingertips as it slowly turned red. His eyes snapped with hatred. "You're mad, Dalton," he growled. "First you call me in for help, then use your own queer methods and refuse to let me proceed with the accepted treatment, but I'll see that you pay for this . . . this insult!"

"How many more ways were y' plannin' t' torture him? I'm not the one who's mad, McColl, you are! You and all your kind who practice such atrocities in the name of medicine! And I did *not* send for y'. I sent for Doc Foulger, though I'm not too sure his methods're any less grisly than yours! How did it feel, McColl, huh? How do y' like bein' burned? Do y' think Dan here likes it any better than you do?" With each accusation Rye took another menacing step forward until he'd forced the apothecary back almost as far as the linter room doorway. There, Rye snarled, "Now take y'r fancy black bag with y' and get the hell out and never darken my door again!"

"B . . . but my cups!" McColl's wide eyes wavered toward

the hot kettle still sitting on the bedside commode.

"Will stay right where they are!" Rye finished for him.
"Out!" A shaking finger pointed the way.

McColl grabbed his cape, turned tail and ran.

A wide-eyed Laura, her face ashen, was bending over Dan,
sickened by the unnecessary wound forced upon a man too ill
to be able to object to such treatment.

As Rye turned back to her, he immediately noted that the
circular burn was brilliant red and already beginning to blister.
"Oh, Christ, would y' look at what that damn fool's done."
Without pause, Rye strode out of the room and returned a
moment later with a handful of snow, which he laid on the
burn.

Immediately, it began melting, and Laura found the cloth
with the brandy stains and dabbed away the rivulets as they
formed.

"Oh, Rye, how could McColl do such a thing?" There were
tears in her eyes.

The hand holding the snow shook yet with anger. "The
man's an ass! He and all his ilk. What they get by with is
criminal—leechin', cuppin', rowelin'—every last one of 'em
should be made t' suffer their own *cures*, and they'd soon stop
subjectin' others t' them."

"I'll mix up an ointment for it. How are Dan's fingers
doing?"

Laura's question diverted Rye's attention, and his nerves
stopped jumping. He checked Dan's fingers, which were
warming now and beginning to bleed. He lifted his eyes to
Laura's, and there was pain in the blue depths. "I won't lie to
y', love. He'll do plenty o' sufferin' before this's over."
Together they looked at the man on the bed, then at each other
again.

"I know. But we'll be here to see him through it. Both of
us."

The long lines of weariness at the sides of Rye's mouth were
accented in the dim candlelight. And from where she stood,
Laura made out each pockmark on his face as a round shadow
while he answered.

"Aye, both of us."

A tremulous silence passed while they seemed to solemnize the vow, then Laura silently turned and left the room.

They wrapped Dan's hands in linen strips and covered them with a pair of mittens, then applied a balm of witch hazel to his burn, then covered it with a square of soft flannel before they bundled him in a feather tick and went back to the keeping room to wait.

Laura turned toward the fireplace to rewarm their tea, but she glanced over her shoulder at a soft word from Rye.

"Look."

Rye stood beside Josh's bed, gazing down into the alcove's shadows. Laura came up behind his broad shoulder and peered around to find Ship sound asleep at the foot of the bed, curled against Josh's feet, while the child, too, slumbered peacefully.

Rye turned his eyes from the bed to the woman beside him. She lifted her face, and for a moment he read peace there. He watched her coffee-colored eyes rove over his features, pausing on his hair, his eyes, lips, sideburns, and homing again to his eyes. Outside, the wind rattled the shutters while behind her a log broke and settled to the grate with a soft shush. More than anything in the world, Rye wanted simply to circle her with his arms and rest his cheek on top of her hair, close his eyes for a moment, and feel her face pressed against his collarbone. But he didn't. His thumbs remained hooked at his waist while he invented inanities to bridge the compelling moment.

"I'm sorry, Laura. I remember y' don't like dogs on y'r beds. Should I make 'er get down?"

"No. Josh needs her just as badly as . . ." She caught herself just in time before saying, *as I need you.* But Rye's sharp glance made her realize the words were clearly understood between them. Again she groped for something to say. "Thank you for coming, Rye."

"Y' don't have t' thank me, Laura, y' know that. Nothing could've kept me away when you or Dan needed me." He paused thoughtfully for a moment, then his mouth formed a rueful quarter-smile. "Funny, isn't it? Everyone on this island knows the truth of that. I was the first one they thought o' runnin' to when they found Dan, just like he was the first one they went runnin' to when I was supposed t've drowned."

They stood silent for a minute, once again pondering the reversal of the two men's roles in Laura's life, then she admitted, "I don't know what I'd have done without you. I would never have been able to stand up to McColl the way you did or know what was best for Dan."

Rye sighed and glanced toward the linter room doorway. "Let's *hope* we've done what's best for him." Then, looking down at Laura's hair, he asked, "Have y' got that tea ready?"

She led the way back toward the fireplace while Rye slumped to a bench at the trestle, and she placed two hot mugs on the boards, then sat down opposite.

Quite naturally, their thoughts roved backward five years to the last time they had shared this table. Laura looked up to find Rye watching her as he lifted the cup to his lips. He sipped, then the crease deepened between his eyes. He looked down into the cup. "The honey—you remembered." Again his blue-eyed gaze met hers over the cup.

"Why, of course I remembered. I must have fixed you tea with honey and nutmeg a hundred times."

The spicy, hot brew brought back at least as many memories now, but they knew it was dangerous to revive them. "When I was on the ship and the ice storms came on a night much like this, I'd think of sittin' with y' this way beside the fire, and I'd've given my entire lay t' have a cup o' y'r tea then."

"And I'd have given the same to be able to fix it for you," she added simply. It was the first time he had expressed regret over the choice he'd made. She tried to keep her eyes on anything except him, but it was as if they were unwilling to obey her wishes, and time and again, Laura's gaze got tangled up with his. They raised their mugs, drank deeply, and suddenly, beneath the table, Rye shifted his long legs and his knee bumped hers. Her knee jerked back to safety while he simultaneously sat up straighter.

For the first time Rye became fully aware of the pungent scent of bayberry permeating the room. He glanced toward the hearth, along the stones to one side, noting the candle forms, the baskets of berries, one of them spilled, the kettle and long-handled ladle for dipping the melted wax. Slowly, he turned back to look at her.

"Y've been makin' bayberry candles."

She nodded, her eyes flickering up, then quickly down again.

He let his eyelids drift closed, pulled in a deep lungful of evergreen-flavored air, and dropped his head back slightly. "Ahh . . ." The sound rumbled from his throat in a long syllable of satisfaction before he looked at Laura once again. "The memories that scent brings back." The perfume of the bayberries seemed to shift about his head like rich incense, bringing with it recollections of himself and Laura, younger then, seeking privacy in the bayberry thickets. And after they were married, there was the time she had made candles, and that night, in an orgy of excess, they had lit six of the fragrant tapers and placed them all around the bed, then pleasured each other within their circle of flickering golden light while the essence seemed to flavor their very skin.

Sitting now with that same smell filling their senses, the two were aware of each other as man and woman as they'd ever been in their lives. The dancing firelight sent shifting highlights over their faces, and lit the sleeve of Laura's pink wrapper to a deep melon color. Her mug was empty, she had taken refuge in it so often, and she told herself to go get the kettle, to break this spell. But before she could, Rye lowered his right hand and laid it palm up on the table between them. Her gaze moved from his long fingers to his sea-blue eyes, which remained steadfastly on hers. Her heart tripped and thudded, and she clutched the handle of her mug while looking down again at the callused palm that waited in invitation.

"Don't worry," he said, low and gruff. "I wouldn't do that t' Dan when he's lyin' unconscious. I just need t' touch y'."

She moved her own hand slowly until it rested on his, then his fingers closed gently around hers and she searched for something proper to say, but so many intimate things came to mind instead.

"Rye, I got the message you sent about Josh. I meant to thank you for sending it that day I came to the cooperage to order the cover, but my temper got the better of me and I—"

"Laura, I'm sorry for what I said that day, and for not comin' downstairs the day y' came t' pick up the cover. I knew y' were down there, and I heard y' tellin' the old man y' wanted t' talk t' me."

"Oh no, Rye, I'm the one who should apologize, for what I said that day about DeLaine Hussey. I realized later how unfair it was of me to put restrictions on you when I'm . . . well . . ." She let the thought go unfinished, and asked instead, "How did you find out that Josh knew you were his father?"

"He came t' the cooperage and denied it, then punched me in the stomach and took off, cryin'."

Unconsciously, Laura covered Rye's hand with her free one. "Oh, Rye, no." Her eyes were sad and her lips drooped compassionately.

"I could see he was terribly upset, and I worried about him day and night after that, wonderin' what was goin' through the little tyke's mind, and through yours. Then when y' came to the cooperage, I . . . I didn't even bother t' ask how he'd found out and how he was takin' it."

"He found out from Jimmy . . ." Laura relayed the happenings of that day, and as she finished, Rye was staring at their joined hands while his thumb stroked her knuckles.

"Did y' tell him about us? About the beginnin'?"

"I did. I tried to explain everything so that he'd understand, about our childhood and why you went on the voyage and what it was like when I thought you were dead, right up to the time you came back."

"And what was his reaction?"

"He wanted to know if I was married to both of you, and if you both . . ." But she decided it was wisest not to finish.

Rye shot her a sharp look, and Laura sensed that he knew, even though she hadn't said it. She understood intuitively that what Rye sought was some assurance that Josh was growing to accept the knowledge of his paternity. Laura's forehead showed lines of concern.

"Oh, Rye, his security has been so badly shaken. I can see changes in him as time goes on, and I believe he's coming to terms with the truth, but I really can't say what his feelings are. I think he's still very mixed up about all this."

Rye sighed, then absently watched his mug as he moved it on the tabletop in circular motions.

Laura freed her hand and went to fetch the kettle once more. When she was again seated across from Rye, she purposely cradled her mug with both hands, gazing down into the wisps of steam as she stated quietly, "So you've been seeing DeLaine Hussey."

She looked up. Rye's face was somber, and he studied her as if trying to decide how to answer. At last he sat up straighter.

"Aye, I have . . . a few times."

Her gaze dropped to the tabletop, where his hand rested. She concentrated on the back of it, where two engorged veins branched beneath the firm, brown skin. "It hurt when I heard that," she admitted thickly.

"I didn't do it t' hurt y'. I did it 'cause I was lonely."

"I know."

"She kept comin' to the cooperage—"

"You don't have to explain, Rye. You're free to—"

"I don't feel free. I've never felt free of y'."

Her heart raced with renewed feelings, and though she'd said there was no need to explain, she could not stop herself from asking, "Did you enjoy being with her?"

"Not at first, but she . . . aw, what the hell, forget it, Laura." Rye looked away. "She means nothin' to me, nothin' at all. When I kissed her, I—"

"You kissed her!" Laura's startled eyes flew to his and her heart seemed to lurch.

"Y' didn't let me finish. When I kissed her, I found myself comparin' her to you, and when I realized what I was doin', I suddenly felt . . . I don't know what it was . . . disloyal, empty, I guess."

"Yet you saw her again after that?"

"Aw, Laura, why are y' askin' such things?"

"Because DeLaine Hussey has had her eye on you for years."

"I tell y', I've no designs on her, even though she all but asked me . . ." But Rye abruptly halted and took a deep draft of tea.

"Asked you what?"

"Never mind."

"Asked you what, Rye?" Laura insisted.

His lips tightened, and he scowled, cursing himself for letting his tongue flap. Laura's lips dropped open as if her tea was too hot, but when he chanced a quick glance from beneath lowered brows, he found her face pinched with disapproval.

"What did she all but ask you, Rye?"

"Oh all right! T' marry her!" he admitted in exasperation.

In that instant, Laura tasted the bitterness Rye had been expected to swallow each time he saw her with Dan or thought of the two of them together. There was instantaneous jealousy tinged with a fine edge of anger at the idea that another woman could presume to make claim on the man she had considered *hers* most of her life. Laura's stomach did cartwheels and the color surged to her face.

"I told y', she means nothin' to me," Rye said.

"Is that why you've been considering leaving Nantucket and making a new start on the frontier with her—because she means nothing to you?" Laura was only groping in the dark, but she studied Rye carefully for his reaction. Her head seemed to go light and fuzzy when Rye failed to deny it.

Instead, he drained his cup, ran the back of his hand across his lips, and lurched to his feet. "You're tired, Laura. Why don't y' try to get some sleep and I'll sit up with Dan. If anything happens, I'll wake y'."

Laura felt suddenly bloodless and cold as Rye rounded the table, took her elbow, and urged her to her feet. Tell me I'm wrong. Oh, Rye, don't be considering such a thing.

But she knew he was, and they need not discuss it further for Laura to know *why* he was. Jane had come right out and said it: this island wasn't big enough for all three of them. And Rye was the one who was finally taking steps to give them all more space.

Laura lifted her eyes to him now as they stood in the bayberry-scented keeping room with the fire dwindling to lazily waving fingers of orange. The wind buffeted the house and snow hissed against the siding.

But though she still hoped he'd deny it, Rye only suggested, "Why don't you snuggle up beside Josh for a while? I think there's room for one more."

There was nowhere else in the house for her to lie. But though she didn't want to sleep, neither did she want to think. And she certainly didn't want to face the truth in Rye's blue eyes. Thus, when he turned her toward the alcove and nudged the small of her back, she resisted only halfheartedly as she whispered, "But you're tired, too."

"I'll wake y' t' sit watch if I get drowsy," he promised, and gave her a second nudge. She obediently crept to the bed, pulled back the covers, and slipped in, curling herself around Josh's warm little body. At her feet the dog's bulk pressed down on the quilts, but she pulled her knees up and faced the wall, scarcely caring or knowing how cramped the space was. She hugged Josh close and, behind her, heard Rye moving to take a chair into the linter room. She heard it thump lightly onto the floor, then a long, deep sigh.

She tried not to think about DeLaine Hussey proposing marriage and Rye talking to a stranger named Throckmorton. But behind her shuttered eyelids those images came and stayed and blended with that anomalous picture of Rye, propped on a chair at the bedside of Dan, whose life was now in Rye's safekeeping.

Chapter 19

THE NIGHT WINDS howled and the wrath of a bitter Atlantic beat against the weathered cottages of Nantucket. In the linter room on Crooked Record Lane, Rye Dalton sat in a Windsor chair with his feet propped up on the bed, alternately dozing and stretching. Dan remained asleep, scarcely moving except for an occasional spasmodic twitch of his fingers inside the mittens. Rye leaned forward and placed a palm on Dan's forehead; it seemed hotter. Dan's left hand jerked again, and Rye wondered how long it would be before he woke up. When he did, the pain would be horrendous for him. Would Dan call out? Would Josh hear? Would Laura have to witness Dan's pain, too? Rye wished he could spare them.

He wrapped his left hand around his right, braced his elbows on his knees, and bent forward, resting his chin on cold knuckles and studying Dan. His breathing seemed to come with greater difficulty, and as Rye stared at the rise and fall of Dan's chest beneath the covers, his own thoughts meandered in disconnected fragments . . . my friend, I remember sharing your bunk when we were boys . . . why can't y' control y'r drinking . . . I love y'r wife . . . y' knew we were together that day Zachary died, didn't y'? . . . Jesus, man, look what y've done t' yourself . . . I don't really want t' be sittin' here, but my heart tells me I must . . . I will leave this island, come spring . . . there's no other way . . . easy, friend, don't move y'r hands that way . . . I wish dawn would come . . . I must go down and tell Hilda what's happened . . . Laura read the truth in my face . . . it'll kill part of me t' leave her, but . . . Josh had the best smell t' him . . . y'r breathin' seems worse . . . supposin' y' died, Dan . . .

The dark thought straightened Rye's spine, and he leaped from the chair, horrified at what had crossed his mind. He checked the time—five A.M. He'd been dozing, not fully responsible for the hazy wanderings of his mind. He stretched and made his way silently to the keeping room to add a log to the coals. When the wood caught and flared, he hunkered before it, elbows to knees, staring, thinking the awful thing again. Supposing Dan died . . .

After several long minutes he straightened, sighed, ran a hand through his hair, then ambled across to the alcove bed while massaging the back of his neck.

The three slept soundly, but the only one he touched was Ship, who sensed her master's presence and lifted a sleepy head, then stretched her feet straight out, quivered, and relaxed into sleep again. Rye's gaze caressed the curve of Laura's back, though she was covered by quilts to her chin. Her disheveled braid lay on the pillow and trailed over the quilt top, but as his hand gently slid from the dog's head, Rye resisted the urge to touch her and turned back to his vigil in the linter room.

He folded his long frame into the hard hoop-backed chair once again, but the room had grown chilly as the fire waned, and he wrapped his arms tightly across his chest, lifting his crossed calves again to the edge of the bed. He watched the rise and fall of Dan's chest and wondered if he imagined it had accelerated. But Rye's eyelids soon drooped, and the added log lent a small measure of warmth that seeped around the doorway, and soon he slept soundly with his chin digging into his chest.

Laura awakened and glanced back over her shoulder. The fire still burned and the blizzard still blew. She glanced at the windows, but they were dark, and as she turned the coverlets back and crept from the bed, a strange sound seemed to whisper an accompaniment to the chitter of snow on shingles. Josh did not stir as she silently slipped to her feet and crossed to the bedroom doorway.

Dan lay as before, on his back, covered to his neck, but with the mittened hands on top of the feather ticks, while Rye slumped beside the bed with his head drooping and his elbows propped loosely on the arms of the chair. The strident sound, she suddenly realized, was that of Dan's labored breathing. She inched nearer to the bed, gazing at his face, but it seemed to glow and fade in rhythm with the candle stub that guttered on the bedside table.

For nearly a full minute she stood utterly still, watching the quilt rise and fall, listening to the faint wheeze, trying to recall if his breathing had sounded like this before. She compared Dan's breathing to Rye's and found Rye's much slower and lacking the strident sound.

"Rye?" She touched his shoulder. "Wake up, Rye."

"What?" Disoriented, he opened his eyes and lifted his head. "Laura?" Still fuzzy from sleep, his head bobbed slightly before he jerked erect and ran his hands over his face. "Laura, what is it?"

"Listen to Dan's breathing. Doesn't it sound strange?"

Immediately, Rye leaned forward and came to his feet, bending over Dan and placing his palm on the hot forehead. "He's got a fever."

"A fever," she repeated inanely, watching Rye's hand test the skin of Dan's neck, then slip to his chest.

"He's hot all over. Why don't y' fix a vinegar compress for his forehead?"

She left the room immediately to do as Rye suggested. When she returned and placed the cloth on Dan's head, his breathing seemed no worse. The candle was nearly out, and she fetched a fresh bayberry one, lighted it, and placed it in the holder, giving the room a renewed brilliance.

"I'll stay with him for a while. Why don't you go get some sleep?"

But Rye was wide awake again. "It seems I did. And any-way, there's noplace for me t' lie, so I'll stay, too."

He went into the keeping room and got another chair, which he placed on the opposite side of the bed from his. As they settled down across from each other, they both studied the man between them. The constant rush of his breathing grew more labored as dawn crept nearer. Dan's chest seemed to strain for each bit of air, and soon the sound of his inhalations became like that of a bellows with a piece of paper caught in its intake.

Laura lifted troubled eyes to Rye. He hunched forward with his lips pressed to his thumb knuckles, staring intensely at Dan's chest. As if he sensed her watching him, he glanced up. But her eyes skittered down; she was unable to look at him.

A pale thread of gray seeped over the windowsill, and with it the breathing of the man on the bed became more labored, carrying a distinct wheeze now.

This time it was Rye who looked up first. Laura raised her eyes, too, as if compelled by his gaze. Her eyes appeared larger than life-size, unblinking.

"I think he has pneumonia." The words fell from Rye's lips in a coarse, scratchy whisper that scarcely reached the opposite side of the bed.

"I think so, too," came her shaky reply.

Neither of them moved. Their eyes locked while between them the chest of the man lifted painfully, the new hissing sound whistling even more sibilantly with each breath that escaped his dry lips. Outside, a limb tapped the eaves, and in the other room their son rolled over and murmured in his sleep. On the walls of the linter room a bayberry candle cast two shadows while lifting its bittersweet and nostalgic fragrance above the bed they had once shared. For an instant they were transported back to a time when nothing stood between them. And somewhere in a place called Michigan, a new beginning waited for Laura and Rye Dalton. A place of high, green trees, where a cooper could make barrels for a hundred years and never run out of wood; a place where a boy could grow to manhood without reminders of the past; a place where not a soul knew their names or their histories; a place where a man and wife could build a log house and sleep in the same bed and shower each other with the love they were longing to share.

And in that moment of clarity, as Rye's and Laura's thoughts communed, as the pounding realization descended on them, their hearts hammered with the sheer magnitude of what they were considering. There was fear in their eyes as they understood with startling lucidity that this—all this!—could be theirs.

All they needed to do . . . was . . . *nothing*.

The solution to their problems. The obstacle removed. Fate taking over to give them back what it had robbed them of.

The cognizance struck them both at once. They saw comprehension settle, each in the other's eyes, while poised for that reckless moment in time.

Nothing. All we need do is nothing, and who would there be to blame us? There was Ephraim Biddle to swear he'd stumbled on an unconscious drunk in the snow, and if nobody would take the word of a drunk like Eph, there was Hector Gorham to verify the condition of Dan when he'd been laid out like a plank in the Blue Anchor. Even the confrontation between Rye and Nathan McColl was proof that Rye cared immensely for the outcome of his friend. And wouldn't the whole island know Doc Foulger was stranded somewhere on the far side of the island in this blizzard?

Like two wax mannequins, Rye and Laura stared at each other across Dan's struggling body, the list of justifications parading through their minds, each aware that this profound moment would change every moment that followed for the rest of their lives.

I love you, Laura, the somber blue eyes seemed to say.

I love you, Rye, the troubled brown eyes answered.

The moment lasted but several seconds, the realization smiting them swiftly, alarmingly, as they strained toward each other from the seats of the hard, wooden chairs.

Then suddenly, as if some wicked sorcerer's spell had at last been broken, they simultaneously flew to their feet, two blurs of motion.

"We have t' move him nearer the fire."

"I'll help you."

"No, y' get Josh and bring him in here. We'll switch beds. Y' have extra sheets, don't y'?"

"Yes."

"And plenty o' bayberries left t' boil down into wax?"

"More than enough!"

"And onions t' fry for a poultice?"

"Yes, and if that doesn't work, there's oil of eucalyptus and mint and mustard packs, and . . . and . . ."

Suddenly they halted, their eyes meeting with a new intense fire of dedication.

"He'll live, by God," Rye vowed. "He'll live!"

"He's got to."

The two sleeping bodies were interchanged without mishap. Josh's bed was ideal as a steam tent, with its hinged wooden doors. There they placed Dan, and while Laura rubbed eucalyptus oil on his chest, Rye built up the fire and unceremoniously dumped a basketful of berries into the iron kettle, then hung it on the crane. Laura made a thick poultice of fried onions and covered Dan's chest with it, while Rye worked to construct a makeshift funnel of linen sheets through which to direct the steam from the boiling bayberries into the opening of the alcove bed. They warmed bricks, wrapped them in blankets, and slipped them beneath the covers to keep Dan warm.

The pain in Dan's hands began infiltrating his semiconsciousness soon after the steam thickened above him. He moaned and tossed, and Laura drew her eyebrows together in concern. "How will he tolerate the pain?"

Scarcely looking up, Rye answered brusquely, "We'll keep him drunk. For once it'll do him more good than bad."

And they did.

Thus yesterday's bane became today's blessing. The analgesic quality of the liquor numbed Dan, and the lengthy time required to render clear candles provided a steady billow of aromatic steam that worked to loosen the congestion on Dan's chest. They forced him to drink brandy hourly, opening one of the hinged doors only briefly in an effort to keep the steam contained within. The combination of alcohol and the warm, steamy room was as effective as a narcotic in subduing Dan. He remained in a bleary stupor during the hours when the worst of his agony would otherwise have been sheer torture as his fingers burned and throbbed and his breathing turned to a thick rattle, followed by a racking cough that curled his shoulders and seemed to roll him into a tight ball as the expectorant did its work.

They waited for the first dread sign of dead skin on Dan's fingers: the flaking away of thin layers of flesh. None appeared. His fingertips were swollen and red, and obviously circulating healthy blood. When their worst fears were put to rout, Rye told Laura, "I'll have t' go down t' let Hilda know. And Josiah, too. He'll be wonderin'."

She took a moment to study him. Rye's beard had grown overnight, shadowing his chin and upper lip. His hair was messed and his eyes red. "As soon as you've had something to eat. You look a little peaked yourself."

"I can grab somethin' at the cooperage."

"Don't be silly, Rye. The fire's hot, and I've thawed some fish."

She fried him bass dipped in cornmeal, the way he liked it best, but as he sat for the first time at his own mealtime table, it was not under the circumstances he'd earlier imagined. Josh sat across from him, assessing all the goings-on, but once again keeping his distance from Rye. Laura tended the fragrant black broth that gurgled away on the hob and could not be abandoned for long. And from the alcove bed came the repetitive hacking of Dan, interspersed with an occasional weak moan or mumbled utterance too obscure to be distinguishable.

The storm had not abated by midmorning, when Rye was preparing to leave the house. Laura watched him as he stood near the door buttoning his jacket, pulling the knit cap low over his ears, and donning mittens. Ship stood at his knee, looking up and wagging her tail.

Rye turned to Laura. "We'll be back soon. Is there anythin' y' need?"

For just a moment the spoon stopped moving in the bayberries and their eyes met.

Is there anything I need?

Her eyes lingered on his, but she was conscious of Josh studying them both and she only smiled and shook her head, continuing to stir.

In a flash of memory, Rye was swept back to the beginning of spring and a day when he'd stepped to this door and found her standing just where she was now, with a spoon in her hand like that. It would take discipline he was not sure he possessed to leave Nantucket for good.

He turned and pulled the door open, and a flat wall of snow collapsed and fell into the keeping room, for it was piled up hip-deep around the building. A delighted Josh came running to eat a handful as Rye stepped back and looked at the floor. "The snow's made a mess—"

"I'll see to it." Already Laura was crossing the room with a broom. When she reached Rye's side, she looked into his eyes and murmured, "Keep warm."

"Aye."

Then Ship made a dive into the world of white, and Rye followed, securing the door behind him.

The windows were running with steam that collected in corners and formed triangles of ice. Laura cleared a small spot on a pane, to watch Rye and Ship trudge through the drifts of snow, Rye taking giant steps and Ship resembling a dolphin leaping and surfacing on the ocean. She breathed a silent prayer of thanksgiving for having Rye here when she needed him, then turned back to sweep up the snow.

Josh took up sentry duty at the window, eager to have Ship back again. An hour later, he called, "Mama, there's *two* people coming!"

"Two people?"

"I think it's Gramma!"

Laura crossed to stand behind Josh's chair and peer outside. It was Hilda Morgan who braved the elements with Rye and the dog. Laura opened the door and welcomed the distraught woman with a brief touch of cheeks. Snow and wind swirled inside, sending the fire dancing and ash lifting to the hearth in a backdraft.

"How is he?" Rye and Hilda inquired together as soon as the door was closed.

"There's not much change."

They stamped the curds of snow from their feet, and Hilda surveyed the makeshift tent around Dan. "It looks like you two have been busy," she noted while handing her coat to Laura, then she moved toward the alcove bed.

Hilda stayed until dusk. She proved to be a great help to Laura, taking turns with the bayberries, loading the forms with wicks, and helping with the pouring. She was an astute woman who immediately sized up the situation and read it correctly. Though Laura and Rye would have spared her the truth about how Dan had come to such a pass, Hilda was the antithesis of Dahlia Traherne, meeting life head-on instead of nursing self-delusions. She had deduced that Dan's drinking was responsible for his state, even before Josh informed her of all that had taken place here last night. She noted, too, the careful way Rye and Laura avoided looking at each other or crossing paths as they moved about the house.

But as the three of them paused in the late afternoon to share hot apple cider together before Hilda went back home, the woman surprised both Rye and Laura by forthrightly admitting, "My son is a fool. No one realizes that better than I. He knows perfectly well the two of you belong together, yet he refuses to admit it. I told him the day you came back, Rye, that if he kept Laura, it'd be against her wishes. I warned him—'Dan,' I said, 'you got to face reality. That boy is his, and that woman is his, and the sooner you come to terms with that, the better off you'll be.' "

She examined the surprised faces before her and went on crisply. "I'm not so blind I can't see what took place here. And I'm not too ignorant to figure out that you could just as easily have let him lose his fingers or wheeze himself to death. I only hope and pray that when he wakes up, he'll realize how much love it took—from the *both* of you—to do what you done for him." She reached across the table and covered one of each of their hands with her own, gave a firm squeeze, and added, "I thank you both from the bottom of my heart." Then, pretending to ignore their self-consciousness, she took a last gulp from her mug and pushed herself to her feet. "Now, I'd best get these old bones home through the snow before nightfall." Her tone changed to mock sternness. "Well, Rye Dalton, you gonna sit there all day, or you gonna see me safely to my door?"

To Rye's further amazement, Hilda said but one thing after

that. They'd trudged through the snow with heads low against the gale-force winds, and when they reached Hilda's house, he hunched his shoulders, waiting for her to go inside so he could turn back toward home.

Hilda swung to face him. The wind licked her scarf and painted her nose bright red as she shouted above the storm, "That Hussey woman ain't for you, Rye, just in case you was thinkin' she is." And with that, she opened the door and disappeared. Rye stared at the panel, dumbfounded. Was there anyone on this island who thought Laura belonged with Dan?

Rye made a sudden decision to stop at the cooperage again and let Josiah know how things were going. But as long as he was there, he took the opportunity to wash, shave, change his clothes, and comb his hair. Only then did he realize his loyal dog had remained with his son.

When he opened the door of the saltbox on the hill, the first thing he noticed was that Laura, too, had taken a few moments out for grooming. Her hair was wound into a neat nutmeg swirl at the back of her head, and she'd changed into a clean, simple dress of gray broadcloth, over which a white floor-length apron was tied. Rye hung up his jacket on the coat tree and stomped the snow from his trousers, and as he passed the table, noted it was set for three. Josh and Ship were preoccupied in a tug-of-war with a rag, and Laura was turning muffins out of a cast-iron form. For a moment Rye indulged in fantasizing that all was as it appeared—a man returning to his own abode, to a son, a dog, a wife who moved about their kitchen putting supper on their table. How ironic, Rye thought. It *is* what it appears, even though it isn't.

A restless movement from the alcove bed reminded Rye that Dan was there. "How is he?"

"His coughing is worse, but it's looser."

"Good . . . good." Rye stepped near the fire, extended his palms, and rubbed them together. Laura moved about, doing small domestic preparations at his elbow. Hilda's comments lingered fresh in their minds, and it suddenly seemed neither of them could look at one another.

"Wind might've gone down a little," Rye ventured.

"Oh, that's good news!" She looked up brightly, then instantly turned away when she found his eyes on her.

Rye studied the fire. She had stopped boiling bayberries to make room on the hearth for supper. He looked back over his shoulder at the three places set at the table and counted the months, the years, he'd been waiting for this night.

"Josh, supper is ready. Come to the table," she called.

Rye turned from the hearth and stood uncertainly, watching Laura place the last of the serving bowls on the table, then settle Josh in his place.

Laura looked up to find Rye watching. In the subdued light of the candle and the fire glow, his pale blue irises looked like lustrous sapphires. "Sit down, Rye," she urged softly.

His heart did a stutter-step, and suddenly he felt boyish, perhaps a little uncertain, like the first time after their marriage when she'd prepared a meal for him and called him to the table.

When they all were seated, she passed Rye a familiar tureen; it had been his grandmother's. He lifted the cover and found one of his favorites: thick nuggets of venison covered with rich brown gravy.

There was, Josh noted, something different about the way Rye and his mother looked at each other and the way Papa and Mama looked at each other. Though Josh understood Rye was his real papa, he still relegated the title to Dan only. But watching the exchange of glances between the two who sat at the table with him, he puzzled over his mother's pink cheeks and the cooper's satisfaction at each bite he took.

The meal was strained. What little there was of conversation was stilted and came to sudden stops until finally they forsook talk altogether. When supper was finished, Rye checked Dan, changed the dressing on his burn, and noted how Dan was now expectorating green phlegm—a good sign. He spread a square of flannel on his pillow, turned Dan onto his side, and propped several pillows behind his back.

"Why you doin' that?" Josh asked.

"So he won't choke," Rye answered, and Josh wondered how a man could know so much, then added this newest detail to his growing list of observations of how carefully Rye and

Mama took care of Papa. There were many things Josh noted about the tall cooper that puzzled him. There were many that intrigued him. Sometimes it took a great effort to keep from talking to him, but Josh still felt that to do so would be to divide his loyalty, and in his childish mind, this seemed wrong somehow.

Thus, the supper conversation had been thwarted by Josh's refusal to take part whenever Rye tried to include him. Also, there was a childish guilt at work within the boy for what he had said and done the day he'd run away to the cooperage.

Now, in the dim keeping room, Ship had finished her supper and Josh could not encourage the contented dog to play, so he watched guardedly as Rye crossed to the coat tree and extracted a piece of wood and a knife from the pocket of his jacket. Without a word, Rye placed a chair near the fireplace, sat down, stretched his legs out, and rested his heels on the hearth. He whistled softly between his teeth while the short knife bit into the wood and scraped off a loose curl that fell to his lap. But though Josh's interest was piqued, he remained guarded.

Another kettle of bayberries was hung on the crane, and Laura and Rye took turns tending them. In between times, Rye sat contentedly, whittling.

Josh was put to bed in the linter room, and as he kissed his mother, he inquired, "Is Rye staying here tonight?"

"Yes. We have to take turns watching Papa."

"Oh." Josh looked thoughtful for a moment, then asked, "What's he makin'?"

Laura brushed the silky bangs back from his forehead and smiled. "I don't know. Why don't you ask him?"

Josh seemed to think it over briefly, then posed a surprising question. "How come you look at him funny all the time?"

Startled, Laura replied with the first words that came to her mind. "I didn't know I did!"

When Laura returned to the keeping room, Rye had set aside his whittling and was stooping over Dan, checking him again. He straightened, unaware that Laura stood behind him, observing how he braced his back with one hand, his nape with the other, arching backward with a deep sigh.

"Rye, you haven't really slept for forty-eight hours."

He snapped erect and turned. "I'm doin' fine. And I slept some last night."

"In that chair beside the bed?"

"There're berries left t' boil yet, and we'd best keep steamin' him at least till mornin'."

"You need some rest."

"Aye, then . . . in a while." Dan coughed. Rye turned to wipe his lips, then closed the hinged door so the steam could build up again.

Laura moved to the fireplace, doggedly taking up the spoon to stir the berries. She sensed Rye moving up quietly behind her. "You know—" She laughed tiredly. "I used to love this job, making bayberry candles. But I don't think I'll ever make another one as long as I live, once these are done."

She felt Rye's hands surround the tired muscles that sloped from her neck to her shoulders, and Laura's eyes sank shut, the spoon drifting to a stop. She sighed wearily, tipping her head back until it touched his hard chest.

"Laura," he murmured, gently turning her around.

"Oh, Rye . . ." She met his eyes for a moment, then closed her own and let herself rest against the hard bulk of his torso while his cheek pressed against her hair and their arms circled each other very loosely. The embrace was one of exhaustion rather than desire, a drawing of strength, an affirmation of support, and perhaps a consolation.

For a long time neither spoke. Laura rested her palms against the back of his sweater and felt its coarse knit texture beneath her cheek. Again she smelled the lingering essence of cedar trapped in the wool and, through it, felt the warmth of his body.

Rye breathed the scent of bayberry and turned his lips lightly against the silken skeins of her hair while his palm closed loosely over her upper arm, then rubbed reassuringly.

"He's goin' t' live," Rye murmured into her hair.

"Thank God," she said with a sigh of relief. Suddenly, Rye's knees trembled in sheer exhaustion. She felt it and backed away to observe his bloodshot eyes. "I've got a few good hours left in me yet. Please, Rye, will you rest? I'll wake you at midnight, I promise. Just go stretch out beside Josh.''

Rye's brain could scarcely function, and he felt powerless to resist the temptation of closing his eyes and drifting into oblivion. And so he slept in his own bed for the first time in five years, though, again, not in the way of which he'd dreamed, not with Laura beside him. Rye slept instead with the gentle breath of his son falling peacefully against his wrist, which was flung out on the pillow between them.

He awakened in the deep of night, listening to the sounds of the storm losing strength and Josh's rhythmic breathing, then the persistent hack of Dan's coughing. Sitting up, Rye came alert, glanced back at Josh, then crept to the doorway on stockinged feet. It was well after three in the morning. The coals were glowing; a new batch of candles hung by their wicks on a lathe resting between two chairs. A candle burned on the table beside Laura, who was slumped across the trestle with one arm flung out, fast asleep.

Dan's coughing subsided, and he mumbled incoherently, then fell still again. Rye went to the side of the bed, tested Dan's forehead, found it cooler. Then he turned to Laura, slipped his arms beneath her knees and back, and lifted her from the bench.

Her eyelids fluttered open, then slammed shut as if they were weighted. "Rye . . ." Her forehead dovetailed within the curve of his neck and her right hand lifted to curl about his collarbone while he carried her toward the bedroom. Incoherent, more asleep than awake, her voice came again, thick and muffled. "Rye, I love you.''

"I know.'' He gently laid her down beside Josh and tenderly pulled the feather tick up around her ears.

Through her last vestiges of consciousness, Laura felt his warm lips pressed to her forehead as she snuggled into the bed that still held the warmth of his body.

The following day, Rye and Laura were revitalized as their vigil continued. One of them was always at Dan's side. When Rye took his turn, he often propped his feet up, took up the soft whistling and his whittling knife, pretending to be unaware of Josh's increasing interest in the project.

But as the mysterious object came to resemble an ice skate, Josh lost his will to remain stoic. He managed to creep nearer and nearer Rye's chair until finally, when his curiosity grew too great to contain, the child questioned, "What you makin'?"

"What . . . this?" Rye twisted the nearly finished skate back and forth in the air.

When his eyes fixed on the double runners, Josh nodded five times in succession—hard!

"Why, this's an ice skate."

"For you?" Josh's transfixed eyes grew even wider.

"Naw, I got a pair o' skates already."

"Y' do?" Josh could scarcely drag his eyes to Rye's face.

"I'm just passin' the time, like I used t' do on the ship, skrimshanding." Rye took another swipe at the wood with the blade, then he studied the results critically and suddenly started in surprise. "Why, this skate looks like it's just about the size o' your foot, boy!" It was all Rye could do to hold a straight face while Josh glanced down at his small feet, then back at the skate. "Here, let's see." Rye leaned over to compare the skate to Josh's boot, and when the two complemented each other ideally, Rye mused, "Mmm . . . seems t' me I heard y' had a birthday this week." Without looking, Rye sensed Laura's smile.

After that, Josh hung beside Rye's chair, asking questions, pointing, showing an interest in anything Rye had to tell about his years at sea. The cooper told him about the doldrums and how they were responsible for many a sailor taking up skrimshanding to pass the time. He described the Nantucket sleighride, that heart-stopping ride in a whaleboat just after the whale's been harpooned, when it tows the whalers through the boiling waters in a life and death struggle sometimes lasting for days. Eventually, Rye's stories came around to some of the tall tales exchanged by members of the New England Whalers' Liars Bench. Josh sat wide-eyed and eager through the fantastic yarns about the fabled deepwater sailorman Old Stormalong, who measured four fathoms from the deck to the bridge of his nose, took his whale soup in a Cape Cod dory,

favored raw shark meat with the skin still on and ostrich eggs
scrambled with their shells, then lay back after breakfast and
picked his teeth with an oar of white oak—"Twenty-two feet
long for good leverage!" Rye ended, subduing a grin as he
eyed Josh askance.

"Aw, you're just makin' that up!" But Josh was grinning
and eager for more of such spoondrift.

During those shared hours, as Rye entertained his son with
brig yarns, he carefully slowed the speed of his whittling to extend the time while he got to know Josh better.

Toward the end of the third day, the funnel of sheets was
taken down and the rations of whiskey stopped. The blizzard
had run itself out, leaving a total accumulation of fourteen
inches of snow over which Dr. Foulger's cutter delivered him
safely from the far side of the island. He examined Dan and
pronounced that there was nothing more he could do that had
not already been done, but that Dan was definitely out of
danger.

Laura and Rye had spoken of nothing personal since that
first night. They sat now, on the fourth night of their vigil, on
chairs pulled up facing the fireplace. Josh had been put to bed
in the linter room, and Dan seemed to be resting more comfortably, the doors of the alcove bed open.

Laura was knitting a woolen stocking for Josh. Rye was
pondering the fire, slumped down low in his chair with an
ankle crossed over a knee.

The click of the needles went on and on in the silence until
Rye hunched forward, resting elbows to knees. "About the
Michigan Territory . . ."

The needles stopped clicking. Laura held her breath. She
looked up at the side of Rye's face, where the rough side-
whiskers were burnished by the light of the fire as he stared
into it.

Slowly, he turned to look back over his shoulder. "I won't
be goin' with DeLaine Hussey," he announced in a deep, quiet
tone.

"Y . . . you won't?" Laura's heart seemed to be slamming

against her ribs hard enough to break them.

"I'll be goin' with you."

The blood rushed to her face. Without thinking, she glanced at the open doors of the alcove bed while her heart thrummed on as if powered by some superhuman source. Her lips dropped open as she struggled for breath, then took up knitting with a new, frantic energy.

"That is, if y' think y' can leave this island." He continued studying her over his shoulder. Still she made the needles race. "Will y' stop that infernal knittin'," he ordered with quiet impatience. Her hands fell to her lap, and her gaze followed. Rye sat back again, but did not touch her.

"Laura, we've paid our debt t' Dan. He's going t' live. But what about us?"

She looked up. Rye watched her intensely.

"I've been here with y' for three days and nights, and I've seen for myself what fools we've been t' let duty and guilt tell us what t' do. We belong together. I don't give a damn if it's here in this house on Nantucket or in some place we've never seen. All I know is, *you* are *home*. For me, home is where y' are. I love y', and I'm through apologizin' for it. I want no more misunderstandin's between myself and Dan. When he wakes up, I want t' be able to tell him the truth so we can all plan accordingly. Y' see, I've already written Throckmorton and agreed t' join his party. It leaves from Albany on April fifteenth, which means we'll have t' take the packet out of here at the end of March. That's only about three months from now, and there's a lot t' prepare for. I'm askin' y' for the first and last time, Laura. Will y' come with me t' Michigan in the spring, you and Josh?"

He did not smile. His eyes did not waver. His voice, though low, was steady, determined. She believed what he said . . . and what he didn't say: he would go in the spring with *or without* her. She knew in her heart that Rye was right. They had done the honorable thing. They'd saved Dan's life. But then, had there really been a choice? They both loved Dan, and they both always would. But Laura had learned in the past three days that love sometimes mainifests itself in frightening and awesome ways.

She saw again the awl sinking into Dan's flesh, wielded by Rye's steady hand, then Rye's trembling shoulders when reaction set in. She heard the rage in his voice as he slapped the hot cup out of McColl's hand, felt again the pity of witnessing the unnecessary burn on Dan's chest. She relived the terror of that moment when her eyes had met Rye's across Dan's racked and wheezing body. Somehow during that emotionally charged instant when they'd considered letting Dan die, they'd both recognized the truth: they'd had to save Dan to save themselves.

Rye was still waiting for her answer. He studied her face while the weariness of their long fight for Dan's life was reflected in it. Yes, Dan would live, and so must they. There was only one answer Laura could give.

"Yes, I'll come with you, Rye. Both of us will come with you. But until then, we will not dishonor Dan in any way."

"O' course not."

Strangely enough, they agreed to these terms in the most businesslike voices. The time for hearts to sing was not now, while Dan still lay ill. There would be time for that later, as spring came, the season of rebirth.

Chapter 20

DAN MORGAN AWAKENED on the fourth morning after his fall. He opened his eyes to find himself in the strangest place— Josh's alcove bed. His hands hurt, as if each of his fingertips had been slammed in a door. He felt as if he were trying to breathe at a depth of twenty-five feet, with the water pressing painfully on his lungs. His tongue was stuck to the roof of his mouth as if he had a horrendous hangover, and the clanging in his head went on and on like a bell buoy on rough seas.

He turned his head gingerly. There beside the bed sat Rye.

"Well . . . hello," Rye greeted. He looked utterly relaxed, elbows resting on the arms of a Windsor chair, an ankle slung over a knee.

"Rye?" The word was a mere croak. Dan tried to lift himself up on his elbows, but failed.

"Rest easy, friend. Y've been through an ordeal."

Dan let his eyes blank out the bright daylight that hurt his already throbbing head. "What are you doing here?"

"Waitin' for y' t' wake up."

Dan lifted an arm that felt as heavy as waterlogged driftwood. He rested it across his forehead, but the movement made his fingertips throb anew. "Is there some water?" His voice cracked.

Immediately, Rye leaned over, slipping a hand beneath

Dan's head to lift it as the blessedly cool drink soothed his parched throat. The effort left Dan aching and breathless. "What happened?" he managed to say when the weakness passed.

"Y' got roarin' drunk, fell off y'r damn feet in the worst blizzard t' hit Nantucket in ten years, hit y'r noggin on the cobblestones, and lay there till y'r fingers froze and y' caught pneumonia."

Dan opened his eyes and peered at Rye, who'd again settled back into the chair, his fingers laced over his belly. For all his brusque and scolding tone, there was a note of the old Rye once again in his voice. Somehow Dan sensed the animosity was gone. "I did it up good, did I?"

"Aye, y' did."

"How long ago was that?"

"Four days."

"Four! . . ." Dan turned his head too fast on the pillow and he grimaced at the resulting ache.

"I wouldn't move so fast if I was you. We've kept y' stewed t' the gills all that time, and y're bound t' have a hangover that'll put all y'r others t' shame."

"Where's Laura?"

"Out t' the market. She'll be back soon."

Dan lifted and examined the fingers of his right hand. "What did you do to these? They hurt like hell."

Rye chuckled. "Be happy y' still got 'em hooked to y'r arms. They'll heal."

"I take it you aren't wasting any sympathy on me, huh, Dalton?"

The corner of Rye's mouth quirked up. "None at all. Pullin' a trick like that, y' shouldn't by rights have either fingers *or* toes. Y' ought t' be six feet under, and y' damn well might be, except the ground was frozen so we didn't know where the hell we'd put y'."

In spite of his monumental aches and pains, Dan couldn't help smiling. He studied Rye carefully. "You've been here all that time?"

"Laura and I."

Dan was suddenly gripped by a spasm of coughing. Rye

pressed a cloth into Dan's hand, then sat back again, waiting for the paroxysm to pass. When it had, Rye offered Dan another drink, this time of hot ginger tea laced with vinegar and honey. He gave Dan a moment to rest, then began speaking in a straightforward manner.

"Listen, Dan, I've got some things I want t' say before Laura comes back, and—granted, the time is not exactly appropriate, but it may be the only chance we'll have t' be alone." Rye pressed forward in his chair, absently chafing his knuckles together, frowning at the coral stitches on the patchwork quilt. Then he met Dan's eyes directly. "Y've nearly died here in the last few days, and it's all been y'r own doin'. I've watched it comin' on, you and y'r asinine drinkin', and there's not a soul on this island that'd be surprised if y'd frozen t' death where y' dropped." Rye leaned on his knees, scowling into Dan's eyes. "When're y' going t' see the light, man?" he demanded impatiently. "Y'r squanderin' y'r life! Wallowin' in self-pity and wastin' the most precious commodity that'll ever be given to y', y'r health!

"Now, I'm not sayin' y' haven't had reason to worry, but do y' know what y'r drinkin' does t' Laura? She's torn by guilt every time she sees y' stumblin' through that door, and the majority of it's not her fault.

"I'm bein' honest with y', man, and I'm trustin' y' to understand it's not because of the rivalry between us for Laura, but because I want t' see y' pick up y'r life and make somethin' of it again."

Rye's voice rumbled on as he studied his hands, joined between widespread knees. "When spring comes, I'm goin' to the Michigan Territory and Laura has agreed t' go with me . . . and Josh, too. Now y' can accept that and make a man o' yourself between now and then, or y' can go back down t' the Blue Anchor and drink y'rself into another stupor that lasts till spring. I don't care. For myself, I don't care. But I care for Laura, because if she leaves this island believin' she's the ruination of y'r life, it'll be a guilt she'll carry forever. I'm askin' y' to send her off without that burden. And the only way y' can do that is t' give up y'r drinkin' and . . . and . . ."

Suddenly, Rye exhaled a gushing breath and covered his

face with both hands. "Goddamnit, I thought this'd be so simple . . ." He lunged to his feet, jammed his hands into the back waistline of his pants, and stood facing the trestle table.

His head dropped forward while Dan watched and felt a rush of something warm and nostalgic flood through him. It was the same feeling he'd had as he'd watched the *Massachusetts* sail away with Rye aboard.

The tall blond man turned back toward the alcove bed. "Damnit, Dan, I don't want t' hurt y', but I love that woman and we've done our damnest t' fight it, but some things can't be changed. I swear by all the saints in heaven, I haven't laid a hand on her while I've been in this house and I won't till spring. But then, I'm takin' her with me, married or not. But I want us t' go . . . if not with y'r blessin', at least without y'r scorn."

Something indefinable had changed between the two men. As Rye stood now beside Dan's bed, they each sensed the tether of lifelong sanguinity binding them together with a strength that superseded their rivalry for the same woman. They would both always love her, but—the realization hummed between them—they would both always love one another, too. To remain on this island together was to sentence themselves to certain hurt. The time had come for final separations. The pain in Dan's chest was, at that moment, more than just physical, and the softening of the expression in Rye's pale blue eyes did not quite disguise a sudden glitter there.

But at that moment the door opened and a rush of cold air ushered Laura and Josh into the keeping room. Something in Rye's stance told the two Dan was awake.

Josh rushed to the bedside, hung over it on his belly, and cried happily, "Papa! Papa! You're awake!"

Laura was right behind him, leaning to touch Dan's brow. "Dan, thank God you've made it. We've been so worried." She smiled down tenderly, a wealth of concern etched on her brow, but lifting somewhat as she saw his revived color. "Josh, come. We mustn't bring the cold near Papa with our coats. Warm up by the fire first, then you can talk with him again, but only for a while. He's got to rest."

"But, Mama, I got to tell Papa about my skates and about

how Rye brung him here and Mr. McColl tried to—''

"Later, Josh."

Dan noted Laura's swift interruption and how assiduously she sidestepped crediting herself or Rye for saving his life. But from Josh, Dan was to learn, during the days that followed, all that had transpired. The child painted the facts very vividly, until the information formed a concise picture of all Rye and Laura had done during the time he himself had been unconscious.

Dan's recovery was slow and painful. He was confined to bed for two weeks, racked by a cough that at times threatened to choke him. But he grew stronger as the days passed, and he had hours and hours to lie and ponder the curious fact that when he himself was in dire need, the islanders found Rye the natural one to turn to for help; the fact that when the local apothecary proclaimed his fingers lost, Rye refused to accept his word without a fight; the fact that when McColl would have covered his chest with vicious burns, Rye's anger raged out of control; the fact that for four nights and three days Rye and Laura had fought tenaciously to save his life. And had won.

Dan watched the two of them together, having plenty of time to do just that, for Rye came every day to carry wood and water for Laura, to bring fresh milk from town and greetings from the islanders and an analgesic balm for Dan's fingers and a potent medicine for his cough, though he offered no more alcoholic spirits, not even for medicinal purposes.

Dan's mother came every day, too, and from her Dan pieced together the few fragments of the story he was unable to glean from Josh.

Dan could not help but note the change in Josh's attitude toward Rye. The boy had clearly accepted Rye's daily presence in the house, and though it was Dan whom the child still refered to as Papa, there was a camaraderie between Rye and Josh that somehow had little to do with bloodlines.

There came a day in mid-December when Josh was hunkering crosslegged at the foot of Dan's bed and Laura was sitting in a chair nearby, hemming sheets.

"Papa, when will you teach me to skate?" Josh inquired.

Laura looked up and scolded gently, "Josh, you know that Papa's not well enough yet to go out in the cold air."

Dan had not questioned Laura about Rye's claim that she was going to the Michigan Territory in the spring, but by his closest count, this was the seventh sheet he'd seen her hemming. He watched the needle flash as she raised her hand and drew the thread tight. Then Dan turned back to Josh.

"Why don't you ask Rye to teach you to skate? He's a very good skater."

Laura looked up in surprise.

"He is?" Josh's voice went several notes higher whenever skating was mentioned.

"Oh, he's every bit as good as I am. We did plenty of skating together when we were boys."

"And Mama, too?"

Dan's eyes moved to Laura. "Yes, and Mama, too. She went everywhere we went, Rye and I."

There was no sting in Dan's words. Instead, he went on in a mellow tone, relating the story about the time they'd built a fire on the frozen surface of the pond and it melted the ice and fell through into the spring-fed water, nearly taking them all with it.

As Dan talked, Laura felt the breath catch in her throat, and a fierce gratitude grip her heart. Dan, oh, Dan, I understand the gift you are giving, and I know what it is costing you.

Though he would not meet her eyes, she knew Dan was aware of her studying him, listening to his every word. He was still talking when Rye arrived, to be immediately assaulted by Josh, who pitched himself against Rye's legs, looked up, and begged, "Will you take me skating, Rye? Will you?"

Rye glanced from Laura to Dan, then back down at the boy with the untamable rooster tail. Absently, Rye smoothed it down. "And whose idea was this?"

"Papa's. He said you and him skated all the time when you was little."

"Papa's, huh?" His eyes moved to the alcove bed where Dan was resting. "You sure about that?" Still with an eye on

Dan, Rye started shrugging out of his jacket.

"Sure I'm sure. Just ask him!"

But just then Dan cleared his throat. "I . . . ahhh . . . I promised I'd teach him, but there'll be no getting out for me for a while, so I thought maybe . . . well—" Dan gestured with his palms.

Rye moved nearer the bed. Though he stood with thumbs hooked at his waist, it took an effort not to reach out and squeeze Dan's shoulder. "Say no more. I'll have him on the ice before the week is out."

Their eyes met and held, then wavered, and finally parted in the face of indomitable emotions that suddenly sprang up between them.

Before another hour was up, Laura found herself alone with Dan, for Josh had been so persistent, Rye had finally agreed to take him to the cooperage to pick up his own skates, then on to one of the island's many ponds to make use of the last couple of hours of daylight.

The house grew still when the two were gone, and Laura sensed Dan's eyes following her as she moved restlessly about the keeping room, folding sheets, putting away needle and thread, adding a log to the fire. It was the first time they'd been alone in the house in weeks. A spasm of coughing gripped Dan, and Laura turned toward him as she always did, offering a cup of soothing tea. When she brought it, he shifted into a sitting position with the pillows plumped behind his back, accepted the cup, then captured Laura's hand before she could escape.

"Sit down."

She perched on the edge of the alcove bed, and for a moment Dan kept her hand, rubbing it distractedly with his thumb, finally releasing it to hold his mug with both palms.

"Rye tells me he's going to the Michigan Territory with the first thaws and that you're going with him."

It was curious how calm Laura felt at this moment, after weeks of anticipating a great gush of guilt. "Yes, Dan, I am. I wish . . . I wish there was another answer I could give that wouldn't hurt you, but I believe it's time for honesty among all of us. Perhaps I should have told you two weeks ago, when

Rye and I made the decision, but I was waiting for you to get stronger."

"I've got eyes, Laura. I've been watching you hem those sheets to take along."

She stared at her lap and groped for something to say. "They say it gets very cold in the Michigan Territory this time of year, and . . . and settlements are remote."

"So I've heard." His voice was deeper and gruffer than usual from days of coughing, but as he spoke now, the words were very quiet.

She looked up and met his eyes squarely. "We'll be taking Josh along with us, Dan."

"Yes, I know."

The room grew still. Outside, a soft snow had begun, but inside the fire glowed gold and pink. Dan's face was pale, but he was growing stronger each day, yet Laura understood—it took more than physical strength for Dan to face the truth.

"And I know why you sent him off with Rye—so the two of them could have some time alone, to get to know each other." She lightly touched the back of Dan's hand, which lay on the quilt. "Thank you."

For a moment Dan's eyes were tormented, then he quickly erased the drawn lines from his face, but continued gazing at Laura. "I know everything you two did," he said. "I know how Rye picked me up off the street and brought me here and saved my fingers, and how angry he got at McColl, and how the two of you tended the fires day and night to keep me from dying of pneumonia." His voice fell to a murmur. "Why did you do it?"

Her eyes caught and reflected the light from the fire and met Dan's with an openness and lack of guile that told the truth with an eloquence no words could convey. "Don't you know?" she breathed. But to say she loved him—they both loved him—would be to cause Dan unnecessary hurt, thus she only studied the play of emotions that turned his eyes soft with understanding.

"Yes . . . I guess I do."

Self-consciousness suddenly mushroomed between them, for the words need not be said to be felt. He took her hand, squeezed it in a grip that demonstrated surprising strength for a debilitated man. "Thank you," came his gruff words. For a moment they both concentrated on their joined hands.

"Don't thank me, Dan, just . . . just please don't jeopardize your life like that again." She beseeched him with her eyes. "Please, don't drink anymore."

"I've already promised Rye I won't."

She sighed and slumped her shoulders in relief. Then she gently withdrew her hand. "Dan, there are some things, some *other* things, we must talk about that are very hard to say."

"I think I know, Laura. I'm no fool. I don't need to sleep out here in this alcove bed anymore. I know the real reason why you and Josh sleep in there." He nodded toward the linter room.

Laura felt the blood press upward to paint her cheeks a discomfiting red. She nervously pleated and repleated the skirt over her knees, unable to lift her gaze to Dan as he went on.

"Laura, I found the busk a long time ago."

"You did?" Her eyes flew up and her face flared to an even brighter hue.

"I did."

"Oh, Dan, I'm so sorr—"

He presented a palm to cut her short. "We've been doing enough feeling sorry around here, don't you think? There's been you feeling sorry for me and Rye feeling sorry for you and me feeling sorry for myself, and Lord knows I've been the worst of the lot. At first when Rye came home, it was impossible for me to face the truth, then after I found that busk, I guess I knew this was inevitable."

"This?"

"That I'd lose you to him."

Hearing him voice it brought a great, crushing feeling to Laura's heart. He looked tired and beaten and for a moment the urge to protect was there again within her.

As Dan studied Laura, he saw a weariness to match his own. "It's been hard on you, being caught in the middle. Most of the time I forgot that and thought only of myself."

"Dan, I want you to know that I . . . I tried very hard to avoid Rye. You were so good to me, and you deserved—"

Again he silenced her with a movement of his hand. "I know. Rye told me. He laid it all out in the open the day I woke up. I've thought a lot about it since then, and I realize you can't help your feelings any more than I can help mine. That's what I fought against for the longest time. But after I had seen the busk and had proof of your feelings—both of yours—I went to see Ezra Merrill and initiated divorce proceedings."

Laura's teeth caught her lower lip and she stared at Dan in disbelief for several seconds. "Y . . . you've already seen Ezra?"

Dan nodded. "In September. I was angry at . . . at you and Rye. Oh hell, that's the only way I could make myself go talk to Ezra—if I got angry enough. But once I'd talked to him I wasn't able to carry through with it, and that's when I . . . well, I started staying at the Blue Anchor in the evenings. Then the rumor started about Rye and DeLaine Hussey and I got hopeful again and went back to Ezra and told him to stop everything."

Laura's heart was thumping hard. She remembered the time Dan had manhandled her, venting his frustrations. Yes, it would have taken anger to make Dan act.

"Ezra, of course, knows the whole history of the three of us, and I suspect he had the foresight to guess exactly how unsettled the situation was. He said he'd already filed the proper papers and had explained the situation to Judge Bunker, but he advised me that even though I wanted to withdraw the papers just then, maybe I ought to wait until . . . well, just wait and see. He said nothing would be acted upon without both of our signatures and an appearance before the judge, so we—"

Just then Dan was clutched by a spell of coughing that doubled him over. When he reclined against the pillows once more, he was winded. During the pause, Laura's mind reeled with questions, but finally Dan went on.

"The papers are still there, Laura, up at the town building, in probate court."

Their eyes met, and unconsciously she counted the months until spring.

Dan's voice grew even more raspy as he went on. "Even my own mother realizes I've held you against your wishes ever since Rye's return."

There was no soothing response Laura could offer. She remembered very clearly the things Hilda Morgan had said.

"And do you know what else she told me?"

Laura only stared at Dan, not moving a muscle.

"She told me you and Rye had given me back my life and that it was time I gave you back yours."

A poignant silence fell. A sense of impending ache settled between them. Faraway, a bell tolled as evening came on, and in the candlelit room all was silent but for his words hovering between them. "Christmas being the season of giving, I thought it might be the appropriate time to . . . give you what I know you want most, Laura—your freedom."

Laura felt a lump gathering in her throat. She swallowed, but the emotion could not be gulped away. No matter how badly she'd wanted her freedom, she'd never expected this overwhelming sense of loss at getting it.

Sensibly, Dan hurried on. "As I said, the papers are still there, and the circumstances being what they are, Judge Bunker would never deny the dissolution of this marriage. He's known us all our lives, too." Dan cleared his throat, continuing with an assumed dispassion. "Anyway, my mother said she'd welcome having a man around the house again to cook and do for, so as soon as I'm well enough, I'll be moving back there . . . until things can be properly settled in court."

Laura was speechless. What could she possibly reply? Thank you? The noble gesture was painful enough for Dan without adding the insult of a gratuitous response. Then suddenly Laura felt as bereft as she knew Dan must be. The tears she had been trying to hold back became a deluge. Without warning, she was overcome and dropped her face into both palms while sobs jerked her shoulders. Though she'd neither planned nor anticipated this reaction, there could have been no more fitting response to Dan's words. The end of five married years that had been basically harmonious and loving deserved this moment of mourning.

She sat on the edge of the bed, crying softly for several minutes, and when the tears stopped, somehow Dan was holding her hand. With a gentle tug, he pulled her sideways until she fell into the shelter of his arm with her head tucked beneath his chin. There were no more words. But as they lay in silence, their unspoken thoughts became the requiem for all they'd shared, not only during the past five years, but for nearly two decades before that.

When Rye and Josh returned, Rye immediately noted the constrained atmosphere. He could see at a glance that Laura had been crying, and for a moment felt the clutch of dread weight his stomach. Josh scampered straight across the room to Dan, bubbling with excitement over his first skating lesson. Rye attempted to catch Laura's eye, but she assiduously avoided glancing his way, so with a worried scowl, Rye prepared to leave.

Dan's words stopped him at the door.

"Rye, I have a favor to ask."

The tall man turned back into the room. "Of course, anything."

"I hate to ask after all you've done already, but Laura goes out to Jane's every year a few days before Christmas to take her some bayberry candles and things and have a visit before the holidays. And I . . ." Dan raised his palms helplessly. "Well, of course I won't be able to take them this year, so I was wondering if you'd mind driving her and Josh out there one day soon."

Rye's glance swerved to Laura, but she was studying Dan with an expression warning she was having difficulty keeping from breaking into tears again. "Of course," Rye answered. "I'll rent a cutter and be here whenever Laura says."

At his words, Laura could no longer avoid meeting Rye's eyes. She thought that if this day didn't end soon, her heart would certainly crumble. It had been flooded with emotion so many times already, this seemed the final stroke that might shatter it. She wanted to cry out, Dan, don't be so damnably noble! Instead, she could only suffer an overwhelming sense of injustice for him and answer Rye. "Any day . . . whenever you can find the time."

"Tomorrow, then, at midafternoon?"

"We'll be ready."

The following day at the appointed time, Rye came to collect Josh and Laura in a sleek black cutter pulled by a gray and white piebald mare. With warmed bricks at their feet and a heavy sealskin fur across their laps, the three set out across the snow-covered moors. The breath of the horse billowed and formed a cloud that appeared the same color as both land and sky. The jingle of harness rang out with the clarity of a glockenspiel in the cold, cold air. As the runners of the vehicle sliced through the dry snow, they squeaked out an unending syllable and left behind a pair of tracks with hoofprints between.

There was room on the black leather seat for no more than two, thus Josh sat on his mother's lap, with both of his knees bumping Rye's left thigh. Josh did more talking than either his mother or father, and when he asked if he could hold the reins, Rye laughingly complied, settling the boy between his legs and placing the lines in Josh's smaller hands. The horse sensed the difference and turned a blinder sideways, then headed straight again, her trot never wavering as Rye kept a watchful eye.

With Josh seated between his spraddled thighs, Rye's warm leg now rested firmly against Laura's. The contact was thrilling, though neither turned or looked at the other.

When they reached Jane's house, Josh immediately scrambled from under the laprobe. But when Rye began shifting, Laura placed a hand on his forearm. "Josh, you run in and tell Aunt Jane we're here. Rye and I have to talk for a minute." Then Rye suspended Josh over the side of the rig by one arm and lowered him till his feet touched the ground.

When they were alone, Rye and Laura looked at each other fully for the first time.

"Hello," he murmured.

"Hello." Will I ever grow tired of looking into his pale blue eyes? she thought. Never . . . never.

"You were very sad yesterday."

"Yes, I was."

"Can y' tell me why?"

Against her thigh, his was pressed, warm, secure.

"I told Dan that I'd be leaving with you in the spring, and he told me that he was giving me a Christmas gift." She paused, knowing he had guessed what it was. "He told me he is giving me my freedom. Mine and Josh's."

The wisps of whitened breath ceased falling from Rye's nostrils for a long, long moment. Then he breathed again, a huge sigh. "When?"

"He will be going to live at his mother's house as soon as he's well enough to make the move. As for legalities, he spoke to Ezra Merrill last September and filed divorce papers then. Right after he found the busk."

Rye slowly turned to face forward, his sober expression anything but victorious. Laura laid her mittened hand on his forearm. The reins remained laced through the fingers of his leather gloves, but he seemed unconscious of the fact. "He sent us out here today so we'd have a chance to tell Josh— both of us, together."

Rye said nothing. He seemed to be staring at a point beyond the horse's head, then he sighed again and dropped his chin, and sat for a long moment, lost in thought. The horse shook her head and made the harness jingle, and it seemed to drag Rye from his reverie. "Why don't I feel like celebratin'?" he asked quietly.

She only squeezed his arm, for they both knew the answer to his question.

The visit to Jane's passed in a haze of distraction, for Laura's thoughts were on their ride home. When the three were again settled in the cutter, she felt apprehensive. Josh's acceptance was vital, and as she studied the back of his head, wrapped in a thick knit cap and a scarf whose fringes shimmied in rhythm to the hoofbeats, Laura closed her eyes, hoping.

"Joshua, Rye and I have something to tell you."

Josh, with his ripe-apple cheeks and wind-reddened nose, turned to look up at her. Beneath the fur, Rye's leg flanked hers in firm support. "Rye and I . . . well, we . . . we love each other very much, dear, and we never wanted to . . . to . . ."

When she faltered, Rye took over. "I'm goin' t' marry your

mother, come spring, and the three of us'll be goin' t' the Michigan Territory together, along with my father.''

For a moment Josh's face reflected his lack of comprehension. But when understanding dawned, it brought no smile. "Is Papa comin' too?"

"No, Dan will stay here."

"Then I ain't goin'!" Josh declared stubbornly.

Laura's gaze skittered to Rye, then back to her son. "I know it's hard for you to understand, Josh, but Rye is your real father, and when I marry him you'll be our son. You'll have to live where we do."

"No, I don't want him to be my papa!" Josh stuck his lower lip out belligerently, and it began to tremble. "I wanna have the one I always had and live in our same house!"

Despair weighted Laura. "But wouldn't you like to go off on an adventure to the Michigan Territory, where you've never been before?"

"Is it far away?"

Laura was afraid to tell the truth, but knew a lie would only make matters worse, eventually. "Yes, it is."

"Do we have to take the ferry to get there?"

Oh, much more than the ferry, Josh, she thought, but answered only, "Yes."

"But then how could I see Jimmy?"

"Well . . . you wouldn't see him, but you'd make new friends where we lived."

"I don't want new friends. I wanna stay here with Jimmy and Papa and you." The belligerence had disappeared from Josh's face, and the tears he'd been valiantly trying to control whispered over his golden lashes and down his red cheeks.

Laura pulled him back against her and tucked his head beneath her chin. Holding Josh, she wondered how to make him understand, but suddenly she realized something Rye had said. She turned to look up at him.

"Josiah's going along—for sure?"

"Aye. He says his bones've had all they can take of this dampness and fog. Though I suspect he just doesn't want t' miss out on the adventure.''

The idea of having Josiah along was pleasing, but still, it

could not dispel the cloud cast over their plans by Josh's reluctance.

In an effort to win his son's approval, Rye now asked, "Would y' like t' drive the team again, Josh?"

But the boy only shook his head and burrowed closer against his mother. All the careful buildup of trust between father and son seemed to have been for naught. Lord, Laura thought, would things ever be easy? Would there forever be obstacles between her and Rye?

Chapter 21

IT WAS AN afternoon in late January, crisp but cloudy, when a wagon drawn by an aging sorrel mare pulled up at the foot of Crooked Record Lane and was loaded with the clothing and miscellany of Dan Morgan. It would have been easier for Laura had she conveniently planned to be absent from the house when Dan left it, but that would have been the coward's way out. Instead, she stood beside the dray while the last items were secured and Dan came around the tail end to stop before her and pull his gloves on tighter. He glanced at the house, then down at the icy bay, and once again needlessly tugged at his gloves.

"Well . . ." The word hung in the cold air like the ting of a bell in a winter woods.

"Yes, well . . ." She spread her palms nervously, then clutched them together.

"I'm not exactly sure what one says at a time like this."

"Neither am I," Laura admitted.

"Do I thank you again for saving my life?" He sounded not bitter, only resigned.

"Oh, Dan . . ." Suddenly she realized they were standing like wooden soldiers, and reached to lay a hand on his forearm. "Thanks aren't necessary, surely you know that."

He studied her right shoulder, and she his eyes. He glanced

toward the house and spoke with false animation. "I fixed that loose hinge on the back door and put a shim under the leg of the dry sink so it won't rock anymore."

"Yes, thank you."

"And remember, if there's anything you need, just . . ." But if there was anything she needed, Rye would see to it from now on.

"I'll remember."

"Tell Josh I'm sorry I missed saying good-bye to him, but when he comes back from Jane's, I'll stop by and see him."

"I'll tell him."

"Good . . ." He fell silent for several long, long seconds. Then came the same word, scarcely audible. "Good." He squared his shoulders, but just then was hit by a spasm of coughing, the last lingering vestige of his illness.

"It's bad for you to be out in the cold any longer than necessary, Dan. You'd better go."

"You're right." His eyes found hers at last, and for a moment she thought he meant to kiss her. But in the end he only nodded formally, clambered aboard the dray and said simply, "Good-bye, Laura."

"Take care of yourself, Dan."

The dray moved off, and she watched Dan's back until a sharp shiver reminded her that she herself wore no gloves or hat. Clutching her cape, she stared at the ice-encrusted scallop shells while making her way back to the house. When the door closed behind Laura, she sighed and sank back against it, closing her eyes, feeling momentarily forlorn and guilty of something not exactly nameable. The silence of the house imposed itself on her and she opened her eyes, scanning the keeping room, noting the absence of Dan's humidor on the table, of his coat and hat from the tree beside the door, of his shaving strop from its peg.

But on the heels of her guilt came immense relief. Alone. How long had it been since she'd been alone? There was a rich healing revitalization in having time to oneself. No one to cook for. No one to answer to. Nobody whose chest needed poulticing or whose shoes needed tying or whose bruises needed kissing. No eyes to either meet or avoid.

Laura was suddenly grateful Josh was gone—they were all gone! Countless times she'd wondered how she'd feel at this moment. Never had she expected this weightless sense of release. When she was a girl she'd known an extraordinary amount of freedom, and having reveled in it as she had, Laura now became aware of how changed her life had become after marrying Rye, bearing Josh, and subsequently marrying Dan. There had always been someone around, someone either relying on her or on whom she relied. Now, for a short time, there was no one.

Laura felt reborn.

She put an extravagant three logs on the fire at once, poured a generous serving of apple cider and set it on the hob to heat, closed the door to the linter room, adding an extra coziness to the main room, dragged an upholstered wing chair from the far end of the keeping room to the hearth, replaced the spermaceti candle with one of bayberry, fetched a fat goose-down pillow and threw it onto the chair, flung her apron off and searched for something to read, coming up with a three-month-old copy of the *Fireside Companion* she'd never taken time to open.

Two hours later, when a knock sounded at the door, Laura was dozing in her cozy nest. She stretched, flexed, and reluctantly left the chair to pad across the room on stockinged feet.

Rye stood on the step, dressed as usual in his pea jacket and knit bobcap. "Hello. Come t' do the chores."

"Oh!" Her eyes widened in surprise.

"Well, you goin' t' let me in or not? It's cold out here."

"Oh, of course!" She stepped back and closed the door as he entered and headed immediately for the water pail across the room. Halfway there, he caught sight of the chair, pillow, and book, her discarded shoes, the trestle table pushed away from its usual spot and positioned nearby with a bayberry candle and mug easily within reach.

Without a word, Rye took the pail and headed out back. When he returned, he lifted the filled pail to the dry sink, glanced at the alcove bed, then at the closed door of the linter room.

"Where's Dan?"

"Gone."

"Gone?" Rye glanced sharply at Laura. She seemed twitchy, standing on the far side of the trestle table as if intentionally keeping it between them.

"To his mother's."

"For a visit?"

"No, for good."

Rye's assessing gaze moved to the spot where the humidor used to be, then he boldly stalked to the door of the linter room and flung it open. She watched his eyes take inventory of the room before he spun again to face her. "He moved out?"

Laura nodded silently.

"And where's Josh?"

"At Jane's."

Without another word, Rye closed the bedroom door and strode out back to return in two minutes with an enormous armful of wood, which he deposited in the woodbox before heading out for another load. After the third trip the box was full, and he brushed the bark from his sleeves, then swung around with impatience emanating from every muscle of his body. "The back path needs shovelin'. It won't take long."

While he was gone, Laura put more cider to warm, added logs to the fire, and put a ring of spicy barley sausage on to cook.

When the back door opened again, Rye paused to ask, "Is there anythin' else that needs doin' today?"

"No, that's all."

He hesitated, watching her lift an arm to the mantle but keeping her back to him.

"I've put some sausage on to cook if you'd like to stay."

"Is that an invitation?"

"Yes." She turned at last to face him squarely. "To supper." The implication was clear. For a moment neither of them moved. Then Rye casually sauntered toward the fire while unbuttoning his jacket with one hand. He shrugged it off and flung it across the trestle table, eyeing the chair as he circled it.

"Looks like somebody's been spendin' a lazy afternoon

here." He stopped beside the arm of the chair, leaned over from one hip, and picked up the magazine from atop the pillow.

"I confess. And it felt wonderful."

With the tabloid in his hand, he next took stock of the candle, her cup, her apron tossed across the trestle beside his own jacket.

"Aye, I c'n see that." His mouth quirked up at one corner. "Mind if I try it out?"

"Not at all. Just don't make yourself too comfortable."

He plucked the pillow from the seat of the chair, took its place, and plopped the puffy thing onto his lap, watching Laura while she ladled hot cider.

"Here, I thought you could use this." She offered him the mug, but when he reached it was with both hands, taking the drink in one hand and her wrist in the other. Twisting around, he set the mug on the table, then tugged her toward his lap.

"I'll tell y' what I c'n use." She landed on the pillow with a soft plop. "And it's not a cup o' cider." He still wore the navy blue knit bobcap. It rested against the tall back of the wing chair while his elbows indolently hooked its arms, and his palms contoured her waist.

"What, then?" she asked in a voice no louder than the hiss of the fire.

His lips opened. His glance dropped to her mouth. His hard hands left her waist and traveled up Laura's sleeves to her shoulder blades before drawing her against his chest. She fell into the accommodating nest of his shoulder with a palm resting on Rye's heart, looking up into his face as he bent his head over her. Even before his lips touched hers, she felt the tumultuous hammering through his thick, cable-knit sweater. It was at first less than a kiss, rather, a reunion after their long separation, a hello again, as his mouth met hers lightly, lightly. The tip of his nose brushed her cheek, cold yet, as were the lips that moved in a silken exploration across her own while his warm breath created dew on her skin. Then her head was moving slowly from side to side in answer to the movements of his, with only the crests of their lips brushing, as if in reacquaintance. Their tongue tips met and passed, moving on to dampen the perimeters of their mouths. The kiss widened, deepened, and with an easy turn of her body Laura sought the thick cords of his neck, riding her palm inside the high turtle-neck of his sweater while Rye slipped a hand beneath her knees and drew them over the arm of the chair.

Slowly, minute by minute, the ardor of the kiss grew until his tongue brushed the inner walls of her cheeks, and hers, his. Cradled in his arms, she felt the hand beneath her knees spread wide, then slide up along the underside of her thigh to her buttock, where it pressed, warm and firm, learning her contours once again as his moist, full kiss rocked her senses. Laura's hand moved from Rye's neck to his hair, and blindly she slid the knit cap away to thread her fingers into the thick strands at the back of his head.

Long moments later, when the first kisses and touches had ignited an emotional fire, Rye lifted his head to look into Laura's lambent brown eyes and whisper thickly, "I can't believe we're really alone at last."

She caressed his warm skull, shifting her fingers in his hair until the aroma of cedar seemed to lift from it. "It's been five months, two weeks, and three days."

"Is that all?"

"But, Rye, before you came I was—"

"Later. We'll talk later." His mouth descended to hers again and he shifted her weight in his arms, turning her so that one breast pressed against him, leaving the other free. She held her breath as he withdrew the arm from beneath her knees and slowly brushed it up her thigh, hip, and ribs until at last her resilient flesh was taken warm within his palm. A shudder of delight quaked through her limbs as he caressed her breast, squeezing, then releasing repeatedly while his tongue dipped into her mouth and hers played a circle dance around his. Through the cotton covering of her garments, his fingertips explored the projecting nipple until it stood up all the more boldly with desire.

Against her open mouth, he muttered, "Let's go t' bed, darlin'."

She shook her head in slow motion while his mouth fol-lowed. "No, I tried to tell you—" But his mouth closed tightly over hers, cutting off the words and inundating her with the wet, sleek texture of his tongue.

When he lifted his head again, it was to murmur, "If y' won't say yes, I swear we'll do it right here in this chair." A trail of miniature kisses passed along the side of her nose.

"Mmm . . . that sounds wonderful," she approved throatily, and felt him smile against her neck. "But we're not going to do it anywhere, not until I'm your wife."

"You are my wife," he went on imperturbably, shifting their positions so that he could bend forward to cover her far breast with his mouth.

"No I'm not."

"Mmm . . . y' smell good enough t' eat. Y've smelled like bayberries y'r whole life long. Did y' know that?" he murmured, ignoring her protest.

She was draped over the arms of the chair like a dust cover, head slung back limply while his mouth took possession of the crest of her breast, deliberately wetting the fabric of her dress and camisole, then biting the engorged nipple until it sent up an incredible aching. He twisted his head from side to side, playfully ferocious as he tugged at her hidden flesh, until a guttural sound escaped Laura's throat and her hand sought his hair to urge more of the same. But a moment later she insisted again, "Rye, I'm not going to make love with you." With her head slung back, the words were strident and forced. She pulled herself up, finding some hidden source of resistance, until she sat on his lap again.

"Who're y' tryin' to fool?" he questioned, still teasing the hardened nipple with the backs of his fingers. The point of flesh pressed outward against the wet circle on her dress front —it was silly to deny that she was tempted.

"I'm as human as you are. I could no more have stopped myself from kissing you than I could when we were sixteen. But I'm being honest with you, Rye."

Still he didn't believe her, but grinned engagingly. "Well, while you're bein' honest, do we have t' have this damn pillow between us?" He manipulated her as if she were no heavier than a rag doll, lifting her up and jerking the pillow away to toss it onto the floor. Then he unceremoniously grasped one of her ankles and swung it across his stomach until she found herself straddling him in the chair with her most intimate parts settled obligingly against the bulging mound of his arousal.

"All right, where were we?" he asked coolly. "Oh yes, you were being honest with me and telling me that y've no intention of makin' love with me until you're legally divorced from Dan, is that it?" But as he spoke, Rye tugged at the copious skirts of her dress and petticoats, which were pinned beneath her, hauling them hand over hand till she felt the lumpy hems scrape along her bottom, then slide free.

"Yes, that's it," she claimed, meaning it. But Laura sat on him now with only his trousers and her pantaloons between them. Unperturbed, he adjusted his hips, settling them more comfortably in the chair until his hardness and her softness fit together like two pieces of a jigsaw puzzle.

"Mmm . . ." His hands slid beneath the billows of cotton and found her two ankles, pulling them against his hips, then continuing to caress them through her scratchy wool stockings. "And y' intend t' hold out on me till March?"

"Exactly," she replied in the calmest voice she could muster while his mischievous eyes glowed, partly in amusement, partly in desire.

"Do y' mind if I test y'r will a little bit, Mrs. . . . ah, Morgan, is it?"

"Not at all," she answered with a firm smirk. "Test away. As I said before, nothing more till we're married." She carelessly looped her wrists about his neck and laced her fingers together, accepting her bawdy pose with a blitheness Rye could imagine in no other woman.

"Y' know I'd never be one t' entice y' into doin' anythin' against y'r will." His warm palms slid up her calves to the shallows behind both knees, then back down, pushing the wool stockings to her ankles. He inserted thumbs and forefingers inside the ruched wool, caressing the hollows above her heels, then squeezing gently, massaging.

"I know." Tingles sizzled up her legs. He was, as he'd always been, the consummate lover, inventive, irresistible. He could stir her senses in ever-new ways, as he was doing now. Oh, Rye, I want to go the limit with you . . . but I can't and won't until he's truly gone from between us.

Rye tipped his head to one side, lolled back against the chair with a lopsided grin, and requested in a husky voice, "Tell me again, then, what it was y' invited me t' stay for." But beneath her petticoat his hands slid to her hips, tipping them back slightly until she felt the warm knob of masculinity meeting the feminine pulsepoint that couched him.

Her eyelids slid closed. Her breath fell harshly. "Sausage," she murmured, following his lead in precisely the fashion she knew he expected.

"Then maybe we ought t' eat. I think I smell it cookin'."

Her eyelids fluttered open and her lips curved. "You're a nasty man, Rye Dalton."

"Aye, and don't y' love it. Come here." With total disregard for the state of her clothing, his arms tightened across her back—skirts and all—and he pulled her forward until their tongues met, as did their bodies, his lifting in invitation, hers pressing in answer. His right hand roved down her spine, caressing it through the rough cotton of her pantaloons, then sliding lower, around the curve of her buttocks, as she leaned forward, kissing him with an ardor that set their pulses pounding. When temptation was transformed to torture, they pulled apart and spoke simultaneously.

"Laura, let's go t' bed . . ."

"Rye, we have to stop . . ."

His hands squeezed her hips, but hers pressed his chest. Their eyes were so close together their lashes almost brushed.

"Y' mean it, don't y'?" he questioned. "Y' mean t' hold me off until y'r name is legally Dalton again?"

She backed farther away. "I told you that when we started this."

"Why?"

"Partly because of what happened the last time we made love, partly—"

"Y' mean Zach's death?"

When she nodded, his frustration at last surfaced. An expression of annoyance darkened his features. "Laura, that's ridiculous!"

"Maybe to you, but —"

"And anyway, you're splittin' hairs!" he interrupted. "What's the difference between what we're doin' and what we want t' do? You're only justifyin' your actions, that's all."

Singed because he'd hit on the truth, she immediately jumped from his lap and whisked her skirts down, facing him with the flares of embarrassment coloring her cheeks. "Rye Dalton, don't you sit there accusing me when I'm the one that's trying to do the honorable thing here!"

"Honorable! Ha!" Angry now, he sat sharply forward in his chair.

"Yes, honorable! We made a promise to each other not to dishonor Dan!"

"While he was in this house!"

"No, while he's still legally my husband. But you conveniently forget that now."

"Because you've got me in the state of a . . . an appendix ready to rupture! I ache, damnit!"

Laura's frustrations of the past nine months had built up until now, without warning, they fought their way out. She stood before Rye's chair, little understanding that their tensions, both emotional and sexual, naturally sought release. Her temper blazed, then erupted in a rich, relieving spate of shouting.

"Oh you . . . you oversexed . . ." She searched for an adequately scathing word. ". . . goat!" She pointed a shaking finger at the door. "Dan hasn't been gone half a day and you're right at my door to take his place. Well, did you ever stop to think that maybe I need a little time to myself, without one man pushing me to stay and the other pushing me to go! I'm sick and tired of both of you fawning over me like I'm some prize at a fair. And who asked you to come here anyway, Rye Dalton? I was sitting here just as contented as a calf in clover when you came charging in here, and . . . and . . . ooph!" It felt so wonderful to yell that she went one step farther and yanked him by the front of the sweater. "Get out of my chair! I was perfectly happy in it all by myself, so just *get out*!"

Rye was on his feet. They squared off almost nose to nose. "Oversexed goat!"

"Yes . . . oversexed goat!"

"Y're one to talk. I didn't see y' puttin' up much objection! And I did not come here t' claim y' like a prize at the fair! I came here t' do y'r chores, y' ungrateful hussy!"

"Hussy? . . . Hussy! Don't you use that name on me, Rye Dalton, not when you've been fooling around with her while I was *unavailable*." Though she didn't know it, Laura looked very much the hussy with her fists on her hips, clothes wrinkled, voice raised.

"I never *fooled around* with DeLaine Hussey," he sneered.

"You expect me to believe that—a man with the *drive* you have?" She scooped the pillow off the floor and fluffed it with irate jerks.

"Maybe I should've! The lady was willin' enough!"

Laura gaped at Rye. Her mouth dropped open in surprise. "So you *were* fooling around with her! Damn you, Rye Dalton!" She threw the pillow at his head and he ducked too late. But when he straightened, he held it in a fist and swung it back at her, catching her on the side of the head, forcing her back a step.

"I scarcely touched the woman, fool that I am. Instead I remained *honorable* because of you, and what do I get for it but the sharp side of y'r tongue." The pillow was still clenched in his huge fist. He thrust it against her chest, letting go, and turning to scoop his hat off the floor.

She was nearly knocked off her feet, but recovered her balance in time to reach his jacket before he did. Instead of handing it to him, she swiped it at him. "With a tongue as sharp as mine, maybe I won't be wanted in the Michigan Territory."

He stood as still as a statue for several endless seconds. "Does that mean y' don't want t' go?"

"It'd serve you right if I didn't."

He shrugged into his jacket. "Suit y'rself. Y' can let me know when y'r mind's made up." He headed for the door. "Meanwhile, y' can find someone else t' do y'r daily chores. I got all I can handle down at the cooperage, gettin' ready for the trip, without wastin' my time up here where I'm not wanted."

The door slammed behind him.

Laura stood for a full minute, staring at it, wondering what had happened. Then, in utter childishness, she stuck her tongue out at the door. But a moment later she fell to her knees, burying her face in the pillow upon the seat of the chair, bawling and blaming him. You don't understand what I've been through, Rye Dalton! You don't have the vaguest notion what I need right now!

She howled to her heart's content and socked the pillow with a fury that felt wonderful! Cathartic!

But never for a moment did Laura doubt that she would leave this island with Rye in only nine short weeks.

Rye Dalton stormed down home, cursing all the way, calling her names he didn't mean, bellowing deprecations at women in general and her in particular, feeling masculine and self-righteous and thoroughly purged. He kicked at hunks of snow in his path, promised the Almighty that Laura Dalton would never feel his hardened member against her again—not if she begged till he was feeble and impotent—knowing even before he reached the cooperage that he didn't mean a word of it, and she'd damn well better be ready to make up for lost time when she was Mrs. Rye Dalton again!

Within a day's time they both came to understand what it was that had caused the irrational anger. The sexual tension and frustration had been building up for months, with a myriad of human emotions having been brought into play: desire, guilt, love, recrimination, hope, fear, impatience. And with at least two months to go before the situation could be resolved, their anger was a natural vent.

She stewed for a week.
He stewed for a week.
He felt revived.
She felt refreshed.
Damnit, but I love that woman, Rye Dalton agonized.
Lord in heaven, but I love that oversexed goat, Laura
    fumed.
I'll give her a couple weeks to realize what she's lost.
I'll give him a couple weeks to admit I was right.
Let her carry her own wood and water for a while!

Let him eat Josiah's cooking!
Three weeks till March.
Three weeks till March.
I wonder what she's doing.
I wonder what he's doing.
Sausage . . . (he smiled) . . . ah, what a woman.
Smelled it cooking, did he . . . (she smiled) . . . probably
    the steam off his own body.
Two weeks till March.
One week till March.
Damnit, but I miss her.
Wait till we're married, Rye Dalton. I'll make you pay for
    this misery!

They waited for the courts to set her free, and meanwhile, Josh remained belligerent, often scowling at Laura, angry because Dan was gone from the house. She grew sick and tired of looking at his lower lip protruding as if a weight were attached to it, and often had to keep herself from speaking out in self-defense when he watched her making preparations for Michigan and acted as if she was doing him some grave misdeed with every stitch she took, every item she stockpiled.

She readied an ample supply of clothing, for once they left the convenience of New England's mills, that commodity would become precious. She bought great hanks of yarn for socks and mittens and heavy cloth for sewing longer pants for Josh next winter. Garden seeds were carefully tucked into small cotton bags and packed between layers of clothing, where they could not freeze. She took inventory of her household goods, making decisions about which to take and which to abandon—any item made of wood was automatically left behind, for Rye could fashion a new one when they reached Michigan. It was glass and metal that would be precious on the frontier. She kept a growing list of necessities: needles, paper, ink, schoolbooks, mosquito netting, enough soap to last during their trip, lanolin, spices, herbs, medicinal ingredients, candle wicking, bedding, soft cotton for bandages, and wire—more simple home repairs were made with wire than anything else.

Meanwhile Rye, too, was preparing to leave. He and Josiah

built up as large an inventory of barrels as possible, for when they left, the island would be without a cooper until one could be enticed away from the mainland. For their own use, special waterproof barrels were fashioned for that all-important commodity, gunpowder. Larger ones were constructed for clothing, and medium-sized barrels to carry their coopering tools. He purchased a new John H. Hall percussion rifle and bought molds for bullets. He made lists also, though his were concerned with survival and providing rather than with domestics: knives, spades, spare metal parts for harnesses, hoof trimmers (for horses would be necessary in Michigan), unguent, grease, and oil.

And Rye worried every day that the court would drag its feet and leave him and Laura in a quandary when it was time to leave. But then came the news that the hearing was scheduled six months to the day from the date Dan Morgan had first filed papers.

The probate court of the county of Nantucket, Commonwealth of Massachusetts, had been in existence since 1689. Throughout its history, it had dissolved many marriages by proclaiming missing seamen dead. But to the best of his knowledge, Judge James Bunker had never before heard of one being dissolved because a missing seaman was declared alive.

In his chambers on the second floor of the Town Building on Union Street, the Honorable Judge Bunker reviewed the case before him on this windy mid-March day in 1838, attempting to disassociate his personal knowledge of Rye Dalton, Dan Morgan, and Laura Dalton Morgan from the legal aspects to be considered. Bunker's Puritanical leanings made him averse to divorce. But in this case, knowing the history of the three and considering the bizarre set of circumstances cast upon them by fate, Judge Bunker found it impossible to do anything but grant the dissolution of the marriage.

As his gavel fell, its reverberations echoed through the high-ceilinged room. Ezra Merrill inserted the relatively few papers into a leather portfolio and reached for his greatcoat. Dan and Ezra shook hands and exchanged a few low words Laura couldn't hear, then the lawyer turned to her, wished her his best, and left.

In the ensuing silence, Laura met Dan's eyes with a wan smile.

"And so, it is done," he stated with an air of resignation.

"Yes, I—"

"Don't thank me, Laura. For God's sake, don't thank me."

"I wasn't going to, Dan. I was going to say I doubt that Judge Bunker has ever come up against a case like this before."

"Obviously not." Silence fell again. Dan reached for his coat, buttoned it slowly, then stared at the tips of his shoes while asking, "How soon will you be leaving?"

"At the end of the month."

He looked up. "Ah, that soon."

"Yes." The guilt she'd once felt was gone, but she hastened to add, "You'll want to spend a little time with Josh before we leave. I'll let you know exactly when that will be."

"Yes. Thank you."

Again that discomfiting silence settled between them. "Well then, I guess there's nothing left to do but go our separate ways. Shall we?" He turned, took her elbow in a courtly manner, but dropped it long before they reached the street.

They bid each other good-bye, and Laura turned toward home. Down below the shrill whistle of the steamboat *Telegraph* lifted with an ear-splitting shriek. The *ka-whoozh* of the whistle rattled the air again, and suddenly Laura's heart seemed to soar like the sound.

I'm free! I'm free! I'm free!

She stopped in the middle of the street, whirled around to see if she could spot the *Telegraph*, but though she couldn't see it, she knew it was picking up passengers at Steamboat Wharf, as it did every Monday, Wednesday, and Saturday. And one day soon it would take her away with Rye. All at once it came to her that she was totally free to go with him at last. She suddenly smiled at the memory of the spat they'd had. *Good lord, Laura, you fool! You've never even asked him exactly what day you're leaving!*

She turned and her feet flew up the street toward home. Her bonnet brim fluttered in the stiff March wind, and a thousand unasked questions danced through her mind. She'd never felt right about asking those questions of Rye, about discussing their plans while she was still Laura Morgan. But now she could ask Rye anything. As she hustled up the shell path to the house there was one—only one—question of utmost importance filling her pounding heart.

The message arrived at the cooperage late that afternoon, and Rye tossed a coin to Jimmy Ryerson, recognizing Laura's writing on the note. He took the stairs to the living quarters with great impatience and perched on the edge of his bunk while tearing the seal.

Dear Rye,

I'm sorry. Will you marry me anyway?

Love,
Laura

His face burst into an enormous smile. She's free! He let out a raucous whoop of joy and sent Chad up to the house with an immediate reply.

Dear Laura,

I'm sorry, too. I accept your proposal.
Can I come and carry your water?

Love,
Rye

Dear Rye,

Stay away from me, you oversexed goat.
It's not my water you're after.

All my love,
Laura

Dear Laura,

Then can I carry your wood? Or how about steaming up a sausage?

> All my love,
> The oversexed goat

Dear Rye,

Not until we're married. When do we leave?
Everything is ready to be packed.

> With love,
> The ungrateful hussy

p.s. I need three big barrels, maybe four.
But don't bring them, send them!

Dear Laura,

Am sending Chad with the first of four barrels. If you need more than four, let me know. We leave on the Albany packet, Thursday, March 30. What do you say to getting married by the captain?

> I love you,
> Rye

Dear Rye,

Yes, yes, yes! Everything is all ready. Have room left in one barrel for any of your clothes if you're short of space. When will I see you again?

> I love you, too,
> Laura

It was two days before they were due to leave when the final message was delivered to Laura's door. But this time it was delivered by Rye himself.

She answered the knock to find him not on the wooden step, but backed off about ten feet, standing on the scallop shells. "Rye?" Her heart seemed to stop up her throat at the sight of him. He was dressed in a rugged ecru sweater and the body-conforming sailor's breeches with belly flap and bell bottoms. On his tangled hair nested a Greek fisherman's hat of black cheviot wool, its shallow visor dipping at a jaunty angle across his tan brow. The rakish tilt of the cap set off his brawny handsomeness to great advantage, and as her dark eyes met those of sea-blue, Laura's face brightened into an enormous smile that was immediately reflected in Rye's.

"Hello, m'love." He swallowed, then said no more, only hooked his thumbs in his waist flap and gazed up at her as if he could not get his fill, the smile having softened into something far more eloquent upon his rugged features.

"I've missed you terribly," came her hearty admission.

"I've missed y', too."

"I'm sorry for the things I said."

"Aye, me too."

"Aren't we foolish?"

"Nay, just in love, wouldn't y' say?"

"Yes, I'd say." She smiled wistfully. Still he didn't move, so she invited, "Would you like to come in?"

"More than anything in the world." But his black boots remained firmly planted in the white shells.

"Well, then—"

"But I won't."

"Y . . . you won't?"

He shook his head slowly. A grin eased up along one side of his sculpted mouth. "Two more days . . . I'll wait."

She released a shuddering breath and glanced at the harbor, then back at him. "Two more days." Then she admitted, "I'm a little scared, Rye."

"So am I. But excited, too."

She let her eyes linger on his. "Aye, excited," she agreed softly, intentionally slipping into his nautical vernacular.

He cleared his throat and shifted his feet. "Well, Josiah's all ready t' go. How about Josh?"

"Josh has been treating me like I just kicked his dog. I don't know how he's going to act when it's time for good-byes." They thought of Jimmy Ryerson, Jane, Hilda . . . Dan. And for a moment shadows crossed over their faces.

"Aye, the good-byes're goin' t' be hard, aren't they?"

She nodded, then forced herself to smile, for his sake.

"Well, then . . ." He backed away two steps.

The closer it came to departure, the more the finality of the venture gave them pause. So many uncertainties lay ahead, miles to cross, dangers to face. And what would Josh's attitude be? But as brown eyes met blue, Laura and Rye drew from each other the reassurance that together they could conquer whatever the future might bring.

"I'll come for y' myself around nine on Thursday."

"We'll be ready."

Still he remained on the path below, gazing up into her deep brown eyes, reluctant to leave. Finally, with a small guttural sound in his throat, he crossed the distance between them and lifted the palm of her ringless left hand to his warm lips. "Josh'll come 'round," he reassured. Then he spun away and ran at a forced trot down the hill.

At that very moment, in a yard near the foot of the lane, Josh was on his knees on one side of a marble pit circled by a line drawn in the sand. Taking aim with a cat's eye balanced on his thumb, he suddenly straightened and looked across the circle at Jimmy.

"Hey, Jimmy?"

Jimmy Ryerson was counting the marbles in his cache and stopped at the interruption. "You made me lose count. What?" he demanded.

Josh scratched his head, leaving a gray smear of dirt on the blond hair, and finally asked the question that had been puzzling him for weeks. "What's a adventure?"

Chapter 22

THE LITTLE GRAY LADY of the Sea was as good as her nick-
name on Thursday morning. A thin haze of fog covered the
shoreline, and above the island, the sky was a somber iron
gray. The town came awake to its never-changing sounds—the
morning chimes of the Congregational church tower, the clang
of the smith's hammer, the crackle of canvas catching wind,
the *shushh* of waves beneath pilings, and the rumble of
wooden wheels on cobblestones.

A pair of freight wagons pulled up before the gaping door
of the cooperage, where only the fireplace and tool bench remained as before. Two stevedores jumped down and headed
inside to begin rolling heavy barrels out and loading them. A
gnarled old cooper with a head of hoary curls stood beside a
long, lanky younger one, whose blond mane tangled about his
face like beached kelp. A slow coil of blue smoke lifted above
their heads as the younger man put his arm around the older
one's shoulders, squeezing hard.

"Well, old man—"

A stretch of poignant silence slipped by.

"Aye, son, she's been a good ol' place."

They lifted their eyes to the rafters, the small window above
the tool bench, the worn steps to the lodgings. The voice of a
woman dear to both of them drifted back in memory, calling

them to breakfast, to supper, to bed. Together they stood in the confines of the building that smelled of cedar and pipe smoke and always would.

Josiah removed the fragrant brier from his teeth and spoke quietly. "I'd like a few minutes alone with y'r mother. Go on now, get y'r woman."

Rye drew a deep, quivering breath, let his eyes pass one last, lingering time across the walls of the cooperage, then answered throatily, "Aye, then, we'll meet y' at the wharf." He squeezed the burly shoulders once more, then turned quickly toward the street.

With a long-legged leap, he mounted a wagon, gave a single sharp whistle, and peered back over his shoulder to find a large yellow Labrador bounding onto the scarred boards behind him. The dog jogged eagerly to the forward end of the wagon and rested her jaw over the back of the driver's seat, gave a few wags, and they set off.

At the bottom of Crooked Record Lane, the vehicle lurched to a stop while the man squinted up at a quaint little saltbox with silver-brown weatherbeaten shakes. A woman appeared at the door. She was dressed in a traveling cape of dove gray wool over a simple dress of lemon yellow gingham and a matching bonnet with a satin bow knotted just behind her left jaw.

She raised a gloved hand to wave in greeting, and a boy slithered around her skirts, caught sight of the lanky cooper, and stared at him with a surly expression. But at sight of the child, the dog broke loose and loped forward in her aging gait. The sullen look changed to one of surprise. The winsome eyes and mouth opened in dawning delight, and Josh could resist no longer. He came to meet the dog halfway, falling to his knees in the middle of the path, scrunching his blue eyes shut as the Lab bestowed a wet hello to the rounded curve of the boy's face.

"Ship! Ship!" Instinct made him begin to ask the man, "Is Ship . . ." Then, remembering, he turned to ask his mother instead. "Is Ship goin' with us?"

"Why don't you ask Rye?"

He looked up at the tall cooper he had once liked so much.

"Is Ship goin' with us?" Josh asked at last.

Rye came near, dropped to one knee, and gave the dog's flat head an affectionate rumple. "Why, o' course she's goin' with us. Nobody should be without a watchdog where there're wolves and bears and raccoons t' raid the storehouse."

"W . . . wolves 'n' b . . . bears?" Josh's eyes widened. "Really?"

"Aye, but we won't have t' worry, not with Ship along."

"Is it really gonna be a adventure?"

"Aye, son. And have y' made up y'r mind yet if y'r goin' t' talk t' me while we make it, or are y' bound to keep a button on that lip?" Lowering his voice, Rye added, "It hurts y'r mother and me a lot, y' know. Especially y'r mother. She wants t' see you happy again, but she wants t' be happy, too." He paused, then declared softly, "We both love y', Josh."

Josh's eyes dropped to the dog. In a small voice, he said, "Jimmy, he said . . . well, he said your papa . . . well, if he's goin' along, he'll be my grampa."

Rye's expression softened, and his voice went lower. "Aye, son."

"And . . . and you'll be my father?"

From the doorway Laura watched, her heart filling her breast with wingbeats as the man in the dark breeches, light sweater, and jaunty black fisherman's cap bent near his son with one arm braced upon a knee.

"Aye, son. I am y'r father, as y've known for some time."

Josh raised uncertain eyes, very much like those that looked down on him. "Will I have to call you Papa?"

Rye swallowed, studying the piquant face of his son, realizing how difficult it was for the child to accept the sudden changes thrust upon his life. In a kind, caring voice, Rye answered, "Nay, Joshua. I think there'll only be one man y'll ever think of as Papa. Nothin's goin' t' change that, you know. Y' can keep on lovin' Dan as much as y' ever did."

"But I won't see him no more, will I?"

"Michigan's a long way from Nantucket, Josh. I'm afraid not. But maybe when y're grown up, Nantucket won't seem so far. Then y' can come back for a visit."

Unmoving, Laura waited, willing the child to make peace

with his father so that their lives might know their rightful share of contentment.

Josh was silent for a long time, hunkered before Rye half despondently. The dog took a desultory lick at Josh's chin, but he seemed unaware. At last he raised his eyes to the blue eyes in the tan face above him. In a very businesslike voice for a five-year old, he declared, "I decided I'll call you Father."

Their eyes searched, questioned, and Rye's body strained with repressed love for the boy. Suddenly they moved as one, Josh shooting to his feet, Rye's arms widening, and for three thundering heartbeats they were chest to chest as love had its irrepressible way.

Seeing father and son healing at last, Laura's eyes misted. Joy burst through her heart, and she thought now the best time to intrude upon the scene.

"Are you two going to stay down there all day or are you going to come up here and help me carry things out to the wagon?"

Josh backed away. Rye looked up toward the top of the path, then slowly got to his feet. Stretching his long legs into a calculatedly lazy stride, he began moving toward her while commenting in an undertone, "Y'r mother's lookin' quite saucy t'day."

The child looked up the long man beside him. "What's saucy?"

But only Rye's rich laughter answered his son's question as they mounted the path together. At the step, Rye hooked one boot over its edge, leaned on the knee with both palms, and let his gaze rove over the floor-length cape and the long triangle of yellow gingham it revealed.

"And what are you laughing about, Rye Dalton?"

"Is that any way t' greet y'r groom on his weddin' day?"

Her jaw dropped. "Today!"

"Aye, t'day. If I have t' commit mutiny t' get the captain t' perform the ceremony. That is, if we don't miss the Albany packet while we stand here yammerin'."

With a gay smile she swung inside, followed by Rye, Josh, and Ship.

The house was stripped of all its former warmth and appeared forlorn now, its furnishings having been systematically rifled. Those that remained were to be sold by Ezra Merrill, and appeared sadly abandoned in the small rooms, which had been divested of all personal items. Rye avoided analyzing his surroundings, quickly tipping a barrel instead and shouldering it through the door. It was a day that would, by its very nature, repeatedly plunge them from optimistic joy to nostalgic sadness. The best they could do to get through the difficult moments of tugging memory was to put them behind as quickly as possible and look forward.

But when the last of the barrels was loaded and Rye returned to the house for the two black satchels that remained, he found Laura with her back to the door, running her gloved fingertips reminiscently along the edge of the fireplace mantel. Nearby, the doors to the alcove bed were opened, its tick and quilts gone, leaving it nothing but a hollow wooden box. Rye watched Laura's eyes turn to it and linger. Next she moved to the beckoning door of the linter room, and he stepped up quietly behind her shoulder. She glanced back at him, unsmiling, then together they gazed inside at the wooden bedstead.

"I'll make y' a new one," he promised softly, understanding that she truly did not pine to take the old one along, but that it deserved this moment of elegy. Upon it their marriage had been consummated. From it he had gone to sea. Upon it Joshua Dalton had been born. And to it Dan had come.

For the first time today, Rye touched her, in much the same fashion he had touched his father. "Come," he encouraged softly. "It's time t' go."

They turned from the bedroom doorway, crossed the keeping room with lagging steps that echoed in the still space where once their laughter had lilted. There was no laughter now. They stepped from the house, shut its door for the last time, closing it on a phase of their lives both sweet and sad. The stark white scallop shells clicked together in the familiar crunch that had meant home for so long. Halfway down the path, they turned one last time to impress the image of the little saltbox into their memories.

If it was difficult saying good-bye to their dwellings, the scene on the wharf was impossible. Everyone was there—Jane and John Durning and all six of their little stair-steps; Jimmy Ryerson and his parents; Dahlia Traherne; not only Hilda Morgan, but Tom and Dorothy as well; Chad Dalton and his parents, along with a large entourage of Dalton relatives— even Cousin Charles with his wife and three children. Joseph Starbuck had come, and Ezra Merrill and Asa Pond.

And standing in the background at the fringe of bravely smiling faces, looking as if she was trying to hold back tears, hovered DeLaine Hussey.

And, of course, there was Dan.

He was one of the last to arrive, and at first as he stole up quietly behind DeLaine, Rye and Laura were unaware of his presence. Laura was in the arms of Dahlia, who pressed a cluster of recipes into her daughter's palm. "These're your favorites from when you were a little girl." The tears started then and grew more insistent as Jane bestowed the next good-bye, a fierce hug in the middle of which she released a shattering sob beside Laura's ear. Rye was being passed from aunts to uncles while Josh and Jimmy Ryerson knelt one on either side of Ship, surrounded by Josh's cousins, all of them for the moment jealous of Josh's adventure, his acquisition of the dog, and the possible dangers of bears and wolves.

But then Cap'n Silas motioned the crowd to clear space for the stevedores to drive the wagons to the gangplank and unload them, and as the crowd parted, Rye and Laura glanced up the chasm to find Dan there, the thumbs and forefingers of both his hands slipped inside his vest pockets, a beaver hat on his head, and an expression of tight control on his face.

The eyes of the departing couple swerved to each other, then back to Dan, and a hush seemed to fall over the crowd before a self-conscious chatter swelled again.

The last of the barrels was loaded aboard the *Clinton*, and suddenly everyone winced as the deafening steam whistle blew over Steamboat Wharf.

The sudden jarring sound was so overwhelming it set Laura's heart thumping—or was the reaction caused by the sight of Dan, still hesitating twenty feet across the wharf, restraining himself just as she was?

But then Josh spied Dan and lurched to his feet, running the length of the wharf. He flung himself into the arms of the man who knelt down, then scooped the child up, and clung to him a last time while a woeful wail carried above the wharf.

"Papa . . . Papa . . ."

Cap'n Silas commanded, "All aboard!"

The steam whistle shrilled again while over Josh's shoulder Dan Morgan blinked and tried valiantly not to let his tears spill over.

Laura lifted pleading eyes to Rye, and even as her feet began moving, she felt Rye's hand grasping her elbow, hurrying her toward Dan. Dan set Josh on his feet and met Laura halfway. As her arms went around him, his hat was knocked onto the silvery boards of the wharf, but nobody seemed to notice. Rye's eyes had locked with those of DeLaine Hussey, and he nodded a silent good-bye while she pressed trembling fingers to her lips.

Laura felt Dan's heart slamming piteously hard against her breasts before she pulled back to look into his face. His lips were set grimly against his teeth, but his nostrils trembled while he blinked repeatedly. She lay a gloved hand on his cheek and managed two shaky words. "Good-bye, Dan."

He seemed unable to trust himself to speak. Then, to Laura's dismay, he suddenly pulled her against him once more and kissed her full on the mouth. When he put her away, her tears had wet his cheeks, and she realized Josh was standing alongside, looking up at all three of them.

Rye's hand met Dan's in a solid handshake, and their eyes joined in a last farewell.

"Take care of them, my friend."

"Aye, y' can be sure of it."

Their voices were unnaturally deep with emotion, and their four hands clung, gripping so hard the knuckles turned white.

From the gangplank, Cap'n Silas called, "Got a schedule t' keep. All aboard!"

Then Josh was on Rye's arm, looking back over his father's sturdy shoulder at his papa. Tears streamed down his freckled cheeks, and the rooster tail at the back of his blond head bobbed with each long-legged step that bore him away. Laura, too, felt Rye's commanding grip on her elbow and passed the sea of faces toward the boat with tears now blinding her completely.

* * *

They stood at the rail of the steam packet—Rye with Josh in his arms, Laura beside him, and Josiah on her far side. Ship whined and nudged between them, lunged up and caught her front paws on the port beam. There was a clunk and a lurch, then the cumbersome packet began to move, shivering to life with ponderous reluctance until the rhythmic clunk picked up speed and became the incessant heartbeat of the vessel.

Each of those at the rail had singled out a face on which to linger. For Josh it was Jimmy Ryerson, who waved one freckled hand and wiped his eyes with the other. For Laura it was Jane, who held her youngest and pressed a cheek against his hair. For Rye it was Dan, who had picked up his hat but seemed to have forgotten to put it on his head. But Josiah turned from the faces on the wharf to lift his gaze over the top of the bait shack and the candle shop beyond to the roof of a small wooden building scarcely visible in the distance. He dropped his hand to Ship's head and stroked it absently. The dog whined, raised doleful eyes to Josiah, then watched the shore slip away into the mists of Nantucket Harbor.

They remained at the rail for a long time, with eyes cast astern toward the little spit of land they loved. As they passed the shoals, the projecting fingers of Brant Point and Coatue seemed to want to pluck them back and hold them. But the *Clinton* headed into the sound toward the long tip of Cape Cod, chugging along steadily until Nantucket appeared no more than a pebble floating on the surface of the water before it dwindled, then disappeared altogether in a haze of distant fog.

Laura shivered, glanced up, and found Rye studying her.

"Well, would y' like t' see our quarters?"

Our quarters. If anything had the power to wrest Laura's dolorous thoughts from the place they'd just left, it was those two words.

"I guess I'd better, since we'll be spending two weeks in them."

The five passengers headed belowdecks. The *Clinton* was far less luxurious than the steamboat *Telegraph* would have been, for though it hauled a capacity of thirty passengers, the chief purpose of the Albany packet was transporting cargo, thus the accommodations could scarcely be called cabins. Rye led them to two rooms that were little more than partitioned spaces, offering thin-walled privacy but little else.

As he opened the door and stood back in the narrow companionway, Laura peered inside to find, to her dismay, a pair of single bunks, berthed one above the other, a small bench seat bolted to the wall, a tiny shelf above, and a whale-oil lantern swinging from the overhead beam. But her eyes were drawn to the sight of her suitcase sitting beside Rye's sea chest.

Before she could react, Josh pushed at his mother from behind. "Let me see!" He squeezed past and headed into the cubicle, but a restraining hand fell on his head and forced him into an abrupt about face.

"Not so fast there, young man! Y'rs is the next one!"

Laura's heart reacted with a flutter, and she wondered if Josh would put up any objection to being separated from her in the midst of all these strange surroundings and events. But she had little time to speculate, for there was a moment of confusion while she dipped inside the open door to let the three, plus Ship, pass along the companionway to the next door.

"Y' and Josiah will be sharin' this compartment," she heard, then poked her nose around the doorway to find a second cubicle identical to the first.

"Me and Josiah?" Josh looked up dubiously at Rye.

"Aye, y' and Josiah."

"Where's Mama gonna be?"

"Right next door." Rye nodded toward the first cabin.

"Oh."

At Josh's unenthusiastic grunt, Josiah spoke up in his slow New England drawl. "Got somethin' here I been meanin' t' show y', Joshua."

Josh's expression was skeptical as his glance passed from Rye to Laura. It was one of the weirdest moments of Laura's life, hoping for approval from her son to sleep with his father! But just then Josiah bent to retrieve a small wooden carton with airholes along its sides. He sat down on the lower berth and gave the container his full attention, carefully placing his hands on its cover as if it were a magician's box. Josh's attention was captured.

"What is it?" The boy moved nearer his grandfather's knee.

" 'Tain't much. Just a couple little companions f'r the long trip."

The wooden lid came up in Josiah's hands, and from within the box came a duet of *cheeps*.

"Chicks!" Already Josh was reaching eagerly, smiling and fairly squealing, "You mean we can keep 'em on the boat?"

"We'd better. The way I heard tell, there ain't many chickens in Michigan. Thought we'd best start up a flock right away so y'r mother'd have eggs f'r her cookin'."

Ship nosed forward and sniffed at the puff ball in Josh's hand. Already Josh seemed to have forgotten Rye and Laura. Josiah reached into his breast pocket and found a cold pipe, clamped it between his teeth while studying the boy, the chick, and the dog. He raised laconic eyes to Laura while continuing drolly, "Y' know, Joshua, I c'd use some help pamperin' them chicks, so I hope y'r mother don't mind if y' sleep in here with 'em."

Josh spun around and all but climbed Laura's skirts in enthusiasm. "Can I? Please, can I? Me and . . . me and Grampa, we got to take care of 'em and keep 'em warm and stuff, and make sure Ship don't eat 'em up!"

Rye and Laura laughed. She managed to catch Josiah's eye, found a charming twinkle there, and hoped he understood the wordless message of thanks she flashed.

"Yes, of course you can, Josh."

Immediately, he turned back to the box on Josiah's knees. "We gotta name 'em, don't we, Grampa?"

"Name them chickens? I never heard of no chickens with names!"

"Well, I can see you two don't need us, so we'll get settled next door." Rye took Laura's elbow and a shaft of fire seemed to sizzle up her arm. Josiah and Josh didn't even look up as they made their exit.

Inside their own cabin, the door was closed and all was silent but for the pulsating throb of the steam engine shimmying up through the floor. There was no porthole, only the oil lamp swaying on its hook, and Laura knew, to the exact highlight and shadow, what Rye's face would look like by its golden light should she turn and lift her eyes. But she stood facing the bunks, feeling him close behind her shoulder.

"It's not very fancy," he apologized, but she heard instead the note of tight control in his voice.

"When have I ever needed anything fancy?" She felt both of Rye's hands move up her back and circle her neck.

"Never," he said thickly. Then, as if he didn't trust himself, he dropped his hands from her.

"Were the chicks your idea?" she asked.

"Nay, my father gets the credit for that."

"Josiah is very astute."

"Aye."

She wanted to turn, but felt as shy as a violet blossom. Her heart was giving the engine some competition, throbbing so powerfully she thought surely it was her own pulse shaking the boards beneath the soles of her shoes.

Rye cleared his throat. "Well . . . I have t' talk t' the captain, so why don't you—"

"Josiah didn't dream up those chicks for nothing, Rye," she interrupted, turning at last to face him. "Don't you dare run off to the captain without—"

His mouth cut off her words, and she was in Rye's arms at last! His kiss was a rich, sensual welcome while his arms slipped within her cape to haul her up tight against his chest, and hers looped about his neck as her feet left the floor. Then Rye's warm, wet tongue was all over and around Laura's, and she whisked the cap from his head and held it in one hand while the other threaded his coarse hair.

He turned, backing her up against the cabin door, pressing the length of his body against hers while their kiss became a wild search for relief. She ran her tongue along the sleek texture of his teeth, then explored the moist depths of his mouth, missing none of its familiar landmarks.

He let her slip down only far enough that their stomachs and hips met and used his tremendous strength to wedge her between the door and his body, pressing so hard the breath was forced from her lungs. He was fully tumescent and wasted not a moment letting her know. His hips made figure eights as they ground against hers, thrusting the hard male ridge against the equally hard rise of her mons.

Desire sent a liquid rush of feeling to the part of her against which Rye pressed. She felt it, gloried in it, welcomed it! But Laura was impaled against the door, unable to transmit her own tacit message of arousal.

"Rye, put me down," she managed.

"If I do and my hands are free, there'll be no stoppin' them."

"I don't care."

"Yes y' do. Y' want t' get married first, so I'll put y' down, but then I'll go see the captain about arrangin' it, agreed?"

"Blast you, Rye Dalton," she murmured against his lips, provocatively inserting her tongue into his mouth between words. "What a time . . . for you to do . . . the proper thing."

"Agreed?" he repeated, moving his head back only far enough to escape her darting tongue.

"Oh all right, agreed."

She felt her toes regain the floor, and his hands steadied her for a moment while her skirt still clung to his trousers. He backed a step away and the skirt fell properly into place.

His voice seemed to throb like the engine while his impassioned blue eyes fixed upon hers. "But I'm warnin' y', t'night will be a different matter."

She rose up on tiptoe and placed the wool cap on his head, adjusted its narrow visor to a raffish angle, and studied her effort. "It had better be," she rejoined softly.

They kissed once more, Rye's hands running possessively up her ribs while she touched his jaw. Then he put her away and backed off a step. "I'll be back as soon as I can. Meanwhile, get y'rself ready for our weddin' . . . again. Only this time when he says *till death do us part*, y' can believe it."

Then he turned and was gone.

She smiled at the door, then spun around. Her body felt combustible! This restraint was playing havoc with her composure. She took four deep breaths, but found it did little good, and at last ran a hand down the front of her skirt and clutched herself in an effort to quell the throbbing begun by his caress.

What time is it? Barely noon. How many hours to wait? Until at least eight o'clock, when we can respectably retire for the night. Goodness me, how will I last that long?

She removed her bonnet and cape and prowled about the small cabin, testing the mattress, pushing the suitcase and sea chest against the wall. There was no unpacking to do because no place was provided for the storage of extra clothes. Time crawled.

When Rye returned, he found Laura sitting on the edge of the lower bunk. She flew to her feet as he stepped inside, closed the door, and leaned back against it.

"Four o'clock," he announced without preamble.

"Four o'clock," she echoed like a litany.

"Aye. In the captain's cabin." His eyes assessed her yellow dress with an expression of strained forbearance.

"Well," she said breathlessly, raising her palms and glancing around as if expecting some diversion to come jumping out of the cabin walls.

He sucked in an enormous breath, let it out slowly while tilting his cap back beyond his hairline with a thumb. Then he heaved himself away from the cabin door, opened it, and stepped back. "Let's go see how the chicks're doin'."

Laura's knees felt watery from relief.

The four of them spent a pleasant half hour watching the chicks and the dog, who by now was less inquisitive and allowed the tiny yellow birds to be placed between her paws and even on her head.

Shortly after noon, a bell announced dinner, which was served in a long forward salon as lackluster as the rest of the craft. Tables and benches filled the room, and there was little space for the galley help to pass between them with the hot seafood chowder and hard dark bread that comprised the meal.

Laura sat next to Rye, scorchingly aware of every brush of his thigh against hers. The conversation around the table ran on brightly as passengers compared destinations and home ports. It was unnecessary to reveal that Laura and Rye were to be married that afternoon, for everybody took them to be a married couple, since Josh was with them, and Josiah, too.

In the afternoon, Rye left Laura in the cabin to rest if she wanted, while he excused himself, taking his suitcase next door. But she was keyed up so tightly it was impossible to relax. She found herself continuously checking the tiny gold pendant watch pinned near her collarbone, and finally, when it read three o'clock, she went next door to fetch Josh, ordering, much to the boy's dismay, that it was time for him to change clothes and get ready.

She had decided to wear the yellow dress, had recombed her hair into a flattering nutmeg top knot, but was nervously indecisive about whether or not to wear her bonnet.

"What do you think, Josh?"

But Josh was little help. He merely shrugged and wondered why his mother was acting as flappy as a fish out of water.

At ten to four, a knock sounded and Laura sucked in a quick breath and whispered, "You answer it, Josh!"

The door opened upon a freshly combed, freshly shaved Rye Dalton, decked out in the same splendid suit he'd worn the night of Joseph Starbuck's party. The green trousers clung to his thighs as the skin hugs a grape. The jacket delineated his shoulders' breadth and musculature with awesome precision. His sienna skin was temptingly foiled by the snowy ruffles that fell to his knuckles and the tightly wound stock that climbed his neck nearly to his side-whiskers.

"Are y' ready?"

I've been ready since I was fifteen.

Laura reined in her wild thoughts and managed to utter hoarsely, "Yes, both of us."

He nodded and stepped back from the door, through which Josh immediately began to precede his mother, only to be halted in midstride by his father's strong hand.

"Ladies first, young man."

They were joined in the companionway by Josiah, and the four made their way up to the main aft deck and the captain's quarters.

Captain Benjamin Swain was a burly mutton-chopped man with red cheeks and a raw scrape to his voice. He stepped back to allow them entrance, raspily welcoming, "Step inside! Step inside!'' But he was surprised to see the shortest of the quartet, who followed on his mother's heels. ''Well, now who have we here?''

Josh looked up. ''Joshua Morgan, sir.''

''Joshua Morgan, is it?''

Josh nodded, giving the captain no further enlightenment.

The ruddy-cheeked captain closed the door and cleared his throat with a thunderous rumble. ''This is m' first mate, Dardanelle McCallister,'' Captain Swain announced. ''Thought y' might need a witness.''

Rye and the first mate shook hands. ''Mr. McCallister, I thank y', but we won't be needin' y'. My father will act as witness.''

''Ah, very well, sir, then I'll take m'self off to other duties.''

Other introductions were made all around, and Laura's hand was crushed in the tight grip of the captain.

His cabin was the most luxurious part of the craft. It had rich walls of waxed teak and finely crafted fittings such as the belowdecks cubicles hadn't. A carved bedstead covered one end of the room while on another was a long pigeonholed desk and closed storage cabinet resembling a chifforobe. The center of the room was monopolized by a table over which were strewn maps, ledgers, a brass sextant, and compass. There was more space than their own cabins afforded, but still, with five people in this room, it was undeniably crowded.

Captain Swain motioned them to stand to one side of the desk while he stooped to fetch a Bible from its lower drawer.

Laura stood between Rye and Josiah, while Josh took up a place before them, with Rye's hands resting on the boy's shoulders. The captain began paging through the book, but before he found what he was looking for, Josiah leaned forward and whispered something in his ear. Rye and Laura exchanged curious glances but were left unenlightened as the whispered exchange continued, then the captain nodded his head, found his place, and looked up with a second clearing of his throat.

''All ready, then?''

Josh's rooster tail bobbed as he nodded enthusiastically. The captain puffed out his chest and began reading a simple prayer. Beside Laura, Rye's elbow seemed to quiver as it brushed hers. She stared at the gold buttons on the captain's protruding stomach. The prayer ended, and the rotund man dropped the book and extemporized.

"Y've come to me on this, the thirtieth day of March, eighteen thirty-eight, to join together as man and wife. Is that correct, Mr. Dalton?"

"That's correct."

"Is that correct, Miss Morgan?"

"That's correct—Mrs. Morgan."

The captain arched a brow. "Mrs. Morgan, yes," he amended. "And to the best of your knowledge, is there any reason why the Commonwealth of Massachusetts should not grant its seal to your wishes?" He looked first at Rye, then at Laura. In turn, they answered, "None."

"Marriage is a state into which you must enter with all intentions of making it last a lifetime. Do you both so intend? Mr. Dalton?"

"Yes, I do," Rye answered.

"Yes, I do," Laura answered.

"And it is also a state into which none should enter without the bond of love. Do you promise to love each other for the rest of your lives?"

"I promise . . ." Rye turned loving eyes on Laura, "for the rest o' my life."

"I promise," she echoed, meeting his blue eyes, "for the rest of my life."

"And who will witness this union?"

"I will," Josiah stated. "Josiah Dalton."

The captain nodded. "And who gives this woman?"

"I do," Josh piped up.

The captain quirked an eyebrow—obviously this was the part of the ceremony about which he'd been prompted. "And you are?"

"I'm Josh." He looked up over his left shoulder. "She's my mother." Then he looked up over his right. "And he's my father."

The captain forgot protocol. "What!"

Laura bit her lip to keep from smiling. Beside her, Rye colored and shuffled his feet.

"She's my mother and he's my father, and I give 'em permission to get married."

The captain gathered his wits and proceeded. "Very well, and are there any rings?"

There was a sudden flurry of activity as Laura pulled open the drawstring of a tiny reticule and the groom—to the captain's utter amazement—pulled a gold wedding band off his finger and handed it to his bride. Then they faced the captain as if nothing unusual were taking place here.

The captain's mouth hung open as he realized the groom would be wearing the same wedding ring again.

"You gonna marry 'em or not?" Josh asked, fidgeting now.

"Oh . . . oh, yes, where were we?"

"Are there any rings," Josh reminded the captain, who harrumphed in an effort to cover his confusion.

"Oh yes, so repeat after me while you're placing the ring on her finger. 'With this ring I take you, Laura Morgan, for my wife, forsaking all others, loving only you, till the end of our days on this earth.' "

Laura gazed at Rye's calloused fingers holding the gold band on the appropriate knuckle. His own trembled, as did his voice while he repeated the words of the captain. Then he slipped the gold band onto her finger for the second time in her life.

She took Rye's left hand in hers and held the ring he'd just removed. It still held the warmth of his flesh, captured in the polished gold. She held it shakily while Captain Swain dictated the words again and her subdued voice repeated them.

"With this ring I take you, Rye Dalton, for my husband, forsaking all others, loving only you, till the end of our days on this earth."

She slid the ring on securely and her face lifted to find his pale blue eyes waiting as the captain sealed the union.

"By the power vested in me by the . . ." He took a moment to glance out the cabin window at the shoreline and verify their location. ". . . by the Commonwealth of Massachusetts, I now pronounce you man and wife."

"For once and for all," Josiah mumbled, smiling in satisfaction as his tall, strapping son bent over the woman who lifted her lips for his kiss. He watched the couple part, then break into two of the most beaming smiles Josiah had ever seen as they impetuously hugged each other one more time.

"Well, you goin' t' keep her all t' yourself or y' goin' t' let an old man get in on this?"

While Josiah hugged Laura, Rye shook hands with Captain Swain, but suddenly realized Josh's short stature put him well below the action. Rye leaned down and scooped the little one up.

"I think the bride deserves a kiss from her son." Perched on Rye's powerful arm, the child leaned to kiss his mother. The joy reflected in her face brought a bright smile to his face, too. Her laughter lilted through the cabin before she looked into Josh's eyes and spoke softly. "I think the groom deserves a kiss from his son, too."

For a moment Josh hesitated, his small hand resting at the back of Rye's collar, his other behind Laura's neck, uniting them into a trio. When he moved to touch his rosebud lips to Rye's for the first time, a current of joy swelled the man's heart. Josh straightened, and with their eyes so close together and so very much alike, the two studied each other. The moment seemed to stretch into eternity. Then suddenly Josh's hand left Laura and he flung both arms around Rye and buried his face in the strong neck that smelled of cedar. Rye's eyes closed as he breathed deeply to control the floodtide of emotion generated by the embrace.

The captain cleared his throat. "I believe a little toast is in order, after which I'd be honored to have you at my table for supper. I've asked the cook to see if he can't scratch up something besides stew for the occasion."

Laura and Rye might have been eating sawdust for all they cared. The conversation was sprightly, and the salon seemed much gayer than it had at noon, once Captain Swain announced to the other passengers that he'd had the honor of performing a marriage ceremony. But in spite of the chatter around them, Rye and Laura were conscious of only two things—each other and the time. It seemed to slog by on leaden feet. It took a conscious effort to keep from getting lost in each other's eyes. They were surrounded by people and were approached repeatedly by total strangers offering congratulations. Though it was impossible for Laura to check her pendant watch without being observed, she noted that, more and more often as the evening progressed, Rye pulled his watch out under cover of the table. Each time he snapped its cover shut and tucked it away in his vest, he would move his eyes to hers and she would feel the heat travel up her cheeks. Once as she listened to a female passenger relating an anecdote about a millinery store in Albany, Laura felt Rye's gaze and turned slightly to find him staring at her left hand, which was unconsciously fingering the pendant watch at her collarbone. She dropped the hand immediately and turned to pay attention to the woman. But Laura heard not a word the stranger said, for beneath the table Rye shifted his leg until a long, hard thigh pushed hard against hers, even as he turned to face the opposite direction and answer a man on his far side.

Several minutes later the leg shifted again, and Rye's heel began bouncing in an unconscious jitter of impatience. The motion quivered its way up Laura's leg and increased the heavy-hollow feeling of arousal deep within her.

At a point when she thought her patience couldn't hold out another second, Josh—bless him!—turned to Josiah and put a hand on his arm.

"Grampa, I think we better go check our chickens."

"Aye, I think y'r right, boy. Been lollygaggin' here long enough."

Beneath the table Rye's heel stopped jumping. He stretched his long form up off the bench with a feigned leisure that made Laura smile inwardly, then took her elbow to urge her to her feet. As if I need urging, she thought.

The handshakes and good nights seemed to take a monumental amount of time, but at last the group broke up and the Dalton party filed through the companionway to their quarters.

At Rye and Laura's door, Josiah stopped and gestured at them with the stem of his pipe. "Y' best sleep late in the mornin'. Don't worry about Josh and me . . ." His hand felt for Josh's shoulder, found it, and squeezed. "We'll be busy feedin' the animals."

Josh took the wide, gnarled hand and dragged his grandfather toward the next door. "C'mon, Grampa! Ship is whining!"

"'I'm comin', I'm comin.'" Josiah let the boy tug him away, knowing a sense of well-being he hadn't felt since the day his son sailed off on the whaleship *Massachusetts*.

Chapter 23

THE LATCH CLICKED behind them. Laura paused in the middle of the room, Rye a foot from the door. Through the wall came the muffled sound of Josh greeting Ship enthusiastically, answered by two canine yips of excitement, then silence, but for the steady, throbbing beat of the steam engine that churned in the bowels of the boat. They'd left the lantern burning. It swung now above Laura's head, throwing her shadow across Rye's legs, up the wall, and back to his feet again.

Laura studied the narrow single bunks, comparing their inadequate length to Rye's, coming up short by a good six inches. She was slipping the drawstrings of her reticule from her wrist when Rye's low voice came from behind her.

"Mrs. Dalton."

She turned slowly to face him. He stood with feet planted wide apart, knees locked, one hand hanging loosely at his side while the other untied the stock at his throat.

"Yes, Mr. Dalton?" She tossed the reticule toward the bench without bothering to check where it landed. Her heart did a mating dance along her ribcage. Her breath was in short supply.

"Can I make love t' y' now?" He leisurely unwound the stock but let it hang loosely around his neck. Pushing his jacket front back, he hooked it with both wrists and rested wide hands on slim hips. His stance revealed why his foot had been jumping under the table earlier, though he stood now boldly, hiding nothing. The masculine ridge pressed outward up the center of his green trousers, and he watched her eyes travel down to it and back up to his mouth.

"I thought you'd never ask," came the husky reply.

They paused on the brink of forever, tarrying that last scintillating moment to relish the anticipation of the embrace before the embrace itself.

"Then come here and let's get started."

But they moved of one accord, meeting halfway, heart to heart, mouth to mouth, man to woman, in a union preordained by the years through which not even the frowns of fortune had been able to keep them apart. Their impatient tongues met, sleek, silken members joining husband to wife in an oral imitation of what was to follow. His kiss forced her head back against a solid shoulder as he bent low, savoring her taste, texture, and the ever-clinging essence of bayberry trapped in her clothing.

He smelled of fresh linen and the woodsy tang his body seemed to have captured from the furlongs of oak and cedar he'd shaped down through the years.

His body was warm, the flesh resilient within his clothing, as she slipped an arm between loose jacket and tight vest, contouring his wide ribs, then spreading her palm wide over the silk fabric that stretched taut across his shoulder blades as he bent into the embrace.

The months had been long, testing their rectitude time and again. But restraint was no longer necessary, hands need not delay. His moved to cup a waiting breast while hers measured and caressed the warm column of flesh along Rye's stomach.

A grum sound of passion rumbled from his throat while her answering murmur was swallowed by his kiss and the tongue that stroked the satin reaches of her mouth. Their hands began moving and delight to build.

When he moved his head at last, Rye's hand was atop Laura's, increasing the pressure and following her strokes. "Ah, m' love, I was beginnin' t' think I'd never feel y' touch me again." His palm left her knuckles and moved down her yellow skirt, clasping the mound of femaleness hidden beneath layers of cotton. "Or me you."

His touch fired her blood and transformed the simple act of breathing into a most difficult labor.

"I thought supper'd never end," he uttered against her throat.

"I kept wanting to ask you what time it was."

Rye's lips brushed Laura's and he straightened her with a deft sweep of an arm. Eyes as blue as the Atlantic's deep waters smiled into those as dark as rich loam. "Time t' get y' out of that dress, Mrs. Dalton."

"And you out of that suit, Mr. Dalton."

He dimpled engagingly and scratched a sideburn. "Aye, come t' think of it, it has grown a bit uncomfortable."

"Then please allow me," she intoned sweetly, pushing his lapels back over his shoulders.

Obligingly, he turned his back and slipped from the jacket. She tossed it to the bench while he swung again to face her, unhooking the watch fob from its vest button while her eager fingers also moved to Rye's chest. His arm reached wide to place the watch more securely aside while she freed the vest buttons and nudged the garment from his shoulders, heedless of how it fell.

She was reaching for his collar button when her forearms were grasped firmly and held. "What's y'r hurry, darlin'? You're gettin' ahead of me." His rough thumbs stroked the bare flesh of her inner arms, where pale veins seemed to throb beneath his touch. His eyes held blue sparks of impatience that put the lie to his words while he forcibly restrained himself from rushing. Keeping his eyes locked with hers, he kissed first the heel of her left palm, then of the right, before running his tongue lightly along the sensitive skin of her inner arm to the edge of her elbow-length sleeve. He placed her hands at her sides and lifted his own to the row of buttons running from the shallows of her throat to her hips. When the dress was open, he brushed it from her shoulders. It caught on the petticoats at her hips, where it lay forgotten while Rye delicately touched her beneath both earlobes with only the tips of his middle fingers, then ran them with agonizing slowness down the sides of her neck, along its sloping base to her shoulders, hooking the straps of her chemise and dragging them over the alluring curves.

While his fingertips made their journey, her eyelids trembled shut. A breath was captured and held deep within Laura as Rye's feather-light touch sent a hot arrow of fire down her belly. It seemed to pierce some vessel of liquid contained deep within her body, releasing it in a warm, sensual flow of desire and preparedness.

She shuddered and opened her eyes. His were deep and watchful, certain of what was happening within his bride as he sketched invisible tendrils around her collarbone, then over the soft, warm swell of her chest, ending at the lacy top of her chemise. Her hands came up beneath his, and with a single tug, the bow disappeared from between her breasts and the chemise lay reefed around her waist. She grasped the backs of his hands and filled their palms with her breasts, leaning against him with a pressure that still could not quell the almost painful aching in her flesh.

Again her eyelids dropped; her head was thrown slightly back and to one side as strained words whispered past her lips. "Rye, I've thought of this every day since last August. Kiss me, darling, please."

His head dropped forward, and warm lips opened over an ivory globe of flesh, which he lifted and reshaped until its pink tip thrust into his engulfing mouth. He suckled it, bathed it, and rolled the nipple between his teeth before they closed gently upon it. She moaned and grasped his shoulders, pulling back while his teeth held the aroused bud and stretched it. And when the sensations of pleasure bordered on pain, she lunged forward again, moving her shoulders sinuously, making his mouth seek and follow the nipple.

Suddenly he growled, grasping her hips and burying his face against her fragrant flesh, capturing the breast again and holding her still while his hands freed the button at her waist, then pushed chemise, pantaloons, petticoats, and dress into a lemon-colored billow at her ankles.

"Sit down. I'll take off your shoes."

She fell back with a soft plunk onto the cloud of garments and perched there like the pistil in the center of a yellow-and-white daffodil, while he knelt before her and quickly loosened the strings of her shoe, slipped it from her heel, and peeled off her stocking before at last looking up.

"The other one," he ordered, impatient now. It was caught in the waistband of the petticoat, but he freed it, then began baring the foot without a wasted motion.

While he deftly tugged at the strings, she caressed his hard thigh with her bare foot, studying the top of his hair as he bent over his task. "Have you any idea how badly I wanted to make love that day you had me on your lap in the chair?"

He looked up, surprised. "The day y' threw me out," he recalled.

"Yes, the day I threw you out," she said, then went on seductively, "I went to bed that night and pleasured myself."

His jaw dropped. A look of stunned disbelief held his face immobile. Then the shoe thudded to the floor. "After five years y're still full o' surprises."

She turned her knees to one side, rolled to a hip, and leaned nearer him with a palm braced on the floor. "Well, don't tell me you didn't do the same thing plenty of times all the years you were on that whaleship." While she spoke, her hand reached for the buttons of his trousers.

He manipulated his shirt buttons at the same time, grinning down into her face. "I won't deny it. But I thought of y' every time I did it." He grabbed the front panels of his shirt and, with an impatient jerk, thrust it from his shoulders. His grin grew bolder. "I don't think there'll be much need for self-pleasurin' in the future, d' you, Mrs. Dalton?"

"Oh, I hope not."

His trousers were unbuttoned, and he dropped flat onto his rump, began tugging at a long, black boot while her eyes caressed his face. The boot stuck. He muttered a curse, straining at it while she raised on both knees, grasped the ends of his stock in both hands, and hauled him close, then passed the tip of her tongue along his left eyebrow.

"This goddamn boot—" But just then it came free. Immediately, he hoisted the other one up while she went to work on his other eyebrow, nearly forcing him backward as she tantalized him, caressing his eyelids now with her moist tongue tip, moving to the side of his nose, and finally biting his upper lip.

"Do you need some help with that boot?" she murmured, closing her teeth on an unruly clump of side-whiskers, tugging gently before nuzzling her way toward his ear. Her tongue dipped inside, and Rye gave a vicious yank, sending the second boot flying across the room.

He spun on his hips, knocking her flat to the floor beneath him with her breasts crushed under the curled hair of his chest. He grabbed the sides of her head, plundering her mouth with his own, slipping his impatient tongue along her teeth, beneath her tongue, atop it, plunging it again and again with suggestive rhythm.

His disheveled trousers still clung about his hips, but her naked back was pressed to the raw wood of the cabin floor, through which the throb of the engine shuddered. She felt its beat drive up into her muscles while Rye adjusted himself until he fit securely against her length. Somewhere deep in the boat the valves of the steam engine plunged into the pistons and the steady thrum of its power reverberated through the wooden craft with a faint ongoing *ka-thunk, ka-thunk, ka-thunk*.

Laura's arms circled Rye's shoulders and her fingertips caressed each bone along his spinal column as far as they could reach, while Rye's hips began moving in rhythm with the powerful litany of the machinery that could be both felt and heard.

Their movements synchronized as she joined him in a cadence of thrust and ebb, then maneuvered one foot until it caught at the waistband of his pants and began working them down past his buttocks. He reached back to give a helping hand, and when the trousers shimmied from his heels, the soles of her feet silkily caressed the backs of his thighs and explored the hollows behind his knees.

He braced both forearms on the floor, cradling her head in his wide palms, dropping a garland of kisses across her face. "I love y' . . . Laura, Laura . . . all these years. . . I love y' . . . ." His hips undulated, finding their complement within her own. Her body lifted in greeting while her fingertips slid along his skull and drew his head down above her own.

"Rye . . . it's always been you . . . I love you . . . Rye . . ." Her moist lips pressed his eyelids closed, adored his hollow cheek, and found his dear mouth once more, knowing its shape, its warmth, its treasure even before it closed over her own.

He rose.

She reached.

He poised.

She placed.

He pressed.

She parted.

He sank.

She surrounded.

To the uncountable and ceaseless rhythms of the universe, they added one more.

Her body opened like an oyster shell, and his silken strokes sought and grazed the pearl within, that precious jewel of sensuality whose arousal unleashed some magical force that fired Laura's limbs. She met each thrust with one of equal might, and together they reached for the reward they had earned with the long winter of solitude.

They were buoyed by love but powered by a lust as rich and demanding as their hale bodies deserved. Laura's teeth were bared as Rye drove into her with a puissance that soon set off the first pulsations deep within.

Unknowingly, she reached above her head, palms pressed flat against the cabin door as the explosions of feeling gripped her muscles. The sensations triggered a shuddering reaction and dotted the surface of her skin in a thousand tiny shivering pinpoints, as a breeze ruffles the smooth surface of a pond.

A growl sounded in Rye's throat as he lifted her higher, his wide hands spanning her hips while Laura's clasped her elbows above her head and the powerful muscles of his arms corded as tight as rigging under sail. He called out an unintelligible utterance of release as he lunged a last time, then shuddered against her, the hair over his forehead quivering for an interminable moment while his tense fingers left ten bloodless stamps of possession on her hips.

Then his arms went lax, his eyes slid shut, and his head dropped forward, open lips coming to rest on her shoulder.

Beneath them, the engine continued to throb. Above them, the lantern still swung. Beyond them, the two-tiered berths remained untouched. She brushed his damp shoulder to recall him from the lethargy into which he'd sunk.

"Rye."

"Hmm?" His weight was a gift that lay unmoving.

"Just Rye, that's all. I always want to say it . . . afterward."

The lips at her shoulder parted, pressed firmly in wordless accolade, and the tip of his tongue wet her skin.

"Laura Adele Dalton," he returned.

She smiled. He rarely used her middle name, because she disliked it. But hearing it now from her husband's lips, it took on a new note, sitting side by side with *Dalton*.

"Yes, Laura Adele Dalton forever."

They lazed in afterglow, thinking of it, until the boards beneath Laura spoke their piece.

"Rye."

His eyes opened and his head came up. "Hmm?"

"This floor is harder than the one in old man Hardesty's loft."

With a smile he pulled her up until she straddled him with their bodies joined. "Mmm, but it works good, doesn't it?"

She looped her arms around his neck and draped herself around him. "Wonderful."

"Y're wonderful. Y're better than wonderful. Y're . . . *stupendous*."

She laughed silently against his chest. "Either stupendous or stupid. My hipbones are chapped, I think."

He laughed, rubbed the bruised parts, and warned, "Better get used t' it, woman."

She drew herself back and peered up impishly. "Oh, I brought lots of lanolin along."

Rye's teeth gleamed startlingly white behind his wide smile as he chuckled appreciatively. "Nevertheless, hang on, and we'll move t' more comfortable quarters." He locked his wrists beneath her buttocks and she her ankles behind his hips, and he struggled to his feet, then crossed to the bunks.

"Pull the blanket down," he murmured, kissing her jaw,

and she leaned sideways in an effort to follow orders, but suddenly her eyes widened and she squirmed against him.

"Rye! You're slipping!"

"Aye, that's the general idea."

"Rye!"

But she squirmed again and they managed to stay together while he backed onto the lower bunk and fell, taking her with him. Unfortunately, when he stretched out, the space fell just short of accommodating his feet. He rolled them onto their sides and made himself as comfortable as possible.

"When we get t' Michigan, I'm goin' t' make us the biggest bed y've ever seen."

She snuggled against him, burying her nose in the thatch of gold hair on his chest. "This one's big enough to suit me."

"Ah no, we'll need an enormous bed for the lazy mornin's when all those young ones come pilin' in with us."

She reared back and stared. "All *what* young ones?"

"Why, all the young ones we're goin' t' have." He caressed her satin hip and buttock. "As often as I intend t' do this with y', I expect there'll be a pack of 'em in no time."

"And what do I have to say about that, Rye Dalton?"

He placed a lingering kiss on the end of her nose, another on the space between it and her upper lip, then on the lip itself. "If y' can say no, feel free to, m' love. But from the demonstration y' just put on on the floor down there, I'd say y' better get used t' knittin' booties."

"Demonstration!" She socked him one on the shoulder. "I did not put—"

His mouth cut off her words. He was smiling, nuzzling, spreading breathy warmth across her chin and lips. "Mmm . . . you were buckin' like an unbroke horse, now admit it, and I thought f'r a minute I'd have t' gag y' t' keep my father and Josh from hearin'."

"*I* was . . . well, what about you?"

"I was feelin' a little like a stallion m'self."

He hugged her close, she squeezed her legs tightly around his middle, and they laughed together. Once again silent, they lay entwined, listening to the beat of the engine, their breathing, an occasional creak of timbers. The lantern light fell across Laura's shoulder, gilding the bone structure of Rye's face, the tumbled hair across his forehead, the swooping whiskers on his cheek, his earlobe, his lips. Studying him, her heart swelled anew with love. She ran her fingertips along the outline of his upper lip, the expression in her eyes softening to reflect a profound depth of feeling.

"Rye, do you really want a lot of children?"

He didn't reply immediately, but looked into her brown eyes and into the past. His reply came softly. "I wouldn't mind. I've never seen y' carryin' my babe." He ran his hard palm across her stomach. "I've thought about it so many times, of how beautiful y'd be that way."

"Oh, Rye," she said almost shyly. "Women aren't beautiful when they're carrying babies."

"You'd be. I know you'd be."

Without warning her eyes stung. "Oh, Rye, I love you so much, and yes, I want lots of your babies."

He saw the tear, touched it with a fingertip, then placed the wet saltiness on his own lips. He drew a deep, uneven breath, spanned her cheek, ear, and jaw with one hand while his thumb stroked her chin. "Lau—" But his voice cracked, and the remainder of her name went unspoken. His strong arms pulled her once more against the hair of his chest, and beneath her ear she heard the racing beat of his heart. "I love y', Laura Dalton, but sometimes it seems like just those words don't say it all. I can't . . . I want . . ." But Rye found himself speechless in the face of an enormous tide of emotions. So he closed his eyes against her hair, his arms around her shoulders, and rocked her wordlessly.

She swallowed the thick knot of love that pushed high in her throat, understanding what he felt, overcome that for Rye it should be as magnificent as it was for her.

"I know, Rye, I know," Laura murmured. "Even now I can't quite believe you're here, you're mine, and we don't ever have to be apart again. I want to hurry, make up for lost time, crowd a thousand emotions into each minute I'm with you . . . and . . . and . . ." But neither could she adequately express this multitude of feelings.

His hand was heavy as it stroked her head. "Sometimes I

feel like I don't know what t' do with it all. Like . . . like I'm a glass o' rich wine that's filled right up t' the top, and one more drop and I'm goin' t' spill over.''

Words seemed suddenly pale and inadequate, none eloquent enough to relate the splendor they shared at that moment.

But Rye and Laura Dalton were mortal, and thus they held within their bodies the ideal manifestation of the emotion whose description eluded them. It needed no words. It required no verification. It simply happened, in all its wonder, in all its glory.

His body hardened, still within hers. And hers became liquid as it sheathed him. Their eyes, those windows of the soul, met and clung as she rose to meet him. She was lithe and passionate, and he, tensile and deep, while they moved harmoniously in the expression of love that supersedes all others. The act—this wondrous gift bestowed by nature—said all their hearts were feeling.

Rising and falling, like the engine that drove them through the Atlantic toward a new home, Laura understood fully what Rye had meant the day he'd asked her to go to the Michigan Territory. Home was not Nantucket, not Michigan. Home was the essence of love, one heart residing within another.

She felt the pulsations begin deep in her body and the last and longest possible reach of his body within her own, and beneath her palms his skin grew damp.

They shuddered.

They dissolved.

They were home.

From the *New York Times* bestselling author
of <u>Morning Glory</u> and <u>Bitter Sweet</u>

LaVyrle Spencer

One of today's best-loved authors of bittersweet
human drama and captivating romance.

___	THE ENDEARMENT	0-515-10396-9/$4.95
___	SPRING FANCY	0-515-10122-2/$4.50
___	YEARS	0-515-08489-1/$5.50
___	SEPARATE BEDS	0-515-09037-9/$5.50
___	HUMMINGBIRD	0-515-09160-X/$4.95
___	A HEART SPEAKS	0-515-09039-5/$5.50
___	THE GAMBLE	0-515-08901-X/$5.50
___	VOWS	0-515-09477-3/$5.50
___	THE HELLION	0-515-09951-1/$4.95
___	TWICE LOVED	0-515-09065-4/$5.50
___	MORNING GLORY	0-515-10263-6/$5.50
___	BITTER SWEET (March '91)	0-515-10521-X/$5.95